MOON FATED

(SKY BROOKS WORLD: ETHAN BOOK 5)

MCKENZIE HUNTER

A J CONNOR

This is a work of fiction. Names, characters, businesses, places, events, and incidents are either the products of the author's imagination or used in a fictitious manner. Any resemblance to actual persons, living or dead, or actual events is purely coincidental.

McKenzie Hunter

Moon Fated

ISBN: 978-1-946457-10-3

Logan sat watching us with the casual confidence of a creature in complete control. His smile and the twinkle of his lavender eyes could almost have seemed friendly, but there was a monster lurking beneath this imitation of humanity, and like the animal inside me, it could not remain concealed forever. Logan might still have his pretty looks, but he had just revealed the ugliness within.

Logan had betrayed us. Worse, he had betrayed the woman I cared about. Just as he'd been asked, he had found the Tre'ase that had created Maya, the spirit shade that lived within Sky and to whom her life was tied. But he had returned from his mission with only the Tre'ase's heart, a macabre thing that kept beating with magic linked to his own life, a pulsing piece of meat in a domed jar, and instead of handing it over, he clung to it as his own.

I shouldn't have been surprised. Tre'ases were tricksters by nature and betrayal was in their blood. The signs had always been there with Logan—the swirling marks across his skin, where magic had been used to limit his power; the restriction that had kept him from leaving his home. He was dangerous enough that powerful magic users had tried to contain him. Working with him had been playing with fire from the start.

Of course he wanted to make a deal. Traitors always did. They treated the world as if it was full of idiots, people who they had tricked once and could easily trick again. I wanted to lash out, to punish Logan and take the heart by force. But if I killed him, then Sky would die, too, and I couldn't stand that.

Silent seconds of waiting turned into minutes, the tension in the room tightening around us. Bargaining was one of Sebastian's strengths, one of the reasons why he was our alpha, and I waited for him to make his move.

"What do you feel you need and want?" Sebastian asked at last.

Logan's smile widened, a smug streak of self-importance. He tapped the container that held the heart of the Tre'ase, a reminder that Sky's life was in his hands, that he could reach into that jar, squeeze that heart, and kill her. The thought made me sick, and that in turn reminded me just how much Sky had come to matter to me. Was I even falling in love? There was a brightness to her, a light and innocence that my life had been lacking for years. Now that light was in danger of being snuffed out on the cruel whim of a monster.

"Please, have a seat, we have a lot to discuss," Logan said.

"I'll stand," Sebastian said, staring at him with deep disdain.

"Have it your way," Logan said with a shrug.

Beside me, Sky shifted from one foot to the other. I could sense her fear and the courage with which she flattened it. There was a reason I would go to any lengths for this woman.

"What do you want?" Sebastian asked, his tone heavy as a tombstone. Any hint of friendship or common courtesy was gone, replaced by the barely restrained hostility of beasts circling one another, looking for an opening.

Logan smiled. He had the advantage here and he knew it.

"Very simple," he said. "One, I'd like these cursed marks removed from my body. They do make things difficult for me."

He gestured at the tattoos that swirled across his skin, magical restraints that others had placed on him. I had wondered what he did to earn them. Now that he'd revealed his true colors, the answer was clear.

"Why?" asked Josh, pacing the room. "Because they alert people that they are being magically bound to a contract and don't allow you to trick anyone into anything?"

"Exactly," Logan said, the smile never leaving his lips. "You've noticed I'm the only one who has them. Why should I bear the marks of past mistakes that were forced on me by the dreadful witches?"

"How many did it take to invoke the curse?" Josh asked. This was his territory, my brother and our resident witch revealing the insights that made him so useful to the pack. If anyone could find a way to break Logan's magic, it would be him.

"Thirteen," Logan said with a frown.

"If these marks were given to you by thirteen witches, how are we, with one witch, going to remove them?" Sky asked.

Instead of looking at her, Logan shifted his gaze to me. There was a knowing malevolence there. He knew our history, knew what Sky and I had achieved, saw how much she meant to me. He was going to use that against us, and there was nothing I could do about it.

I had never hated anyone so much.

"You removed a curse done by witches before, so it stands to reason that you can do the same again," Logan said, his attention returning to Sky. "But frankly, how it is done really isn't my problem as long as it is."

Of course. We had the Clostra, the set of spell books with

which we had removed the witches' death curse on Sky, and in the process unwittingly unraveled other magics, including the one containing Logan in his home. Logan assumed that we could do the same thing again, but we only had two of the three books, and getting the third wouldn't be easy, no matter what we had led Logan to believe before. Even if we wanted to agree to his terms, there was no guarantee that we could fulfill them.

Sebastian's eyes narrowed and his lips pulled back, baring the edges of a predator's deadly sharp teeth. His breath became a rumble, so quiet it could barely be heard.

Logan just laughed, placed a possessive hand on the jar, and smiled. He knew that any threat we made now would be hollow. None of us would risk Sky's life by attacking him. He took a deep breath, as if he were inhaling our anger, relishing the taste of the tension that hung thick in the air. Then he let go of the jar and stood, clasping his hands behind him.

He paced the room, his footsteps a mocking shadow of Josh's, and Josh stiffened in response. Logan turned his back on us and on the jar, his contempt on open display. He didn't need to watch us, didn't need to keep that bloody portion of the Tre'ase in his hand. His link to the heart was deep and magical, like the ties that bound the pack together. He could kill Sky without lifting a hand, crushing my own heart as readily as the Tre'ase's.

"Should I go on with my second request?" Logan asked.

When no one responded, he turned to Sebastian.

"Should I go on with my second request?" he asked again, a dark edge in his voice.

Sebastian fixed Logan with the same hard stare.

Logan resumed his pacing, moving with a grace he would never have had in his true, monstrous form. He flicked his hair—pale blond today with hints of silver—and smiled haughtily at Sebastian.

Josh had stopped pacing and stood still, his attention

focused on the jar. His fingers flickered and his lips twitched as he cast spell after spell, magic inching out from him toward the trapped heart. The blue of his eyes was eclipsed by a dark smoky gray as stronger magic flowed through him.

For every spell Josh cast, an equal force emerged to dissipate his magic as he and Logan engaged in a silent battle of wills. Josh's power wrapped around the jar, and for a moment I thought that he had won. I allowed myself a small smile of triumph. But then the magic evaporated, and Logan let out a dark laugh.

"Ah yes, did I expect anything less than the witch attempting to remove the spell?" Logan asked. "Tell me, are you having any success?"

Josh glared at Logan, his face tight with frustration.

"I assure you," Logan said, "I've mastered the spell to ensure that it cannot be lifted by anyone but me. Shall I continue?"

"Go on," Sebastian muttered through clenched teeth.

Seemingly indifferent to the angry predators facing him, Logan continued to slowly walk the length of the room, his back to us in open mockery. He paused for a moment, then continued his demands.

"Sky made a deal with me, one that she didn't fulfill. I would like her to fulfill that deal. That's my final request."

He turned to look at us, smugly self-satisfied, the look of a weak creature that thought it finally had its hunter trapped.

I could hear Sky's heartbeat race as the focus of the conversation turned back to her. She was the one who had originally sought out Logan, in hopes of removing a death spell cast on her by the witches. Logan had wanted her to cast a *servus vinculum* in exchange, binding my ex-girlfriend Chris to her so that Sky could hand Chris to Logan. Of course, Sky hadn't done it—she was better than that—but Logan wasn't letting go of his desires.

"No," Sky said firmly, heading for the door. "We don't have a deal."

"Ms. Brooks," Logan said, "I don't believe you have much of a choice."

"Yes, I do have a choice, and it is to leave. I'm not giving you anything. You live your miserable life as it is with your goddamn marks to show that you are truly a demon and remain alone, because I refuse to give you a person to keep as a pet. And know that I will be doing everything possible to make sure that the ward is replaced, and you are confined here in your home as was intended."

I felt a surge of pride. This was the Sky I knew—strong and determined no matter the cost.

"I do believe you are underestimating the situation." Logan's velvety soft voice contrasted with the deadly glare he shot at her.

"No, I understand the situation just fine."

"Then you understand that you aren't really in a position to bargain." Logan's smug grin returned. "At this juncture, the only thing you should ask is how much time you have to deliver."

Sky hesitated, one hand on the door frame. As I watched, I wished that I could take the burden of this moment for her, that I could be the one who bore the danger and the terrible decision that had to be made, whether to sacrifice another's happiness in order to survive.

"No deal," Sky said. "If I have to die just so that you can continue to live this miserable life, then so be it."

She started out the door.

Logan's hand twitched.

Sky dropped to her knees, her face screwed up in pain, clutching her chest as she gasped for breath. Her heart thumped hard once then stopped, thumped again a few seconds later, its beat arrhythmic and shallow.

I watched in horror as Sky battled the pain running

through her. She tried to rise to her feet, staggered, and fell. I moved toward her, but Logan held up a hand.

"Stop right there," he said. "I can do far worse than this, and I will if you come a step closer."

I froze, watching helplessly as Logan stroked the jar holding the heart and Sky kept writhing on the ground. The only thing keeping me from ripping out Logan's throat was the fear that he might kill Sky before I reached him.

"Let her go," I growled.

"Hm." Logan looked around the room, casting a slow, disdainful stare up and down each of us, before settling his gaze back on me. "I wonder, do you really think that's something I'd consider right now?"

"Stop it, or I'll make you regret it."

Logan curled his fingers and Sky screamed.

"I don't think you're taking the point, Ethan," he said. "Every time you threaten me, you make things worse for yourselves. None of this is stopping until you learn that lesson."

"We don't respond well to threats," Sebastian said, his tone cold.

"And yet you give them out so easily," Logan said. "Not that I'm complaining—hypocrisy is food and drink to a Tre'ase, as rich and filling as your pain. Speaking of which..." He raised a finger. "Step back, Ethan, or this is going to get a lot worse."

I looked at Sky, lost in her own private world of agony, then at Logan, that raised finger curling around toward the jar. Hate flashed like fire through me, but I took a step back.

Sebastian took my arm and drew me to the side of the room. He, Josh, and I huddled together, talking in whispers while Logan watched Sky and laughed maliciously to himself.

"Can you break this magic?" Sebastian asked.

"Maybe, eventually, given time and research," Josh said,

frowning. "But here and now, no chance. I've never seen anything like this, and Tre'ase magic has a strength that I can't punch through by brute force."

"I'm going to kill him," I hissed, shooting a look of pure hatred at Logan. "I'm going to rip off his head and shove it down his throat."

"This is not the time, Ethan," Sebastian said. "We need solutions, and violence isn't one right now."

"Give Logan what he wants," Josh said. "It's the only solution we have."

"And bind the pack to empowering Logan?" Sebastian asked. "We would be making a bigger problem for further down the line."

"If we don't, there is no further down the line for Sky."

"And if I do, then the pack is bound to this deal. What we agree isn't just about those of us in this room, it's about the whole pack. As Alpha, I have to consider them."

An awkward silence fell between us, punctuated by Logan's low laughter and the sound of Sky twitching against the floor.

Sebastian stood up straight and looked Logan in the eye.

"If you kill her, you'll get nothing from us," he said. "Worse than nothing."

"Is that a threat again?" Logan flicked his hand and Sky's back arched as she twisted in fresh pain. "You remember how I feel about those."

"Not a threat, a statement of fact. You can manipulate us by torturing Sky, but there's a limit, and you should be careful you don't cross it."

"A wise point." Logan lowered his hand and Sky curled forward again, still whimpering in pain but no longer bent over in terrible spasms. "You see, we can both be reasonable. Now get back to your pups and make a decision before my patience wears thin."

Sebastian turned to me and Josh.

"That's one of our pack lying there," I said at last, pointing at Sky. "You said you had to consider them all, but what about considering her?"

"I am, and one of the things I'm considering is her view on this. She refused the deal with Logan. Do you want us to go against her wishes?"

"If it saves her life, yes!"

I'd had enough. I couldn't stand any more of us pointlessly arguing while Logan tortured Sky.

"Stop it!" I bellowed, striding toward Logan.

Sebastian grabbed my arm and hauled me back. I swung my fist, missing Logan's mocking grin by a fraction of an inch.

"I will stop when we have an agreement."

He held his hand out, fingers hovering over the jar. The heart within pulsed, then went still, and Logan raised an eyebrow at me, as if challenging me to come at him again.

I could barely contain my anger, which snapped and snarled like a living thing inside me. He had hurt Sky, a woman I cared about more than any other I had met in my life. For all I knew, he was killing her, snatching away the one person in the world who made me truly happy. My vision clouded as a red rage descended. But Sebastian still had hold of my arm, his cool and steady grip a reminder of the terrible reality we faced. If I attacked, it would just make things worse. Killing Logan would kill Sky.

I was helpless, unable to do anything to save Sky. My whole life was about protecting the people around me, and now, when one of those people most needed me, any action I took would only make things worse. I was so used to being able to take control, to tear through the problems facing me, that this moment became unbearable, a knife twisting in my heart. I had to find the patience Sebastian had taught me, but it was impossible to stay calm while frustration twisted me into knots.

"No," Sky panted. "Don't agree."

"We agree," Sebastian said.

Logan's smile, already insufferable, somehow grew wider. With a flick of his wrist, he released the magic surrounding Sky. I heard her heart return to a swift but steady beat, accompanied by deep, ragged breaths as she lay on the floor, finding her strength once more. At last, she stood.

There was another magic in the room now, not a spell but just as powerful. Sebastian's agreement had bound us to Logan not with the simple social and legal bonds on which humanity relied, but with something far more potent. A sick look of satisfaction crossed Logan's face as he pulled the magic tight, binding us to him through our agreement. Not for the first time, the fate of the pack was tied to an outsider who meant us no good.

I watched Sky as the reality of the situation sank in. She stood tense, angry, determined. Despite what Logan had just done to her, the proof he had provided that her life was his to extinguish, it seemed that she might still leap at him.

I shrugged Sebastian off and moved over to Sky, so close that when I leaned in my lips brushed against her ear.

"Come on, let's go," I said.

We walked to the car, every one of us heavy with the burden of what had just happened. These days, it seemed that we couldn't get through a morning without finding a fresh threat to the pack.

"Are we really going to do this?" Sky asked.

"We don't have a lot of options, Sky," Sebastian said.

"Of course we do. We don't do it."

"Do you think he was bluffing in there?" Sebastian snapped, his features crumpling in frustration.

"He was going to let you die," I said, fighting to contain the fury those words conjured. "What were you thinking?"

"I was thinking that I didn't want to give him the upper hand."

"He has the upper hand!"

"We don't even know where Chris is," Sky said. "And do you think Samuel is going to give us the third Clostra again so that we can remove a curse from a Tre'ase?"

I slid into the driver's seat of my SUV and sat there tense while Sky got in, thoughts about what had just happened racing through my mind. It was my job to face any threat that came at the pack or its members, but how could I keep doing that when we were bringing the threats on ourselves?

Lifting the curse on Sky had been the right thing to do, not just because she was Sky, but because that was what the pack did—we looked after our own. But in doing so, we had undone magic that upheld the delicate balance of the supernatural world. Vampires walked freely in the daylight. Elven creatures had burst out of the dark forest, unrestrained by the barriers around it. The ward that kept the Tre'ases tied to their homes had fallen, and now they were free to commit whatever atrocities they saw fit, to once again twist the world to their dark ends, just as Logan was twisting us to his. We had given him a taste of freedom, and he had used it to threaten and kill. What more would he do if we took away the remaining restraints?

In a way, it didn't matter. Whatever came at the pack, it was my job to deal with it.

Sky's seatbelt clicked into place. I turned the key in the ignition and heard the comforting sound of a well-tuned engine stirring to life. As I headed out onto the road, the car moving to my will, my racing thoughts started to settle.

I could deal with this.

We drove away from Logan's in silence, just the rumble of the engine and the hum of the road beneath my wheels.

Every time my thoughts started to settle, I flashed back to the image of Logan's face and my fury rose again.

I needed this silence, but apparently it was too much for Sky.

"What—"

"Sky, please. Not now."

I kept my eyes on the road, finding my focus in the drive. On instinct, I headed back toward Sky's house, accelerating as we headed along the country roads. When we reached the house, I stopped in the driveway and sat, hands gripping the wheel, battling to keep my calm without the road to steady me.

Sky got out of the car and headed for the front door. I wanted to follow her, to find comfort in her presence, to talk about what had happened and to reassure her that things would be all right. But my body trembled with rage and frustration, and there could be no peace or comfort in that.

I got out of the car and went around to the back of the house. There, I stripped off my clothes and stood staring into the wilderness of the forest, the place where the animal within me lived.

The wolf rose inside me and I gladly gave way to it. My body buckled, bones stretched and twisted, muscles spasmed, and I sank to the ground, a creature of fur, claws, and killer instinct. I could smell the wood sap, hear rodents rushing through the undergrowth, feel every faint stirring of the wind through my fur.

I took to my paws and ran.

Like the woods behind my own home, this was a safe space to run. Few of Sky's neighbors bothered to come out here, too caught up in their human lives to recognize the joy of this densely wooded land. The only one I ever saw was David, who already knew what I was, and I could tell by his distant scent that he was safely at home with his partner

Trent. No one would stand in my way as I ran. No one would ask why a wild wolf was here.

I raced between the trees, losing myself in the rhythm of the run.

As I ran, images of our encounter with Logan flashed through my mind. The malicious grin on his face. The glee he had taken in torturing Sky. The terrible realization of what control he had over her. I had seen the woman I cared about almost die, and that image tore me apart inside. I had to run away the grief, the frustration, the fury clouding my mind.

The dread and pain at the thought of losing her coursed through my veins, powering my every movement through the woods. One day, I would have revenge on Logan, but for now there was nothing I could do against him, and that made things even worse. I couldn't fight for what mattered to me, and without that fight there was nowhere for my fury to go. The only way to burn off my emotions was to run.

I pictured Sky lying on Logan's floor, writhing in agony, and I wanted to howl in hurt and pain, to vent my anguish. But that howl would be heard all around and might draw unwelcome attention. Instead, I quickened my pace, running until my muscles ached and the breath burned in my lungs, trying to chase that terrible image from my mind.

As my head began to clear, I thought about how we could make Sky safe. There wasn't an easy answer to this situation, but that didn't mean that no answer could be found. Logan had a hold over us and he thought he could bend us to his will, but he clearly didn't understand the ways of were animals. We weren't pets to be coddled or controlled, we weren't livestock to be herded and tamed. There was a reason we came in the forms we did—wolves, panthers, snakes, coyotes. We were the wild, forceful and independent. We bowed our heads to no masters.

To some people, the fact that it was Chris who Logan

wanted might have mattered. But there had never been love between me and my ex, and now there was nothing. Whoever Logan wanted, I would have denied him in just the same way. I wouldn't make my worst enemy into a magic-bound slave to a monster's lust.

I understood why Sky had considered it. She had been desperate, trapped, looking for a way out. But she was better than Logan, and she had denied him in the end.

Sky filled my mind as I swerved between the trees, the mulch of fallen leaves flying from my paws, filling my senses with a soft, earthy scent. Things were changing between me and Sky. When she had first come to the pack she had seemed like a liability. She refused to follow the rules, to obey the hierarchy, even to bow to common sense. It had taken her a year to even accept that she needed to be part of a pack, and when she did, she had been a source of constant disruption, with her untamed emotions and her wild behavior.

That same behavior and those same emotions that had frustrated me had eventually drawn me to her. They were the signs of a strong spirit, a woman of passion and empathy who refused to let the world break her.

Now our relationship was changing. Our romantic involvement brought me joy but also uncertainty. Could this last? Was there a way to make it work between us?

For that to happen, I needed to disentangle our personal relationship from our pack one. I was the Beta of the Midwest Pack and she was one of its members. When I gave an order, she needed to obey, whatever her instincts. But we were lovers, too, and I needed to keep that power imbalance from spilling over and ruining what we had.

Even as I thought about her, I could feel Sky's presence behind me at the house. We'd been bound together ever since we performed the spell to remove my grandmother's dark elf magic from me, and she had become a constant in the back of my mind, always drawing me toward her. I turned and dashed through the trees. We had endured the confrontation with Logan together. We should enjoy the run together now.

Emerging from between the oaks and pines, I saw Sky standing beneath a tree, her tablet in her hand. She smiled at me as I approached close enough to bump her lightly with my nose, then grab her pants between my teeth and tug.

"I don't want to change," she said.

I pulled my lips back and snarled my displeasure.

"Yeah, yeah," she said. "You're scary. Vicious. Terrifying. Carry on."

She waved dismissively toward the woods, then settled down next to a tree and started looking at the tablet.

I got it. She was looking for comfort in something familiar after the tension of confronting Logan, losing herself from that grim reality in a book. But a run would help clear her mind and help bring us closer together. I leaned over and bumped her leg with my head.

"I said no. Ethan, I don't want to change. I need to stay like this."

I growled.

"Eek. Now you're super scary." She rolled her eyes and returned to the book.

Frustrated, I shoved the tablet out of her hands and onto the ground. Even as I did it, I knew it was a mistake. This was the domineering Beta emerging again, trying to bend a weaker wolf to his will. But that couldn't be how this part of our life worked. I didn't want Sky to run with me because I'd forced her. If she ran with me, it should be because she wanted to, and if not, I would just have to run alone.

"Real mature," she shouted as I trotted away. "Bad wolf!"

I ran again, but no matter how far or how fast I went I couldn't outrun my frustrations. I was angry at myself for not managing my feelings around Sky better; angry at Logan for the hurt he had inflicted on her; angry at Sky herself for constantly putting her own life in danger. The vampires, the witches, the elves, everyone had earned my fury over the past few months, and it ran together into a deep pool of rage that I couldn't drain no matter how far I ran.

At last I gave in. There was no peace to be found in the forest, but at least I could find some comfort with Sky.

At the edge of the woods I paused to change back into my human form. I emerged from the trees and approached Sky, who was still sitting and reading beneath a tree. She stood as I approached, her eyes running up and down my body. The scorn and mockery she had once thrown upon the casual nakedness of the pack was gone. If she still had a problem with me showing up like this, then it certainly didn't show.

I stopped close to her and took a deep breath, drinking in her scent. My skin tingled and my heart beat faster at the intoxicating smell.

I opened my eyes and walked toward her until we were only inches apart. She was a thing of beauty, with thick waves of mahogany hair falling around her oval face, full lips parted just a little as she looked up at me with those deep-green eyes. I laid a hand on her waist and walked her back until she was pressed up against the tree, then ran my gaze down her body, taking in every last curve.

Slowly, I leaned in and pressed my face against the smooth skin of her neck. She let out a long, wavering breath and ran her fingers through my hair as I moved up to kiss her on the lips. My kiss was gentle at first, and she responded in kind, rousing my passion. I kissed her more deeply, losing myself in her presence.

But the thoughts that had assailed me before returned. I was as frustrated by her as I was drawn to her, as furious as I was aroused. She had endangered herself, endangered us all through the way she dealt with Logan.

I drew my head back and looked at her, trying to make sense of this woman and of my own complicated feelings toward her. It was impossible to separate good from bad, joy from frustration. They became a heady mix in Sky Brooks, a sweet but potent cocktail that I couldn't resist despite myself.

Again, I buried my face in the curve of her neck, resting there while I tried to steady myself, to work out what I needed to say. I kissed her on the neck, unsure how she would respond to any of this. She let out another soft breath, and so I kissed higher, across her cheek, over her jawline, back to her lips. Then I kissed her with all the passion and all the fury running through me, pouring out all my feelings.

At last, I willed myself to pull back, lingering for a moment as I did so to taste her lips. Then I steeled myself for what had to come next.

"Don't do anything like that again," I said, still thinking of her and Logan.

"Ethan," she responded, our lips brushing against each other as she spoke, keeping that precious contact between us. She ran a hand across the side of my face, and I could tell that she was going to find some distraction or some way to try and debate this. But her behavior around Logan wasn't a thing between the two of us, and on that I had to be firm. I took both of her hands in mine and cradled them gently against my chest, clinging to something of our personal relationship as I fought to focus on the pack one.

"No," I said firmly. "There is nothing to discuss. Next time we are anywhere near Logan, you say nothing. You do nothing. You sit there with a smile and, if you need to, clamp your hands between your legs and don't do a damn thing. I don't care what you do, but you will remain silent."

I pushed away from her, grabbed my clothes from where I had left them on the ground, and headed for the house. I hated fighting with her and knew making demands would only result in her digging her heels in more. She hated our rules and my role in protecting the pack. I couldn't let her put herself in danger, and I couldn't let a pack issue become a debate. If I stayed with her here, then I wouldn't be able to stay strong, so I had to walk away.

We had only been together a short time, but already our relationship was becoming uncomfortably complicated.

"Ethan," she called out after me. "Ethan!"

The living room of the house was tidier than I had seen it in some time. Steven's absence was making all the difference. I pulled on my clothes and went to lean against the kitchen counter, even as Sky stomped up to the house.

"Wait a goddamn minute," she barked as she stormed in. "I am not a child. You don't just tell me to sit down and shut up. Today didn't go as expected. I can't change that. I was trying to fix the situation."

"But you didn't fix it!" I snapped. "Instead I watched you writhe on the ground for thirty-six minutes, trying to stay alive. No, Skylar, 'sit down and shut up' is exactly what you will do in any meetings dealing with Logan that you accompany us to. This is not a suggestion. It's not up for discussion. It's a command. As a member of the pack who is responsible for the safety of it, I have spoken. End of discussion."

I could hear her heart racing, could see her fury reddening her cheeks. Well, tough. She wasn't the only one here who was mad as all hell. She was a pack member and I was the Beta; that made me responsible for her safety. I had to make her understand the importance of compliance in building a strong pack and keeping us all safe. She could be as wild and willful as she wanted on her own time, but not when we were acting as a pack, and most of all not when it was going to put her in danger. I couldn't stand to see anyone hurt Sky—not even herself.

All she had to do was one simple thing—say yes and accept her place in the pack. She couldn't even do that, could she?

I was the Beta of the Midwest Pack, and as such I was used to being obeyed. When I gave an order, pack members did as they were told, just like Sky should. It was even harder to accept this disobedience from someone so much closer to me, someone who had more power to hurt me than the rest. The person I relied on to provide peace and calm was instead creating stress and tension.

"Ethan." Her tone softened and she stepped closer, caressing my cheek with her hand. I turned my head away, unable to even look at her.

She stepped back into the middle of the room and took off her clothes, casting aside her t-shirt and then letting her jeans drop to the floor. It was all I could do not to look at her naked body. Then she shifted into her wolf and walked back over to me, nudging at my leg, tugging at my pants just like I'd done to her.

Dammit, she knew how to get under my skin, but this was what I'd wanted—a chance for us to bond as wolves. With a sigh, I took off my own clothes and shifted.

She retreated to the center of the living room and lay down on the floor. I longed to join her, to lie together in the comfort of our animal forms, but I was wary. Was I giving too much ground by letting her draw me in like this? Could I really let the anger go?

I approached her cautiously, drawn in by the sight and scent of her. With one tentative paw I reached out to touch her, and when she didn't resist I lay down across her, our bodies fitting perfectly together. I licked her face and she snuggled back into my chest. We lay like that for a long time, resting in the rhythm of each other's breath.

Sky was the first to shift back, her fur receding and her body twisting as she became human again. I lay there a few minutes longer, reluctant to let go of what we just had but unable to resist that body. Then I shifted as well, returning to my human form with my arms wrapped around Sky.

I rolled on top of her, our bodies pressed together, her olive skin warm and soft against mine. We kissed, my tongue exploring her mouth, then my lips drifted across hers, along her neck, across her shoulders and breasts, tasting the sweet salt of her skin.

My hips pressed against hers, gently at first, and she let out a deep, trembling breath. Her legs widened and I pressed on, slow and gentle, easing into her. Her nails dug into my back as she pulled me in as I moved faster, harder. I grabbed her hair and pulled her to me, kissing her as I gripped her tight. At last she gasped and arched her back, a moment before pleasure grabbed hold of me and we both cried out.

I rolled onto my back, closed my eyes, and pulled her onto me. I ran my fingers across her, enjoying the contours of her curves, the smoothness of her skin. For the first time all day, my anger was gone. There was just me and Sky in the whole world.

"Ethan," she said, running a finger over me.

"Hmm." I opened my eyes just a little to look up at her.

"If you ever command me to do anything like that again, you won't like what happens next."

I laughed. Even now, Sky's willful spirit was showing through, the spirit that drew me to her. Despite her words, she seemed relaxed, and I wondered if this was how we should deal with every argument between us.

"What exactly will that be?" I asked.

"Probably something like you screaming you can't believe I kicked you in the balls," she said, looking straight at me. The green of her eyes was like the forest, a piece of wild nature lying here in my arms.

I smiled at this fresh display of Sky's fiery will. It seemed I'd pushed things too far and was at risk of being kicked in the worst possible place. But as Beta I still had a duty to make her understand.

"It was an order," I said, the words flowing from me now that they weren't bottled up behind a layer of anger. "In the pack, I'm over you. I have an obligation to keep you safe. Yes,

I will order you to do things, and your only response should be 'yes.' You're welcome to add 'sir' to it if you'd be inclined."

"That's not going to work for me."

She sat up, grabbed a throw off the sofa, and wrapped it around herself. Disappointed by this sudden move away from nudity, I sat up too and tugged at the cover until one of her breasts was exposed. I ran my hand down her side, but she slapped it away, pulled the throw up, and wrapped it tighter around her.

"I'm serious. You were angry. I get it. Things didn't go as planned."

Suddenly, the anger was back, flashing through me like a spring flood. I clung desperately to the peace we had just found, using the memory as an anchor to keep myself from being swept away.

"I watched you almost die," I said. "Don't ask me to be okay with that or the fact that you might do it again, because it's not going to happen."

She frowned and looked away, pulling the throw tighter around her, as if it might protect her from me. I kept forgetting how new this all was to her—not just our relationship but any relationship. Fear of her animal side had kept her from finding anyone before we met, and that could have created an imbalance between us, if I had ever met anyone quite like Sky before.

"Sky, this is new for me, too," I said. "You..." I hesitated, struggling to find the words. "You challenge me in ways that I'm not used to. I don't know how to deal with you—with this."

"Telling me I need to sit down and shut up definitely isn't the way."

I nodded and smiled. Of course it wasn't. This was Sky.

"I'm not backing down; you can't do anything like that again, Sky. You can't. You can't put yourself in danger—"

The breath caught in my throat at the thought. I lay back

on the floor and Sky settled next to me, burying her face in my chest. This sort of moment was meant to be simple, but it never could be between us, could it?

"I know that wasn't handled well," Sky said, "but Logan is the last person we want to have us in his pocket. We can't remove his marks or give him Chris. We just can't. Not even to save my life. We have to figure something out."

"I know. But for now we have to at least let him think he's going to get what he wants. If we don't put up a good faith display that we are working on it, he'll try to kill you."

An uncomfortable silence descended. I wished that I knew what Sky was thinking. Was she happy with how things were changing between us? Could she be content with her place in the pack? It had already become hard to imagine my life without her in it, but that was what would happen if we couldn't find a way to make this work.

I wasn't used to being with someone like Sky, someone for whom relationships were just about the connections you made, not about power. I'd spent so long around weres, witches, and vampires, their lives a constant struggle for dominance, but Sky had grown up with humans, and she had a kindness only they could possess. It led to moments of incredible compassion, but it could lead to foolish naivety as well.

Sky was frowning, gazing across my body with a half-focused expression. It was as if she was in the room with me but looking at something I couldn't see.

"What's wrong?" I asked.

"Nothing."

Her heart rate increased, as it always did when she lied. I tensed, ready for another round of arguing, but then I real-ized that I had seen other people wear that expression she had now. Josh wore it, and other witches, too, when they were sensing the magic around them.

Was Sky exploring the magic around me?

I sat up quickly. There were things she still didn't know, about the spirit shade, about how Josh had been saved, about my past and the power dwelling inside me. Things that were too dangerous to tell, for her, for me, and for the whole pack.

"I need to get going," I said, keeping my voice level. "I really need to talk to Sebastian and Josh."

She nodded and sat up, too, the throw sliding off her shoulder. I wished that we had more time together, just the two of us, naked and alone. But there would be other chances for this, and that thought made me smile.

I stood and started to dress.

"Do you plan on showing Josh and me the spell you used on Ethos?" Sky asked. "It might be something we need in the future."

So she had been pondering my magic. I couldn't quite suppress a smirk at realizing that I'd gotten inside her head.

"Of course, it's easy," I said, quickly thinking up an excuse. "It was just a spell—an archaic one. I'm pretty sure our mother showed Josh before, but he wasn't always as interested in old magic as he should have been."

As I headed for the door, I caught a glimpse of movement through the window. A young-looking woman, her black hair decorated with lavender extensions, stood in the driveway—the psychotic vampire Sable. For once, she didn't look like she was out for blood. Sky's propensity for picking up strays was showing again.

"Your other vampire is here to visit," I said.

I nodded to Sable as I headed out the door, letting her know that I had seen her here, and if there was trouble, I would know who to blame. Then I got into my car and drove away.

I drove up to the pack's retreat, a large building on its own forested patch of land, well away from the bustle of Chicago and all the major routes in and out. This place wasn't exactly a secret anymore—too many other supernatural visitors had been here, whether as friends or foes. But it was at least discreetly tucked away out of ordinary human sight.

Josh was in the library, as was so often the case these days. Ours was one of the most impressive collections of magical texts in the United States, with some books that even the witches didn't possess. Anyone looking for a solution to a magical problem would do well to start here.

"What's up?" Josh looked up from a pile of books he'd scattered across the table in the center of the room. While not as bad as Steven, my brother still had a way of spreading out to fill the available space. Order and organization could wait when there was a goal to be pursued.

"Working on ways to beat Logan?" I asked, looking over the selection of books. There were tomes on Tre'ases, magical bindings, and the workings of pacts and promises. It wasn't hard to draw the line from where we'd been a few hours earlier.

"You'd better believe it." Josh ran a hand through his tousled hair. "There's no way I'm letting him hurt Sky again."

I gave him a sidelong glance. It wasn't so long since Josh had taken a romantic interest in Sky, but he genuinely seemed to have abandoned those thoughts since we got together. His concern for her now held a more brotherly tone, one friend looking out for another.

"While you're digging around in this, could you keep an eye out for something else for me?" I asked.

"Seriously?" Josh asked, looking indignant. "You think I'm going to let you distract me from looking after Sky?"

"This is for Sky, too," I said. It wasn't true, but I couldn't tell him the truth—that his own survival was tied to a spirit shade, one that lived inside me and I'd been hiding from him.

When we were young, the power of the spirit shade inside me had been used to hold back a curse cast on Josh. The curse was still in him, as was the magic restraining it. My spirit shade would die if someone killed the Tre'ase that made it, and then Josh would die, too. I needed a way to make my brother safe, and that meant securing the Tre'ase.

Josh narrowed his eyes as he looked at me.

"What am I missing?" he asked. "Or rather, what haven't you been telling me?"

I sighed and sat down in a chair across the book-littered table from him.

"Is there any way to sever the link between a spirit shade and a Tre'ase?" I asked.

"Not that I've ever heard of, and I've been delving deep into this stuff." Josh slapped one of the books for emphasis.

"What if I could track down a Tre'ase and bind it somehow—could we find a way then?"

"It's a long shot, but maybe."

"Then I need you to look out for that: ways to find and bind a Tre'ase."

"Okay." Josh tore a sheet from a notebook and scribbled something on it. "I'd be looking in the same books anyway. Might as well kill two terrible monstrosities with one stone."

"Thanks."

"Finding a way to track the Tre'ase should be relatively straightforward. The other part..." He shrugged. "If there's a way, I'll find it."

He pulled a book toward him and started reading again, making notes as he went. Despite my own magical abilities, inherited from our mother just like his, I wouldn't be able to understand what he was scribbling. My magic was instinctive. Josh's had been shaped and channeled through years of study and practice. He could grasp the fundamental principles of magic and use them to create a new spell. To me, those principles were as incomprehensible as quantum physics. I just worked with what I was given.

"One more thing," I said as I headed for the door. "Don't tell Sky about this. It might take us years to trap a Tre'ase, if we ever can. I don't want to give her false hope."

CHAPTER 2

Sebastian leaned back in his seat and stretched. We'd been talking in his office for over an hour, going over the details of the encounter with Logan. With the patience and focus Sebastian brought to so many of the pack's problems, we were picking the situation apart and putting it back together, making sure we understood what we faced.

"He's not one of the most powerful Tre'ases in the area," I said, passing Sebastian a sheet of paper listing known manifestations of Logan's power. I kept dossiers on all the significant supernatural players in our territory, assembled using scrying magic, reconnaissance by pack members, rumors among other locals, and even modern surveillance technology. As far as possible, I knew who our competitors were, what they could do, and where they could be found. "Or rather, he hasn't looked like one of the most powerful. The problem is, he was locked away in the woods for so long, he might not have shown us his full strength."

"So he could have powers we don't know about?" Sebastian asked.

"He caught another Tre'ase and tore out its beating heart.

There's got to be more to him than just changing his appearance and a little light soothsaying."

Sebastian frowned.

"I don't like not knowing what we're dealing with," he said. "Sky's life is at stake here, and thanks to the deal we struck for her, so is the security of the pack."

"You think I don't know that?" I remembered Sky writhing on the ground as Logan inflicted pain on her. Frustration and anger flared through my mind. "I saw what he did. I was there for the deal."

"It's more than that," Sebastian said. "Logan represents a new force in the region, one who could disturb what passes for a balance of power around here. If we don't deal with him effectively, he could end up working with our enemies, and we don't even know what he could offer them. I need you to get better intelligence on him, Ethan. We know he has dark magic, but we need to find out what he can do with it."

"The problem is that he's been trapped for so long, not using much of his power. No one we know has seen what he's capable of."

"Then dig deeper. Ask old powers. Look into the historical records. Do whatever it takes."

I would try, but it wasn't going to be easy. We had other issues to deal with, and only so many hours in the day. I rubbed the side of my head, trying to drive out the tension building there.

"We wouldn't have this problem if we hadn't lifted that curse," I said. "He's out for the same reason the vampires can safely walk in daylight—the side effects of our actions."

"You did your best with what you knew," Sebastian said. "That's all we can ever do. Now tell me about Chris."

"So far, I've heard nothing about where she is, but I've got one of my human agents on it. Chris isn't like a Tre'ase, she needs society to function, and that means she'll leave a data trail."

"Good. If we can't counteract Logan quickly, we may need to hand her over."

"It's not much of a backup plan if we can't even find her."

"It's better than nothing." Sebastian set his elbows down on the desk and leaned forward to look directly at me. "How is Sky responding to the situation?"

I knew that this was a particular concern for Sebastian. It wasn't just the chance that Sky might do something to put her life at risk. There was her mood to consider as well.

The emotions of the pack's members were always affected by one another. Part of that came from living in close proximity and relying on each other for our lives. But it was also about our animal natures and the magic that created them. It led to links that were deeper than those between ordinary humans and that sometimes worked in unexpected ways, like the bond between a newly made were and the one who had turned them. Sky's emotions were particularly powerful. They radiated from her, affecting the mood of everyone in the pack. She was a wild card in a deck that was already rigged for danger.

"I've done my best," I said. "Tried to make clear to her that she needs to rein herself in, for all our sakes."

"And how did that go?" Sebastian asked with a mocking smile. "Was Sky as sweet and obedient as always?"

I sighed wearily. "It went about as well as you'd expect."

Sebastian laughed quietly, but I could see the same weariness in him that I felt at dealing with Sky. It was difficult to deal with someone who refused to fit in with the community of the pack.

"I like Sky. She's quirky and she's kind," Sebastian said. "But I need you to get her under control, Ethan. If my Beta can't control the members of the pack, then that undermines my authority, and with it our stability."

"You think I don't get that?" I snapped. "But it's Sky. She's stubborn, strong-willed, and doesn't listen to anyone."

Now Sebastian smiled. "You mean she doesn't always do as you say?"

"Exactly. And that, as you said, is the problem."

"Fair point. Let's leave this for now." Sebastian looked down at a note in front of him. "We have one more issue to discuss."

"And I've still got no news on that."

A moment of sadness crossed Sebastian's face. Like everyone in the pack, he was very fond of Kelly, the human nurse who worked in our infirmary. Her disappearance hadn't just stressed out Dr. Jeremy, the pack's physician, who now had to deal with all of our frequent injuries alone. It had upset everyone who knew Kelly, a bright, innocent, lively young woman who sparked joy wherever she went. Her absence had become one more dark undercurrent upsetting the equilibrium of the pack, and a personal hurt that affected us all.

"I thought that Gavin and Jeremy were looking for her?" Sebastian asked.

"They are, but we don't even know where to start. There's no sign of trouble with family or an ex-boyfriend, no unusual behavior before her disappearance, no trouble at her other job."

"And no trace of where she went?"

"I'm not saying that no one caught anything on camera; the country's riddled with surveillance. But we've picked over every piece of footage we can find, and we've had no luck."

Part of the problem was that we'd left it too long. At first, neither of us had believed that Kelly was missing, despite Gavin's insistence that something was wrong. We had let the situation drift while leads grew cold. It had seemed like the right call at the time, but now it was high on my list of regrets.

"Isn't there something else we can do?" Sebastian asked.

"Kelly is practically pack. She deserves all the help we would give one of our own."

"I could try hiring an investigator or two," I said. "But what if there's something supernatural behind this, or it's about our politics? We could end up pointing a human straight at the things we hide from them."

"You could investigate."

"And when this Logan business is over, I will, but unless you want me to prioritize Kelly over Sky…"

"I'm not even suggesting it."

Sebastian growled deep in his throat. He was better at accepting things he couldn't control than I was, but that didn't mean he liked them.

"Keep an eye on Gavin," he said. "He's been even more difficult to deal with since she's been gone. I can't have one of our weres tearing the pack apart when we've already got so many outside threats."

I nodded. Everyone knew that Gavin had a special fondness for Kelly, and we'd been giving him some leeway on that account, but the pack could only bend so far to work around a difficult member.

"I'll deal with it," I said.

⁎

The library wasn't exactly my favorite place in the pack's retreat. I didn't mind hitting the books, but I preferred to be out and about, whether in action or dealing with people. I'd become a lawyer for the challenge of mastering others, not learning the details of old cases. It just happened that one relied on the other.

Despite this, I seemed to be spending more and more time in the library. I'd found myself there again, going through heaps of magical texts with Josh, looking for insights into dealing with Logan and the Tre'ases, even as I wondered how my brother had found time to add to the mass of tattoos that now marred almost every inch of his arms.

"Most Tre'ases have a distinctive magical signature," Josh said, pointing at a diagram in one of the books. It showed arcane symbols arranged in formations that I was sure were meaningful to him but that I would have had to spend hours decoding. "It's in their nature and shapes the powers they can use."

"So we could use that to track down a specific individual?" I asked.

"Sure, though that's not really needed in this case. We know where Logan keeps that Tre'ase, or what remains of it. What's important here is that it affects the sort of magic you need to fight, trap, or even protect an individual Tre'ase."

"So it's more than just a magical fingerprint?"

"Much more. If you can understand their magical pattern, you can understand their strengths and weaknesses. It's the basis of any attempt to track and trap one of them."

I looked at the book, my eyes running over the symbols while I considered what this meant for us. General advice on fighting Tre'ases wouldn't be enough. We needed specifics on what we were dealing with.

"Mind if I join you?" Sky asked, appearing in the doorway.

"Sure." I gestured to a seat. "We're looking for ways to remove the curse on Logan."

"Really?" Sky asked, incredulous.

I shrugged. "It might not be what we want, but we should at least put on a good show. Plus, it gives us a backup option if things go wrong."

I shot a glance at Josh, who gave me a small nod of acknowledgment. No more talking about the topic we'd been pondering a minute before—how to track and trap a Tre'ase.

Sky sat down, pushed aside some of the litter of pens and coffee cups, and opened one of the spell books. Soon the three of us had settled into a rhythm, each working on our own parts of the research, sometimes sharing useful things we'd read or references the others might find useful. Sky and Josh kept passing a laptop back and forth, as he looked up obscure pieces of theory and she struggled to translate spells from Latin. At last, with Josh busy on the laptop and Sky forced to reach for her phone for a translation, I went around the desk to help. I didn't want to cramp Sky in her work, but we needed to get this done.

"A spell for the eradication of boils," I read over her shoulder. "I don't think this one is going to help."

Sky frowned and tapped a pen against the table. She shot Josh a look.

"This would go faster if you had your own book," he said, grinning at me. "Sky's done this before—many times. Even before you decided you wanted to start helping. So if you plan to help, then help."

I took a step aside and glared at Josh, biting back a retort about Sky's reading speed and his own chaotic approach to research. Now wasn't the time to pick a fight.

Josh clearly disagreed.

"Have a seat, brother." He flicked his finger and a chair hit my legs from behind, knocking me into it. A childish attempt to show his power, when his very presence in the pack came on my authority. It wasn't long ago that I would have shown him where he could stick that trick and even the chair itself, but I was intensely aware of Sky's presence and of the scornful way she viewed these brotherly disputes. Once again, I bit back my anger and settled to work.

A few minutes later, Josh looked up at me from his book. I braced myself for another challenge.

"Have you had any luck getting a lead on Chris?" he asked.

Not a question I'd expected, but at least it wasn't a jab at me. I leaned back in my chair and shook my head.

"How long has she been gone?" Josh asked.

"I'm not sure," I replied. "I wonder what the hell Demetrius did to her to make her leave and go underground."

"Are we really going to do this?" Sky snapped. "You're going to find Chris to give her to Logan like she's property?"

"Sky, don't do this," I said, keeping my voice low in hopes of calming her.

"Don't do what? Have ethics that get in the way of what you're thinking about doing?"

"Sky, this isn't a black-or-white situation. It's not about morals, it's about survival."

"I understand what you're saying, I just don't agree with it. I thought we were going to present the illusion that we were looking and not actually look for her." She took a deep breath and her voice emerged more level. "Why don't we work on a way to remove his marks first?"

Josh frowned at me, looking aggrieved.

"You didn't tell her?" he asked.

"Tell me what?" Sky glanced back and forth between us.

"Don't you think you should tell her?" Josh asked in a low drawl. "I didn't agree to this. We've done some crappy things before, but this is low. Very low. His obsession should not be our obligation."

"You know I don't want to do this," I said. "We don't have a lot of options."

"Not yet, but we can keep looking."

"While he holds his power over us? While he could keep torturing Sky?"

"While we buy time. We've done it before."

"We've not dealt with power like this before, we can't keep assuming that—"

"You all are looking for Chris to give her to that monster?" Sky butted in, standing to glare down at us, as stern as any judge. "Are you insane? She escaped from one, only to be handed over to another."

I took deep breaths, calming myself as Sky's fury washed across the room and out through the building. I could feel my body respond to it, the turmoil that her emotions brought, and I was glad that at least none of the other weres were in the room.

Sky's naivety, which could sometimes be so charming, was becoming an obstacle where Chris was concerned. The survival of the pack, like that of any supernatural group, was only possible through politics and pragmatism. We couldn't always afford to do the right thing. Sometimes all we could do was take the least bad choice, and in this case those choices had been shaped by Sky herself.

"How can you do this to her?" Sky continued. "You know she's hiding from Demetrius because of what he did to her."

Just mentioning Demetrius, the Master of the Northern Seethe, brought my own deep-seated anger to the fore. The vampire leader was as vile a figure as I'd ever had to deal with, cruel and ruthless. His desire to break the independent Chris was entirely in character with a man who wanted everyone's obedience no matter the cost. The fact that she defied him after he had created her only made him more determined to rein her in. But while I might not like the guy, I could at least understand the impulse. A seethe, like a pack, needed some sense of order to survive.

"I know, Sky," I said, keeping the anger out of my voice. "I have no intention of handing her off to him, but if we need more time, well—"

"Well what, Ethan?" She looked at me like I'd just brought a mutilated body in and dumped it at her feet.

I leaned in and took her hand, seeking the connection we had, hoping to cut through her hostility and get her to listen to reason.

"Sky, I give you my word," I said, "we will not be giving Chris to Logan."

As long as we could find another solution, that would remain true, and I was confident that something could be found. With Josh's skills and this whole library at our disposal, Chris was very much a last resort.

"You have to promise me that under no circumstance will you do this," she said. "I'll concede to removing his marks, but we can't give him a person. We can't devolve into monsters."

It was hard to stay angry when the situation was so absurd. These weren't Sky's decisions to make, a point she was constantly forgetting. And as long as she failed to challenge anyone and take a formal place in the pack, none of that was going to change. The irony was that she could gain some influence over this business if she just stepped up, like other weres did. But irony, like pack politics, was lost on Sky.

I smiled at her and she looked away.

"Concede?" I said. "Sky, I do believe you have misunderstood your position in this pack. We consider your desires, but Sebastian and I make the decisions. You don't concede anything."

Her lips twitched, but whatever response she was considering, it didn't come out.

Sky would almost certainly get her way. Handing over Chris might get us off the hook with Logan, but it could bring a heap of other troubles down on our heads. Not just Chris's own response, using the skilled and brutal violence she had spent years honing as a hunter, but Demetrius's response. He might not like Chris defiant, but he would like her to be controlled by Logan even less. Such an affront to his authority would risk triggering a war between us and the Northern Seethe if he ever found out we were behind it. Much as I wanted to kick the ass of every vampire in the territory, that wasn't a fight we needed.

Handing over Chris was a Hail Mary move—better than nothing, but only just.

The problem was getting Sky to accept that. No matter how many times the rules of the pack were explained to her, she seemed unable to wrap her head around them. Important decisions were made by Sebastian, supported by the ranking members of the pack. That hierarchy was bound by strict rules, without which any pack risked descending into bloody anarchy. We lived or died by the rules, and even Sky Brooks wasn't immune from them.

For once, she seemed to accept that, bowing her head. When she looked up, I leaned in and kissed her on the cheek.

"I promise you," I said, "I will do everything to come up with something you can live with. Okay?"

She nodded.

"At what point should I be offended that I didn't get any kisses and promises?" Josh said with a mocking grin. "I said something very similar to you this morning, and not once did you cuddle me, and I damn sure didn't get any gentleness or sweet kisses. I'm starting to feel like you like Sky a little more than me."

"As if there's a contest," I said, laughing. I set the book I had been reading down and headed for the door. "I definitely like her more than you."

I let the door fall closed behind me, and a second later there was a thud of flung books colliding with wood. I laughed. Let the pair of them get this out of their system, let them sit and moan about me now. As long as they followed the line and got the work done, all would be well.

I pushed through the glass doors of my legal firm, nodded to Aaron the receptionist behind his cherrywood desk, and headed down the corridor toward my office. It was a quiet afternoon, with half the senior partners away at a conference and other staff relaxing in their absence. That made it the perfect time to use office resources for pack business.

Stacy, my paralegal, followed me into the office and closed the door behind her. As I sat down behind the desk, she opened a document on a tablet.

"I presume you want to talk about Chris first?" she asked.

I nodded. By long habit, my off-the-books business always came first on our agenda; that way, there was less risk of getting interrupted as we discussed werewolves, vampires, or cyberattacks.

Stacy's skills went well beyond law and administration. When I'd first met her, she had been a low-level attorney at a firm in New York, using her computing skills to discreetly siphon off money from clients' retainers. Those funds hadn't gone to her own accounts, but a gang of Russian-American gangsters who had gotten their claws into her. I had surprised her not just by catching her in the act, but by believing her wild story, getting her out from under that gang, and providing her with a new job and a new life here in Chicago. In return, she had become one of the most loyal and valuable humans I employed, working not just as my paralegal but as my hacker, gathering information I couldn't access by other means.

"Chris is definitely in town," Stacy said, setting the tablet down in front of me. "The problem is working out where."

A slideshow of images appeared one by one on the tablet's screen. Hotel bills in the names of Chris's known aliases. Bank records with names and transactions circled in red. Images from security cameras, some grainier than others, all of them showing the same familiar face.

"She's not at one of these places?" I asked, pausing the slide deck and skipping back to the hotel bills.

"Not anymore," Stacy said. "She doesn't stay anywhere more than one night, doesn't use the same alias more than twice in a row. I'm pretty sure she's ditched the cards she used for the first three places, but I'm still tracking them just in case."

That was just like Chris—careful to the point of paranoia. It was one of a hundred reasons why things hadn't worked between us, reasons why we never should have been together at all. For all the tensions between me and Sky, our relationship was a breath of fresh air after that madness. It helped that Sky wasn't a mercenary killer turned vampire.

"You wouldn't be showing me all this if you didn't have a lead," I said, looking up at Stacy.

"You know me so well," she said with a smile, tucking her hair back behind her ear. "I've put together a list of other places she might be hiding out, ones that fit her past patterns or where she has known contacts. It's in the secure virtual folder."

There was a knock on the glass wall of the office. Without waiting for a response, Eileen Harper opened the door and walked in.

If anyone less than a named partner had acted like that, I would have put them firmly in their place, but this place was Eileen's and she knew it. One of the founding partners of the firm, she had been a driving force of the Chicago legal scene for thirty years and showed no sign of slowing down. Steely eyes swept over me from beneath a blond bob as sharp as her immaculately tailored suit.

"Yesterday was the Wadritsky meeting," she said, without preamble or concern for Stacy's presence. "Where were you, Ethan?"

"Busy with another case," I said. "I knew that the rest of you would have it. We always overstuff the room with attorneys when Wadritsky comes around. He won't notice that he's one lawyer short."

"Cut the crap, Charleston," Eileen said, tapping a lacquered nail against the glass. "We have to show respect to big wallets like Wadritsky, and I wanted your insight on the deal."

"I'll read the files again and get you an updated opinion."

"That's a start, but I want more. This isn't the first meeting you've missed recently. We give you a lot of leeway because the clients like you, but that means they notice your absence, and that makes things harder for everyone else. If you can't get on top of your work, then I need to know."

The threat hung unspoken in the air between us. There were a thousand lawyers in the city who were itching to take my seat at Wendell, Harper, and Holmes, at least a dozen of them in the firm itself. We might not spill each other's blood, but law was still a cutthroat business, and if I didn't pull my weight, then I would be tossed to the curb.

There was no denying that I'd been less reliable of late. The troubles around the pack, which had intensified alarmingly since Sky arrived, were throwing not just my life but my work into chaos. Stacy had done well at covering for me when things went unexpectedly wrong, but there was only so much she could do, and sooner or later it came back to me. I needed this position, not just for the money and the legitimacy it provided but for the influence it gave me to cover the pack's tracks. I couldn't let my supernatural side ruin my mundane life.

"I'll get on top of it," I said. "I promise."

"Promises are bullshit," Eileen said. "Just do the job."

And with that she was gone, letting the door swing closed behind her.

I took a deep breath as I considered my next move.

"So, you'll be going to the Maxwell meeting this afternoon?" Stacy asked.

I groaned and sank back in my seat. A property developer's dispute with a concrete producer was small fry by the standards of the firm, but the last thing I needed right now was to miss another meeting. On the other hand, I needed to get hold of Chris before she vanished from the city entirely.

"Can you find an excuse to delay?" I asked.

"I'll do one better," Stacy said. "A software issue at Maxwell's office. He's such a control freak, he'll postpone the meeting so he can spend the day screaming at his staff to get it fixed. That way, this one won't be your fault."

"Perfect," I said. "I'd be lost without you."

"Don't forget that at bonus time."

I pulled out my phone and opened the list of addresses Stacy had provided.

"I need to go look into some of these places," I said, getting out of my seat.

"Do you want a hand?" Stacy asked. "I know my way around seedy hotels, and a couple will raise fewer questions than a handsome executive cruising the dive districts on his own."

"I work best alone," I said. The streams of my life had gotten crossed enough already, I didn't need to tempt fate. Besides, someone would have to take all the calls I was ignoring while I hunted for Chris.

Sure, there were other things that I could have been doing with my time. Looking for Kelly, researching spells, even meeting with the odious Maxwell. But Chris was the most reliable plan I had to keep Sky safe, even if that safety came at a cost, and right now nothing mattered to me more.

Leaving behind my responsibilities as a lawyer, I headed out the door.

CHAPTER 3

*S*tacy had done her job thoroughly, as always, providing an extensive list of places Chris might be. It was late at night by the time I was halfway down that list.

The Bellhop was a roach hole hotel in the borderland between two equally rundown neighborhoods. Once upon a time, it had played host to traveling salesmen and tourists looking for an inexpensive room. These days, its clientele was almost entirely junkies and hookers, looking for somewhere to do their business where the police didn't care to interfere. That made it the perfect place to go unseen.

Everything about The Bellhop was cheap. Cheap paint peeling off the walls. Cheap carpet worn through and showing its stains. A cheap neon sign out front that shone erratically into the darkness, its light flickering enough to trigger every epileptic for a mile around. Even the receptionist was cheap, giving up the room number of a woman matching Chris's description for the sake of a twenty.

A security camera hung in the corridor leading to that room, but it wasn't one that had fed into Stacy's file of photos. Leads dangled, disconnected from the back, and the lens was covered in dust. I doubted that the hotel's owners had ever bothered buying a security system to plug the camera into. It was cheaper just to bluff.

I stopped at the door of room 403 and listened. Down the corridor, a couple were arguing, and someone was pacing back and forth two doors down, but the only sound from inside Chris's room was the inane chatter of late-night TV hosts with the volume turned down low.

I slid a set of lock-picks from my pocket and crouched in front of the door. I'd learned this work from a former master thief, but even an amateur would have had that door open in seconds. The tumbler clicked around, and I turned the handle and walked slowly into the room.

The place was everything I'd expected. Dusty carpet, lumpy mattress, cheap art prints covering the stains on fading wallpaper. A quick glance out the window showed a four-floor drop to the ground, without a fire escape to ease the way. There was no one here, and the TV had probably been left on to cover that up. I opened the window to try to clear out some of the mildew smell, closed the door, and started looking around.

Chris had definitely been here. The scent of her lingered in the air, particularly around the bed. She'd spent the night, but probably only once. The wardrobe and drawers had been cleaned out and there was nothing under the bed except dust balls and a cockroach.

I went to the bathroom, turned on the main light and the one above the sink, and scrutinized all the fittings. If Chris had gotten into trouble, then there might have been traces of blood where she'd cleaned up or toiletries abandoned in her rush to get away, but none of that was here. Chris had moved on quickly, but at her own pace.

A movement in the room behind me made me spin around. A figure stood by the window, tall and slightly built in black slacks and a button-down shirt. Dark wavy hair was swept back from cheekbones that caught the flicker of the neon light outside.

"Demetrius," I growled, tensing at the sight of the Master of the Northern Seethe.

"Ethan," he replied, raising one eyebrow. "What are you doing here?"

"I'd ask you the same thing, but a seedy hotel is very fitting for you."

I emerged from the bathroom, approaching Demetrius at a slow prowl until we stood inches from each other, tense and glaring.

We both knew why we were there. Each of us had an interest in finding Chris, and though our reasons were quite different, Demetrius had no way of knowing mine. That was good, because I didn't want him having the leverage of knowing what had happened between the pack and Logan.

"Come to rescue her, have you?" he asked, his voice a menacing hiss. "To save your precious ex from the clutches of the bloodthirsty vampires?"

"Maybe."

"And you think she'll appreciate that, do you? That she wants rescuing by some shining knight in wolfskin armor, who'll whisk her off her feet and carry her away to his fairy-tale fortress in the woods? You don't know her at all, do you?"

His sneering tone set my teeth on edge. Anger rose inside me, hot and pounding as the blood in my veins.

"I know her better than you," I snapped. "I know she wants out from under your control."

"You're wrong," Demetrius said, leaning closer to me. He tapped himself on the chest. "She wants the darkness. She wants the strength and superiority we represent, civilized creatures of power and restraint, not dogs in heat running out of control."

"If she wants you, then why was she here?"

Demetrius took a step back, lips twisting into the narrow thread of a frown. I'd cut to the heart of him with that last point, in as far as Demetrius even had a heart, and it felt good.

"She doesn't understand herself yet," he said. "But she will."

Demetrius's hand clamped down on my shoulder. I grabbed it, twisted, and flung him through the air. Dust flew as he slammed into the wall, but he landed on his feet, fangs bared and fists raised, spoiling for a fight.

"Don't touch me," I growled, feeling the wolf rise.

"Don't tell me what to do," he hissed, dark eyes gleaming with menace.

We stood for a long moment staring at each other, two creatures of power and fury. I wanted to end him then and there, to bring a close to years of strife, to save the world from Demetrius's violence. But I knew how much that would unsettle the political equilibrium in which we existed. We couldn't afford a war with the vampires. Not yet.

"Leave Chris alone," I said. "How she lives is her choice, not yours."

"Just the sort of words I would expect from you and your pack," Demetrius said. "Condescending and hypocritical. You think you're better than the rest of us, but you're the ones running out of control, bringing trouble for everyone else. All the chaos of the past few years has stemmed from you. You keep dabbling in powers that aren't your own, that you don't understand and can't control. You act, the rest of us suffer, and then you try to tell us that we should do as you command."

"Are you done whining?" I asked. "Because I've got better places to be."

"Chris is one of my people now," Demetrius said, setting one foot on the window ledge. "That means it's my job to stop her running wild. You need to stop worrying about her and start paying attention to your pack, because if you can't bring them into line, then the rest of us will, by whatever means it takes."

With that, he leapt out the window and vanished into the night, leaving me to silently curse at the empty air.

When I ran out of places to look on Stacy's list, I started chasing up ideas of my own, going to places I knew that Chris had hung out back in the day, the sort where the criminal and supernatural underworlds intersected. These were the sorts of bars where the less ethical hunters found their prey, taking on mercenary jobs tracking down humans as often as they hunted dangerous beasts.

"Sorry, bro, I haven't seen Chris in months," Ernesto said as he slid a glass of bourbon across the bar. Ernesto owned the Black Door, a discreet cellar bar with low lighting and cheap drinks. He always took the late-night shifts, as he said it was easier to keep staff if they didn't have to work those hours.

I sipped at the bourbon. It was the third one I'd had since arriving at the Black Door, filling time while I waited for Ernesto to be free. One taste had been enough to remind me why the drinks here were so cheap, but I preferred to drink bad spirits than to risk whatever came out of the beer taps.

"Is there anyone else around who might have seen her?" I asked. "Anyone from the old days?"

Ernesto stroked his mustache and looked around the room.

"Try Sofia," he said, nodding toward a table in the darkest corner of the bar. "I heard they still talk from time to time."

I paid my tab, along with a generous tip for the information, and headed over to Sofia's table, my glass of bourbon in one hand and a bottle of vodka in the other. I set the vodka down on the table and sat down across from its only occupant.

Sofia looked out from behind her choppy blond fringe and gave me a mischievous grin.

"Ethan Charleston," she said in her low Estonian accent. "Long time no drink. You feeling lonely and decide to look up an old acquaintance?"

"In a manner of speaking," I said. "I'm trying to get a hold of Chris."

Sofia gave a short, bitter laugh, emptied her glass, and reached for the vodka bottle. She poured herself a good two fingers of the sharp-smelling spirit, downed that, and poured again before she spoke.

"I thought you and Chris have let each other go. Was bad for both of you, and for your business, yes?"

"It's not like that," I said. "Chris might be in danger and I need to let her know."

There was truth in that. Chris would be in danger if Demetrius caught up with her, and probably if Logan ever got her under his control. The fact that I was considering letting one of those things happen didn't make it any less true.

"Only danger Chris is in is she ends up sleeping with wrong wolf, I think." Sofia's eyes flashed indigo, a reminder that she was still an elf, even if she scorned the rest of her kind. I knew that the scars she hid behind her hair came from elves in her home country, and that she'd been disappointed to find that as many lived in the States as in the Old World. Her life wasn't one that inclined her to trust, but I'd seen before that alcohol inclined her to talk.

"I don't need to know exactly what's going on with Chris, just some idea of what she's up to. That way, if things get worse, maybe I'll be able to get a message to her."

"Fine." Sofia poured herself another drink. "Chris is in

town, you know this, yes, or you would not be here. She is looking for work also."

"Hunter work?"

"Of course hunter work. What else would that girl do, become stripper?" Sofia laughed. "She does not have the patience for it, or the legs."

I knew firsthand that last part wasn't true, but I could keep those memories to myself.

"Do you know what her plans are other than hunting?" I asked. "Is she going to stay in Chicago for long?"

Sofia slid a hand across the table and ran her fingers up my arm. She was leaning over her glass, long hair framing a sloppy grin.

"You come back to my place, yes? I see what else I can remember. Maybe we have ourselves a party while we are there. I have wig, can dress up as Chris if you want."

Even before Sky, I would have been wary of getting cozy with a drunken and crazy elf. Now, I had someone I cared about waiting for me, and that thought got me out of my seat before Sofia could get any closer. The whole reason I was pursuing Chris was to keep Sky safe, and Sofia had clearly given all the help she could.

"Thanks for the chat," I said. "Enjoy the rest of your vodka."

Sofia let out a mewl of disappointment as I walked away, but I ignored it. There were still other places to check out.

I walked up the stairs, through the door for which the bar was named, and out into the street. To my surprise, I found myself blinking in broad daylight. I'd spent the whole night looking for information, and the best I'd gotten was that Chris was being Chris, looking for a chance to hunt.

My phone buzzed, a call from Sebastian.

"Cole's called for a council," he said as soon as I answered. "I need you back at the retreat."

"Have I got time to go home and change first?" I asked. I

didn't want to face the ranked weres of the American packs wearing a shirt that reeked of bars and booze.

"You've got until midday," Sebastian said.

The driveway of the pack's retreat was full of cars when I arrived, not just the familiar vehicles of pack members, but ones with out-of-state plates, and even a pickup truck that had come all the way from Canada, hidden away behind the SUVs and sports cars. Niimi's pickup wasn't my sort of ride, but I admired her commitment. On the rare occasions when she made one of these meetings, she made sure to remind us that life was different up north.

The grin that thought put on my face disappeared when I saw who else was here. Cole, the Alpha of the East Coast Pack, stood in the doorway of the retreat, his back to me. He was dressed in dark jeans and a deep-red button-down shirt, with the carefully calculated poise of a man pretending he was just one of the guys, a buddy you could relax with. But I knew Cole better than that, a political beast who had been aiming for control of the larger Midwest Pack for years. He had even tried to challenge me for Beta twice, probably thinking that his best way into Sebastian's shoes was through my position, but Sebastian had refused to allow those challenges. Cole had stirred that into a small political storm that had led to a change in the rules governing all our lives, meaning that Alphas could no longer protect their Betas from outside interference. The guy was trouble, and just the sight of him made me tense.

As I prowled closer, I saw who Cole was talking with. Sky stood in the doorway, dressed in a pair of yoga pants and a shirt that only just fit, looking like she'd been dressed by Winter, who was also there. Cole was leaning in close to Sky, flashing her that innocuous smile that I knew ended in trouble. One more predator closing in on her.

I walked up behind Sky. Normally, her subtle scent would have lifted my spirits, but Cole had hold of her hand and the sight put me even more on edge.

"Cole, we'll be meeting in Sebastian's office," I said.

Cole dropped Sky's hand and looked over at me. For a moment, I saw a flicker of something that could have been frustration, but then his usual welcoming smile appeared.

I wrapped my arms protectively around Sky, pulling her close, and rested my chin on her head as she settled against me.

"It's probably a good idea for you to go in and grab a seat now," I continued, locking eyes with Cole.

His smile faltered and he stepped back, heading toward Sebastian's office. If Sky hadn't been there, I thought he might have answered back, turning the conversation into another of our power struggles, but he had put on the pretense of sweetness and light for her, and he seemed set on maintaining it. I clung to Sky until he turned and headed around the corner, then I took a step back.

She turned to look at me, and I realized that she was injured. There were scratches on her cheek and dark bruises showing at the gap between her shirt and the yoga pants.

"How did you injure yourself?" I asked, kneeling down to lift her shirt and look at the bruising. She'd been beaten with some sort of blunt weapon, but while the purple of the bruises was alarming, I didn't think that the damage was too bad. I ran my hands across her skin and she didn't wince, so I released the shirt and stood. I wanted to know who had done this to Sky, so that I could make them pay.

"That's why we're here," she said, but she kept looking past me as other people drove up and headed for Sebastian's office.

"Ethan?" Sebastian appeared in the corridor, looking

straight at us. He looked weary, a bad sign for what was to come.

"Is it possible for us to discuss how you got the bruises later?" I asked, looking back down at Sky. I needed to know what was happening, to reassure myself that she was all right, but right now my duty to the pack came first.

"That's fine," she said. "We really just needed Josh."

"He'll be in the meeting as well," I said. "It will need to wait. Just until later. Okay?"

"That's fine." Sky fell into step with me as I headed for the office. "I'll talk to him after our meeting."

I couldn't help smiling at her less than subtle attempt to get in on the council, but I also couldn't give her what she wanted. I closed the space between us and kissed her softly on the lips.

"That was a good try," I said.

In spite of all the past evidence, it seemed that Sky could take a hint. She stopped where she was, and when I glanced back at the corner, I could see her turning to talk with Winter.

By the time I got to Sebastian's office, every seat was taken. The Alphas and Betas of the major packs were there, along with Josh, invited by Sebastian as our in-house magic expert. They'd come here to meet because Sebastian was the Elite Alpha, boss not just of the largest pack in North America but of all the weres in the region. If there was an issue we all needed to consider, then out of respect to him, the meeting happened on our home ground.

I shut the door behind me and took a place leaning in the corner of the room, giving me a good view of everyone there. The seating gave away some of the politics of the packs. The Canadians sitting off to one side, arms folded defensively across their chests. Joan and her Beta from the Southern Pack sat closest to Sebastian, lending him their support.

Others sat between Cole and Sebastian, waiting to see what our two most powerful leaders had to say.

"You called for this meeting, Cole," Sebastian said, watching his guest thoughtfully. "Why don't you explain?"

"I've received a prophecy," Cole said. "It was meant to be a prediction about my own future, but it touches on all of us, and so I thought I should bring it to the council. Forewarned is forearmed, and I didn't want to leave friends in the dark."

"Who did this prophecy come from?" Niimi, the Canadian Alpha, leaned forward as she spoke. She came from the Anishinaabe people, and like many weres from the First Nations, she took the issue of prophecy very seriously.

"From a Fae," Cole replied.

He paused to let the words sink in. Fae were the weaker descendants of the Faeries, and nowhere near as dangerous to deal with, but they always had an agenda. If Cole had sought out their prediction, then he had been playing with fire. If they had come to him, then we had to worry about what they were playing at.

"Why?" Sebastian asked.

"Repayment of an old debt," Cole said, brushing the question away with a wave of his hand. It was the perfect answer to avoid further scrutiny. We all had secrets in our pasts, obligations we didn't like to talk about, and no one was going to dig deeper in case they faced similar questions at some point. It could simply be the truth, or it could be a manipulation, and I couldn't see any reason to trust Cole.

Others did though. Niimi and her Beta watched Cole eagerly, waiting to hear what he had to say.

"I was told that I would be cursed," Cole said. "That the packs would fall at the hands of the wolf who isn't anchored to this life."

He gave Sebastian a significant look.

"You mean Sky," I said, feeling anger rise inside me. One moment Cole was flirting with her, the next he was trying to blame her for endangering us all. Either way, I wasn't going to stand for it.

"I can't think of a better interpretation," Cole said. "And believe me, I've tried. I don't want to believe that one of us is going to bring down some terrible curse, but…"

"The Fae could have been lying," Joan said. "Trying to divide us for some reason."

"Fae do not lie about prophecy," Niimi said, and her muscular arm tightened as she gripped the arm of her seat. "It is the one way in which they can be trusted."

That left the possibility that Cole was lying, but a glance from Sebastian told me I shouldn't say that out loud.

"Maybe this prophecy doesn't mean what you think it does," I said. "There are plenty of ways to deceive people while still telling the truth."

Cole turned to look at me.

"That sounds like pedantry," he said. "Splitting hairs to avoid facing the truth."

"I'm a lawyer. I know better than to dismiss details as pedantry."

"And I'm an Alpha. I know what it means to have a whole pack's lives depend on you."

"I have people who depend on me."

An arrogant smile crept up Cole's face.

"You seem defensive, Ethan," he said.

"Of course I'm defensive. This is turning into a threat against a member of my pack."

"According to the prophecy, I'm the one who's threatened by your pack member, not the other way around."

I glared at him. He had an answer for everything, which left me even more convinced that this business was a carefully constructed fiction.

Even if the prophecy was real, it didn't have to be about Sky. My own dark elf blood and the spirit shade bound inside me meant that I could also be considered unanchored from this life. There were probably other weres who could find reasons why it might apply to them. But Sky was a lightning rod for trouble, and the prophecy fit her like a second skin.

"Prophecy is a difficult magic to handle," Josh said. So far, he had sat quietly on the sidelines of the meeting. Now all eyes turned to him. "The theory of it is poorly understood, the practice inconsistent. Sometimes two prophecies say seemingly contradictory things, and it's only later that we can see how they fit together. Some prophecies have been shrouded in mystery for centuries, only decoded after years of work by the world's smartest witches."

"You're saying we're too stupid to understand prophecy?" Cole asked, raising an eyebrow along with the tone of his voice. "That we should leave it to experts like you?"

Several of the weres glared darkly at Josh. I could practically smell the indignation coming off of them, the outrage at the implication of their own stupidity.

"That's not what I said," Josh replied. "Just that this is complicated and might not be as clear as it first appears."

"I think we all understood what you were saying," Cole said. "The only thing that's not clear to me is why there's a witch in this meeting."

"Josh is our in-house magic expert," Sebastian said. "You brought us an issue rooted in magic, I brought you the person best placed to help understand it. Or do you only take outside advice when it comes from the Fae?"

Cole gave Sebastian a forced smile.

"I'm happy to take advice. I just want to make sure that our decisions are our own."

"They will be. And if you don't think I can enforce that, then you should challenge me."

Cole's expression became even stiffer. "I have every faith in you, Sebastian."

"Then what do you want us to do about this?" Sebastian asked.

"Mostly, I just wanted you to know." Cole looked around, meeting each were's eyes in turn, like he was taking them into his confidence. "Beyond that, I feel that we should make some decisions as a group, if not now then later. If there's a threat to all of us, then we'll be stronger tackling it together."

"We should be watching this Sky," Niimi said. "Learning all we can about her."

"And we should make plans," someone else said. "In case we need to contain her."

Anger boiled up inside me. They were talking about Sky as if she was theirs to make decisions for, without consideration for how this affected her. And they were disrespecting Sebastian, letting Cole draw them into meddling with the business of the Midwest Pack.

"This is an overreaction," I said. "People proclaim prophecies all the time. When they even come true, it's never in the way anyone expects."

"The visions of the Fae are not to be so lightly dismissed," Niimi said.

"Neither is Claudia," I said, referring to my godmother, one of the most accurate fortune-tellers anyone had ever known. "She's talked about the future of people in the pack on numerous occasions, and she's never foreseen anything like this."

"Better to have a plan we don't need than not to have one we do," said one of the other Alphas.

"We're not making plans to treat one of my pack as a threat," Sebastian said, looking at the weres who had spoken. "Not on the basis of so little evidence. We have a vague prophecy that might or might not be about Sky, given by a Fae for reasons we don't know. That's not grounds to start plotting against anyone."

There was something else he didn't say: We only had

Cole's word for it that this prophecy was real. Implying that another Alpha might be lying would stir up a storm of trouble. It was the sort of thing that I would have said out loud, but Sebastian was more cautious. He was keeping Sky safe for now, sowing the seeds of doubt about Cole's prophecy, not giving the other weres a reason to act against us.

"You're dismissing my concerns?" Cole asked, a hard edge beneath the calm politeness of the question. His apparent determination to put Sky in danger made me want to leap up and punch him in the head. I clenched my fist at my side and took long breaths, staying calm while Sebastian did his work.

"Of course not," Sebastian said. "As soon as you bring me something more solid, we'll act on it. Until then, thank you for keeping us all informed."

The others started getting up to leave. As they went, I stood staring at the back of Cole's head. He was up to something with this line about a prophecy. I didn't know what, and I had no way of proving anything yet, but I needed to keep an eye on him.

CHAPTER 4

"Ethan, stay behind," Sebastian said as the rest of the council were leaving.

I closed the door and sat facing him across his desk.

"Well done for keeping your temper with Cole," Sebastian said. "That couldn't have been easy."

"Just doing my job as Beta," I said.

He was right, it hadn't been easy, not with Sky's safety at stake. But I trusted Sebastian to make the right call on this.

"We'll have to keep an eye on Cole," I continued. "And watch out for signs that he's manipulating the others."

"You're right, but that's not why I asked you to stay." Sebastian leaned back in his chair. "The tensions in the pack are getting worse."

I shrugged. This was hardly news. We'd discussed it only days ago.

"Sky should be challenging for a ranked position," he continued. "She's strong enough for it, she's well established in the pack, and she's central to some of our most important business."

"I agree," I said. Sky more than deserved the recognition she would get as a ranking member, and while it wouldn't remove the strain on our relationship, it would at least bring us closer to an equal footing.

"So, what's stopping her?" Sebastian asked.

"Steven," I said wearily. "Challenging him for the rank of fifth would be her first step into the hierarchy, but they've become good friends. She practically treats him like a brother."

"Would you not challenge your brother?" Sebastian asked with a mocking smile. He knew full well that Josh and I were always competing, and that if we were both weres we would be tearing into each other practically every day, battling for dominance. Our different spheres of supernatural influence helped keep what passed for peace between us.

"Sky doesn't think like we do," I said. "She's not scared of fighting for a ranked position—I'm not sure she's scared of anything—but it appalls her, and as long as she likes the people above her, there's no reason for her to overcome that."

"She could at least have the good judgment to dislike one of us," Sebastian said with a laugh.

"She didn't like me at the start, but now..." Neither of us needed me to explain that one out loud. "Winter is her sparring buddy, Gavin and her have this weird mocking friendship, and even if she wanted the Alpha spot, she respects you too much to take you on."

"So she's never going to step up?"

"She should but she won't. It's very Sky."

"Then you need to find some other way to integrate her into the hierarchy, because a were with all her influence and no clear place is a liability to all of us. Plus, settling her down might convince Cole that she's not the one he should worry about."

I snorted derisively. Nothing was going to change Cole's tune—he was just saying what suited him.

"There's something else I should tell you about," I said. "I'm looking for ways to track down and trap a Tre'ase, the one that created the spirit shade in me. If I can do that, then I can make sure no one does to me what Logan is doing to Sky, and I can protect the magic keeping Josh alive."

"I can help with that," Sebastian said.

I blinked in surprise. Sebastian knew about a lot of things, but this didn't seem like his area of expertise.

He swiveled around in his chair, pulled a book from the bottom row of shelves behind him, and laid it down on the desk.

"Allen Ginsberg?" I asked. "I don't think the Beats can help us with this."

Sebastian opened the book and took out several sheets of loose paper. Some of them were the product of an old dot matrix printer, but others were handwritten, their paper brown with age.

"I was given this years ago," Sebastian said, handing me the papers. "Information on the magic of Tre'ases. This is dangerous territory, so I've kept it hidden instead of putting it in the library. I wouldn't trust anyone else with this, but if you're going to take on a Tre'ase, then I want to make sure you do it right."

"Thanks," I said, sliding the papers into the pocket of my jacket. "I'll let you know what I find."

"Happy hunting."

I was up half the night, going over the notes Sebastian had given me. They were an odd mix: accounts of unusual inter-actions with Tre'ases; historic stories about people hunting or tracking them; some magical theory that I didn't under-stand. It was going to take a lot of time and thought to piece these fragments together, but when combined with Josh's insights, they were giving me a better understanding of the workings of the Tre'ases and of how to track one down in practice. The difficult part would be working out where to start on the trail of a specific Tre'ase. In the stories, the hunters always had a starting point, and that was something I was missing.

My phone kept buzzing with calls and texts from Sky, but I didn't answer. It wasn't that I was avoiding her—amid all the frustrations of the day, I couldn't think of anything better to soothe me than the two of us together—but we had serious issues to discuss and I wanted to do that in person. By the time I finished my work, it was too late to head over to her place, so I burned off some of my frustrations with a workout then slept for a few hours in the pack house.

The next morning, I got up and drove straight to Sky's place. I thought I'd gotten an early start on the day, but Sky had done better. When I got to her house, the door was open and she was in the room where Steven had once stayed, in the middle of some serious rearranging. Curious, I peered around at the piles of boxes.

"Steven's moving back in," she said, without a hello to precede it.

I tried to hide my frown. This would just make her place in the hierarchy more complicated, the dynamics of the pack more confused.

"Foi ideia tua ou dele?" I asked, shifting to Portuguese, hoping that her mother's language might help Sky relax into a difficult conversation. *Your idea or his?*

"Minha," she replied. *Mine.*

We stood awkwardly, each waiting for the other to say something. I needed an explanation to help me understand, but as a member of the pack, the onus was on her to make herself clear.

"He's under the impression he needed your approval," she said, then waited a long time before offering me a smile. "Bobo, certo?" *Silly, right?*

Not for the first time, I stifled the urge to snap at the flippant tone with which she treated such serious issues. She was playing with the delicate dynamics our lives were built around. That wasn't a laughing matter.

"I miss him," she admitted, genuine sadness entering her voice.

"What do you miss: having all your food eaten up, finding his books tossed about in your living room, or following him with a vacuum to ensure that your house doesn't look like a sty?" I smiled, trying to match the lightness of her tone, but I could tell immediately that it hadn't worked, and I could have kicked myself for adding to the sadness on her face.

"There were other things," she said. "My life didn't consist of just that."

"Then what is it?" I'd never fully understood the bond between Sky and Steven, who we had sent to keep an eye on her in the early days. Something had grown between them. I was glad that it brought her joy, and I wanted to better understand what went on in the heart of Sky.

"He's fixated on the fact that he needs your approval. Give it to him so he'll move back."

"Sky—"

"Steven makes things…" She waved a hand in the air, like she was trying to snatch words out of the ether. Whatever they were, they kept getting away. "He's comforting."

I took a moment to process those words, so simple and yet so revealing. It was easy to forget that Sky was relatively new to the world of the supernatural, and just how hard it could be to adjust. If Steven's presence took away some of that discomfort, maybe the problems it created were a price worth paying.

"I'll take that into consideration," I said.

Before Sky could respond, I walked out of the bedroom and into the living room, where I settled down on the sofa. I couldn't get into a debate on this at the moment. If she wouldn't show consideration for the ways of the pack, she could at least give me time to make my decisions. But I could see from her face that Sky was building up to argue back, unable to accept that this was a Beta and pack member issue, not an Ethan and Sky one.

"It's good that you're thinking about it," she said. "But since it's not your decision, it really doesn't matter."

Once again, I held back the rebuke any other pack member would have earned, but I could feel my face crumpling in frustration.

"It's not your decision to make," she repeated coldly.

I took three long breaths, calming myself, mustering the right words, trying to find a place of clarity amid the increasingly blurred lines of our relationship. What terms might she accept? What line of reasoning could cut through this?

"But it is," I said.

"Ethan—"

"This discussion is over. I don't want another man living with you."

"Another man? It's Steven, not some random guy."

My whole body was responding to this challenging behavior from a member of my pack. Muscles tensed. Pulse quickened. I felt the angry howl of my wolf. I took another deep breath, pushing down that fighting response.

This whole conversation was nonsense anyway. If I told Steven that he shouldn't move in, he would accept that. I could have my way here without an argument. As long as I remembered that, I could keep my wolf in check.

"As I stated before, I'll take your request under consideration."

"Just call him and tell him now," she said, unable to let it go.

"No." I held my hand out to her, a peace offering, but she stared at it like I was dripping in filth. "We have more pressing things to deal with."

At last, Sky relented and took my hand. I pulled her down

to straddle me, then leaned in and took a deep breath, relishing her scent.

"See, if Steven lived here, we couldn't do this." I ran my hands up under her shirt, kneading at her skin, stroking it. The bruising of the previous day was gone, and she showed no discomfort at my touch. Far from it, her hips shifted as she settled against me.

"Of course we can," she said with a smile. "In fact, I owe him a couple of uncomfortable moments. I can't tell you the number of times I found one of his stray one-nighters in the house. At least I know your name. That's more than I can say for him and the random half-naked women I had to have my coffee and breakfast with."

I laughed. It was classic Steven.

"I'm sure he knew their names."

"A couple he couldn't give with certainty. He was reduced to calling them 'sweetheart' or 'hon.'"

"And yet you miss that?"

"No, I don't miss that. But I do miss him."

My mind moved on. I still didn't know how Sky had gotten those bruises.

"What happened yesterday?" I asked.

"Winter and I went out looking for Kelly. We thought her disappearance might be connected to the animal person we saw near the woods—the not-were. There were torn clothes and signs of a sedative, so we headed deeper into the woods. Chase and Gabriella were there, and we had another little clash, but I don't think Chase will bother me again anytime soon."

I laughed at that. It was good that Sky could put some of the most troublesome vampires in their place. But there was something else as well, something she had left out just before that, a lie of omission that I could sense in the racing of her pulse. I didn't like being lied to, by my partners or pack members. Sky should have known better by now.

I sat back and waited to see if she would tell me the truth.

"After that, we found another of those creatures, part woman and part animal. Her name was Carol. There was another woman with her, someone who wielded power but didn't feel like a witch. She had backup—that's how I got those bruises, once things turned nasty. It's also how they got away."

I was proud of her, holding her own against strange forces as if it was no big thing. I kissed her, soft and soothing, then leaned back a little so I could watch her face. Her eyes darted back and forth, but if she knew that I had caught her in a lie, then she wasn't letting on, and I could only think of one reason Sky would lie to me: to protect someone else.

"Who did you see, Chris or Quell?" I asked.

There was a chance she would keep an encounter with Chris quiet, if Chris had asked her to, but Quell seemed the more likely option. Sky knew I didn't approve of her twisted friendship with the misanthropic vampire, a creature so steeped in his own misery that he had even turned his back on his own kind. He didn't even have the merit of feeding off plants instead of people anymore, and the fact that Sky was the one he fed off only added to my worries.

Sky's heart beat faster, caught in the lie. Her eyes went wide as she struggled to find a way out, then she brushed her lips against mine in a desperate attempt at distraction. I pulled her closer, happy to enjoy the moment, kissing her hungrily as my fingers ran through her hair. But I wasn't going to be put off that easily. A flame of anger was starting to burn in me, born of frustration at her obvious lie, someone I cared about and who should have known better trying to deceive me. It wasn't something I would stand for, and even my desire for Sky couldn't suppress my determination to get at the truth.

"Who did you see, Chris or Quell?" I asked again.

Tense, silent seconds stretched out into minutes, neither

of us speaking. I could wait as long as it took, but Sky shifted uncomfortably, fingers twitching. At last, she looked past me, unable to hold my gaze any longer.

"The witch or mage or whatever was strong," she said. "Standing next to her was like standing next to Josh, but the magic was different. I haven't been around enough mages to—"

"Seventy-seven," I said, holding back my rising temper. "Your heart rate has increased to seventy-seven. You're lying to me. Answer my question and then finish. Tell me everything. I know it had to be either Chris or Quell because those are the only two people you would be reluctant to tell me about. Which one was it, Sky?"

There was another long pause, but Sky's heartbeat settled as she accepted the inevitable.

"Chris," she muttered.

I closed my eyes, unable to even look at her. The one person we knew could keep Sky safe, the woman I'd spent a whole night seeking, and she'd lied to me about it.

"You can't keep things from me, Skylar."

"I don't agree with her being brought into this, not even to appease him for a moment. Even if it buys us more time."

"It's a last resort. No one wants this, but so far, Josh hasn't found anything. What do you suggest we do, Sky? If you have an idea, please share it with me."

"Steven had one." Her voice became more animated as she sought a way out of the corner we had talked ourselves into. "If we could get hold of a Tod Schlaf, we could use it to paralyze Logan and get him under our control. Then he won't be able to harm the Tre'ase that made Maya."

The Tod Schlaf, an elven parasite that could put its victim into a coma, had been used against us before. The idea of turning it to our advantage was as appealing as it was ingenious.

"That's a great idea. I could talk to Gideon about going into the dark forest, and then we—"

"Actually, I was thinking that Winter and I could handle this. Or more specifically Winter…"

A long debate followed, as Sky set out the case for dealing with the Tod Schlaf her way. I argued back, partly on principle because pack decisions were mine not hers, and partly so she could feel like she'd won when I let her have her way.

Once that conversation was over, Sky settled against me, face pressed into my neck, while I gently stroked her skin.

"What was your meeting about?" she asked.

"Nothing, really." I didn't like to keep things from her, especially not when I'd just insisted that she share her secrets with me. But this was pack business, and I had to treat it that way. Telling Sky about the prophecy would only worry her.

I wrapped my arms around her and lightly kissed her on the head. She moved back, creating distance between us.

"A meeting with all the Alphas was for nothing? That's really hard to believe."

I shrugged, trying to shake the moment off. "Cole called the meeting. He tends to be more inclined to overreaction than most."

"What is he overreacting about?"

I leaned in, kissing her neck. It wasn't just a distraction technique. Spending time around Sky stirred me in a way no one ever had before. Every moment we were together, I wanted to touch her, to kiss her, to feel her body moving against mine. Even when we were arguing, desire was there, a pulsing presence between us.

Sky moaned as I ran kisses up her neck. I ran a hand up her thigh, under her shirt, rising higher…

She bolted out of my lap and stood glaring down at me.

"I'm not that easily distracted," she snapped. I just smiled. "Cole, being over-reactive and dramatic, called a meeting for what reason?"

I rubbed my hands over my face, then leaned forward and looked up at her. She wasn't going to let this go. She wasn't going to let me protect her from the truth.

"Cole was told that we would be cursed and the packs would fall at the hands of the wolf that wasn't anchored to this life."

"We are going to be cursed because of me. Who told him this?"

"A Fae. One with foretelling gifts like Claudia's. The East Coast Pack has a good relationship with them. It was a warning."

"Why do you think it's an overreaction? It's possible."

I shook my head. "You have control of Maya. You have this. I have no concerns. And anything a Fae sees is never going to be as accurate as what Claudia knows. She isn't concerned, so I'm not."

"You've seen what I'm capable of. Maya has unlocked a lot of magic in me. When we removed Marcia's curse, that unleashed magic, too. Maybe we've activated other curses or unleashed other powers. The impact of what we did keeps on unfolding, and each revelation is more terrible than the last."

"It's nonsense."

"Nonsense you all spent hours debating?" She stood with her hands on her hips, glaring down at me. "Nonsense you think is about me?"

She stared at me, her expression one of frustration bordering on fury. I had no idea what was going through her mind, but I could feel the mounting hostility radiating from her.

"You're different, too," she said.

I waved the words away. The spirit shade, the dark magic that writhed within me, was a presence that even I dreaded. Its power kept revealing itself in new ways, risking exposure to the world, a world which would fear and hate what I had. It was hard keeping something so important from her, the one person in the world I felt I could be open with. But there were some secrets that had to be kept, for my safety, for hers, for the whole pack.

"Are we going to have this discussion again? It's really getting old."

"I don't think you're being honest. You did magic that not even Josh knew to kill something that couldn't be destroyed with a spell from the Clostra or Faerie magic. You want me to believe it was just a spell that Josh forgot to learn?"

"I never said he 'forgot' to learn. Josh wasn't always as assiduous as he is now about magic, so there are spells that I know that he doesn't."

"I feel a lot of things would have to transpire for you to be a danger."

I had to get out. Sky was chipping away at the secrets I was keeping from her, ones I had to preserve for all our sakes. If she kept going, then either she would draw something out of me or she would know for certain I was lying. Both my secrets and our tentative relationship were at risk of being broken.

I stood, kissed her quickly on the cheek, and started for the door.

"You're not staying?"

I shook my head. "I'll be back tonight."

But Sky stopped me before I could go out the door.

"Don't look for her," she said. "She can't be part of this, Ethan."

It took me a moment to realize what she was talking about. She thought that I was leaving to go hunt for Chris, rather than to get away from her. Maybe it was better this way. I grunted a response—she might as well be right for all the difference it made—then stepped out and closed the door behind me.

"And don't forget to let Steven know he can move in!" Sky shouted.

I sighed, turned back, and opened the door.

"Steven's not moving back," I said firmly, then raised my hand to quiet the inevitable response. "Steven will never do anything to hurt you. He just doesn't have it in him. Like my brother, he coddles you. Which leaves me being the bad guy—"

"You're good at it."

There was the quick wit that drew me to her. I smiled in response.

"He's happy where he is, and that is where he will stay."

"How do you know?"

"Because Joan said he is." Steven's mother must count as an authority on this, even to Sky. "She has no reason to lie about it."

Sky nodded and I hovered in the doorway, waiting to see if she had any more to say. She looked so disappointed, I thought the truth might finally be sinking in. This wasn't just about her, it was about Steven, over whom she held such powerful influence.

"If he wanted to come back as well, I would be okay with it because it is what you both want," I said. "Your wants can't override his."

Despite those final words, she smiled. I'd offered some hope that she could have her beloved roommate back, and I was happy to have given her some comfort. It was tinged with jealousy at the closeness between them, a comfortable bond that the two of us didn't have, but I was starting to accept that I couldn't keep Sky to myself, any more than she could keep Steven.

I closed the door and left.

CHAPTER 5

If Chris was looking for hunter work, as Sofia had said, then she would be hitting up her old contacts in that world. Having exhausted Stacy's leads, I figured that those contacts were the best next step.

Eliza was an old school hunter from a family that had been battling monsters for generations. Her base was a farmhouse built in the 1930s, a solid building lacking in flash or flare with a few acres of land attached. As I pulled up on the dirt driveway, she appeared in the doorway, dressed in camouflage trousers and a sweat-stained t-shirt, a shotgun hanging from her right hand. Though the gun wasn't aimed at me, I knew she could bring it up and get a shot off in less than a second, and that it would be loaded with more than mundane shot.

"What you doing on my land, Charleston?" she growled.

"I wanted to ask a few questions," I said, smiling as I walked over to the porch. "I know you're a busy woman. I can make it worth your time."

"Don't try to butter me up, wolfy. I can smell the lies coming off of you."

"Really? Because that's my trick, too."

Her eyes darted around, scanning me, my Venom GT, and the woods fringing the open ground around her house. They narrowed for a moment, then she shifted the gun to her left hand and held the right one out.

"Guess it's good to see you," she said.

I took her hand to shake, but as I did that, she gripped tight and pulled. I stumbled forward, her other arm came around, and she slammed me face-first into the wall.

"All right, you bastards!" she shouted, pressing the barrel of the shotgun against the back of my head. "You show yourselves or I blow his brains out."

"What the hell, Eliza?" I snapped.

"I know a trick when I see one. Whoever else you've brought to attack me, tell them to come out."

"Why would we attack you?" I eased my free arm around slowly, trying not to draw attention. Eliza was as twitchy as a flea and I didn't want that gun going off.

"Revenge for Ezalius."

"Ezalius was a vampire. We were glad you killed him."

"Just what one of you monsters would say."

She turned the angle of the gun, ready to fire. I needed to act fast.

I jerked my head back. The barrel of the shotgun grazed my scalp. There was a roar as the gun fired, blowing a hole in the canopy of the porch. Then I was spinning around, grabbing Eliza with both hands and twisting her arm up. She shouted in alarm as the gun fell from her hands and I forced her to her knees.

We stood for a moment, my ears ringing from the shotgun blast so close to my head, Eliza panting in pain and grimacing up at me.

"Finish it," she said.

"I told you, that's not why I'm here."

I let go of her, scooped up the gun, and took two long

steps back. Eliza, still looking at me with suspicion, rose to her feet.

"Then why are you here?"

"I'm looking for Chris. Did you know that she's back in town?"

"Know? Ha! She came to me, looking for shelter and help finding work. I gave her the same warm welcome I gave you."

"I thought she was your friend?"

"The human Chris was, but Hell will freeze over and the seas will boil before I let a vampire in my house."

"You attacked her?"

"Almost staked her. Would have been doing the woman I knew a favor, and saving the world from one more monster, but she's even faster than she was. After that she ran, and good riddance."

It had never crossed my mind that Chris's transformation, while saving her life, might have cut her off from her past. But hunters were hunters, and not many of them were on friendly terms with the supernatural, especially not with vampires. Many of her old colleagues and friends would kill her as soon as talk with her.

In spite of everything, I felt sorry for Chris. Being cut off from the pack, from everyone I really cared about, was such a terrible thought that I could barely begin to imagine how it would feel.

Chris was alone and without help in the city she called home. I felt even worse knowing that we were planning on using her as a bargaining chip in our efforts to control Logan. But none of that would stop me from doing what I had to do.

"Thanks, Eliza," I said, stepping off the porch. "Always a pleasure."

I dropped the shotgun in the dirt, climbed into the Venom, and drove away.

An hour later, I was standing in Claudia's gallery, looking at an abstract expressionist piece by an up-and-coming artist from Brazil. I didn't know much about art, but my godmother had a knack for finding eye-catching pieces, and the swirling maelstrom of red and black oil paint had me transfixed.

"It's a reflection of the trauma Francisca experienced in the favelas," Claudia said, appearing at my side. "Amazing that she was able to develop as an artist at all, living in those conditions."

"Amazing," I agreed, still trying to make sense of the patterns in the paint. "But not why I'm here."

"Of course not." Claudia, sharply dressed as always, took hold of my arm with one gloved hand and led me on a slow stroll through the gallery, away from the handful of customers perusing the pieces by the door. "How can I help?"

"I need your advice on a couple of things. One of them is tracking down and containing a Tre'ase."

"And the other?"

"That's more of a long shot. I was hoping you could help me find Chris."

Claudia sighed.

"I can't help with the first issue," she said. "Too many other things tie my hands. But I might be able to do something about Chris."

That caught me by surprise. Claudia was a Moura and an empath, empowered with magic I barely understood. Of all the people I knew, she'd seemed like the one most likely to know how to tangle with a Tre'ase, whereas Chris barely even moved in the same circles she did.

Then again, she hadn't said that she didn't know about the Tre'ase, but that something was stopping her from using that knowledge. I decided against prying; if she wanted to tell me what it was, then she would, and if not, maybe things would change. In the meantime, I would take whatever help I could get.

"Do you know where Chris is staying?" I asked.

Claudia patted me on the arm. "Give me a few days and I should have something for you."

"Thanks, Claudia. You're the best."

"Is there anything else you want to discuss?" She looked up at me with concern. "You seem unsettled."

I hesitated, then shrugged. I might as well tell her.

"Cole says he has a prophecy from the Fae. It says that he will be cursed and that the packs will fall at the hands of the wolf who isn't anchored to this life. Could that be about Sky, or even me?"

Claudia gave a small shake of her head.

"Most Fae prophets are unreliable at best," she said. "Some are little better than cold readers, telling their customers what they think they want to hear. They wrap their so-called prophecies up in riddles to hide the limits of their skills, which is why their prophecies are always open to interpretation. Never trust a blood bank run by vampires or a prophecy from the Fae."

"And you haven't seen anything that would back up this prophecy?"

"Certainly not. I would have told you if I had."

"Thanks." I smiled. "That was exactly what I needed to hear."

I unhooked my arm from hers, kissed her on the cheek, and headed out the door.

While I was trying to track down my vampire ex, Sky and Winter had been working another angle on dealing with Logan—getting hold of the Tod Schlaf. Liam, the haughty elf who controlled access to the dark forest, had granted us permission to go in to find one of the paralyzing creatures. I didn't know how they had managed to persuade him, and I didn't much care as long as we could do what was needed.

Sky, Sebastian, Winter, Josh, Steven, and I were met at the doors of Elysian by a pair of elven guides, identical twins with red-flecked amber eyes and long fiery-red hair. They had an uncanny way of completing each other's sentences and moving in unison, tucking back their hair in the same way or matching footsteps as they walked. I wondered if they were creations of the dark forest, just as much as the beasts they had brought for us to ride, which unnervingly combined features of a horse, cat, and giraffe.

They lined us up in single file, putting me and Sky at the front. I looked around, trying to work out why they were going to the effort of arranging us like this, and saw the elves looking at me.

"I sense magic," they said together. "It will help keep the rift open longer."

The last time we had been to the forest, it had tried to draw me in, to claim my dark elven magic. As we approached, it was clear that the place was still interested in me. The edges of the wall formed finger-like vines that stretched out to brush against me, making my skin crawl. I laid a hand on the bags hanging from my shoulder, in which were jars to capture Tod Schlaf, a reminder of why we needed to be here.

Sky touched my arm and looked at me in concern.

"It's fine," I whispered.

It wasn't, but we didn't have much choice. We needed to go in.

The others were still lined up behind me, with Josh a few feet away. He would stay behind, our anchor to the outside world, to help us escape if things went wrong.

The ward containing the forest parted and I stepped

through the gap. Sky followed behind me, but before the others could join us, there was a sudden rustling and the ward closed.

I clenched my teeth and glared in fury at the place where our exit had been. The elves had set us up.

Sky thrust her sword into the ward then drew it back. The magic simply closed over the wound. We were trapped. For some reason, the elves only wanted the two of us in here, and I didn't think it was for our own good.

I took a deep breath to calm myself and looked around at the forest. Despite its name, it was a bright and verdant place. Flowers with brown and yellow stems as wide as tree trunks towered over us, swaying as if to the rhythm of a beating heart. Between them rose florets of greenery, while small man-made ponds lay still and sparkling between their roots. The air was filled with the scents of spring blossoms and freshly spilled blood.

Footsteps padded through the forest, the slow, purposeful movements of a predator on the prowl.

"Stay close," I said as we set off into the woods. We had come this far, so we were going to get what we came for before we worked out how to escape.

A creature appeared between the tree-like plants ahead of us, while others spread out to either side, a pack preparing to close in for the kill. These weren't beasts that nature would ever have allowed. Curved horns sprouted from wolf-like heads. Their mouths contained too many large teeth to properly close, so that saliva dripped constantly onto the forest floor, bubbling and steaming as it touched the grass. Long, sinewy bodies ended in stout, muscular legs with cloven feet.

"There are more," I said, drawing Sky's attention from the one in front of her.

When we had sent people into the forest before, they had been told that the antidote they sought was on the vilest creature. Knowing the elves, that would be true of what we were seeking now as well. These creatures were unpleasant, but I doubted they were the worst thing here—more likely an obstacle set in our way.

The pack of uncanny beasts closed in around us.

"Do you think the horns are poisonous?" Sky asked.

Before I had a chance to reply, the creatures charged.

I held myself still, waiting until the last possible moment. The first creature lowered its horns as it thundered toward me, a howl rattling from its throat. Just as it was about to hit me, I darted aside. As it ran through the space where I had been, I punched it hard in the chest. It staggered, stumbled, and I leapt on it, battering it until it fell, bloody and broken, to the ground.

Another of the beasts was almost on top of me. I grabbed it by the horns and twisted. There was a crack as its neck broke, and it fell limp.

More creatures closed in. I tried to shift into my wolf form, but some magic of the forest held me back. Instead I fought with fists and feet, beating and kicking the creatures, driving them into each other, wrestling them to the ground. One almost caught me with its horn, the tip tearing through my shirt. I grabbed the horn, snapped it off the creature's head, and drove it into its eye.

Beside me, Sky was fighting them with her sword. Months of training with Winter had paid off, turning her from a passable fighter to a gifted one, and bodies lay littered around her.

As Sky readied her sword again, the last of the creatures leapt through the air. I caught it in mid-lunge and slammed it into the ground, knocking it out.

The sky darkened, casting the forest into deep shadow, but I wasn't going to be intimidated by cheap tricks. Ignoring the growls and grunts coming from all around us, I strode on into the forest

"Why are they allowed to do this?" Sky asked as we

watched the silhouettes of twisted creatures prowling through the undergrowth.

"I've wondered the same thing," I said. "It has never been an issue, so we never got involved."

"I don't think they should be allowed to do this. Not anymore."

I stopped walking and turned to look at her. Yet again, Sky was missing the big picture.

"But if they weren't allowed, then what would be our option to stop Logan?" I asked.

She frowned. "Let's just get what we need and get out of here."

With a whoosh, a winged reptile with dagger-like teeth and gleaming claws swept through the air. It was the most fearsome creature we had seen so far. If the wolf-beasts had been hard to fight bare-handed, this would be a hundred times worse. Sky raised her sword and I steadied myself, ready for a fight.

The creature looked at me with fiery eyes, lips drawing back from those deadly teeth, and I felt a connection between us, some lingering remnant of elven magic. For a moment, it hesitated, and I seized upon that opportunity.

I drew upon the magic within me, the dark power of the spirit shade that had been emerging more and more over the past few months. Instead of using it just to break a ward, I channeled it down the path of that elven connection, a surge of deadly energy.

The reptile gargled, choked, and fell to the ground, wings twitching.

I walked over to the creature. If the thing we sought was on the vilest creature here, then this seemed like a good place to look. The beast breathed faster, choking and gasping as the energy that had struck it down drew close. I ran my hands over its scales and felt its life slipping away beneath my hands.

Sure enough, our prize was here. Not just Tod Schlaf but also its leech-like antidote carriers nestled in the joints of the scaly body. Taking care not to let it latch onto me, I removed one of the Tod Schlaf and put it in a jar.

The reptile gave one last gasp and fell still. All around, the mutated beasts of the forest fell silent and drew back from me. They had seen me bring death on one deadly creature and they didn't want to face the same fate. I wasn't the only one who dreaded the power inside me.

"What happened to it?" Sky asked, pointing at the winged reptile.

I shrugged and handed Sky the bag with the Tod Schlaf jar in it. Now wasn't the time to explain this. I took her arm and guided her back the way we had come, toward the exit of the forest.

As we approached the ward, I could see our companions waiting for us on the other side. The ward was thinner than it had been, but it was still strong, and as Sky tried to step through, it pushed her back into me. She pushed again, and I saw magic spark around her fingers as she tried to force an opening, but it wasn't enough.

Around us, an uncanny silence settled in.

Her jaw set in determination, Sky took my hand and reached out for the ward a third time. I felt magic pulse around her, then the ward ripped open.

Sky stepped through, pulling me after her. But the moment she was through, the ward closed again, sealing itself around my wrist.

For a moment I stood staring frustrated at the ward. But then I realized that, whether it meant to or not, the forest was giving me an opportunity. The creature I had fought carried numerous Tod Schlaf and antidote slugs. Why leave all those resources here when they could be a valuable tool for the pack in the future?

Sky was tugging at my hand, trying to drag me through

the ward. Instead of leaning into her effort, I let go, drawing my hand back in. The barrier thickened, closing off my view of the outside world, and I turned back toward the depths of the forest.

I ran through the shadows, splashing through shallow pools and jumping over raised ridges of root. The flowering plants swayed faster above me, the heartbeat of their rhythm accelerating. The smell of blood grew strong as scarlet pollen scattered from the flowers and drifted around me in a thick cloud.

There was a swift zipping sound and something shot through the cloud inches from my face. Then came another and another, a swarm of creatures as thin as paper and the size of beer mats. Their wings shimmered, not with the beautiful colors of a butterfly but with a dark sheen of silver over black, like pools of oil spilled across the air. Mouths opened at the front of each one, catching the red pollen as they swept through the air.

One of the creatures touched me as it flew past. It was a brief, glancing blow, but a painful one, the edge of its wing slicing through my shirt and scoring the skin below. Another one flew straight at my face. I swatted it from the air and trampled it underfoot.

More of the fliers were closing in. Pain lashed at my forearm, my thigh, the back of my neck, as they caught me with the edges of their wings.

I stopped. If I kept running through the cloud of razor wings, then I was going to be shredded. I tried to swat them down, hitting at the flat sides with my hands, but there were too many of the creatures. It was like trying to catch snowflakes in a storm.

Through it all, I could feel the forest reaching out for me. Someone had told it to stop me, but it felt the connection between us, my elven blood and the darker power that was mingled with it. The forest wanted me to give in to our connection, and so I did.

The minute I let the forest's spirit in, I could sense every one of the razor-edged fliers whizzing around me. I reached out to them and let my own power flow. It was more than they could stand. Shimmering wings exploded in spatters of silver-black goo, coating the ground like an oil slick. The pollen on which they had been feeding turned to ash.

I set off again. I could see the body of the fallen reptile lying where I had left it. I was only twenty feet away when something lumbered out between the stalks. It had the head of a bull set on the body of a mountain gorilla, some elf's twisted recreation of a minotaur. It roared and beat its chest as it advanced toward me.

I reached out through the forest again, but the minotaur's spirit was stronger than the tiny fliers. It twitched as the magic hit it, but instead of stopping in its tracks it ran at me faster, bellowing with fury.

Its vast fists swung down at my head. I jumped back and they hit the ground instead, making the earth tremble beneath my feet. I lunged in, punching the creature in the nose, but its skull seemed to be made of iron and all I got were bruised knuckles.

Another swing of the beast's fists caught me in the side, flinging me into the trunk of one of the flower trees. I forced myself to my feet and rolled clear again as my opponent jumped on the spot where I had landed.

The minotaur landed off balance, swaying on its short legs. I seized my chance, swung my leg around in a low kick, and knocked it to the ground. It roared, twisted, and grabbed at my foot. I kicked again, catching it in the chest this time. It gasped for breath, but it grabbed my leg and dragged me in.

I kicked with my other foot, battering at the minotaur's face. Its snout might be solid but other parts weren't. Teeth broke loose, fur flew, and then I got a solid kick in its eye. It screamed, let go of my leg, and scrambled away to huddle at the base of a plant.

The minotaur clutched its face and stared at me. It was catching its breath, steadying itself, and I could see it building up for another attack.

I ran to the fallen reptile and grabbed a Tod Schlaf. There was a thundering of feet as the minotaur charged at me. I turned, ducked, and dived down between its legs, slapping the Tod Schlaf against its thigh as I passed. The minotaur stopped next to the reptile, wobbled for a moment, and then fell.

For now I was safe, but it wouldn't last. The dark forest could hold all manner of other monsters. I quickly drew a fistful of small containers from my bag. I tugged antidote leeches off the reptile and dropped each one into a container, until I had them all bottled up. My prize in hand, I ran back to the edge of the forest.

The ward was still up when I reached it. I was a prisoner here, and perhaps that was how the elves wanted me. Was this why Liam had let us in, so that he could take me captive?

I touched the ward and the magic trembled but held. Summoning all my inner strength, I closed my eyes and let the darkness within me flow. The elven magic was strong, but what lay inside me was stronger. For a moment, the two forces pressed against each other in almost unbearable tension. Then the ward exploded, power bursting out into the world.

Through the gap I had created, I looked out into Elysian. My friends stood with their backs to me, fists and weapons raised for a fight. Winter stood in front of Sebastian, blood trickling from her arm. Arrows were scattered on the ground around them.

Facing them was Liam, slender and gray-haired, his silver eyes shimmering, riding a midnight-black horse with eyes that glowed like the heart of a volcano. Other Makellos, the so-called pure-blood elves, stood around him, weapons raised, while more lay on the ground in front of Winter. Liam's hand was in the air, as if about to signal an order. Whether he had planned to end or resume the fight with the pack I didn't know, but he sat motionless now, staring at me.

As I stepped out of the forest, there was a howl and something leapt past me—one of the wolf creatures, racing past the ward and into the world. Some of the elves ran to catch it, while others rushed to the ward, hands weaving through the air as they sought to repair it before all the creatures they had made escaped.

I walked over to Sky, relieved to see her again. My first impulse was to reach out and kiss her, but the magic was still flowing through me and I knew how deadly it could be. I pressed it back down, and as I did so I felt all the energy flow from me. The exertions of the past hour were catching up, and I leaned against a tree to keep myself upright, my head pressed against the bark.

The forest was reaching out, trying to lure me back in with its power. I closed my eyes and focused, building a ward of my own inside me, one that would cut off my connection with the forest. I wouldn't be able to affect its inhabitants again, but it would lose its power over me. I would be safe.

When I looked up, a pair of elven twins, one male and the other female, were glaring at me from the backs of a pair of strange beasts. They were urging us impatiently down a trail that led out of Elysian, while all around their comrades tried to rein in escaped animals or muster the magic to repair the broken ward. The hostility in our guides' eyes made it clear that we were no longer welcome here. They suspected what I knew—that there was powerful magic inside me, and that if I had to, I would unleash all its fury against them.

Once we were out of Elysian and free of elven scrutiny, we stopped to muster ourselves. Sebastian was having firm words with Winter, who had apparently risked herself for him against his orders. Sky stood scrutinizing me, and for once she didn't look away when I held her gaze.

"I liked it more when you found me intimidating," I said, half joking.

"I'll drive," Josh said, holding out a hand.

I would never have let him normally—my cars were precious to me and Josh was not a careful driver—but the rush of physical and magical energy from my body had left me trembling. I handed him the keys, gave my slug containers to Sky, and slumped into the back seat.

"What are these?" asked Sky, who sat in the front passenger seat, examining the containers.

"The antidote for the sleeper," I said. "We have them all now. If anyone wants to use one, they will have to go through us. We need to give them to Dr. Jeremy."

"Is this why you allowed yourself to be pulled back in?"

I nodded, gazing distantly at the road outside the car, remembering the feeling of my mind linking magically with the forest creatures, the sight of the reptile collapsing beneath my power, of the shimmering fliers exploding.

"Why do some creatures and Tre'ase respond to you the way they do?" Sky asked.

I shrugged.

"We removed the dark elven magic," Sky continued.

"I know," I said. "I was there."

"But you still have magic. I felt it and saw it."

"My mother was a witch, remember?"

"I'm very familiar with witch magic. Your magic was distinctively different from anything I've felt on Josh or any witch. Darker, deadlier."

I didn't like to close Sky out, but I had bigger issues to consider than our promises to be honest with each other. The safety of the whole pack depended upon me, and other beings would react badly if they ever knew what I was. I had taken enough of a risk using those powers today, when the elves could see the results. I wouldn't talk openly about what lay inside me, especially not while Josh would hear. After all, there was a secret about him tied to this.

"All magic can be considered dark and deadly, Sky," I said, finally looking back at her. "Please don't find a problem where there isn't one."

CHAPTER 6

Josh drove us straight from Elysian to his place. The whole way, he kept glancing at me curiously in the rear-view mirror, like I was a puzzle he was struggling to solve. I felt like a lab rat snatched out of my cage and placed in front of an audience, an audience that was now expecting me to respond when all I wanted was to be left in peace.

For most of our lives, I'd been hiding the power inside me, keeping it from my brother as much as from the wider world. Hiding that power had been a strain, but it had felt achievable. Now things had changed. I'd had to unleash that power to get out of the forest with the Tod Schlaf, and it had clearly drawn Josh's attention. After today, it would be harder to keep my story straight.

Of course, this scrutiny could be about concern for my health. I'd emerged from the forest drained and battered. If I'd seen the same thing happen to Josh, wouldn't I have been watching him with protective concern? I sat up in the back seat and gave him as reassuring a smile as I could manage. That was enough to keep him from asking questions, for now at least. Josh had apparently been more concerned about the forest's effect on me than about anything I might have done, and seeing me recover my strength settled whatever questions he had.

Josh parked outside his place, got out of the car, and nodded goodbye. I took his place in the driver's seat and started heading for Sky's home.

I hoped for a quiet drive while I gathered some energy, but I could see from Sky's expression that wasn't going to happen. It was all of six minutes before, with all the inevitability of her character, she spoke.

"Ethan."

I sighed. Better to get my explanation out first than to be subjected to a barrage of questions.

"I can do magic," I said. "This isn't a secret. Just like Josh, when I need to, I can use more. You saw it's not readily available to me. It tires me as well. I responded differently in there, too. I have no answers as to why."

It was enough of the truth to give Sky something to think about, without giving away secrets I still needed to protect. Most importantly, it bought me enough quiet to get to her house.

I pulled up into the driveway and saw an unfamiliar man leaning against the door. For a moment, I wondered what new stray Sky had befriended, but then I caught a flash of amethyst eyes and his vicious smile, and I knew exactly who this was. He might have changed his appearance to something more Hollywood, with a square jaw, wide brow, and carefully sculpted brown hair, but Logan was still the same old monster inside.

Sky got out of the car first, drawing Logan's gaze, but when I emerged he turned his whole attention on me. He pushed himself away from the door and prowled toward me, his expression a mixture of menace and intrigue. The intensity of his focus was unsettling, a hungry look that I didn't appreciate from a creature of such darkness.

Then I realized, he wasn't just reacting to me, he was reacting to the magic that still hung around me, the dark inversion of an afterglow from the forest and what I had unleashed there. Logan was captivated by pain, by death, by all things dark and dreadful, and now he sensed darkness on me.

He stood inches from me, lips parted, fingers twitching by his sides, staring at me as the minutes dragged by and I glared back at him. I didn't want him in my city, never mind my personal space. On top of that, Sky had already asked about the power inside me, and there was a risk that Logan's interest might draw questions from her that I didn't want to answer.

Logan raised a hand toward my cheek. I grabbed him by the wrist, then wrapped my other hand around his throat and lifted him off his feet.

"Don't touch me," I growled, feeling the magic swell within me.

Logan's smile only deepened, his eyes widening, as though in doing so they could somehow stare into my soul. That look of longing sickened me, but I was more focused on my anger. How dare he come here, threatening Sky once again with his presence? I would have made him pay for this, if it weren't for the fact that he would then hurt Sky.

"Why are you here?" Sky asked.

I growled and squeezed Logan's wrist, but he kept staring at me, apparently lost to everything else in the world. Then Sky's question seemed to sink in and he turned his gaze to her.

"I wouldn't expect such rudeness, from either of you," he said. "This courtesy is a friendly reminder that you have a job you need to complete and something you need to return to me."

So this was about Chris, not Sky. Fine. I dropped him,

indifferent to how he landed, and walked past him to the door.

"We never agreed to a time," I said, my back to Logan. I was worried that, if I looked at him, I might lose my temper and lash out. Given his hold over Sky, that was too dangerous to risk. "You'll get everything when we are able to deliver it. We told you we would do it, and we will, we just need time."

"Time is one thing I have plenty of, but do you?"

I spun around in anger, baring my teeth. That menace would have been enough to wipe the smile off any sane face, but Logan kept grinning smugly as he backed away. At last, he turned his back on me and walked away, a swagger in his stride.

Sky stepped past me, a curious look on her face as she opened the door. I could see more questions coming, and part of me wanted to open up to her, to break down the walls between us and let her in. But I kept my secrets to protect all of us, including Sky, and forcing her to keep them with me was too much to ask. It was getting harder and harder to maintain those defenses as the two of us grew closer, and the fear of losing her made me feel defensive, ready to snap at any moment. If I was to keep my temper, then I needed to get over the confrontation with Logan first.

I wanted an excuse to put the conversation off, so I headed to the shower. I'd gotten sweaty and dirty enough in the forest that this really was something I needed. I cast off my clothes, turned the temperature of the water up high, and let it run over me, so hot that my skin turned red. The intensity of that feeling drew me away from the emotions I'd been swimming in, the anger, frustration, and resentment. Through the billowing steam, I took deep breaths, brought my temper under control, and considered how to respond to Sky's inquiries, while the water washed away the blood and dirt of the elven realm.

At last, I stepped out of the shower, toweled myself off, and put on clean clothes that I'd left after one of my previous stays. When I emerged, Sky was waiting. She wore a look of determination that I'd grown all too familiar with, one that was appealing in itself but usually meant we were heading into a conversation I didn't want to have.

"I'm sleeping with a stranger," she said. "What are you hiding?"

I sighed and ignored the flippant comment. "You are making something that isn't into a big deal."

"If it's not a big deal, then you have nothing to hide. I saw you in the forest and the way that creature responded to you. And the way you were after you broke through the ward to get out. Something is off, and you can't just tell me that it's residual magic like I'm a fool. If you're keeping it from me to protect me, I can handle it. If it's something that is confidential, you know you can trust me. I just can't continue to live in the dark. I can't be with you—"

I moved closer and pressed my lips against her face, desperate not to hear her finish that sentence. The thought of losing Sky was so painful that even the words were too much to bear. I ran my fingers across her skin, seeking a distraction for both of us. I wanted her, and I wanted this conversation to be over. Why not kill two birds with one stone?

But Sky was determined to have her way. She tried to step away, and I tightened my grip, pulling her closer. I took hold of her hand, raised it to my lips, and kissed it. Sky only became angrier, jerking her hand from my grasp and pulling away from me, creating a gap between us.

"What are you?" she demanded.

I couldn't do this. Not now. Not when there was so much else we already had to deal with. I needed her to understand that, to give me time to discuss this at my pace. But that required more patience than she was capable of.

"Sky," I said gently, pleading for time.

She opened her mouth as if to speak but froze mid-breath. Her heartbeat slowed to a crawl, sending a jolt of alarm through me. I leapt forward just in time to catch her as she collapsed.

"Sky?" I turned her face toward me. "Sky, talk to me." I raised my voice but there was still no response.

Terror swept through me. Her heartbeat was unnaturally slow, her breath rasping in her throat, and her whole body had gone limp. This wasn't a heart attack and Sky wasn't prone to fainting. What the hell was happening to her?

Still holding Sky close, I pulled out my phone and dialed Sebastian.

"Ethan," he said. "We were expecting you back at the retreat."

"Something's happened to Sky," I said. "She's fainted and she won't wake up."

"I'll send Dr. Baker."

"I don't think he can help. This doesn't look like anything natural."

"I'm on my way," Sebastian said and hung up.

I sat on the floor of Sky's living room, still holding her in my lap, listening to the sound of her heartbeat. Was it fading still? Would I have to face the horror of losing this woman who meant so much to me?

"Sky," I said softly, then raised my voice when she didn't respond. "Sky, can you hear me?"

She lay still, not even a twitch of movement indicating that my words had gotten through.

"Sky, I need you to wake up," I said, shaking her by the shoulder. "I can't lose you. I won't."

For so long, protecting Josh had been the central pillar of my life. But now there were two people who mattered so much I would go to any length to protect them. And now I found myself helpless, frustrated, unable to do anything to revive the woman in my arms.

"Come on, Sky," I pleaded. "I need you here with me."

I pressed my face against hers, hoping that the connection between us would somehow get through, but there was no response. I changed into my wolf form and wrapped around her, letting the animal's regenerative energy flow, but still she lay limp, her breath frighteningly shallow, her skin pale. Was she slipping away from me?

Back in my human form, I took her in my arms and listened to her heartbeat. It was almost back to normal now, slow but steady, yet she stayed lost to the world. Whatever had happened, whoever was behind this, if they hurt her, then I would make them pay.

There was one thing left, one option I hadn't tried. It was the one that scared me most, but for Sky I was willing to risk it.

I closed my eyes and called on the magic lying inside me. It swelled with each breath, a rising tide touched with darkness. I let it flow through me and into Sky, trying to turn it into a protective force, one that could drive back whatever had hold of her. Conflicting spells clashed and there was a stinging in my hand, a physical reflection of that magical battle. Sky twitched and jerked as if in pain, but stayed limp, her eyes closed and breath shallow. Faced with an equal power, my magic was only making things worse. Frustrated at my own limits but unwilling to risk further harming Sky, I drew the magic back in.

There was a screech of tires and a car pulled into the driveway. Car doors slammed, the door to the house flew open, and Sebastian strode in, with Winter, Steven, and Gavin behind him.

"What happened?" Steven asked, sinking to his knees beside me. He took hold of Sky's hand and I could see his distress at how pale and lifeless she was. Behind him, Winter stood staring, grief and anger raging across her face as she saw the state of her favorite sparring partner.

"Tell me what happened," Sebastian said calmly.

I went over the events since we had left Elysian, carefully steering around the details of my conversations with Sky. I needed them to understand what had happened, but some things were private, even in a moment like this.

"Logan," Sebastian said. "This has his stink all over it."

I cursed myself for not having seen it before. I'd been so busy worrying about whether Sky would be all right that I'd missed the obvious cause.

"That asshole," Winter hissed. "I'll rip him full of holes for this."

I felt just the same, but fortunately Sebastian had his own anger in check, just visible beneath the mask of control.

"Threatening Logan will only make this worse," he said. "He felt defied, now he's reminding us what he can do. If we cross him again, this could get a lot worse."

"We're doing what he demanded," I snapped.

"Apparently not fast enough." Sebastian's brow furrowed. "He's going to be even more trouble than we thought."

Sky let out a soft moan and tilted her face closer to my chest.

"Is she awake?" Steven asked.

I leaned in, listening to every moment of her heartbeat, every flutter of her breath. Gavin retreated to a corner of the room as quiet fell.

"I think she's waking up," I said, my voice barely a whisper. I didn't dare speak louder, in case I somehow cursed the moment and she slid back into darkness.

Together we watched as Sky slowly stirred. Overwhelmed with relief, I kissed her on the forehead and drew her close.

"Are you okay?" I asked.

"I can't breathe," she choked.

"What?" Panic grabbed me as she squirmed in my arms.

"You're squeezing me too tight. I can't breathe!"

I relaxed a little, trying to give Sky the space she needed. She shifted and I held her tight, afraid that she was going to fall again.

"I need to stand," she said. "Please."

I was in turmoil—desperate to hold her close, to support her, to keep her safe through everything that was happening—but at the same time I knew that I had to give her space to find her own strength. Reluctantly, I let go.

Sky stood and looked around. Her expression, at first thoughtful, turned suddenly intense and her gaze narrowed in on me.

I realized with a shock what she must be thinking. She knew about the dark elf magic I had inherited from my grandmother, had felt what happened when I lost control of it. She had even seen a glimpse of the other, deeper magic inside me, something coiled and dangerous, ready to strike. Now she was knocked out by magic again, in the middle of an argument. I saw what it had to look like to her, but I needed her to know I had nothing to do with this.

"Logan decided to make a point," I said. "We aren't moving fast enough."

Silence filled the room. I could feel the anger at Logan radiating from Sky, matching my own hatred for him.

Sebastian was calmer, but the weight of the moment was still on him. He spoke firmly and steadily, but I could sense the concern underlying it.

"He'll need something done in good faith. Josh hasn't found a spell to remove his markings, and…"

He let the words end there. We had to find Chris. For now, it was the only way to keep Sky safe.

Sky pressed her lips together. She had that look on her face again, the one that said she wasn't happy with what we were doing. I didn't need her to be happy with it, I just needed her to accept it, for her own good.

"Why can't we try to put the sleeper on him?" she asked.

"Do you really think we can do that without him doing something to Kalese, Maya's creator?" Sebastian asked curtly. "This isn't something I want either, Sky, but it is what needs to be done."

"Why is my life so important to you all?" Sky asked, looking first at me and then at Sebastian. I felt hurt, stunned that she even asked, after everything that had happened between us. Her life was the most important thing in the world to me right now. I would go to any length to keep her safe, to protect her from the darkness surrounding us. I'd risked myself time and again for her sake, and yet she was talking as if I was a stranger. Didn't she know what she meant to me?

"You are part of this pack," Sebastian said. "It is my job to keep you safe."

He turned to Gavin, who stood gazing out the window, bored and impatient at other people's emotions.

"You need to find Chris," Sebastian continued. It made sense. Gavin was our best hunter, better even than me. No one could escape him forever. "We need her retrieved unscathed."

Gavin stood unmoving, his expression blank as he looked at our Alpha without responding. Brown eyes stared out from behind a curtain of long dark hair, giving nothing away about what he thought or felt. Something wasn't right in his response, and Sebastian could sense it as well as I could. He repeated his instruction, and when there was still no response, he repeated it again.

"No," Gavin said softly.

Sebastian's brow furrowed.

"No?"

"I'm busy. We still need to find Kelly, it's been thirty-four days."

Gavin brushed his hair from his face and kept on staring back at Sebastian.

For a long moment, I thought that there would be violence. As the Alpha, Sebastian couldn't afford to let disobedience and indiscipline spread through the pack. He had to not just be in control but show that he was in control. But then I saw what was holding him back: the sadness in Gavin's usually indifferent expression. We all missed Kelly, the humor and the care she brought to the pack, the one woman in the world who could call Gavin "bad kitty" and live to tell the tale. But she was particularly important to Gavin, and now he was making a stand for what mattered to him. I could understand that. I would do the same for Sky.

Sebastian ran a hand over his face. "Okay, you look for Kelly. Ethan, you find Chris."

A worried expression crossed Sky's face.

"I have information," she said. "It's flimsy at best, but I have a hard time thinking this is all coincidental."

I thought that this would be something new about Chris, but instead Sky repeated what she had told me about her encounter in the woods with the feral woman Carol and a possible mage. I hadn't realized that it had any connection to Kelly, and I was surprised to only hear the two things connected now. If they were linked, then shouldn't we have sent someone to check it out sooner?

"There's a building out there," she continued, "warded to keep people out. They've been taking people and carrying out experiments on them."

"A witch and a scientist?" Sebastian asked, frowning.

There had been times in the past when magic and science were combined to terrible ends. None of us wanted to see that happen again.

"I don't think it was a witch," Sky said, "definitely

someone who has magic, a great deal of it, but it didn't feel or smell like Josh's or any witch magic that I've encountered. I think it was a mage."

It wasn't much, but if there was a chance that it was connected to Kelly then we had to look into it.

"Winter, Gavin, Steven," Sebastian said. "You go check out the area where this feral woman was seen. Ethan, you go find Chris."

I nodded. I was already on this task, so it made sense to continue. I wondered if I should tell them about the help Claudia had offered but decided against it. No need to tell the pack that I'd involved another outsider in their business. If it worked out, and everyone was happy, I could let them know then. If not, it wouldn't matter.

Leaving Sky to recover from her shock, we headed out on the hunt.

CHAPTER 7

For the next three days, I scoured the seedy bars, neglected motels, and mercenary watering holes that lay scattered like scars across Chicago and the surrounding area. I worked my way down a list of possibilities, starting with those most likely to hold Chris. Every day brought fresh frustration, with no sign of her and few clues as to where she might be.

"You should ask Claudia," Sky said to me as we sat on the sofa in her house. "She can probably solve this faster than anyone."

Sky knew a lot about Claudia. That she was a cultured art dealer. That she was a respected figure in the supernatural world, one who had stood in for the Fae at conclave. That she, like Sky, was a Moura Encantada, responsible for the care of one of the protected objects, the Vitae that played a vital part in keeping Josh alive. And she knew that Claudia had a gift for finding people. In some ways, it was amazing that it had taken Sky this long to ask.

Of course, what she didn't know was that Claudia was already on the case.

"I don't know," I said, hiding my amusement. "Do we

really want to involve her?"

"Don't want to rely on your godmother?" Sky asked with a laugh. "Worried it'll damage your tough guy reputation?"

I set aside my coffee, picked up my phone, and headed for the door.

"Fine, I'll give her a call," I said, still suppressing a laugh. If Sky thought she had me worked out already, she was missing a point or ten.

Out of her earshot, I gave Claudia a call.

"Any luck finding Chris?" I asked.

"I'm watching her right now through the window of a coffee shop," Claudia said. "Would you like a word?"

I considered my options. Where was the best place for a controlled confrontation with Chris?

"Can you bring her to the pack's base?" I asked.

"I don't think she'll go for that. It gives you too much power."

We couldn't do this in public, with the risk of being overheard. "How about at someone's house?"

"By someone, do you mean Sky?"

"Do you have a better idea?"

Claudia paused for a moment before she spoke. "I'll make it work. Give me a few hours."

While I waited for Claudia, I called Sebastian to tell him what was happening. He came over with Josh and Winter, and the five of us waited expectantly to see what would happen.

At eight on the dot, Claudia arrived, as pleasant and polite as ever, with a furious Chris in tow. Claudia nodded respectfully in Sebastian's direction.

"I do apologize for the meeting being here rather than your office, but I believed this would be more acceptable for Chris." With the same genial smile, Claudia turned to Chris. "I appreciate you for accepting my invitation to this meeting."

Chris glared silently at her, arms folded across her chest.

"Thank you, Claudia," I said, offering her an air kiss by way of goodbye. Josh went to do the same, but as they separated, she grabbed hold of his arm with her gloved hand and stood frowning at the most recent tattoos.

"No more," he promised.

I'd tried to get him to stop ten tattoos ago, and of course my disapproval just made Josh want something more, but one word from Claudia and he completely changed his tune. Not that I was bitter—after all, I'd only accepted a burden of dark magic to keep him alive.

Once Claudia was gone, Chris looked around like she would rather set the place on fire than sit and talk with us. Impatient as I was to secure Sky's safety, I kept quiet, waiting for Chris to start the conversation on her terms.

"What do you want?" she asked in a hard, rough voice. However Claudia had brought her here, it wasn't entirely willingly.

"We need to hire you," Sebastian said, a useful half-truth.

"This is new," Chris said suspiciously. "You had me tracked down to hire me. What job can I do for you all that you can't do yourself?"

She crossed her arms and leaned back against the wall. Next to me, Sky shifted uncomfortably, and I had the horrible feeling that she was preparing to intervene. Her reticence about involving Chris could blow this whole plan apart.

"Logan wants you, and we want you to go with him," I said. There was no sense hiding it. That would only make Chris angrier when we got to the truth.

Chris raised an eyebrow and frowned. "Wants me for what?"

"I have no idea. Just another admirer? Nevertheless, he would like you to visit him for a while, and we want to pay you to do it."

"You're paying me to spend several nights with a man who wants me. Sweetie, that's not my job, that's the oldest profession and I have no interest in it." She pushed off from the wall and started to leave.

"Chris, wait," Josh said. She kept walking, so Josh kept talking. In a rush of words, he told her everything, from us asking Logan to find the Tre'ase who created Maya, to him killing Kalese and linking himself to her heart, and how he'd threatened to destroy it if we didn't do what he wanted.

Chris turned, one hand on the door, and looked across us. I expected her to tell us where we could stick the plan; it was what I would have done in her place. But while her face was impassive, her voice was a little softer when she spoke.

"Bambi dies if I don't go?"

Josh nodded.

"Okay." She looked at Sky. "I owe her, so I'll do it."

From the moment she had walked in, my body had been rigid with tension, uncertain how this would work out. I'd spent days looking for Chris, scouring the city for her as my one hope to keep Sky safe. I'd needed her to agree to the plan, but I knew how strong-willed she could be, and the whole time I'd lived in fear that she would just say no, turn around, and walk away.

Now that I knew we had a way to appease Logan and keep Sky from harm, the tension left my body and I subsided onto the couch, letting out a sigh of relief. This thing with Chris wasn't a long-term solution, and it only dealt with one of our myriad problems, but it was a start.

There was a sharp knock at the door. Chris darted across the room, putting as much space between herself and the new arrival as she could. A familiar scent and the sound of someone moving without a heartbeat made me tense once more, ready for action. By the time Sky reached the door, I was ready to face Demetrius.

"Skylar, I know she is in there," he called out. "Please open the door."

We all looked at Chris, who stood blank-faced, tense and still, before slowly nodding her head.

"Let him in," she said in a small voice.

Sky hesitated, one hand on the door handle.

"I said let him in," Chris said, her old strength and confidence returning.

As Sky opened the door a crack, I saw a familiar shift in her expression. That determination had appeared. She was going to try to get him to renounce any claim over Quell, to make the most of this moment to push for something Demetrius would never allow. She was going to anger the Master of the Seethe, putting herself and our plans in danger.

I got up off the couch.

"Okay, you can come in," Sky said, "but on one condition—"

I uttered an invocation and the ward holding Demetrius out dropped. With one hand I pulled the door open, while I wrapped my other arm around Sky's waist, urging her back. She whipped around and bared her teeth, and I smiled with pride at how fierce she had become, but now wasn't the time to fight among ourselves. I leaned in, her hair tickling my face.

"We'll discuss it later," I said.

Anger visible in her every move, Sky stepped around me and took position at the edge of the room, ready to spring into action if she didn't like what she saw. Chris still stood across the room from Demetrius, staring him in the eye.

"You need to come back." Demetrius's poise was slipping beneath the pressure of his own anger, a thick accent emerging from beneath his usually refined tone.

"I'm not coming back," Chris replied.

Demetrius flashed his razor-sharp fangs.

"You didn't get what you wanted," he snapped. "So what?

The south was never going to be yours even if you had successfully killed Alexander. Your little stunt warranted your punishment. You have no one to blame but yourself. Accept it and your position in the Seethe. I've been tolerant of your tantrums—I won't be any longer. You have two days to return on your own. After that you will be brought back, and it will not be with care. Do you understand me?"

Chris had always been fast, but vampirism gave her an extra edge. Before anyone could react, she shot across the room, grabbed a knife out of the butcher block, slammed Demetrius into the wall, and pressed the blade to his throat.

"I'm not coming back. Not to you. You locked me in a fucking box like I was an animal. For what, because of Alexander? You can't… I don't like… you can't lock me…"

Her voice wavered and blood ran from where the knife bit his skin. Chris gritted her teeth and pressed harder, making more blood flow.

"You can't lock me in boxes!" she said through clenched teeth.

None of the rest of us moved. It wasn't just that we loathed Demetrius, that every one of us would happily have watched Chris decapitate him. That was something we could have set aside to make this negotiation go smoothly. But this was Seethe business, and it was no more our place to intervene than it would have been Demetrius's place to referee one of our challenges.

"You disobeyed me, did you expect something different?" Demetrius said in a low, cool voice, as if the knife weren't even there.

Chris pressed harder. Demetrius winced, then smiled, and raised his hand to touch hers. His thumb stroked her finger, gently, lovingly, and he smiled at her adoringly. Leaving aside the darkness of his kinks, Demetrius had no sense of when not to indulge them.

"I've missed you," he said tenderly.

Chris's hands were trembling, her hate for Demetrius at war with her good sense, an understanding of the terrible consequences that could come from this.

"Chris," Sky said softly, as if she were trying to soothe a frenzied beast. She pulled Demetrius's hand away, then covered Chris's with her own. Slowly, Chris relaxed, letting Sky take the knife from her.

Chris stepped back, putting space between her and Demetrius. Sky stood between them, the vampire's blood dripping from the knife in her hand.

"Demetrius, please leave," Sky said.

He ignored her and stood staring at Chris. I could see the forces at war within him—enchantment, obsession, the need to control his creation. It was like looking at a monstrous form of my own conflicted relationship with Sky. But where our connection was built on affection and admiration, his was twisted and intense, warped by the drive to dominate, and now it had him transfixed. Was this all about control, or was Demetrius drawn to Chris by something more now, some cruel imitation of love?

"Demetrius, Sky asked you to leave," I said. "Honor her request or I'll make you."

Something flickered in Demetrius's eyes, a moment of doubt perhaps, or calculation, or just one last look over Chris. Then he was gone, out into the night.

Several moments passed while we waited for Chris to compose herself. In those moments, she seemed to come to some decision. She headed for the door.

"Where are you—" Sky began.

"I said I will help and I will, but I have to feed."

"I assure you if you leave, you will not be able to come back," Sebastian said. "Demetrius will make certain of that."

"You give Demetrius and his Seethe too much credit. I stayed in business because he's not nearly as good at hunting as he'd have you to believe. I'll be fine."

"You can use me," Sky blurted out, to my alarm.

Chris burst out laughing. "Bambi, I would love to take you up on that offer, but if Quell is any example of what happens when a vampire tastes Bambi blood, then I'll have to pass. Fawning over the cute brunette in the Midwest Pack is really not on my to-do list."

I sighed in relief. I didn't want to have to talk Sky out of that mad and irresponsible offer.

"I'll do it," Josh said.

My heart sank. Had everyone lost their mind?

Chris stepped away from the door and examined him, taking hold of one arm and then the other, looking them over like pieces of meat. She shook her head.

"Ink. I can't stand the taste of it."

Josh tilted his head, exposing his neck while backing into the couch and then taking a seat. Chris approached him slowly, failing to hide her thirst. Her eyes widened and the pupils pulsed at the sight of the proffered vein. The terait, the orange quarter ring around the pupils of the vampire's eyes that spoke to their hunger, shone like amber in her dark eyes.

Chris climbed onto Josh, her legs astride his. My discomfort at watching any woman straddle my younger brother was ten times greater when that woman was a hungry vampire.

"Have you done this before?" she asked, her voice low and seductive, making me cringe. If this was what it took to protect the pack, then so be it, but I wished I wasn't there as a witness. I didn't like to see vampires feed on anyone, least of all someone I cared about.

"Yes."

"Neck?"

"No."

"Okay, I'll be gentle," she said with a trace of humor.

The rest of the world seemed to vanish as I watched her settle onto him, her face pressed into his neck, her fingers curling into his hair as she pulled him close. He groaned, a sound filled with the sort of lust I never wanted to hear from my brother, and eased back on the sofa, exposing more of his neck.

Watching Chris feed on Josh, I couldn't help remembering Quell feeding on Sky. That was something else I hadn't wanted to happen, never mind to see in the flesh. That had been awful to watch because it was Sky and I couldn't bear seeing a vampire leech on her like she was some snack, some plaything to meet his needs. But this was another level entirely. It was something sexual, two bodies wrapped together so close they might as well have been naked. His hands ran up her sides, kneading into her skin, and she thrust herself harder onto him. They pressed against each other, lost in a moment that should have been private, an act that was intimate in a way that Sky and Quell had never been.

It could almost have been reassuring, seeing what hadn't taken place between Quell and Sky, knowing that there really had been restraint. But it was hard to feel reassured by the sight of my ex dry humping my brother.

At last, Chris pulled away. She peered at the puncture marks on Josh's neck, then leaned in again and ran her tongue over the wounds until they closed up. Josh's hands rested on her hips when she finished, and she looked down at his lap, then smiled. There were streaks of red along the bridge of his nose and cheeks, and he was grinning like an idiot.

Chris climbed off of Josh, and he waited a moment, staring intently at some distant spot on the wall, before he stood up as well.

I finally dragged my gaze away from them. If I never saw that happen again, it would still be too soon. At least I had never been subjected to that by Sky and Quell, to my immense relief. If he'd been hoping for the lusty blood and grinding version of a feeding, Quell had been bitterly disappointed.

Chris's face had brightened and her tongue slid over her lips, licking up the last traces of blood. She made her way to her bag across the room, pulled out a pen and a pad of paper, and scribbled something on it.

"This is my fee," she said, handing a note to Sebastian. "It's high, and you're going to be a little pissed. Get over it and wire the money to the account below."

Sebastian stared at it for several seconds before thrusting the paper back at her.

"No."

Chris blew out an exaggerated breath, making her lips ripple. "How many times must I tell you all—we aren't going to haggle. I said I'd do it to save Bambi; I didn't say I was going to do it for free. But if you need time to pretend you don't need me, I'll be around. Apparently, Claudia knows how to find me."

Anger was boiling beneath Sebastian's frown, but he kept it hidden there. He took out his phone, tapped at the screen several times while looking at the note, and finally nodded to Chris. She pulled her own phone out, looked at a notification, and smiled.

"So I visit him and what? There has to be more than that. Do you have a plan?"

"We have possession of a Tod Schlaf," Sebastian said.

Chris smiled. "So, I'm assuming since you all don't want me out and about, I'm staying with Josh?"

Josh shrugged, feigning indifference. A trace of red had reappeared on his cheeks. But to hell with that—I wasn't having her treat my brother like an all-you-can-eat buffet.

"Josh? Hell, no," I snapped.

"Why not?" Josh asked.

"If Demetrius does decide to come and get Chris, I don't want you put in danger."

"I'll be fine. I have a ward that I will set up, and I'm sure Chris and I can handle ourselves if they try."

I glared at him while I tried to muster a better answer. Of course Josh was dead set on this now that I'd objected. And of course he wanted to do the thing that could put him in unnecessary danger, maybe scarring his body along the way. I'd spent my whole life protecting him, and he'd fought back the whole time. There were times when his ingratitude seemed staggering, and this was one of those moments.

"We'll be fine," Chris said, heading out the door with Josh close behind.

I stared after them, but there was nothing I could do. Sebastian had paid the price and now we had to keep the goods safe. I would just have to suffer my discomfort alone.

I woke in the night, unsettled by a sense of something missing. I reached across the bed to find that Sky was gone. A flicker of light under the bedroom door told me she hadn't gone far.

I walked into the living room and found Sky sitting on the couch, watching television with the volume turned down. She looked lost, a small figure huddling in the dark of the night.

"You can't sleep?" I asked, leaning against the wall.

There was no response, just a tightening of her shoulders. I could see the seething mess of emotions work their way across her face. What was she worrying about this time? What necessary act had offended her sense of how the world should work?

"What's wrong?" I asked.

"Nothing," she said stiffly.

I stifled an irritated growl. Was I going to have to drag the words out of her if I wanted to avoid another day of resentful silence?

"You know I hate when you lie to me. Don't do it."

"Do I have to worry? About Chris? Do I have to worry about her and you together? I saw the way you responded to her feeding from Josh. Is her being a vampire the only thing that's keeping you from her? Eventually, that won't bother you so much."

I rested against the wall, rubbing my chin while I mustered my thoughts.

So this was it. On the one hand, the truth would get us out of this. On the other hand, was Sky ready to hear it?

"Chris was easier to be with," I began.

"Nice to hear," she snapped. "You plan on putting that on my Valentine's card? Or do you have something even more insensitive?"

"Do you have more or are you going to let me finish?" I knew this was going to be a struggle. Sky didn't like hearing any view that wasn't the one she already had. I watched her, but she refused to meet my gaze. Her whole posture was an accusation leveled at me. How dare I feel the things she imagined I did?

"Sky," I said softly, and she finally looked at me. "Can I finish?"

She gave the barest hint of a nod.

"Most people didn't understand my relationship with Chris," I said. "It was easy with her, contrary to what others thought. Our relationship didn't extend any further than the walls, more specifically the bedroom. When we were there, we were together. I knew what she was capable of and likewise she of me. Our loyalties and expectations like everything else ended when we went out the door. I'm not saying it was a functional relationship—it was riddled with dysfunction—but it worked for us. What you and I have is complicated and extends further than this bedroom, this house. I've accepted everything about it and about you. I didn't enter into anything naïvely or blindly. I knew what I was signing on to when I decided to be with you."

I felt exposed, talking to anyone like this, most of all Sky. Her reaction could hurt me in ways no one else could, just as she could lift my mood like no one else could. That was why I had to tell the truth, in a way I never had with any other woman in my life. Not just had to do that but wanted to, however hard it was. The openness I shared with her was something special, and it was changing me. I had to help her understand that there was nothing to worry about.

"It's worth the trade-off. All of it." I sat down next to her and she leaned into me. At last, I started to feel safe again. I kissed her on top of her head, feeling the softness of her hair and soaking up the smell of her. "Sky, I don't want to keep having this conversation."

"We've never discussed Chris before," she said.

I frowned. I was sure that wasn't true. These things went around so many times, I felt like I was losing myself in the details, but I had covered this, and it was frustrating to find that she didn't remember. It took such a strain to talk this way. It hurt to find those words had been forgotten.

"We have had this conversation. I told you once, you don't have anything to worry about. You don't. Okay?"

She nodded.

"Now we need to discuss Quell," I said. This was another corner of our relationship that filled me with discomfort, but we had to address it.

Sky pulled away from me.

"Why did you intervene with Demetrius? I was just—"

"I know what you were just going to do, and I won't allow it."

She took a sharp breath. "Allow? Do you want to rephrase that?"

"Okay." I grinned. I preferred the Sky who fought back to

the one staring morosely at a silent TV screen. "I'm not going to let Quell come back. That's not up for debate. He's fine. He settled into a nice house, and from my understanding, he has a donor and she's safe with him."

"What?" Sky stared at me like I'd told her that the Pope lived on the Moon.

"He found a donor, a brunette with curly hair and similar features to yours. Her eyes are blue instead of green."

I watched her, looking for any sign of emotion. I didn't understand her relationship with Quell. She had always said that it wasn't romantic, and after seeing what the Chris and Josh version looked like, I finally felt like that was true. But I also felt like I was missing out on some part of Sky, something she shared with Quell but not me, and it stung that a vampire might understand her better than I did.

"How is he doing?" she asked.

I forced a smile. I wished she didn't feel a need to know, but I had opened up this topic and now I had to face the consequences.

"I find it oddly convenient that he was unable to survive without you, yet he seems to be doing just fine now without you," I said. "I can't help but wonder if it was an excuse he used to have access to you because he knew you would be there if he needed you."

"He's not like that."

I didn't believe that, but I wanted to believe in her, to know she would never respond to Quell in the way that he wanted.

I stood up and held out my hand. "I pose that same question to you. Do I have to worry about Quell?"

She shook her head.

"I need to hear it," I said softly.

"No. You don't have to worry about Quell."

A sense of calm descended over me. Hand in hand, we headed back to bed.

CHAPTER 8

The sound of a car woke me from a restful sleep. I reached out for Sky, only to find her side of the bed empty again. I glanced at the clock—three in the morning. Someone had been struggling to sleep again.

This time, she wasn't sitting in front of the television. I looked out to the driveway and saw that her car was gone. It didn't take much thinking to work out where she was heading. Sky was still troubled by the deal we had made with Chris and wouldn't be happy until she'd forced Chris through a long conversation about it all. She needed everything neat and tidy, with the reassurance that Chris's choice was her own.

I went back to bed and lay in darkness, staring at the ceiling. This shouldn't have bothered me. Sky was welcome to talk with whoever she liked as long as it didn't disrupt pack business. But I felt on edge, anxious about how the conversation between my ex and my current girlfriend might go.

It didn't help that I'd been thinking about the magic stirring inside of me, this dark power from my elven inheritance and the spirit shade. Though it had been there for years, it had been more active recently, more powerful. That gave me opportunities, but it also caused concern. What if the power wasn't mine to control? I tossed and turned, body and mind restless.

If I couldn't get to sleep in this state, then I would just have to tire myself out first. I got out of bed and did one-handed push-ups until both my arms ached, then switch to sit-ups. I kept going until I had no energy left to spend, my mind on Sky the whole time. At last, exhausted, I crawled back into bed.

Still lying awake, I reached out across the bed, and Sky's absence felt more acute. What was going on at Josh's place? What might Sky be learning about me from Chris, and might it change the way she felt?

At last, I heard Sky's Honda Civic pulling back up into the driveway. She crept into the house, discarded her clothes in the dark, and slipped into bed beside me.

"Did you get the closure you needed?" I asked.

Sky just lay there looking at me. I turned my head and smiled, trying to let her know that it was all right, that I understood.

"You're more predictable than I even imagined," I said.

"I know why we're doing it," she said, "but don't ask me to be okay with it."

That was a perfect Sky moment right there, still wishing that she could make life easy for others when sometimes it was just hard. My forced smile turned genuine as I gazed at her soft, sympathetic features.

I wrapped my arm around her and the sleepiness that had evaded me finally took hold. I closed my eyes and moments later I was asleep.

I pulled up in front of Logan's house. In the seat next to me, Chris opened her bag and checked the contents again. She pulled out the small jar holding the Tod Schlaf, peered at the strange, almost invisible creature one last time, then thrust it back down out of sight.

"You ready?" I asked.

"Let's go," Chris replied.

I looked over my shoulder. Sky was sitting in the back seat, arms crossed, glaring at Logan's house. I'd known that she was going to hate this, had tried to discourage her from coming, but she was determined to see it through, just like she was always determined once she set her mind to something.

Chris and I got out of the car. I glanced across the street to where another car sat. Sebastian, Gavin, and Winter had all come along in case there was trouble. I didn't know whether Sebastian thought he needed to keep an eye on Logan or on me more. Either way, they all watched as we headed for the front door.

Just being back at Logan's place unsettled me, reminding me of the sight of Sky writhing in pain, of the terrible helplessness I'd felt. At least this time I was in control. I knew what Logan didn't, knew we had planned a way out of this, and that would have to be enough.

I didn't like that we were giving in to Logan's demands. It felt wrong to give him the satisfaction of a victory, however brief and false that satisfaction might be. I didn't like the risks involved either—throwing Demetrius's favorite toy to Logan could start a war with the Seethe if the vampire master ever found out. Most of all, I didn't like how unhappy this whole business made Sky, who I was sure would sulk until Chris returned.

But I didn't have to like the plan to recognize that it was the best one we had. This was about keeping Sky safe, and I was more than willing to hand Chris over for that cause.

Logan opened the door as we approached.

"Chris!" he said, as if she were an unexpected guest, not a

prisoner he'd been told we would be delivering today. "Come in, come in. It's such a delight to see you."

Chris forced a smile.

"Logan," she said. "Long time no see."

I glared at him, this monster who held Sky's life in his hands, who had used that leverage to get hold of another unwilling victim. He looked so smug, I wanted to knock his teeth out. The look on my face only made him grin more.

Chris smiled at Logan, putting on a pretense of pleasure in his company. Then she looked at me with a coolness that seemed all too real. First I'd opposed saving her life by turning her into a vampire, and now I was responsible for handing her over to this monster. I was sure she understood my reasons, but that didn't mean that everything was good between us. We were working together because we had to, nothing more.

"It's okay, Ethan," she said calmly. "I'll be fine."

Then she stepped past Logan into the house and he closed the door behind them.

I spent the next two days on edge, waiting for the call from Chris that would tell me that she had succeeded and Logan was in our power. My nerves weren't helped by Sky, who paced and fidgeted every hour of the day, not even trying to hide her apprehension. Her tension spread through the pack until everyone felt the same way, snapping and snarling at each other, inches away from outright fighting. Sky, caught up in her own thoughts and feelings, seemed oblivious to the effect she was having, the huge effort of will it took from all of us to keep things civil.

At least we had other issues to focus on, starting with Gavin's investigation of the strange people in the woods.

"What do you think?" he said, looking across the pack's

living room at Josh. The two of them had gone back to where the feral woman had been spotted, and now they were sharing their findings with the rest of us.

"The ward is strong," Josh said. "I felt a lot of strong magic, too."

"Then it has to be the witches," Gavin said, scrabbling for any solid lead.

"I didn't feel witch magic when I was there," Sky said.

"I didn't, either." Josh turned to Sky and Winter. "There isn't any activity in there, either. We were there for several hours, and nothing."

"Not even in the location we told you about?" Sky asked.

Josh shook his head. "Seeing you must have made them more cautious. I didn't break the ward because it would have alerted whoever erected it. But I suspect there is a house deeper in the forest."

He'd done the smart thing by holding back. Breaking a blood ward would have sent a warning to whoever set it, and we didn't want to tip our hand. First learn what our enemies were about, then make our move on them.

"Do you know who owns the property?" Sebastian asked. "If we have that information, we might be able to find out if it's the witches or someone affiliated with them. We don't want to go in blindly."

I shared his unhappiness at the thought that the witches might be involved. The more supernatural powers we ran across, the more complicated this situation would be to deal with, and the witches hadn't exactly been cooperative lately.

Gavin shrugged. "The geek's working on finding out."

"His name is Matthew," Sky snapped.

The geek in question was one of the Worgen, a small pack of twenty weres that we had recently assimilated. It wasn't the first time I'd been through a merging of packs, as it was sometimes necessary to bring smaller, wilder groups under control, or to provide shelter to weres whose packs were in decline. It was never easy, as every pack had its own culture, habits, and ways of working. There were usually clashes of communication and a few months of jostling for position, with bared teeth and claws, as hierarchies combined and the new arrivals looked for spaces near the top of the pack.

Theoretically, the Worgen should have been a tough assimilation. The whole style of their pack had been nerd culture, something they were either unwilling or unable to let go. But ironically, their weird interests had reduced the clash of their arrival. Their computing skills made them instantly useful, and as long as we kept them supplied with Mountain Dew and nachos, they seemed happy to collectively accept a place near the bottom of the pack. Instead of one more problem rising over the horizon, they'd become a potential solution to other issues we had.

Issues like whatever was happening in the woods.

"If there is a house or something behind the ward, you can't be sure that Kelly is in there," Sebastian said, his tone soft as he tried to soothe a pacing Gavin. "We can't just go in without more information."

"We should go in just because there's something terribly wrong going on," Winter said with a look of disgust. "If Kelly is in there, we really need to get her out."

Sebastian sighed and steepled his fingers. He and I had discussed this earlier. Winter was right, not just about protecting Kelly but about needing to deal with whatever was going on. Something obscene was festering on the edge of our territory, and that wasn't the sort of problem we normally let go. Being a pack was about dominance, it was about power, and if we didn't use that power to keep people safe around us, then we would face not only chaos but the threat of humans looking more closely into our lives.

But right now, it was harder to act. We were facing several problems, and if we tried to tackle them all at once, then we risked dealing with none of them well. We were strong as a pack, but we had limits, and we had paid the price of spreading ourselves too thin before. There was a time to just charge in and fight our problems, and I relished that time as much as Winter did, but that time wasn't now.

Before Sebastian could reach a conclusion, his phone rang. A frown briefly crossed his face, to be replaced by his usual steady calm as he answered the call.

"Chris?"

Logan's voice emerged from the speaker, cold, hard, and angry. "I am not amused."

I winced. This could only mean one thing. Chris had failed, and now we would face the consequences of that failure—consequences that could be terrible for Sky. She steadied herself in anticipation of what might come next.

One thing was clear—Chris had risked herself for us, and now the time had come to repay the favor.

———

Sky, Josh, Winter, Sebastian, and I ran up to Logan's home. I could feel the magic in the air, something thick and rotten, as dark and twisted as the creature who wielded it.

I slammed into the door shoulder first. There was a splintering crack as the frame gave way and the door burst open. We charged in, ready to face the worst.

Logan looked up wild-eyed from the floor, his face a picture of rage, magic swirling like a storm around his head. His human disguise, that charming shell he used to trick and manipulate others, flickered in and out of view like a corrupted video file. As those features scattered like static into the air, they revealed the true Logan, with his massive jaw, misshapen features, and jutting horns.

Chris lay on the floor in front of him, her body shriveling as she sank into reversion, that hideous state vampires could fall into somewhere on the brink of death. A stake protruded from her chest, hammered through flesh and into her heart, but Logan clearly hadn't meant to finish her off, as half-empty blood packs were scattered around her. He was bringing her in and out of reversion, bringing her back and forth across the threshold of terrible pain. Most vampires deserved every agony they got, but it was still a monstrous thing to do.

"Step away from her," Sebastian demanded in a steely tone.

"No. She is mine," Logan said, his eyes blazing with anger. "This deceitful little bitch will not get away with her treachery, and neither shall you. The curse of the lunar eclipse will happen, and I will have my vengeance as I watch all of your kind expire in the very way the Faeries saw fit for such treacherous animals to die. You will be put down."

I glanced at Sebastian, but he looked as confused as I felt about Logan's ramblings.

Josh snapped out a spell and magic burst from his hands. It struck Logan hard, flinging him across the room, away from Chris. Dread filled me and I looked at Sky, but Logan's own fury and the suddenness of Josh's attack had distracted him from the one way he could most easily punish us. Instead of using the heart, he drew upon his own magic, the marks on his arms whipping around. He stamped his foot and waves of magic rushed out in every direction, flinging us against the walls.

The marks glowed and I braced myself for another attack. But Josh was faster than Logan again. A flick of his hands sent a sofa soaring through the air. It smashed into Logan, throwing him against the opposite wall. His nose smashed into the brickwork and blood streamed out.

"Careful," I said, seeing Josh's fury rising, a storm of magic gathering around him. "Josh?"

I'd seldom seen him like this. I was the one with the temper, the one who lashed out without control. It was worrying to see bright, upbeat Josh giving in to that same impulse.

Fortunately, my sharp tone cut through whatever feelings whirled around inside him. He took a slow breath, but his magic remained extended, pinning Logan to the wall.

Something shifted in Logan's eyes, a moment of realization that sent a chill through my veins. His body relaxed and his eyes shone, drifting from bright lilac to black. Dark magic swirled around him, and I choked on a sudden stench of rot and death.

Here was the power of the dreaded Tre'ase, unleashed against us at last. Pain pierced me like a red-hot iron spike through my chest. I doubled over and saw the others do the same.

I looked at Sky. Blood was running down her cheeks. Logan's hold over her made her more vulnerable. The magic was destroying her from the inside out.

At the sight of her suffering, my fury overcame my pain. I stood with a growl and grabbed the nearest thing to me, a kitchen table. I hurled it straight at Logan with all my strength, even as the pain in my chest redoubled. The table exploded, filling the air with splinters, as Winter shot across the room in her snake form. She hit Logan straight on, burying her fangs in his flesh, pouring her venom into him.

Logan's face contorted with pain as he clutched at the wall, trying to keep himself upright and conscious. He muttered incantations, but the words came out mumbled and disjointed, a muddle of noises that summoned only the weakest pulses of magic as he collapsed.

Josh ran to Chris. Half her body was consumed by reversion and she grimaced in pain as she tried to move her hands. He pulled out the stake and pressed a blood pack to her lips, but she couldn't even open it.

Sky snatched up another of the packs from the floor and ripped it open with her teeth before handing it to Josh. Sky shivered and for a moment I thought that Logan had hit her with his magic again. But then she turned, licking remnants of blood from her lips, and I realized with a chill that this was something else—Sky's vampire side showing through.

That unsettled me more than the sight of Chris gulping down three more packs of blood, then burying her face in Josh's neck as he whispered to her. I hated to see my brother drawn into some twisted bond with Chris, but the thought that vampirism might take hold of Sky made me sick to my soul. I'd always known that this was part of her, but some naïve part of me had hoped that I would never have to deal with it. That illusion evaporated as I saw a smile twitch unbidden across her lips.

There was no time now to untangle my feelings on what I'd seen. Issues between Sky and I had to wait. We still had Logan to deal with.

"The Tod Schlaf is in his bedroom," Chris said, pulling herself unsteadily to her feet.

Sebastian followed where she pointed and returned a few moments later with the Tod Schlaf held out between his hands. He placed it on Logan and took a step back.

"Now what?" I asked.

"Now we wait," Sebastian said.

We couldn't risk traveling with Logan if he might wake up and start using his powers. As none of us had seen a Tod Schlaf used on a Tre'ase before, that meant we had to wait to see how well it worked.

After two hours of careful scrutiny, with no sign of movement, Sebastian decided that we could risk it. We slung Logan in the back of a car and headed for the retreat.

Dr. Jeremy frowned as we walked into the infirmary with Logan draped over Sebastian's shoulder. He frowned even more deeply when he saw Chris stumble in, her footsteps slow and weary as she struggled to recover from hours of torture at Logan's hands.

"Should I even ask what this is about?" Jeremy said as Sebastian laid the unconscious Tre'ase down on a bed.

"Monitor him," Sebastian said. "Let me know if there's the slightest hint he might wake up."

He nodded to Josh, who would be staying to try to unlink Logan from Kalese, and Sky, who was to stay with him in case she could sense a change in the magic. Then he headed out of the infirmary, followed by me and Winter.

"We need to start preparing in case he wakes up," Sebastian said. "Winter, can you—"

My phone buzzed. I pulled it out of my pocket and saw Stacy's name flash up on the display.

"This could be important," I said.

"Take it," Sebastian said, waving me away. "I'll catch up with you later."

I walked off down the hallway to a quiet corner, then answered the call.

"I've found something on those properties," Stacy said.

I smiled. This felt like the first bit of straight-up good news I'd had all week. The properties were a list of places mentioned in historical stories from Sebastian's notes on the Tre'ases. The places had all been linked to tales of one Tre'ase, and based on the description, I thought he was the one who made the spirit shade trapped inside me. If any of those places still mattered to the Tre'ase, then they might lead me to him.

"Did you know that they're nearly all owned by the same person?" Stacy asked.

I did now, and it made this lead seem a lot more promising.

"Are you sure?" I asked.

"Oh, I'm sure," she replied. "He's tried to cover his tracks, working through proxies and shell companies, but they all come back to the same guy: an investor named K. L. Estevez."

I didn't know the name, but that was hardly surprising. A Tre'ase might go by a hundred different names if it was more subtle and careful than the likes of Logan.

"Anything else?" I asked.

"Not yet, but I'm working on it."

"Thanks, Stacy."

I hung up and stood staring at the phone. All the struggles of the past few days, and now it was some good lawyerly research that had gotten me what I needed. If I could track down the Tre'ase that had created the spirit shade in me, and if I could find a way to contain it, then I would be safe from the same fate Sky had suffered at Logan's hands. That also meant that Josh, whose life depended upon that Tre'ase's magic, would be safe from a threat he didn't even know about.

The struggle to save Sky from Logan had made me more aware of how vulnerable my brother was. After the desperate fight we'd just been through, and with all the danger Logan still represented to Sky, things felt bleak. Stacy's news let me feel hope again.

Logan lay on the bed, his true form revealed. Unconscious and unsupported by magic, he no longer looked human. Instead, we saw a twisted beast with a jutting jaw and protruding horns, its face horribly distorted. Beside the bed, the Tre'ase Kalese's heart sat pulsing in a jar, the same macabre sight that had once decorated Logan's home, and that gave him power over Sky.

Sebastian and I had come to the infirmary to witness Josh's latest attempt to sever the magic linking Logan to the heart. If he could break that link, then Sky would be safe from Logan. If not, and if the Tod Schlaf stopped working, then Sky would be at the monster's mercy.

The problem was that trying to sever the link also brought risks.

"I don't like it," I said, looking at Josh. "You are going to play with Sky's life each time to 'see' if it works."

There had already been two failures, and hearing about them had me twitching with anxiety. Surely there was a safer way to free Sky than to keep risking her life through these half-planned experiments in spellcasting? At least the previous spells had been ones that Josh could control. Now he was relying on Sky's ability to convert natural magic into dark magic, so that she could mimic Logan's abilities and so unravel his spell. I didn't know enough magic to understand all the theory, but I knew enough about people to sense a desperate plan.

I also knew enough about Sky to know that she wouldn't be kept from doing this. Much as it hurt me to watch her put her life at risk, at least if I was here I could help if something went wrong.

My knuckles whitened as my hands clenched on the bed frame and I forced myself not to protest.

Josh drew a knife and I winced as he cut first Sky's hand and then his own. They joined hands and chanted a spell, connecting their magic together, then Sky uttered another invocation. The air tingled and I sensed dark magic entwined around the pair of them and Logan.

The magic rose and so did the chanting. I couldn't tell what was happening, whether it was working or not. Was this saving Sky or scarring her? Did I need to let it continue or stop it right now? I hated having no control, no way of protecting or supporting her. I hated to feel so useless.

Something changed in the way Sky was speaking. The words weren't any language I knew anymore, and her voice barely sounded like her own. The temperature in the room dropped and Sky's breath frosted as it emerged from between her lips. The magic shifted again, something ancient and powerful emerging.

Sky closed her eyes and spoke faster. It was as if two voices were emerging at once. I reached out for her, but a blast of wind hurtled through the room, swirling around Sky and Josh before flinging the rest of us off our feet. My head smacked against the ground and the world went black.

When I came back to my senses, the air in the infirmary was still. I pushed myself up onto my elbows, fighting to control the spinning of my head, and looked around. Sky was at Jeremy's desk, frantically scribbling something down on a piece of paper, while Josh stood over Jeremy, who was groaning softly as he returned to consciousness.

Something else was different. I looked over at the bed. Logan lay limp, not just unconscious anymore but lifeless, eyes rolled back and head lolling to one side. In the jar beside him, Kalese's heart still beat.

I felt a huge sense of relief. It had worked. Josh had found a magic powerful enough to break Logan's hold, and apparently it had broken Logan, too. As far as I was concerned, his death was a bonus. Now we wouldn't have to worry about him coming back with more tricks and threats, we wouldn't need to find a way to forever contain a being of such power and evil. And best of all, Sky was safe.

"What the hell was that?" Sebastian said as he forced himself to his feet. "What language was that?"

No one else seemed to have a clue what the words had been—even Sky herself, who had spoken them. It was an unsettling realization. If she hadn't spoken the words, then someone had spoken through her. That meant Maya, the spirit shade that lived inside her, had taken control. Had we saved Sky from one menace only to give strength to another one? Maya had an interest in keeping Sky alive, but that didn't mean she had her best interests at heart. My relief at the end of one threat was deflated by the appearance of another.

At least I could answer Sebastian's question. Maya had been a Faerie before she had been a shade.

"Faerie, their original language," I said. "It's old, very old."

Sky had spoken in an ancient language she didn't even know. That meant she and Josh hadn't been the only ones performing magic here, that Maya had cast a spell of her own. Now we had to wait and see: was it just to free them from Logan, or had the ancient spirit shade been up to something more?

It seemed that our pack was doomed to keep unleashing unknown powers.

CHAPTER 9

I woke to a strange sensation, like the tingling of a giant insect bite on my left shoulder. Not painful, but distracting.

I looked across the bed, half expecting to see Sky there, but then remembered that we'd both stayed at our own places last night. Much as I loved waking up next to her—and of course everything that came the night before—we weren't yet at the stage of spending every night together. We each had our own lives and needed quiet nights in our own homes from time to time.

It was starting to get light outside. I stretched, climbed out of bed, and went to the bathroom. Standing at the sink, I twisted my arm around until I could see the back of my shoulder in the mirror. The tingling sensation was fading, but something else remained: a mark in the shape of the crescent moon.

I stared at the mark, trying to work out what it meant. Clearly some sort of magic was at work, and magic done on me against my will couldn't be anything good. I carefully checked the rest of my body for further signs but found nothing more. That was a relief, but something weird was going on here, and I needed to work out what.

I got dressed, jumped in the Venom, and headed down to the pack retreat. As I was driving, my phone buzzed. Sebastian was calling.

"I need you at the retreat," he said as soon as I answered. "I think someone's put a curse on me."

"Let me guess," I said. "You woke up with a crescent moon mark on your shoulder."

"You too?"

"Yes. I'm on my way."

When I got to his office, Sebastian was on the phone. He set it down as I entered and gestured for me to take a seat.

"The same thing has happened to Gavin and Winter," he said.

"So it's hit the whole pack?"

"Only the ranked weres, and not Steven."

I paused to consider what that meant. Someone had targeted the pack's leadership, and they'd done it with magic that could cut through our usual immunity. That was a troubling situation to be in.

"I spoke to Cole," Sebastian added. "It's hit him, too."

"We shouldn't tell everyone yet," I said. "It'll only cause alarm."

"I agree, but we need to get those in the know together to work out our next step. That's why Cole's on his way here."

My frown deepened. Cole was turning into a parasite, worming his way ever deeper into the business of the Midwest Pack. Whatever his reasons, I didn't think they were good for us. He was too much of a schemer, despite his surface charm. He flattered and smiled, but there was nothing of substance behind that mask, just someone looking for power and attention.

Twice over the years, he'd tried to challenge me for my position as Beta in the Midwest Pack, even though he had no strong connections here, no loyalty to the people or under-standing of how we worked. Twice Sebastian had refused him that opportunity, and rather than accept how the packs worked, Cole had persuaded the council to change the rules so that Sebastian couldn't stop him from challenging me again. That third challenge hadn't come yet, but the possibility hung in the air every time Cole was around. He was a schemer whose only cause was himself, and while that often led him to do what his pack needed, that didn't mean he was good for ours.

"We shouldn't keep involving him," I said. "He can't be trusted."

"Trust him or not, we have to work with him. Not only has he been hit by this magic, but he's the Alpha of his pack. Until someone successfully challenges him, that's not changing."

"Can we encourage someone to challenge?" I asked.

"Like who?"

I considered the options, but no one in Cole's pack had the strength or the will to take him down, and any attempt we made to build someone up would become a source of more tension.

"If you want to see him challenged, you'll have to do it," Sebastian said.

"No thanks. I like the pack I'm in."

"I'm so pleased to hear it," Sebastian said with a wry smile.

There was a knock on the door and Josh walked in, looking particularly absurd in a slouch hat and a white t-shirt with "Bazinga" written across the front.

"You asked to see me?" he said.

Sebastian quickly explained to him what had happened. Josh examined our marks with a look that was more curiosity than concern.

"Just because it's powerful doesn't mean it's malevolent," he said.

"Really?" I asked. "You think someone went to this effort without telling us it'll turn out to be good?"

"Probably not," Josh admitted.

"I need you two to find out what you can before the others arrive," Sebastian said. "Josh, you're on research. Ethan, call around to the other powerful weres you know, find out how far this has spread. Be careful what you say. I don't want to alarm people by making half the world think that we're cursed."

Josh tapped my shoulder.

"It would help if I could look at this," he said. "Maybe try some spells on it. Can you make those calls with your shirt off?"

"I'd rather have requests like that from Sky, but sure."

Josh grabbed some books from the library, and we headed to one of the spare bedrooms.

Two hours later, I sat shirtless on the edge of a bed, finishing yet another call to a were from a neighboring pack. Behind me, Josh had been leafing through his books, peering at my shoulder, and casting spells over the mark, sometimes muttering to himself or scribbling down a note about the results. From time to time, one of the spells would make my skin tingle or send a blast of magic through the room.

"What are you doing?" I snapped as one of those spells sent a flash of pain down my arm.

"Tests," Josh said, a deep frown furrowing his brow. "Do you really want to know more than that?"

"If you're doing your tests on me, yes."

"Then you'll have to pay attention to what I say in the meeting."

He wrote something down and went back to his books.

I'd just finished a call when Sebastian rang.

"Cole's here," he said. "Be in my office in ten minutes."

I put on my shirt. "Meeting time."

"Can we go via the library?" Josh asked. "I've got something else I want to check."

"Sure," I said. "We've got a few minutes."

We headed through the retreat to the library, where a familiar figure in a button-down shirt was standing in the doorway.

"Great," I whispered, glaring at the back of Cole's head. "God's gift to mediocrity."

"All hail the king of the douches, come to shower us in his smug superiority again," Josh replied quietly, and I stifled a laugh. At least this was one thing we could agree on.

Cole must have heard something, because he turned his head to look at us, and in the moment our eyes met his smile vanished. A small victory, but I'd take it.

Josh and I walked past him into the library to see Sky sitting at a table. I was pleased to see her, but annoyed to realize that this was what Cole had been up to: hitting on my girlfriend.

"What are you doing here?" Josh asked, approaching Sky's table.

He peered down at the books and notes spread out in front of her, then turned away to grab some books off the shelves.

"These should be of more help than the ones you have," he said, setting them down with a thud.

Sky laughed and stared at Josh's hat.

"Really?" he said, looking pointedly at Sky's hair, which had somehow ended up half tied back, with stray hairs hanging loose all over. She looked particularly adorable, her disheveled appearance reflecting the intensity she took to any important task.

"It's not that bad," I said, leaning forward to kiss her. I'd only meant it as a brief gesture, but once our lips locked it was hard to drag myself away. My whole body responded to her scent, wanting to drag her off and find a place where we could be alone.

But there were other people present and other issues to address. I forced myself to pull away.

"Okay, I guess this is my new hairstyle?" she said.

I laughed and looked back to the doorway, expecting to catch a cold look from Cole, but he was gone.

Josh leaned against the wall, arms folded, and treated me to a mocking scowl. "Next time, why don't you just whip it out and pee on her leg to mark your territory?"

I could see why he viewed my actions that way, but I didn't care. I didn't like Cole, I didn't want him lurking around Sky, but I wasn't worried that he would steal her away. Unlike Cole, Sky was someone I could trust.

Josh scribbled something on a sheet of paper in marker pen.

"Let me help you out, brother," he said. "Here, Sky, why don't you carry this? Better yet, pin it on the front of your shirt so my brother doesn't have to mark you with his lips anytime another man's around. It will save us time."

He held up the paper, displaying the words "Ethan's. Don't Touch." I glared at him and his idiotic, self-satisfied grin. If I couldn't even show Sky affection without putting up with mockery, then it was going to be a very long day.

"Should I make another, bigger so they can see it at least ten feet away?" Josh continued. "I'll make sure she has one that she can pin to her back as well. We want to warn the locals."

Josh was so pleased with himself he was almost laughing out loud. I didn't think it was so funny. First I had this mark turning up on my shoulder, then Cole turning up to continue his schemes, and now I couldn't even enjoy a nice moment with Sky without becoming the butt of immature jokes. I growled at Josh, who practically shook as he tried to control himself.

"We have a meeting," I said, shoving Josh out the door.

"No need to manhandle me, I'm just trying to be helpful." Josh twisted from my grasp and poked his head back into the library one last time. "Don't forget to put on the sign."

"No one thinks you're funny," I snapped as I walked away, pushing Josh along.

Judging by his laughter, he didn't agree.

I sat to one side of Sebastian's office, with Winter in the seat next to me. Across the room, Cole had his legs stretched out in front of him, making himself at home in our space. Josh leaned against the wall, hands in his pockets.

Just having Cole in the room set me on edge. I watched him warily, looking for some sign that he knew more than he was letting on. Unlikely as it was, I couldn't help suspecting that he was behind the lunar marks in some way. After all, they seemed to support his story about a prophecy, and with it his influence among the packs.

We'd already filled an hour going through a list of the powerful weres we all knew, listing the ones who now bore the mark, those who had said they didn't, and those no one had managed to speak with yet. It made for a chilling tally. Of those we'd checked, only a handful, five percent at most, were untouched, Steven among them. Other than those few, every ranking member of a pack we'd spoken with had been marked.

Now that we knew the extent of the issue, the time had come to talk about its cause.

Sebastian steepled his fingers and looked across the desk at Josh.

"What have you found?"

"It's mostly a matter of deduction so far," Josh said,

pulling out one hand and waving it through the air. "Backed up with some research on past events.

"To do this took great power. I've tried using magic to modify or remove the mark on Ethan, and it hasn't responded to anything I've used. Even spells designed to provide information are just bouncing off it."

"So we know nothing?" I said, trying and failing to suppress my irritation.

"Did I say that?" Josh grinned. "This spell might have come from someone powerful, but that doesn't make them smarter than me. In fact, that power tells us that this isn't ordinary magic. It's not just a bunch of witches or some elven curse."

"It's a Tre'ase," Winter said, apparently as impatient with Josh's showboating as I was.

"Not a single Tre'ase," Josh said. "But it could be some event that's unsettled their magic, or even that of the vampires. A big curse or spell in one part of the supernatural world could have ripple effects elsewhere."

"So it's a curse," Cole said.

"Almost certainly, yes, and a powerful one. But while it could come from a number of places, given the power level, one is more likely than any of the rest."

We looked at each other, everyone except Cole seeing where this was going.

"What is it?" Cole asked.

"A Faerie," Josh said, his expression grim. "And given the timing, that means Maya."

It made sense. Ever since she helped us beat Logan, I'd been wondering what more Maya had been up to that day. She might share a body with Sky, but that didn't mean she was on our side. The spirit of an ancient Faerie was bound to have an agenda of her own, and the prospect of finding out what it was, though necessary, wasn't entirely appealing.

"She used you," Sebastian said. "Piggybacked on the magic you were doing with Sky to achieve her own ends."

Josh nodded.

Cole sighed. "A lot of people are going to see this as your pack unleashing trouble for the rest of us again."

I suspected they would only see it that way because Cole encouraged them to, but that was hardly something I could prove. I kept my mouth shut, kept my temper in check, and kept on listening.

"It comes down to history," Josh said. "Weres were once a powerful weapon against the Faeries and a big part of why they were defeated. Without weres, the likes of Maya would still be roaming the earth, bending everyone else to their will. If there's a chance to get revenge on you, they'll take it—even a Faerie like Maya who has become a spirit shade."

"But magic doesn't work against us," I said. "That's part of how they were defeated."

"There's an exception, a curse they pulled off once, relying on the power of a lunar eclipse to overcome your natural defenses. It was preceded by marks like the ones that are on you now, and the results are grim. If it's successfully cast again, it will remove your immunity to magic and your ability to heal. It means true death for weres."

There it was. The price we'd paid to save Sky was to risk all our lives. I would willingly have thrown my own away if that was what it took to protect her, but there was a difference between dooming myself and doing the same to half the people I loved.

"Is there a lunar eclipse coming?" Sebastian asked.

"In twenty days." The words fell from Josh's mouth like gravestones, cold and heavy. "In less than three weeks, the Faeries will have their revenge. Every ranked were will become vulnerable to their enemies, literally marked for death."

A dreadful silence fell across the room. We'd faced some terrible challenges in our time, but never anything like this.

"The prophecy," Cole said. "It's coming true."

"Who would have thought it?" I asked, once again failing to mask my bitterness.

He looked at me through narrowed eyes, for a moment unable to hide his hostility, then turned to look at Sebastian.

"You should have listened to me," Cole said. "We could have avoided this."

"I did listen to you," Sebastian replied. "We've been looking into your prophecy, remember?"

"And yet your pack has fulfilled the curse without even considering the risks." Cole stood up. "Whatever we need to do to fight this, I'll stay around to help, but seriously Sebastian, Alpha to Alpha, you need to get your people under control."

Without another word, he headed out the door.

Winter pulled a face at the seat where Cole had been sitting. "What a—"

"Stop." Sebastian held up his hand. "Whatever Cole's faults, he's right. If this is a curse from Maya, then we brought it about, and others have a right to be angry about it. Blaming them won't make it easier to find a solution.

"Josh, get back to your research, I want a way to break this curse. Winter, call around to the remaining packs, check how far the effect of this has spread."

The two of them nodded and left. I closed the door behind them and turned to face Sebastian.

"Cole might be right, but he's still up to something," I said. "Even if he didn't cause this, even if his prophecy is real, he's using it to manipulate us."

"And what do you want to do about it? Start a fight with someone on our own side?"

"Let me investigate what he's up to. At least that way we'll be prepared."

Sebastian tapped a finger against the desk, a thoughtful expression on his face. After a moment he nodded. "Do it, but be discreet."

With the meeting over, I headed for the gym in the basement of the retreat. Some exercise would help me burn off my frustrations and find focus for the work, but that wasn't my only reason for going. I could sense Sky's presence, drawing me to that room like iron to a magnet.

As I approached, I heard the clash of swords, a lively sparring match. It ended with a clang and then a clatter as a weapon fell to the ground.

"Nevertheless, you are quite impressive, Skylar." Cole's voice emerged up the steps to the gym, grating at my nerves despite its soft tone. "Sebastian's prodigy has definitely earned the high regard in which he holds her."

Silently, I approached the doorway and looked in. Sky stood in the middle of the gym, a look like thunder on her face. Cole was at the wall, returning a sword to the weapons rack.

"It has been my pleasure getting to know you," he said, smiling at Sky. Then he turned to me, offering the barest of nods and the smuggest of smiles. Here he was again, trying to encroach on what was mine—my pack, our work, and now Sky.

"I'm glad you've decided to stay to offer your assistance," I said, with as much civility as I could muster. "It's kind of you. But there are certain things that are off-limits to you, and we should discuss it later."

We stared at each other, the air between us thick with the tension that came when two powerful weres faced off. For a moment, Cole's smile faltered, but then it returned, the edges of his teeth showing in an expression more menacing than friendly.

"Of course. I am your guest, and I realize there are boundaries. I have them as well in our home, and I look forward to hearing what yours are." He turned to Sky again. "Thank you, Sky. It was fun playing with you."

I watched through narrowed eyes as he walked past me and up the stairs, away from the gym. I was glad to see the asshole go, but part of me worried what else he might get up to next. Was he off to try and charm other members of the pack, or to ask Sebastian for another chance to challenge me?

Now wasn't the time to worry about that. Sky was here, and I turned my attention back to her. A sword lay abandoned on the floor near her feet, no way to treat a weapon. I picked it up and put it back in its place on the rack.

It seemed that Sky had started training with Cole. Was this another of her misguided whims, or part of his scheme to drive a wedge through the middle of the pack? Perhaps it was both, the worst of both their impulses colliding. Either way, Cole was clearly up to something, even if it was just trying to get a rise out of me, and I needed to stop it from happening again.

"Sebastian has chosen to be your instructor with the use of this type of weapon," I said. "It's best that you continue with Sebastian or me and no others."

I offered her a smile, trying to ease the awkwardness of the moment and the inevitability of her resistance. This was one of those times when our relationship within the pack and our relationship as lovers could easily clash. More difficult waters to navigate for the prize of having Sky.

"Is that anyone, other Alphas, or just Cole?" she asked.

I leaned in toward her, putting my mouth near her ear.

"For now, all listed. We'll revisit the terms later."

She stepped back, frowning. Was this going to turn into another confrontation? I had better ways to spend my energy, but I had to assert my authority as Beta, and Sky had to learn to accept it.

"You know you'll get further with me if you don't

command me to do things and make them seem more like requests than commands."

I raised an eyebrow. This wasn't the sort of talk I would have accepted from anyone else in the pack. But then, I wasn't sleeping with anyone else.

"Fine. Sky, I request that you follow my commands."

Her lips twitched and her face set into an expression of defiance. Fortunately, I was getting used to spotting these moments. I moved in close, feeling the heat of her body beside me, and pressed my fingers against her lips.

"Please," I said, trying to turn the commands she found so objectionable into a gentle request.

"Doesn't really sound like you mean it," she said.

"You're pushing it."

I turned away. It was time to cut this conversation off. I'd gotten as close to agreement as Sky was going to give, and that would have to do. Managing a pack wasn't all about strong-arming people into submission; some of it was about learning their limits and working with those. I didn't expect Gavin to become the karaoke king on a big night out, and I couldn't expect Sky to immediately admit when she knew she had to obey.

Still, Cole's behavior around Sky bothered me. Was it personal, political, or both? Partway up the stairs, I turned to look back, hoping to catch some memory of how he'd looked when I came in, some ghost of past Cole who could help me understand his motives.

"I wasn't practicing with him," Sky said. "He asked to spar, so I did."

"Just follow my request," I said, distracted by my own thoughts.

"How was your meeting?"

I pulled myself back into the moment, forced a smile, and shrugged.

"It was okay. Let's discuss it tonight at dinner."

With any luck, something else would come up before then, and I could avoid telling Sky that her magic might have doomed us all.

As I approached Sky's front door, I checked myself over one more time, brushing a few motes of dust from the shoulder of my navy-blue suit and straightening my cuffs. Amid the madness of recent life, we hadn't had many chances for a proper night out, something resembling a real date. I wanted to make the most of this one.

When Sky answered the door, I knew instantly that it had been worth the effort. Her hair fell in dark waves across her shoulders and down a single-strap green dress that clung to her curves. Her smile lit up the night and her eyes sparkled like emeralds.

"You look..." I stepped back so I could take in the whole effect. "Beautiful. Absolutely."

I wrapped my arms around her and kissed her with wild abandon. The sight of her in that dress and the magnetism of her presence made me want to give up on going out, pull the dress off, and have her there and then. As she moved her body against me, hands running up my back, I wondered if she was thinking the same thing.

But that could come later. If we were going to make this work, then we needed to make some memories together. I took her hand and led her to the car.

The whole way into the city, I struggled to keep my eyes on the road. I could feel Sky in the seat next to me, her scent all around, subtle and intoxicating. I laid my hand on her thigh, feeling the warmth of her flesh, the smoothness of her skin beneath that dress, and listened to her heartbeat quicken at my touch.

I'd picked our restaurant carefully—somewhere large and

impressive, where we could lose ourselves from anyone's attention, but with enough discreet nooks and low lighting for it to still feel cozy. Jazz drifted across the room from a quartet playing live in one corner, and a gentle murmur of conversation filled the air.

"This way, sir, madam," said the maître d', a man I'd helped through some legal difficulties a few years back, and who made sure I got the best seats any night I chose. He led us to a private section at the back of the room, where chandeliers gave just enough light for us to dine by.

Soon, we were sipping at fine wine and making small talk as we looked over the menus.

"I'll have a steak," I said to the waiter who appeared quietly beside us. "Rare, with potatoes and vegetables."

"The same for me," Sky said. "But make it medium rare."

I glanced across the table and saw the orange curve of the terait, the sign of a vampire's blood hunger, gleaming in her eye. While she might deny it, I knew what Sky really needed.

"Make hers rare as well," I said, grinning. "And bring her a slice of red velvet cake with her salad, please."

The waiter bowed his head and hurried away.

"I wanted my steak medium rare," Sky protested.

I shook my head and pointed at my eye. Neither of us might want to admit it, but the vampire was an important part of who Sky was. She had even tried to bite me recently, when that bloodlust was upon her, and if we were going to be together, then we needed to find a way to manage it. I couldn't go to sleep every night worrying that the woman I shared a bed with might roll over and sink her fangs into me.

That thought brought back memories of other vampires feeding. The most vivid was Chris writhing on Josh, caught in some warped combination of lust and hunger, an image that risked putting me off a fine dinner. I took a sip of wine to mask my expression and tried to focus on Sky.

"Whoever started that rumor about me and dessert needs to stop," she said with a smile.

"Is it a rumor if it's true?" I asked, smiling back.

A few minutes later, our salads arrived, and the cake with them. I wasn't much for salad, so I pushed mine across the table to Sky. She in turn slid both plates of greenery aside, picked up a fork, and set to demolishing the cake. The look of innocent happiness on her face made me smile more than I had all day. These were the moments that made Sky stand out.

"Tell me what happened yesterday with the spell," I said. "Be specific."

Sky paused for a moment, lost in thought or possibly just in cake.

"I could feel Maya stirring from the start," she said at last. "The moment I wound my power around Logan's, she responded to the familiarity of his magic. There was something ancient to the power in both of them, something she had missed perhaps, and she wanted to touch it.

"At first, it seemed like she was joining in with my spell. I was working with natural and dark magic, and she was adding ancient power to the mix. But the more it went on, the more she was taking over. Her words, her spell, instead of mine. I kept going because I knew I needed to finish what I'd started, but the air seemed to freeze around me and that wind howled through. I tried to block her spell out with mine, but I couldn't. We both finished. When I looked around, Logan was dead and you were on the floor.

"I didn't know what the words were she had used, but I remembered some of them. I rushed to write them down while I still could, and that's when you woke up."

I watched her as she skewered another chunk of cake. Something had lifted from her as she spoke, but it hadn't done anything to ease my worries. Not only had Maya taken control of Sky's body, she had done it in a way that made Sky powerless to resist. That was a deeply unsettling precedent. What if Maya took control again? Would it even be possible to undo her curse if she could appear among us at any moment?

"Should I be worried?" I asked.

"About what?"

"About the cake," I said, seeing the look of delight on her face. "I think you're cheating on me with it."

"Oh, I'm so cheating on you with it." She laughed.

"And here you wanted me to think you weren't a 'dessert first' type of woman." I leaned back in my chair, gazing at her, her brunette hair hanging loose across that perfectly clinging dress. She looked back, matching my smile.

"Back to what happened," I said. "Have you found anything that resembled the spell?"

"How did you know it was Faerie language?" she shot back.

"Isn't that what we established Maya is, and Ethos? It only makes sense that's what she speaks."

"If it is, and we can't translate it, then what?"

"I don't know." It was a painful thing to confess. It was my role in life to look after Sky, to keep her from the dangers the supernatural world presented. She had been cut off from that life for so long, she didn't know enough to navigate it safely. For all of her power and strength of will, someone had to look out for her.

"Do you ever wonder what became of the other Faeries?" she asked.

"I don't know," I replied, watching her. Was she angling toward something else? I hadn't discussed the curse with her, but the pack was a place where rumors could easily take hold. Perhaps she had picked up on something, and I should tell her the truth before she worried unnecessarily.

Or perhaps I was looking for an excuse to unburden myself by thrusting the weight of this knowledge onto Sky.

Now wasn't the moment for that. Our relationship was just starting to blossom, and this evening was an important one, a chance to have something special to ourselves, away from the pack and politics and everybody else's demands. I didn't want to bring the mood down by telling her what had happened. It was important to me that this evening went well. Important to both of us, I hoped.

"You don't know, or you can't tell me?" she asked.

I picked up my fork, leaned forward, and scooped up some of the cake. I held it out toward her mouth, the ultimate Sky distraction, but she kept her lips firmly together, unwilling to be deterred.

"Skylar."

She pressed her lips tighter, until they were just a line across her face. This was the Sky who drove me wild, for better as well as for worse—a creature of determination and defiance. She challenged me like no one else ever had. Her stubbornness was the only match I'd found for my own.

The server arrived with our food. The fork full of cake still hung between us, only inches from Sky's lips. At last she took the bite and sat back, glaring at me. I smiled at her as the waiter presented our steaks.

The next twenty minutes were filled with fine food, finer wine, and the finest pleasure of all: time with Sky. But eventually, inevitably, she found a way to bring the conflicts between us back in.

"What was the meeting about?" she asked.

There it was, the subject I'd been avoiding all evening.

"We'll discuss it when we get to your house."

That clearly wasn't enough of an answer, not even to get us through our meal. She kept shooting me odd glances, her lips pursed as if she was trying to solve a puzzle. Of course, I knew what that puzzle was. She wanted to know every secret I had, to hear each dark or dangerous thing laid bare. But that wasn't how I worked.

"Sky, I do wish I could be an open book for you, but I can't," I said softly.

"You said we would discuss it," she said sternly. "I refuse to be in the dark about this."

"And you won't be." I looked around the room, but nothing here could save me from the corner I was backed into. "But as I said, we'll talk about it at home."

<hr>

I put the cake we'd brought from the restaurant down on Sky's kitchen counter, took her hand, and led her toward the bedroom. I couldn't put off the curse conversation any longer, but I could at least deal with it in comfort.

"Ethan—" she said, her voice sounding a note of warning.

"I'm about to show you what the meeting was about," I replied.

I turned on the bedroom light and slowly unzipped her dress, letting it fall to the floor. Even looking her skin over for signs of the crescent mark, I couldn't help but smile at her beauty. I ran my eyes and my fingers across her shoulders, her breasts, and on down, kneeling in front of her with my fingers resting on her belly. I kissed her there and then stood, reassured—no mark so far.

"Ethan?"

"Just let me finish," I said, keeping my voice level.

I walked around her, running my gaze up and down, looking for any sign of the crescent moon. As I went, I kissed her skin gently, celebrating each safe, unblemished piece of her. At last, I came back around in front of her with a sigh of relief.

"You aren't marked," I said.

"Marked?" she said in alarm. "What are you talking about?"

I unbuttoned my shirt, pulled it off, and turned to show her my shoulder.

"Most of us have them," I said. "All the Alphas and ranked were-animals, with the exception of Steven and a few others."

I reeled off the short list of untouched weres we'd assembled earlier.

"When did you get it?" she asked.

"Yesterday. Cole noticed it and called Sebastian, and we spent most of the meeting trying to get a tally of who has it and who doesn't."

"What does it mean?"

I sat down on the bed and rubbed my chin, pondering how best to respond.

"We all believed it was just a tale," I said at last. "You know, one of the many tales of our being cursed, which never turn out to be anything but embellished retellings of things that never happen. I can't even count the number of exegeses there are about our origins and whether it was a curse on humans or animals. Our existence has been attributed to everything from a nefarious spell performed by Faeries to a curse for the wrongdoing of a spirit wolf. No one knows how, but we've always been immune to magic. Our ability to change without the call of the moon or Mercury rising, transits of Saturn, or an eclipse is new.

"Immunity to magic has always given us an advantage and has unsettled most."

I rose and paced the room, trying to walk out the tension rising inside me, the growing awareness of the terrible danger we faced.

"No one knows how we got these marks," I said. Technically it was true. We didn't know, though we strongly suspected. "It could be the result of something that happened to the vampires and the Tre'ases, a curse or spell of some kind."

I looked at her, thinking of the spell she had cast, the spell that was surely behind all of this, no matter what other possibilities I mentioned.

"This is a curse or the removal of one?" she asked, standing stiff and tense.

I could see her own worry rising, her anxiety of what this represented and her part in it. I walked over and kissed her softly on the lips, a gesture meant as reassurance but that only seemed to add to her tension.

"It's a curse." I spoke a few words of Faerie, ones I'd found during my research, and watched to see how she would react.

"How do you know that?"

"Did you finish reading the book I gave you about the Faeries?"

Her hesitation told me everything I needed to know. Once again, Sky had neglected learning about her new life. Perhaps that was for the best this time; tales of ancient Faerie atrocities would add to her worries right now.

"Before we became this"—I gestured up and down my body—"we were weaponry against them and a big reason why they were defeated. In an effort to keep us from being used as weaponry, they attempted everything, trying to find a combination that could do magic against us. Nothing worked. It wasn't just their cruelty that led to their demise; their unyielding efforts to try spells to kill us off caused others to come together to defeat them. Apparently one curse was said to work, although it is questionable. Josh read one account that said it's tied to the lunar eclipse. It was the symbolic death of our total immunity. We bear the curse of the lunar. Once that curse is performed again, it is true death."

We stared into each other's eyes while the truth sank in. In twenty days, we would face a curse that could kill me and every other ranked were.

CHAPTER 10

The engine of the Venom GT purred like a contented animal as we drove west, away from Chicago. It was good to be out of the city and in the open, where I could give the engine full rein. The countryside rolled by to either side, interspersed with the occasional farm or gas station, as Josh and I headed out into the wilds.

"I don't get it," Josh said, looking up from the pile of papers in his lap. It contained almost everything I'd gathered so far on the mysterious property owner named K. L. Estevez, and on the Tre'ase that I believed could be hiding behind that name. The evidence was thinner than I would have liked, some of the connections between old stories and modern properties pure speculation on my part. But it was what I had and it was definitely leading to something.

"What's not to get?" I asked, hoping that it was one of my minor jumps of logic and not that he'd noticed what I was leaving out: the evidence connecting the Tre'ase to the two of us.

"For starters, why are we even looking into this guy?" Josh asked, frowning as he waved a copy of an eighteenth-century engraving of our Tre'ase, or at least a Tre'ase that had been in the same place around the same time. It wasn't the strongest piece of evidence, but I'd won trials based on less. Sometimes the pieces were less important than the connections you could draw between them.

"Because he's a Tre'ase," I said.

"That's not much of an answer. Everyone in the pack is chasing clues to this curse of the lunar eclipse, trying to find a way to break the spell or protect you all. You know as well as I do that the curse was caused by Maya. As far as I can tell from your pile of papers, she never even met this guy. So why are we chasing him, when we could be doing something to, oh, I don't know, maybe save your stupid life?"

I couldn't help smiling at Josh's tone of indignation. For all our differences, we'd always looked out for each other, and he was almost as desperate to find a solution as I was.

Of course, that didn't mean that I could tell him the whole truth. I'd been hunting this particular Tre'ase already because of its connection to us, in case someone used it to control the spirit shade inside me, just as Logan had used Kalese to affect Maya and, through her, Sky. It wasn't just myself I was protecting, it was Josh, too—protecting the magic that he didn't even know was keeping him alive. That led into truths I'd been protecting him from for most of his life.

Fortunately, any decent lawyer learns that there are ways to avoid uncomfortable truths without lying, and the truth in this case was that there was another reason I wanted hold of a Tre'ase right now.

"The curse was caused by a spirit shade," I said. "And that spirit shade was created by a Tre'ase. That means that studying the magic of a powerful Tre'ase is our best way of understanding the magic."

"It's one way," Josh admitted. "But library research and

studying the curse marks are also ways to do it, and they seem a lot more relevant right now."

"You've been hiding away from the world, prodding at our marks and scouring the books for two days. How far has that gotten you?"

"Not as far as I'd like."

Josh flicked through the papers again, pausing to read some of them with a studious intensity. It was as close as he would come to admitting that I was right, and I was willing to take it.

A few minutes later, the satnav led us off the main road, up the narrow trail that wound across a ridge of wooded hills. It was a clear day with the trees in full bloom, and as we crested the ridge a gap appeared between the trees, revealing a view of sunlit countryside spreading into the distance.

"Pretty stunning, right?" I said, enjoying the spectacle.

"Eh, it's all right," Josh replied. He'd always been more of a city guy, preferring skyscrapers, coffee shops, and nightclubs to woodlands, rivers, and plains. It was a common preference among witches, who thrived where there were plenty of people to build a coven and use its services. But for a were creature like me, the call of the wild and the thrill of running free through the woods was hard to ignore.

"You have reached your destination," the satnav announced in a woman's sultry voice. I pulled over to the side of the road, switched off the engine, and stepped out of the car.

I'd been expecting something special to explain why Estevez owned this property, but all I could see were trees and a small, open valley where a stream ran down between the hills.

"I don't get it," I said.

"That's because you're still in driving mode," Josh said as he got out of the car. He was grinning, his eyes wide and arms stretched out, as if basking in the sunshine. "You're focusing on what's right in front of you, trying to assert an expectation on it so that you can keep control. But that won't work here. You've got some magic inside you, so open yourself up to the magic here."

"Seriously, that's your answer?" I said, looking at him scornfully. "Some new age crap about opening my heart and mind to the cosmos?"

"I'm sorry, which of us went to magic school? Oh right, that would be me. You're just a lucky amateur."

"And you were a dropout."

"So I don't like tests. That doesn't mean I didn't learn. Now stop trying to put me in my place and pay attention to this place instead."

Annoying as his smug tone was, Josh was right. The moment I stopped focusing on him and instead let my senses soak in the surroundings, I felt a tug of magic drawing me toward the very top of the hill. It was like a guitar string drawn tight across the landscape, vibrating with its own unique note in the key of power.

I followed the strand of magic up the hill, glad that I'd worn walking boots instead of dress shoes. Leafy mulch crunched beneath my feet, letting out an earthy aroma that soothed my spirit despite the sound of Josh blundering along behind.

At the top of the hill was a clearing. A dozen stones, each no more than three feet high, stood in a circle, with a thirteenth stone lying flat in the center. Stepping into the circle, I found myself surrounded by power, dark and ancient, which was channeled by the stones into threads of magic like the one that had led me here. Wary of the intensity of that power, I slowly approached the central stone and looked down to see dark stains spattered across its pale-gray surface.

"Blood," Josh said solemnly, running his fingertips across

the stains. "When it's used to perform magic, even stone is scarred by it."

"What is this place?" I asked.

"An ancient ritual sight, and judging by the resonance of the place, one that's often been used by the Faeries and the Tre'ases. You were right. This Estevez guy was worth looking into."

Josh roamed around the stones, running his fingers through the magical field around us, casting spells and making notes of the results. I just stood, staring down at those stains. Was this how the spirit shade inside me had been formed, through the horrors of sacrifice? Or was this just one more atrocity on the list of those performed by Faeries and Tre'ases down the centuries? I knew that I carried something dark inside me, but seeing this made it feel more real. It was as if I now carried the weight of this stone on my shoulders.

"We should check out the next place," Josh said, interrupting my thoughts.

I glanced at my watch. Nearly an hour had passed while I stood brooding over a lump of rock. Was it the magic of this place that had stolen the time from me, or just the tangle of troubles swirling through my soul? Or worse, was it the spirit shade responding to this place, taking over me as Maya had taken over Sky? Had I been absent and not even known it?

That thought was enough to get me moving, out of the circle and down the hill. We got into the car, I set the next destination, and we drove in silence while Josh scribbled more notes, comparing what he'd found with what I'd supplied.

Our next stop was in a valley an hour's drive to the south. A stream had cut a steep gouge in the land between two hills, exposing rocks that seemed at odds with the flat plains of the surrounding area. It was as if some angry monster had ripped a chunk from the side of a mountain and flung it across the continent, only for it to be buried beneath the earth and then exposed again by the ravages of time. Hell, for all I knew that really had happened—I'd dealt with stranger things.

Once again, I felt a tight thread of magic running along the valley, leading us to a cave halfway up. This time I knew what to expect, so I sensed the pool of dark power in the mouth of the cave before I stepped into it. Other threads of power ran off into the distance.

"None of these places make sense as real estate investments," I said. "You can't exactly build a house down here or set up a gym on top of that hill."

"You think maybe it's about the magic?" Josh said, his voice heavy with sarcasm. He stood in the mouth of the cave, light flowing from his hands to illuminate a series of paintings decorating the walls. With their muted colors and simple lines, they were either the work of prehistoric people or of enthusiastic caveman reenactors.

I pulled out a map on which I'd marked the locations of the properties linked to both the modern Estevez and the historical Tre'ases. They were scattered across Illinois, all within the territory of the Midwest Pack. If one of our competitors, like Demetrius's Seethe or Cole's pack, had bought up these properties, then I would have concluded that they were making a move to increase their power in our area and potentially undermine the pack. But these weren't just modern property purchases; there was some older connection at play.

"Can it just be coincidence?" I asked. "Another supernatural being's power base covering the same territory as us?"

"There's a theory among experts in esoteric geography," Josh said, letting the light from his hands fade away. "They think that there's something inherently powerful about certain regions, something that encourages the emergence of supernatural bands, whether it's a were pack, a witches' coven, or a vampiric seethe. Group boundaries don't have to fit with these areas, but they tend to. It explains why we have several powerful groups all based in Chicago: it's the biggest city in a big pool of supernatural influence. And if the rest of us are unwittingly tapping into that, you can bet the Tre'ases and the Faeries are doing it on purpose."

"You think the Faeries are involved in this?" I asked, pointing at the pattern on the map. That was all I needed, another hostile power backing up Estevez.

"I don't know, but some of the magic around here has their feel to it." Josh pointed at the map. "I want to look at this one next. I think it'll tell me something about the pattern."

We drove on again, east from the valley so that we skirted around the southern edge of Chicago's urban sprawl. As we traveled, I brooded on what the power we had found at these sites meant. Had the Tre'ase, the one I was increasingly convinced now went by the name of Estevez, made some sort of deal with a Faerie to use their power in building up this magical network? Had he stolen it from them in the aftermath of their fall? Was it somehow even connected to the spirit shade inside me? It might not matter, or it might become the key to understanding Maya's curse and to keeping Josh safe.

Our next stop was very different from the others—a large nineteenth-century house sitting inside its own walled estate. We parked down the road and approached on foot, under the watchful gaze of three security cameras and a row of mourning doves.

It had been easy to explore the area around the standing stones and the cave. We could just walk up and wander around. This was very different. Getting to the house itself would take either permission or a break-in, either of which could have serious disadvantages in keeping our investigation on the quiet.

Josh peered through the tall barred gate and up the driveway to the house. With its pillared porch and gothic turrets, it looked like some pre-Civil War money man's idea of a medieval mansion: grand, but also a little absurd.

"Do you need to get in?" I asked.

"Not yet," Josh said, eyes glazing over as he turned his attention to the realm of magic. I did the same and sensed one of the threads we'd seen before, running through the walls and straight to the mansion. We walked along the road and sensed three more before we even reached the corner of the enclosed grounds.

"There's a spell binding all these sites together," Josh said. "That makes the power of each one greater and lets the caster of the spell draw on it to power other magic."

"So it's a giant battery?" I asked.

"That and more. Creating a net like this gives the caster greater awareness of what's going on in the area, and greater control over the whole territory, even the parts they don't own." Josh pointed at one of the closed-circuit cameras on the wall. "Like those, but watching for supernatural events instead of burglars."

"This whole time, we've been living in some Tre'ase's spider web of power?" The thought sent a chill down my spine, and not just because of the power that could give the Tre'ase over me. I imagined what sort of creature, having that much power at their command, would have sat quietly back and let some of the dreadful events of the past take place. That wasn't a creature with good intentions toward anyone but themselves.

"Where next?" I asked, pulling out the map.

"Home," Josh replied. "I need time to think about all of this, to look for precedents and theory that might help me understand it."

Something about his wry smile made me think that there was more going on. Judging by the time and the distance to Chicago, I had a pretty good idea what it was.

"You've got a date, don't you?"

Josh grinned. "Is that a bad thing?"

"If it distracts you from this, then yes."

"Like you won't be going back to Sky tonight."

"No, I'll be going back to my place to do more research, or driving around more of these sites, seeing what Estevez's security is like."

"Good for you. Some of us like to have fun."

"Fun can wait. There are lives at stake." I glared at him, fury rising up inside me. Did he really not understand how serious the situation was, that in a matter of weeks this curse would strike the pack, leaving us vulnerable at best, and more likely dead?

"We can't all be like you, Ethan," Josh snapped. "I've been working flat out for three days, and I need a break before I burn out."

"That was a weak excuse at magical school, and it's a weaker one now."

"You don't know anything about what happened to me there, so quit the high and mighty crap. If you want my help again tomorrow, you're driving me to Chicago now."

Back in the car, I turned the stereo on and cranked up the volume. In that moment, I didn't want to talk to Josh, and I didn't want a stony silence bearing down on us. We drove north to the sound of acid jazz and the low rumble of the car's engine. Josh seemed as willing as I was to continue our journey without talking.

As we were approaching Chicago, he reached out and turned down the volume of the music.

"There's something we have to talk about," he said, his tone somber.

I didn't respond. I couldn't think of anything to talk about that didn't begin with pointing out that he was being a jackass.

"About Sky," he said.

That got my attention.

"What about her?" I said through gritted teeth.

Josh sighed and rubbed his eyes.

"If it goes off, Maya's spell is going to kill a lot of people in our pack and beyond. We're looking for ways to stop it from happening or counter its effects, but there's no guarantee that'll work."

"Great pep talk. Really cheering me up."

"What do you think happens then?"

My grip tightened on the steering wheel. I could see where this conversation was going, but I didn't want to think about it, never mind talk about it.

"Ethan, we can't avoid this forever."

"We can avoid it for the next few weeks, and then it'll be over."

"And you might be dead!" Josh slammed his fist against the dashboard, an act so uncharacteristic I almost swerved across the road. "You think the pack will just accept it? If we can't stop the spell, then they'll want to try another way. They'll want to kill Maya."

I swallowed, fighting down the sick feeling inside me. I didn't understand much about the connection between Sky and Maya, and I didn't think anybody else knew much either, at least no one who was going to explain it to us. But the one clear fact was that Sky and the spirit shade shared a single body, and that their lives were intertwined. Kill Maya and we would end up killing Sky.

"I can't accept that," I said. "I won't. We're not killing one of our own to save the rest. Especially not her."

"I agree," Josh said. "But we've got to be ready for when that idea comes up."

"That means we've got to find another solution, and fast."

"Yep."

The two of us subsided. Now we were in agreement, but the atmosphere between us was still tense, the hostility from our earlier argument filling the car.

Josh sighed, pulled out his phone, and made a call.

"Hi, Sarah. It's Josh. Sorry about this, but something came up at work. Can we reschedule this evening?"

CHAPTER 11

I stood in the woods, concealed by a screen of trees as I watched people come and go from a large building in a warded compound. Beside me, Gavin let out a low, menacing growl, while Winter stood sharpening one of her knives, keeping her hands busy as she waited for a chance to use them on someone.

This was the base Gavin had been watching for the past few days, belonging to the people Sky and Winter had encountered in the woods, the apparent captors of the feral woman Carol. Gavin was increasingly convinced that they had hold of Kelly, and while I hadn't yet seen any evidence, I was inclined to trust Gavin. Weres developed a strong instinct for the people who mattered most to them, and we all knew how much Kelly meant to Gavin.

The familiar scents of Sky and Josh were followed a moment later by rustling in the trees behind us. The two of them silently joined us in our vigil.

"Vans were coming and going the first few days," Gavin whispered. "I don't know what they were carrying."

It couldn't be anything good. From what we'd seen, the owners of this building were experimenting on people, making something that combined the traits of beasts and humans but that wasn't a were. The very woods seemed to have responded to the presence of these terrible experiments and their warped results. There was no chatter of birds or scuttling of small animals, only the rustling of trees in the wind. Nature dreaded whatever was going on in that building, living things retreating into deep tunnels and distant trails to avoid it. If Kelly was in there, then we needed to get her out while she was still intact.

Men in camouflage outfits and webbing emerged from the building, guns at their hips. The first man kept one hand on his weapon while he lit a cigarette. The others looked around with the casual eye of lookouts who had been at a single post for too long. The woods were familiar to them and they were starting to drop their guard.

They were led by a woman in her thirties wearing slacks and a shirt with her hair tied back in a bun. She glanced scornfully at the smoker, then headed toward the fence at the edge of the compound.

Between the guards were a feral-looking man and woman in loose, scruffy clothes. They snarled and stared at their captors while the smartly dressed woman cast her gaze across the tree line. If she was looking for trouble, then she'd missed it. We were still there, waiting, and increasingly angry at what we saw.

"It's a mage," Josh said after a few minutes. There was a note of incredulity to his voice.

That caught me by surprise. Powerful wards ran the length of the tall fence, a magical deterrent to go with the more mundane barbed wire along the top. I'd assumed that magic that powerful would be the work of witches or possibly elves, and it seemed absurd to think that mages, the weak imitators of witches, could have created it. But now that Josh had said it, I noticed a resonance in the magic, something that didn't match the power he wielded.

What was going on here?

Three more humans emerged from the building and went to talk with the woman. I tilted my head and leaned forward a little so I could hear what they were saying. The talk was inane at first, office gossip and chatter about television shows. But it soon took a more serious turn.

"We need to accelerate the program," the original woman said. "He was expecting results by now."

"We have results," one of the others said, with a sidelong glance at the feral people roaming under armed guard. "Just not the results he wanted."

"And for a man like this, that's the same as no results. No more prevarication; it's time to start work on the remaining subjects."

Gavin moved with a panther's graceful stealth out of the dense trees and down toward the compound. I didn't know what he was planning, but it was clearly time to act, and I was willing to follow his lead. He'd been watching this place, observing the guards, listening to their leaders, obsessing over how we could deal with it all. This was his moment.

The rest of us followed, ready for trouble.

We were almost at the wards when the mage smile and nodded her head. The ward fell, the gate opened, and four of the feral man-animals emerged, scurrying toward us. They looked almost human except for their eyes, which were those of beasts, and the speed and strength of their movements, as powerful as a were-animal.

The front-runner charged and Gavin leapt to meet him. They met in midair, Gavin's fist colliding with the side of the guy's head. There was a crunch and the feral man flew back. He skidded across the ground and came to a stop, eyes closed, breath ragged. These things might be strong, but they were fragile, and that gave us an edge.

The other creatures kept advancing with looks that showed no calculation, just pure animal instinct. One lunged at Winter. There was a gleam in Winter's eye, but before she got her chance to respond, the mage tugged at the air and all three creatures jerked back as if on chains, whimpering in pain.

Josh raised his hands and a blast of magic caught the mage in the chest, sending her staggering in the dirt. She returned fire, flinging bolts of raw magic through the air, but Josh raised a translucent shield, a shimmering wall of air in front of him. The mage's blasts burst against his defenses, but she wasn't deterred. She kept flinging magic at the wall, the air sizzling with power, her breath growing ragged as she exhausted herself with her effort, until Josh's defense seemed about to fall.

Behind that shield, I saw Josh clench one hand into a fist and murmur the beginnings of a spell. As the last of the shield exploded beneath a magical blast, he shot his fist out. A bolt of magic shot from it and hit the mage in the chest, flinging her from her feet. She slammed into the ground, raised her hand, and shot one last blast of power at Josh, who deflected it back at her, knocking her flat again.

The mage forced herself back to her feet, the feral people snapping and hissing around her.

"Josh," she said, "you are as talented as you are rumored to be."

"Well, now you have me at a disadvantage. I don't know who you are."

"If you don't leave, you can call me your worst nightmare."

"Fine. Nightmare. Is that Ms.?" He smiled, then shook his head. "Nah, it doesn't matter. Bad girls are only fun for a day or two. Let's get the niceties out of the way. I'm not sure what you're doing, but stop."

Despite the battering she'd just taken, she looked back at him with unyielding calm. "Is that an order?"

"You can take it any way you want."

A flicker of the mage's eyes made me turn my head, just in time to see someone standing in the trees behind us, arms raised. I recognized one of the witches from Marcia's Creed a moment before she lowered her arms and unleashed a wave of magic.

The spell was so powerful it couldn't have been just one witch's work. It hit us like a tidal wave, knocking Gavin off his feet and slamming Sky back into a tree. Magic danced in the air, a dozen different colors, traces of those who had added to the spell.

I cursed myself for being an idiot. We'd been drawn out, deliberately lured into the open outside the wards so that they could ambush us. We had thought we were spying on them, and the whole time we were the ones being observed. Now Sky was hurt and the rest of us in danger. I wanted to charge straight at the enemy and rip them to pieces, except that the witch had disappeared somewhere in the trees.

There was a crackling sound as Josh flung up a field around us, just in time to stop another powerful magical assault. I didn't see where this one came from. The witches were out there in the trees somewhere, gathering their power as they tried to get their revenge on Josh—or Marcia's revenge, at least. How had our one pack ended up with so many enemies?

Waves of magic kept hitting the field, coming at us from every direction. The field wobble, rippled, and finally shattered into pieces, like a glass jar exploding beneath a hammer blow.

Out of the tumbling shards of magic, a wolf came running straight at Josh. He pushed it back with his magic, only for someone else's spell to hit him in the back, flinging him to the ground. The wolf lunged again.

I charged, slamming straight into the wolf. I grabbed fistfuls of fur as we rolled over in the dirt, the beast clawing and snapping at me. There was a burst of pain as it locked its jaw onto my forearm, blood running hot and wet between its teeth. The pressure mounted, ripping through flesh and grinding at bone, threatening to tear through my arm.

I slammed my other fist into the side of its head, but while the grip loosened, it didn't let go.

Twisting my arm around, I grabbed the wolf by the snout and wrenched its head to one side. Claws scrabbled at my body, but it was weakening faster than I had expected. I wrenched the jaws open, pulled my arm free, and pushed its head back with a sharp thrust of my hand. There was a snap as its neck broke and the beast went limp.

I dropped the body in the dirt and clutched my arm, stemming the streaming blood. The others gathered around and we watched as the corpse twisted and jerked, transforming into something half man and half wolf.

The creature I had killed was a were. But if that was the case, why hadn't it been immune to Josh's magic while in animal form?

I looked back at the compound. Its wards were back up, its gate closed, guards, inmates, and staff all hidden away back in the building. We weren't going to learn any more about them now.

We'd come looking for scientific kidnappers. We'd found a werewolf vulnerable to magic and a mage with the power of a full-blown witch. Instead of answers we had more questions, most of which boiled down to what the hell was going on here.

It was time to regroup and consider what we'd learned. Still clutching my arm, I led the others silently out of the woods.

"You're sure it was a were-animal?" Sebastian asked, looking across the living room of the retreat.

Josh nodded.

"And you were able to use magic against it."

Josh nodded again.

It was a sign of how much pressure Sebastian was under that he felt a need to keep asking. Sky, Josh, and I had been over what we'd seen with him, and I could see the strain it had put him under, trying to balance this against the other challenges we faced.

"Were-animals are being used as well as humans," he said quietly. "We have to get in there."

He looked at me and I could see the calculation in his eyes. We couldn't just ignore this, but could we deal with it yet, while the curse still hung over us?

"Thank you, Josh and Sky," Sebastian said. "Ethan, can you come with me?"

We headed down the corridor to his office. Once inside, he closed the door.

"How's your arm?" he asked.

I pulled back the sleeve of the jacket I'd used to cover the wound. Sky had been so dazed from being thrown against a tree, I wasn't sure she'd even noticed how badly I'd been hurt. I was happy to keep her from another worry.

"It's healing," I said. "But I don't think my shirt will recover."

Sebastian paced back and forth, running a hand across his head.

"We don't know enough about this place," he said. "What they're doing. Why they're letting their creations out. Who's funding them."

"I could look into it," I said. "But then..."

"Then you wouldn't be investigating the curse, and that has to take priority."

I nodded reluctantly.

"Gavin's convinced that they have Kelly," I said.

"I know. I'm having trouble stopping him from storming

the place, and I'm going to need something to appease him. Start working on a plan to take that compound, but keep it quiet—until the curse is dealt with, that's our only priority."

I found Claudia sitting in her office, photos of paintings scattered across the desk in front of her and a cup of tea steaming on one corner. She smiled as I walked in and stepped out from behind the desk to kiss me on the cheek and straighten my shirt. I felt like I was ten years old again, a little bit patronized but mostly comforted by her touch.

"Ethan," she said. "What a lovely surprise. How can I help?"

"How do you know it's not just a social visit?" I asked.

"Josh told me about the curse. Don't pretend to me that you have time for social visits."

I frowned. We were trying to keep news of the curse to ourselves, and while some rumors were bound to creep out, I was bitterly disappointed that Josh hadn't shown more discipline.

"Don't blame your brother," Claudia said. "You know full well that I have knowledge and sources you don't, ones he needed to consult."

"And were they useful this time?"

"Not yet, but yet is the word. Now, come and look at these pictures. I'm trying to decide which ones to have sent over from Warsaw. You can't get the full effect from a photo, but you can at least pick the ones worth further scrutiny."

"Actually, I have something else to discuss."

"And you can't look at art while you do it?"

I sighed and followed her around the table. It was usually easier to go along with Claudia than to resist, especially where art was concerned.

To my surprise, I found myself drawn in by the paintings.

The brightness of their colors and the playful curves of their abstract shapes lifted my mood. I found myself smiling, right up until I remembered why I was there.

"I think I've found the Tre'ase who created the spirit shade," I said. "The one in me."

"Really?" Claudia held one of the paintings at arm's length, examining its plant-like mix of yellows and greens.

"He's going by the name of Estevez and he owns a lot of magically powerful properties around here."

"So that's why you dragged Josh out around the roads of Illinois."

"And why I didn't tell him."

She placed a hand on my shoulder.

"I understand. I want to protect him just as much as you do. But you need to be careful." She moved her hand around and settled it on my chest, over my steadily beating heart. "The spirit shade inside you was originally a Faerie, one that other creatures considered too dangerous and malevolent to live. It was killed for a reason, and if you take its shade to its creator, you might find out what that reason was."

She was right. I'd been feeling this darkness swell inside me, its power uncoiling as I faced stresses and threats. Facing Estevez would be a challenge in itself, one made all the more hazardous because of his connection to the spirit. Finding him would put me in great danger.

But not finding him would leave Josh in danger for the rest of his life. There was a line here that I had to cross.

"Where is he, this Estevez?" Claudia asked.

"I don't know," I admitted. "I'm hoping that you might know some way of finding him, based on these properties and the magic connecting them. Find a trail from it to him, or work out where he lives, or... I don't know, but there has to be a way, right?"

I heard the desperation in my voice. I was dealing with

powers beyond my capabilities, taking risks I would never have let Sky or Josh take, but what choice did I have?

"Can you tell me how to find him?" I asked.

"No," Claudia said, and my heart sank. "But with my own power, I might be able to find something." She took a jacket off the back of her chair. "I hope you brought the Venom today—I don't want to be seen around town in an SUV."

As we walked out through the gallery, everyone we passed wanted to say hello to Claudia, to talk with her about the art on display. I waited impatiently as she dealt with each person in turn, until we were out in the street and climbing into my car.

"Do you have a plan for once you find him?" she asked as we headed out of the city.

"Not yet," I admitted. "I'm working on it."

"Then it's a very good thing you came to me. I made a deal since the last time we spoke about this, one that gave me something unique."

"I don't see how art will help."

"This isn't art. It's access to a magical realm, like the dark forest but completely empty. If we can find this Estevez and trap him there, then no one will be able to touch him, and he won't be able to touch you. Your spirit shade will be safe, and so will Josh."

"That's amazing!" I laughed out loud. At last something was going my way. But then another part of what she'd said hit me. "Wait, we can trap him? You know how to do that?"

"Not yet, but just like your plan to track him down, I'm working on it."

***

"That was interesting," Claudia said as we drove away from the hilltop with the standing stones. "I haven't seen magic like this in a long time."

Over the previous few hours, we had been to half a dozen of Estevez's properties. Claudia frowned at the need to tramp up hillsides, through woods, and along mud-caked valleys, but she never complained. She understood the need to do this as well as I did.

"Is there something special about that place?" I asked.

"There's something special about all of them, but that one is particularly well located. It provides a nexus point for much of the surrounding network. That's why it's been used for sacrifices: blood spilled there will empower everything connected to it."

"So if we take that one out, then the network will fall apart?"

Claudia laughed. "Even if you had the ability to destroy such a powerful site, this network is strong enough to heal itself. You might weaken it, but not in any way its creator could not repair. This isn't a problem that you can simply tear apart."

"I don't solve all my problems by fighting," I said in mock indignation.

"I know, dear. Sometimes you sue them into submission instead."

Our final stop on the tour of Estevez's properties was the grand house where Josh and I had finished. I parked down the road, out of sight of the security cameras, and we approached cautiously. There was every chance that we had been noticed before, but that didn't mean that we should draw attention to ourselves now.

As we got closer to the walled grounds, the gates opened and a red Dodge Challenger SRT Hellcat rolled through the opening. It turned right, heading toward us, and was just starting to pick up speed when I recognized the face of the driver.

What was Chris doing out here?

I stepped into the road. Claudia yelled in alarm, but I

knew what the Challenger could manage, and I knew Chris's skill as a driver. The car screeched to a halt so close I could reach out and touch the hood. Skid marks left black trails along the road behind it.

The window rolled down and Chris leaned out.

"What are you doing here, Ethan?" she asked, glaring at me.

"Nice car," I said, running my eye over its fine lines. I would have liked a chance to get inside and drive it myself—I'd heard good things about the Challenger and been considering adding one to my collection. But I couldn't see Chris giving me a go behind the wheel.

"What are you doing?" she asked again.

"I could ask you the same question."

"You could, but I asked first."

I considered what to tell her. As a pack, we'd taken Chris into our trust to help deal with Logan, but there was a world of difference between that and actually trusting her, especially with what I was doing now. She wouldn't believe I was just out for a walk, but that didn't mean she was going to get the whole story.

"I'm looking into some local power players," I said. "And judging by where you just came from, you know one of them."

"I just came to do some shopping." Chris gestured at a small wooden crate strapped into the passenger seat.

"I didn't know this place was open for business."

"It isn't, but I made some special arrangements."

I looked at the crate. It was sturdily built, with solid steel fittings and a hefty padlock on the front. Everything about it screamed weapon, except for the thick layer of dust that had been partially wiped away from the top. I doubted that this was the sort of place you came to buy a handgun, but there were plenty of other ways to kill someone, or something. If this was a supernatural weapon, then Chris must have big plans.

"So you're making a bid for power among the vampires," I said. "Good for you. I can think of worse people to be in charge. Please tell me you're gunning for Demetrius."

"Why would I ever tell you my plans?" Chris asked coldly.

"You asked what I was up to, I figured the conversation could go both ways."

"All you need to know is that this is the last thing I needed, and I'll soon be heading out of town. If you want a sucker to draw into the pack's schemes again, you'll have to find someone else."

I leaned in closer and pointed back the way she had come.

"What do you know about the guy who owns that house?" I asked. This could be a golden opportunity. If Chris had been inside, then she would have seen things I hadn't, might even have met Estevez himself. Any information I got could be invaluable.

"What are you offering for those answers?" she asked.

"Help from me further down the line."

She snorted. "I've had enough of your sort of help."

The window rolled back up, the engine roared, and she sped off down the road.

I turned back to Claudia, who stood gazing at the gate Chris had emerged from. Her eyes had gone black and she held her hands out to either side as she chanted. I expected to feel a shift in the magic around me as she wove whatever spell this was, but there was nothing. The magic was purely passive, taking in what the world offered, observing without changing.

She lowered her hands, blinked, and when she looked at me her eyes were back to normal.

"Your taste in women has certainly improved recently," she said, glancing down at the marks Chris's car had left.

I wasn't in the mood to dissect my love life. Claudia could

be very insightful on human relations, but that was an unsettling experience, and I had enough to think about already.

"Did you find out anything useful?" I asked.

"This was the last node I needed to map out the magic, and it's proven a particularly interesting one. The spell is deceptive; it's not just here to empower the Tre'ase, it's here to protect and hide him, making it harder for enemies to track him down, never mind attack him. We're dealing with someone deeply cautious and immensely powerful."

"Can you break through those protections?" I asked as we headed back to the car.

"Perhaps. I need to work out how the pieces connect and what it all means. Give me time and I'll see what I can do."

"Thank you for all of this. I couldn't do it without you."

"Whatever it takes to keep you and Josh safe."

Winter was waiting outside the dive bar when I arrived, brutal disdain written across her face. I felt the same distaste both for the place and for the man we were about to meet, a mage and businessman named Dexter. Sky had identified him as the owner of the compound in the woods, the money man behind the experiments on humans and were-animals. I'd seen his name come up a couple of times in business deals my firm had helped broker, and though they were nothing I'd worked on, the man's reputation as a lowlife had still reached me. His choice of drinking holes did nothing to improve the image.

"Sky called you too?" Winter asked.

I nodded. Apparently I was here to act as a living lie detector, a tool we would definitely need for dealing with this guy. I assumed that Winter was there as muscle—given that we were facing a hostile foe with surprising amounts of magical power, it made sense to go in heavy.

A car pulled up and Sky and Josh got out. To my surprise, Chris was with them. I'd thought that she was safely out of town by now, but apparently she needed a little more time to enjoy groping my brother first. I clenched up at the sight of her, and her eyes narrowed as she watched me, but I kept from any comment as she led us into the bar.

From the outside this place looked like a dump—battered door, peeling paint, dirt everywhere. Inside was very different—gleaming metal furniture and fittings around a glass-topped bar, behind which smartly dressed bartenders were mixing drinks. It was a place of flash over substance, perfect for a mages' bar.

The regulars looked at us as we came in, hitting us with a wave of low-level magic and casual hostility. Their stares narrowed in on Josh, with that combination of jealousy and desire that came when a celebrity walked into a regular bar.

Josh and I flanked Chris as she strode across the room like she owned the place. Sky and Winter hurried after us, pausing on the way to watch barmen using magic to fling cocktail shakers around.

Chris shoved another pair of doors open and we strode into a second room. This one was as retro as the other one had been modern. There was a wooden bar, a CD jukebox, and a set of pool tables. Padded chairs and a sofa took the place of polished aluminum stools.

Evidently the vintage look wasn't in fashion with modern mages, as this bar was far emptier than the other one. The lone barman had an easy time casually pulling beers and most of the games were currently unused.

Chris headed for a group of three people gathered around one of the pool tables.

"Dexter," she said.

An average-looking guy with a short beard turned to look at her. He grinned and leaned on his pool cue.

"X," he said, looking over each of us in turn. His gaze settled on Winter and his grin widened. "I'm X, and you are?"

"I'm with them," Winter replied with a steely tone.

"I'd still like a name."

"Winter."

"What's in a name? You don't have to be so cold, baby."

The line was so unoriginal it almost made me laugh. I'd seen at least a dozen guys try something like it on Winter, each of them with the same sparkle in their eyes, the look that said they were sure they'd come up with something so novel she couldn't resist. And of course, I'd seen all of them rejected.

Winter glared at Dexter as he approached her, but he seemed determined not to take the hint. I could see her temper about to snap, bringing our conversation to a violent end, when Chris stepped in, blocking Dexter's advance.

"I can assure you that is a bad idea," she said, "unless you really feel like visiting the ER tonight."

Dexter laughed and stepped back, settling himself on the edge of the pool table. He looked around like he owned us all, then settled his attention on the women.

I'd met plenty of people in my life who I didn't like, but I'd never met a human so immediately punchable. From the smug grin to calling himself X to twisting his wrist to draw attention to his Bulgari watch, everything about him was obnoxiously ostentatious. He might be hanging out in the back room, but he was the living embodiment of what we'd seen in the main bar—a desperate desire to be seen as wealthy and cool, an arrogance born out of working twenty-four seven to look better than everyone else, not to become a bearable person.

"What can X do for you?" he asked as his friends headed out of the room.

"I have it on good authority that you own a couple of properties that we are interested in," I said.

"And those properties are?" He started racking the balls for a new game.

"The ones you have over near Camby Lane, in the woods, protected by a ward that a mage couldn't even begin to erect," Josh said, glaring at Dexter.

"Josh—it is Josh, isn't it?" For a moment, Dexter's fake smile faltered, flashing unvarnished hostility at Josh. Then he turned back to the table and started to play. "I've been made aware of your feelings toward us. 'Diet-witches' and 'half-witches' are what you all usually call us, right?"

"I prefer diet-witch," Josh said. "Half-witch gives you all far too much credit."

"And yet I have a ward that you can't seem to break. So I guess you aren't the witch that you are rumored to be." Dexter glanced at Chris. "I will remember you brought them into my house."

"I wasn't aware that you lived here. Hard times?"

"If I own it, I consider it my house."

"My apologies," Chris said with a shrug that announced how little she cared. "They are looking for their friend, and I've been trying to find someone for the past few weeks. I think you might be able to help us."

Dexter didn't feel a need to respond. He just kept on playing pool, ignoring our concerns.

My temper was rising. This little asshole apparently thought he was God's gift to humanity, when all I was seeing was a poser who'd earned more money than taste. If we were right, he was using that money to carry out magical experiments on people—people including our friend. Without my thinking about it, my hands balled into fists, ready to show him what I thought of his damn game of pool.

"Let's not be coy," Chris said. "What the hell are you doing in that house?"

Dexter chuckled.

"I thought you said you didn't want to be coy? Let's not

be." He turned to look at me, and my anger kept rising in line with the smugness of his tone. "Let me guess. I should be honored that you'd deign to come off your little high horse to come visit. Apparently I have something of yours."

"It's not a something, it's a person," Sky snapped.

Dexter shrugged and turned back to the table.

That was it. I'd had enough. I grabbed the edge of the table and flung it aside. It landed with a crash and a clatter of balls across floorboards.

"We need your attention," I snarled.

Dexter glared at Chris.

"Thanks for bringing this into my house," he said, still riding high on his own arrogance. "There isn't a need to play games. We will finish our little experiments and you'll get her back new and improved."

"Unless she dies, like the rest," Sky said.

"There's that. I've had some losses, but things have improved. I hope she's not one of the casualties of this. I can see why you are fond of her. She's kind of cute, quite the fighter. They had a hard time keeping her. She nearly escaped twice. Please know, I had no idea who she was until I was informed of it." He waved a hand in the air. "My bad. I'll make sure—"

I grabbed him by the throat and lifted him off his feet. I wanted to snap his neck there and then for what he was doing to Kelly, but saving her was more important than getting revenge. He scrabbled at my hands and magic flashed from his fingers as he tried desperately to break free, but his power was nothing compared with those I'd faced. I shrugged it off and tightened my grip.

"They will kill her," Dexter rasped, red-faced.

That did what his feeble magic couldn't: it made me drop him.

Dexter collapsed to the ground, rubbing his throat.

"If anything happens to me, they've been instructed to get

rid of all evidence," he said. "If anything happens to me, it is your doing."

Now it was Josh's turn to lose his temper. With a flash of magic, he hurled Dexter against the wall and pinned him in place. "What are you doing with the people there?"

"I guess what you lack in brains, you make up for in magic. A human with were-animal senses is an asset. Like here in my club, as guards. But they also have human fragility and are able to be controlled with magic. I'm sure Chris has already told you how I like to spend my leisure time. Can you imagine the show?"

So the rumors were true. Along with all his other shady businesses, Dexter traded in people, using their bodies to fill brothels and fight clubs. Now he was going to use his experiments to the same ends.

Even trapped by Josh's magic, there was an arrogance to Dexter, an unwillingness to admit that he wasn't winning, never mind that he was in the wrong. His expression twisted between pain, fury, and disdain, like a kid trying on emotions before he descended into a full-blown tantrum.

We knew what we needed to know. Dexter had Kelly, and many other innocent people. He was willing to throw their lives away to protect himself. And he didn't have the power to have created those wards; his magic was too feeble for that. He must have backup from among the witches. We weren't going to learn any more here.

We headed out the door, Dexter shouting curses after us. The mages watched with hostile curiosity as we crossed their gleaming bar room and headed out into the street, leaving their world of petty power and even pettier personalities behind.

CHAPTER 12

"It sounds like this Dexter will deserve whatever loss we inflict on him," Sebastian said. "Do you have a plan ready to take down the compound?"

I leaned back in my chair, looking across his desk. A lot of our time seemed to be meetings at the moment, whether the two of us or larger groups. Had running the pack always been like this, or had something changed over the past few years? It seemed that we were facing one crisis after another. We spent half our time working out what to do about them, and the other half executing those plans.

"I've got it mostly worked out," I said. "We'll need to do a little more reconnaissance first, but if we're not going in until the curse is lifted, then we've still got time."

I hated that we had to wait that long. Now we knew that Kelly was in there, being tortured by Dexter's experiments, and it was dreadful to think that we were leaving her trapped. But the survival of one member of the pack had to be balanced against an attack on all of us, which was what the curse threatened.

These were the sorts of decisions that the likes of Gavin and Sky could never be made to understand. Sometimes it didn't matter how much you wanted something. Sometimes it didn't matter what principle you thought you should be following. Sometimes it was just about the horrible mathematics of keeping as many people as safe as you could. It was a constant burden ratcheting up my anger every time we encountered a threat, and right now that didn't leave me with much mental room to be anything but angry.

"We should talk again about the tensions in the pack," Sebastian said. "Aside from Gavin's desire to go on a rampage."

"I agree," I said. "We need to stop these visits from Cole."

"You think this is about Cole?" Sebastian asked. He steepled his fingers and gave me an interrogatory look.

"Every time he comes here, you can see the tension rising," I said. "He acts concerned about people as a way of playing on their fears and insecurities, building up the things they worry about. He looks for the divisions between us and pushes them wider. And the whole time you can see him eying up the place, planning how he'll change it once he's in charge."

"I'm not saying you're wrong about Cole," Sebastian said. "But he's clearly not our biggest problem."

"Then who is?"

"Sky."

I sat bolt upright, staring at him.

"That's crap," I snapped. "Just because she has to be pushed into line doesn't make her as big a problem as Cole."

"Not while he's here, but that's the difference. Cole comes around every so often and stirs people up. Sky is with us all the time, and that means her actions are proportionally more important."

"This is bullshit." My hands clenched the sides of the seat as I glared at Sebastian.

"Ethan, I need you to calm down. I know this is a difficult conversation, but it's not like it's come out of nowhere. Sky hasn't found her place in the pack. She won't challenge for a position, but she still pushes back against ranked weres. That leaves everyone else uncertain about where they stand. It's destabilizing us and making everyone harder to manage."

"And you think that compares with Cole?"

"You suspect Cole of plotting against us, and I think you might be right, but we know for certain that Sky's undefined position is a problem, and one that's around us all the time now."

"Sky's working hard to fit in. She's learning about our ways, reining her emotions in, joining in with the pack."

"I agree. She's making great progress."

"Then what the hell makes you think she's more of a problem than Cole?"

"Impact. The effect she has on the people around her."

"And he doesn't?" I was practically spitting with rage.

Sebastian took a deep breath, closed his eyes for a long moment, then opened them to look straight at me.

"This isn't a competition, Ethan. We don't get to pick one problem to deal with and ignore the other one. Yes, we'll have to deal with whatever Cole is planning when it becomes clear. But right now, we need Sky to decide how she fits in here. I can deal with that if you want, but given your relationship, I think it would be better coming from you."

I sank back in my seat, forcing myself to calm down. I might not agree with how Sebastian prioritized our problems, but I couldn't deny that this was one of them. I didn't want to deal with it because my relationship with Sky was already complicated enough, but I didn't really want anyone else dealing with it either.

Sebastian's desk phone rang. He rejected the call, but it rang again, and again, the sound interrupting my attempts to gather my thoughts, to work out how we took this forward.

The ringing had its hooks in my mind. A chill ran through me. Something wasn't right.

"Yes?" Sebastian snapped into the phone.

"Oh God, Sebastian!" The voice was a wail of grief and fear, but I still recognized it as David, Sky's neighbor. Dread grabbed me at the pitiful sound. "You have to come! There's blood everywhere, and the magic, and she forced them out, but they might come back and now she won't wake up and I—"

"David," Sebastian said, cutting through the stream of words. "What's going on?"

"Vampires," he whimpered. "Vampires came to Sky's house, they attacked her, and now she's... she's..."

We both leapt to our feet. "We're on our way."

We raced out of the retreat and into my car, then sped through the night toward Sky's house. The whole way, my mind was full of terrible questions and worse images. Which vampires had attacked Sky? How badly had they hurt her? Was she even still alive? What if they had somehow turned her, bringing out more of her vampiric side, dragging her away from me? What would I find when I got there—the woman who meant the world to me, a cold corpse, or something worse? The speed limit vanished into the distance as we tore toward our destination.

The car screeched to a halt in front of Sky's house and we jumped out. There was a ward around the place, not just the one she normally kept up but something stronger, something raw and riddled with dark power. Maya had been at work again, but on whose side?

I pressed my hand against the ward and let power flow from deep inside me. The sound of sobbing from inside the house fueled me, drawing deeper from that well of power than ever before. I had to get inside. I had to make sure that Sky was safe. And if she wasn't, then I would tear apart whoever had hurt her.

The ward was strong, but it shattered beneath my touch.

There was a flash of light as the magic resolved itself and then the way was open.

David was kneeling in the middle of the living room, his button-down shirt stained with blood. He was pale and shaking, tears rolling down his cheeks.

Sky lay with her head in his lap. Her eyes were closed, her body limp, her skin even paler than his, except for the deep red of blood that was smeared across her hands and the side of her neck. David's hands were pressed against that neck wound, staunching the blood flow with a cashmere sweater. He looked up at us with wide, bloodshot eyes.

I sank to my knees next to them and felt for Sky's pulse. It was weak but steady, her chest rising and falling as she drew shallow breaths. Seeing her in this state was like a dagger to my heart, but at least she was still alive. The worst of the images I had conjured on the way over faded. They were replaced by cold fury in my belly, a rage that came from seeing the reality of what had been done to her. I was going to make someone pay for this.

"What happened?" I asked, peeling back a corner of the sweater to look at her wound. As I feared, there were teeth marks, not the neat holes that came when a vampire bit down on a willing victim, but the torn and ugly wounds that happened in a fight. There were other signs of a struggle, too. Overturned furniture, broken knickknacks, and a sword lying abandoned not far from Sky. I was proud to see that she'd put up quite a fight. I would put up even more when I found whoever had hurt her.

"There were these people, and they, and I, and I couldn't, and I didn't know how, but they—"

"Enough," I said, cutting David off. I wasn't going to get anything coherent out of him until he was a lot calmer. For now, the priority was making sure that Sky lived.

I pressed the sweater more firmly against her neck and

tied it in place using the sleeves. Then I scooped her up in my arms and headed for the door.

"Come with us," I said.

David didn't move. He was frozen in place, staring down at his bloodstained hands.

"Get up," I snapped.

Still he was frozen in place, eyes wide, as still as a statue.

Sebastian laid a hand on David's shoulder and leaned in close.

"Do you want to still be here if the vampires come back?" he asked.

David shook his head.

"Then get up and come with us. We're taking you somewhere safe."

<hr>

"She'll be fine," Jeremy said, drawing Sebastian and I away from the infirmary bed. Sky lay there, still lost to the world. The blood-soaked sweater had been replaced with bandages and she was hooked up to an IV drip, but otherwise she looked much as she had when we'd found her at her house: pale and limp. "What she needs now is rest, and having an Alpha and Beta pacing around won't help with that."

"She won't even know," I said, loath to be away from her. "She's asleep."

"And you two are going to have half the pack coming to you with questions. How do you think she'll sleep with that going on?"

He shoved us out of the infirmary and turned back to tending Sky.

I hated to be kept away from Sky, especially when she was in this state, but I wasn't going to argue with Jeremy on matters of medicine. He was one member of the pack whose authority would never be challenged, because it came down to skill, not status.

Sebastian headed for his office, while I made for one of the spare bedrooms. Once inside, I closed the door behind me, took a deep breath, and let out a howl of rage. I pictured Sky lying bloody in the middle of her trashed living room. I imagined the vampires who had attacked her. I felt the red-hot fury that had been rising inside me this whole time, let it flow through me and out into that long, bestial howl.

Windows shook and light fittings rattled. Voices from other rooms around the retreat fell silent. I kept going until my lungs were empty and my throat was raw, then stood panting in the middle of the room, the anger still lying inside me, a force that would drive me into action once we knew who had done this.

For now, the howl would have to be enough.

I walked out of the room, past a couple of concerned-looking weres, and down to the living room where we had left David.

I wasn't a big fan of David, with his silly nicknames and inability to treat life seriously. But Sky would want us to look after him, and I couldn't see anybody else doing it. Reluctantly, I walked over to where he sat in a chair in the corner of the room, his face blotchy and eyes bloodshot. There were still stains on his hands and shirt.

"How are you doing?" I asked.

"I… I don't know. That was just the most horrible, frightening, miserable thing I've ever been through. I was sure I was going to die, and then I was sure that Sky was going to die, and then…" He stared down at his hands. "Oh my, what happens now?"

"Now we get you cleaned up." I led David to a bathroom where he could wash up, then went to find him a spare shirt. By the time I got back, he stood outside the bathroom, no longer bloodstained but soapy, dripping, and shirtless, looking frantically all around.

"Ethan!" he exclaimed. "Thank goodness! You have to go find him!"

"Find who?" I asked, looking around. Had Sky's attacker followed us here?

"Trent," David said. "If the vampires come back and he's still at home, then he could be in terrible danger."

I groaned. David was right. I couldn't imagine anyone more likely to walk into danger than his partner Trent, a man with all the good sense of a lobotomized pigeon.

"Here," I said, thrusting the shirt I'd found at David. "Put this on. I'll find someone to get Trent."

Winter was out by the entrance to the retreat, stalking back and forth with a knife in her hand. She looked at me eagerly as I approached.

"Did you find out who it was yet?" she asked. "Whichever vampires were behind it, I'm going to tear their throats out."

"That can wait until Sky wakes up," I said. "I need you to send someone to get Sky's neighbor Trent, and bring him here. I don't want to leave the enemy with leverage over Sky."

"I'm on it."

She sped off into the darkness and I paused in the doorway, mustering my thoughts. The past two hours had flung me back and forth through moments of terror, uncertainty, rage, and relief. Not for the first time, I'd been faced with the terrible reality of seeing Sky hurt and the worse possibility of losing her. It had filled me with anger, but it also left me hurting, an exposed wound bared to the world. Having her in my life was making me vulnerable, and I hated to feel like that, but I couldn't see any way to avoid it. She mattered too much to let her go, and from now on that would always be one of my weaknesses, even as the calm and happiness she provided became one of my strengths.

There would be anything but calm and happiness for

whoever had done this. I had a strong suspicion, and I was more than ready to act once it was confirmed.

Sebastian appeared in the doorway.

"Jeremy thinks she's waking up," he said.

We hurried into the infirmary, arriving just in time to see Sky's eyes flicker open.

"What am I going to do with you?" Jeremy asked, looking down at her.

"Help me kill Demetrius and Michaela," she croaked, confirming my suspicion. "And can this be done like yesterday?"

Jeremy turned Sky's head, then ran his finger across the bandaged wound. Sky winced.

"Sorry, but it was a bad bite," Jeremy said. "Don't play with vampires for a while. Okay?"

"I'm not sure what type of freaky BDSM things go on in your life that you consider this playing, and I really don't want to know."

Jeremy stopped Sky as she tried to sit up.

"Is she okay?" David asked, rushing into the room. "I'm so glad you're okay. I thought I did the wrong thing."

"How did I get here?"

"I called Sebastian. I wanted to call an ambulance, but I was afraid of"—David lowered his voice—"your condition being found out."

"You don't have to whisper. Everyone here has the condition, too."

"Oh, twinkie, I forgot."

Sebastian took a step forward. "That was a pretty nasty bite."

"It didn't feel good, either," Sky replied.

That should have lifted my spirits. It was the sort of flippant, devil-may-care attitude from her that normally made me smile, a sign that Sky was well on the way to recovery. But all I could think about was her being attacked by Demetrius and Michaela, and the hell I was going to put the two of them through. I lost the thread of the conversation, too focused on controlling my anger to pay attention to David and Sky's chatter. I paced back and forth, letting out what I could of my frustration, while Winter appeared, said something, and led David away.

"Ethan." Sky's voice brought me back into the moment. Somehow she was smiling at me, despite everything that had happened. "I'm okay."

"He's a fucking coward," I said, thinking of Demetrius. He hadn't even stuck around long enough for us to catch him at Sky's place. "He and Michaela were gone."

I crouched beside Sky's bed and she rested her head against my shoulder.

"They probably need to nurse their wounds," she said. "I wasn't very gentle when I tossed them out, and Demetrius will not be looking out his right eye anytime soon."

"What happened?" I asked.

Jeremy and Sebastian walked out, leaving just the two of us in the infirmary. I touched the bandages, and when Sky didn't show any sign of pain, I unwrapped them to see how the wound looked. It didn't seem so bad now that it wasn't freshly covered in blood, and Sky's werewolf healing ability was speeding up her recovery. Now I could see that she was going to be okay, I started to relax.

"It's not that bad now," I said. "There was a lot of blood." I ran a finger lightly over the area, checking for signs that it might scar. "Why did you let him in?"

"He had David and threatened to kill him if I didn't."

Sitting here with Sky, I understood better than ever how that worked. Sometimes the people in our lives made us vulnerable, and sometimes they were worth that cost.

The question now was what Demetrius had wanted.

"Chris?" I asked.

Sky nodded. "He expected me to return her to him as though she's property."

And that was why she had been making plans to get out of town. Demetrius could get very possessive over his creations. While Chris was bound to the vampire life now, there was still a hope that she might not be bound to her creator, and she had to take the opportunity to try.

"She's gone," I said. "Josh seems concerned about that."

I hadn't told Josh about my encounter with Chris outside Estevez's country house. He'd already been growing too attached to Chris, and what I knew would just fuel that flame.

Sky winced.

"What's the matter?" I asked.

"My neck is bothering me. Maybe I need to lie down for a little while."

Even with her pulse weakened by blood loss, I heard the change in it that meant she was lying. Something else was bothering Sky, something that she didn't want to tell me about. Should I force her to explain? I didn't think I should push it while she was like this, recovering from both a shock and a nasty wound.

Sky rolled over to lie on her side, eyes closed, one hand stroking the pillow like a child with a soft toy. Diminished as she was, her presence still seemed to fill the room. I could hear her heartbeat, smell her skin, feel the magic binding us together.

I lay down beside her, our bodies pressed together, and kissed her on the ear.

"If you are going to make lying your thing, at least get better at it," I whispered.

We lay there quietly, just the two of us, and I almost felt calm for the first time in days. Revenge wasn't forgotten, but it was pushed to the back of my mind.

"What happens with Demetrius?" Sky asked, as if reading my mind.

"I'm going to take care of it."

"It's not wise to do anything right now. Let's get Kelly back and remove the curse from the others and deal with everything else later."

I let out a deep breath. I hated to admit it, but she was right. This was another of those difficult decisions, the ones Sebastian and I spent so much time making, and Sky had cut to the core of it. One day, we would have revenge on the vampires, but that day would have to wait.

Gavin and I prowled through the woods, looking down at Dexter's compound. We had a detailed map of the area, to which we were adding the features the researchers had built: the fences, the limits of the wards, where the gates and guard posts were. Every detail we got now could save us time or even lives when it came to attacking this place.

"We should have done this already," Gavin whispered. "We've left Kelly in there too long."

"And we're going in for her tomorrow," I replied. "Like Sebastian said, we don't leave our own to suffer."

I didn't tell Gavin what else Sebastian had said, when we were discussing the new state of the pack after Demetrius's attack on Sky. There was another reason why this mission had risen up our priorities, and that was the need for a win. Whatever the causes of the heightened tensions in the pack, everybody felt them, and we felt like we were losing. The curse showed no sign of shifting, and for now the vampires had gotten away with their attack. We needed a win to raise morale and hold the pack together.

If I'd had my way, we would have been charging in right now, with the whole pack behind us. It hurt like hell to think that we were leaving Kelly there this whole time, at the mercy of these people and their sick experiments. I had to remind myself that hanging on was our best hope, and that made it Kelly's best hope, too.

We crept on through the woods, making notes on the map. The guards were out in force today, ushering batches of test subjects into the woods for reasons I didn't understand, then leading them back in again an hour later, some at gunpoint, others sedated and carried.

"What is this?" I asked.

"Tests," Gavin growled. "Endless fucking tests."

The anger blazing inside him put even my inner fury into the shade. Days of watching this place, many of them with no one else for company, had wound him up tighter than ever. He was desperate to get inside and rescue Kelly, and that colored his view of everything here. The possibility that she was now a test subject was tearing him apart.

Another group of guards went out, leaving the gates open behind them.

"This is our chance," Gavin said, pointing at the opening. "We can go in and get her."

I grabbed his arm, hauling him back just as he was about to charge in.

"Don't be an idiot," I hissed. "There are dozens of them. You'll never make it out."

"There are dozens of them in there with Kelly. I'm not leaving her alone another day."

He swung his arm around, trying to break my hold, but I clung on tight. With his free hand, he swung a punch at me. I ducked, twisted, and came up behind him, wrenching his arm behind his back.

"You think this will help Kelly?" I whispered, staring past him down the hill, watching for any reaction from the compound, any sign that they'd spotted our movements. "If you charge in on your own and get yourself killed, that just means one fewer of us to go in for her tomorrow. Hell, it might frighten them into abandoning this place, and you know full well that they'll kill their test subjects rather than let someone else get hold of them."

"But Kelly," Gavin growled, teeth bared, straining against me despite the pain from his arm.

"We'll bring her out," I said. "I promise. This time tomorrow, we'll be back with the whole pack and we'll take this place by force. Then you can rip these fuckers apart, and we'll be there to help you. But if you charge in now, that'll give them a warning, and half of them will get away. Do you want that, or do you want to make them suffer?"

For a long moment, I thought that he might try to break free again, but then he nodded slowly and I felt him sag.

"Tomorrow," he said, "I'm going to kill every one of them."

CHAPTER 13

*E*ven in human form, I found myself pawing at the dirt, solid boot dragging across the forest floor as my wolf fought to be released. I could already smell something foul from inside the mages' compound—a mix of blood, rot, and medical chemicals. Running through it all was the smell of fear, whether carried by hormones or by magic, the fear of people being tortured and transformed against their will.

Close to me, Josh and Sky were chanting as they pressed their magic against the ward running around the house. The ward was constructed to keep out people, not things, and we'd already reached through it with bolt cutters to make holes in the wire fence that ran along its length. I could see my way clear across a hundred yards of packed dirt to the massive Colonial-era house, its old brick walls scarred with reinforced metal doors, its windows replaced with modern bulletproof glass. This place had been turned into a fortress, but that wasn't going to hold us back.

I growled in anger at the sight of the place, and others around me took up that sound. Not just members of our pack but others who had come to help us, including Joan and

Cole. The sickness of what was going on here had been enough to draw others to our side. No one could be allowed to behave like this. We had to send out a message for all the packs.

For once, I was glad to have Cole with us. For all the disdain I felt toward him, he was a skilled and powerful fighter, both as a human and in his wolf form as he was now. He would help us get Kelly safely out.

The thought of her sent a feeling of nausea through me. We should have done this weeks ago, should have been able to free her straight away. Some people might have taken all our other issues as an excuse, and they had certainly been the reason why we hadn't found this place sooner, why we hadn't come straight to the rescue once we knew it was here. But reasons and excuses weren't the same thing. We had let life slip out of control, to the point where a crime like this could be committed and we weren't there to immediately answer it. We had failed in our duty to a member of the pack, and that was a burden of guilt I would be living with for a long time.

At last, the magic reached its climax. The air rippled as the ward collapsed.

Sebastian barked a command and we poured in. Some of the pack spread out around the house, ready to block any attempts to escape. The rest of us headed straight for the front door.

Josh twisted his hands around and a glowing ball of magic appeared between them. He flung it at the door, which burst in, locks and keypads flying apart, inches of solid steel buckling beneath the force of his magic.

I ran in, the pack close behind. The smells were stronger here, the sense of horror a tangible thing that I could taste in the air. This was a tainted place, corrupted not by dark magic but by twisted abominations against science.

The entrance hall held two staircases—one heading up

and the other down, just like in the floor plan for the house, which we'd obtained from the records of a defunct realty business. I led one group up the stairs and Sebastian led another down, while the rest spread out across the first floor.

We had decided from the start that there was no point including Gavin in the plan to seize the house. As soon as he got in, he would race off after any scent he caught of Kelly. Instead of joining one of the storming parties, he would become a roaming sensor, helping to lead us to our most important objective.

Sure enough, he raced past us on the stairs, roaring as he went, a black blur of fur and claws.

The corridors on the second floor were a sterile white, like the interior of a medical lab. The doors lining them were locked with keypads and some of them had small windows at eye level, to let those in power view whoever was trapped inside. It was like advancing through an asylum for the dangerously insane, except that here the danger wasn't the prisoners—it was the staff.

The place reeked of magic, not just the weak stuff of the mages but the more powerful spells spun by witches. People we had talked with, struck deals with, even worked alongside had chosen to help with this abomination. This wasn't just an atrocity, it was a betrayal, and that thought made me sick with anger.

There was a whine that set my teeth on edge, and a sudden blast of magic. It hurtled past me and struck Sky, slamming her into the wall.

Marcia, the head of the local Creed, had appeared down a side corridor. Behind her were men in camouflage gear, webbing, and army boots, strangely modified guns raised to point at us. Marcia grinned and raised her hands to cast again, but Sky was quicker, flinging out a wave of magic that knocked Marcia back into the mercenaries.

Shaken as she was by the attack, Marcia was still quick to

respond. She flung up a magical barrier in the air, which Sky battered with her magic even as the rest of us charged.

The barrier fell and the mercenaries opened fire. To either side of me, darts hit Steven and Gavin, but the man directly ahead was too slow. I grabbed him before he could take a shot, wrenched the gun from his hand, and slammed him into the nearest door.

The corridor descended into chaos, a wild melee of fists, claws, and guns. There were flashes of magic and screams of pain, the crash of something breaking through the banisters and the thud of something on the ground below.

The man I had hold of tried to slam his elbow back into my face. I grabbed his arm and twisted until the bone snapped and he cried out in pain. Then I slammed his head against the door once more and he slumped unconscious to the ground.

Two more guards came at me, pistols raised, but with so much else going on they couldn't get a clear shot from range. I darted past Marcia, grabbed the first one by the wrist, and yanked him forward as I brought my knee up into his groin. He buckled over and his companion tried to take a shot over his back, but missed, hitting one of his own men. I flung the soldier I had hold of into the other, then leapt on them with a flurry of kicks and punches that sent them staggering back.

I turned just as Gavin, still in his animal form and with a dart protruding from his shoulder, leapt at Marcia. She flung a blast of magic at him and, to my shock, it flung him back. Something in the darts must be overcoming our immunity to magic in were form. Dexter and Marcia had found a way to negate one of our greatest advantages.

It was a chilling thought, but not one I had time to stop and consider. We were fighting for our lives.

The air was thick with magic. Mages had appeared to fight alongside Marcia, and their spells were more powerful than I'd seen from their kind before. Sky and Josh countered their magic and struck back in kind, while the rest of us kept driving back the guards. The scents of blood and magic filled the air.

Some of the pack had broken open doors or unlocked them with swipe cards taken off the guards. The fighting spilled over into the surrounding rooms, animals and men tearing into each other through laboratories, offices, and cells. A man in a lab coat appeared around a corner, eyes wide. His hands went up, and for a moment I faced the question of whether anyone here deserved to be allowed to surrender. But then magic appeared around his hands, the fire of a fighting spell. I jerked up the gun I'd grabbed off one of the guards and fired. The dart went through the scientist's eye and he toppled over in a stream of blood.

At last, I stood without opponents in the middle of the corridor, looking around to see what was coming next. From around the house, the sounds of violence were receding, and weres were emerging from nearby rooms, carrying or supporting the victims of this place. Among them was Gavin, now in human form, carrying a pale-looking Kelly wrapped in a sheet. As he looked down at her, I saw the tenderness that had been missing from his life for too long.

While Gavin carried Kelly to safety, the rest of us split up to explore the house. I walked through labs full of test tubes, sample trays, and scientific equipment I couldn't even name. Still driven by the fury that had fueled me through the fight, I lifted a machine weighing far more than I did and slammed it into another one. I tore out wires and smashed in screens, wrenched open freezers and scattered their contents across the floor. Anything I could break, I did. I wasn't leaving these people with any chance to rebuild what they had done.

Other rooms were worse. There were filthy cages that stank of rot and death, a dissection table, a firing range with pictures of us on the targets. I went through room after room, trashing anything that hadn't already been destroyed.

"Filthy beast," a voice said as I entered another lab.

I turned to see a man in camouflage pointing his gun at me, a look of pure hatred on his face.

"Me?" I growled. "You think I'm the beast when you've done this?"

I pointed to a cage in the corner of the room. Its door had been ripped open to let out whoever was once trapped inside. Above it, blood and tissue samples sat in jars on a shelf, and I doubted that any of them had come from a living donor.

"Your kind need to be controlled," the man said, his finger slowly tightening on the trigger. "Tamed. Directed by real people."

"Real people?" The anger rose in me like never before. This was how they had justified these atrocities, the kidnappings, torture, and murder, the twisting of innocent people into forms they should never have had, creatures who couldn't fit into human society and were too wild and vulnerable to survive in the supernatural world.

He pulled the trigger, but I was already in motion. The dart shot past my shoulder as I charged, hitting him shoulder first, slamming him back against the wall with all my strength. There was a crunch of breaking ribs and he let out a weak, wet gasp.

Despite his pain, the man yanked a knife from his belt and stabbed at me. I blocked the blow, catching hold of his wrist. The two of us strained against each other, the knife blade wavering back and forth, the tip pointing first at him, then at me. With the desperate strength of a man who knew he faced death, the mercenary pressed in, pushing his whole weight behind the knife, and for a moment I thought he might get me. But then I twisted, his body came around, and the blade plunged into his chest.

I left him on the ground, gurgling his last agonized breaths as he bled out. There was no need for mercy here.

Outside the house, I found the others loading the people we'd rescued into SUVs. Jeremy, his face fierce in a way I seldom saw on the gentle doctor, was loading papers, a laptop, and darts from the mercenaries' guns into the back of one of the vehicles.

Marcia had gotten away. It wasn't the result I would have hoped for, but at least now we knew for sure that she was involved. We could track her down later, once her victims were safe.

Sky, Sebastian, and Josh stood by one of the cars. They all looked grim, but the expression on Josh's face was particularly dark. I could understand it. He was a witch, his default loyalty was to the Creed, and here he had seen them involved in something dark and dreadful. Marcia, who should have used her power to protect those around her, had instead used it to support experiments on living people. That sense of betrayal I had felt was ten times worse for him.

We got into the car and led our convoy away from the compound, out through the woods toward the pack's retreat.

"I saw Dexter," Sky said, speaking his name like a curse. "He attacked me and Jeremy, tried to stop us retrieving a computer."

"Is he still alive?" I asked.

Sky nodded sourly. "He got away."

"Not forever."

Josh's face was crumpled in an expression of anger. When he spoke, his voice was heavy with disgust.

"The witches worked with Dexter just so they could create something that would make you all vulnerable to their magic." He closed his eyes and shook his head, as if he was trying to shake off a burden of guilt by association, the knowledge that his fellow witches had done this.

"It looks that way," I said softly, aiming to sooth him. There would be a chance to deal with the witches later. Josh didn't need to keep beating himself up until then.

"They don't even care about the witches anymore, or anyone," he said, and I realized that I had read his expression wrong. This wasn't guilt, it was anger, as pure as my own, all directed at Marcia and the Creed. "It's just about power, and they will do anything to achieve it."

His anger was a physical presence in the car, a swirling vortex of wild magic. It expanded around him, then closed in, and in a moment Josh was gone.

I stared at the space where my brother had been sitting. An hour earlier, I had been worrying about what could be happening to Kelly. Now I was worrying about Josh instead.

The rest of the way back to the retreat, I couldn't stop thinking about Josh. He had to have gone after Marcia, who had escaped us at the compound, and I could understand that instinct. She had been part of something terrible, and in doing so she had betrayed the honest witches who looked to her for leadership. If my Alpha had acted like Marcia, I would have wanted to tear them apart, and I would have expected most of the pack to back me. But Josh was doing this on his own and that put him in danger.

I had to go help him.

First though, I had to deal with the pack and all the innocent people we had rescued. Back at the retreat, I helped unload Dexter and Marcia's victims from the cars and directed them to places where they could rest or get treatment. It was only once a little order started to emerge from the chaos that I let myself think about the next step.

There was a good chance that this was going to get political, so I found Sebastian first. Of course, it could also turn violent, so I grabbed Winter for backup. I didn't know what state Josh would be in when we found him, and Sky was better at managing him than I was, so lastly I headed to the infirmary, where she stood in the doorway chatting with Cole.

I eyed Cole warily as I approached. The conversation looked innocent, but I knew better than to believe that of him. Was he working some angle I needed to interrupt, or making me interrupt so he could use it against me? There was no way to tell and no time to waste while Josh could be at risk, so I wrapped an arm around Sky and drew her to me.

"We have to go get Josh," I said, and she joined me in heading for the door.

Minutes later, we were driving toward the Creed's main lair, Sebastian following behind me. I'd said that this was about Josh, but we all knew that it was something more. In siding with Dexter against us, the Creed had crossed a line. They had attacked us, first indirectly by supporting Kelly's kidnapping, then directly when Marcia had fought against our rescue. They'd pushed us to the edge and Josh had tumbled over. I would follow him no matter what.

I stepped out of the car in front of the store that hid the Creed's main office, and straight away I knew for certain that we would find Josh here. The place stank of blood and spent magic just as badly as the woodland compound had.

I'd been the one who had brought us here, but now I hesitated, trailing behind the others as they headed into the shop.

What was I going to find inside? There was so much blood in the air, this had clearly been a fight to the end. Was Josh dead already, killed in a desperate battle against superior numbers of powerful witches? Was he lying there horribly injured, left to die without mercy like the soldier I'd left in the compound? Could he be badly hurt or even crippled? Some part of me felt sure that he must be in a terrible state, and I advanced reluctantly, not wanting to see what might be there.

As I followed a trail of blood through the shop, I sensed Josh's magic and his anger still filling the space. He was alive, and I should have been relieved, but that anger was so deep, so jagged, so unlike the Josh I knew that a fresh dread came over me. My brother lived, but was he still the man I knew, the one I had protected my whole life?

Sebastian stopped in the door to the back room. As I approached, he stepped aside, revealing what lay beyond.

The witches' meeting room had been utterly destroyed. The walls were sprayed with blood, the mirror at the back shattered into a thousand shards. Broken furniture and twisted bodies lay scattered across the floor. The air was thick with magic, blood held in suspension by its power, creating a scarlet haze in patches around the room. And in the middle of it all stood Josh, stiff and unmoving, looking away from us.

"Josh," I called out softly.

He turned, revealing eyes as black as midnight. His usual smile was gone, replaced by something cold, implacable, remorseless. His breath was labored as if he was struggling against some great force.

A shudder ran down my spine. What had become of my kid brother? Had he drawn on some darkness within himself, or was he now a thing possessed, losing control just as Sky had when Maya took over?

"Hey," I said, keeping the doubts out of my voice, calling to him gently as I walked into the room.

Josh's breath remained strained but a small smile appeared. As I got close, he reached out and pulled me to him. I rested my head against him, felt the trembling of his body, the tension that had him in its grip.

"You kind of made a mess of things, huh?" I said softly.

Josh nodded once and took a deep breath.

He'd trashed the home of one of the most powerful supernatural forces in the region, killed their people, ruined their safe space. He had completely lost control, showing a side of him that shocked me. There was no coming back from this, no undoing the past, and though I would do whatever it took to protect my brother from the consequences, that wasn't what Josh needed to hear in that moment. He was broken, struggling to find himself after what he had done. I could hear the hammering of his heart as I held him close, offering my strength to hold him together.

"It's okay," I said. "We'll fix it."

Josh nodded, accepting the comforting lie, as if there was something here that even remained to be fixed. The anger had faded from his eyes, leaving behind a sense of bewilderment. In his own fury, my brother had shown his power and at the same time left himself exposed, vulnerable, his heart an open wound. I wished that there was some way I could make it better, but he had done the right thing. The blame for all of this lay with Marcia and I couldn't undo her actions. If the only choice was to offer him some comfort, then that was what I would do.

I matched my breath to his, then slowed it down so that he followed along, calming himself, coming back to something like the Josh I knew.

At last he stepped back and looked around at the carnage he had caused. "I guess I should clean up."

Heels clicked as someone strode through the shop and into the back room with us.

"Nah, we got this," a woman said.

A group of eight witches stood around the doorway, surveying the remains of the room. Most of them were dressed all in black and half held crossbows. The strings on the bows were drawn, quarrels loaded, and the women carried them with a casual ease that said they knew exactly what they were doing.

I knew several of the faces, including London, a friend and lover of Josh's, whose cherubic face and pastel-colored hair were at odds with her somber clothes and serious demeanor. But I didn't know the leader, the only one of them dressed in white instead of black.

She strolled through the room, those heels still clicking against the floor. She was a good-looking woman, her shape accentuated by tight trousers and a flowing shirt, and she carried herself with absolute confidence.

"Well, they weren't wrong when they said you were powerful," she said, shooting Josh a forced smile.

She showed no sign of emotion as she held out her hands, magic flaring from her fingers. As she progressed around the room, the blood vanished all around her, clearing the air, the walls, the floor. She stopped when she reached the bodies and looked down at them, a moment's grief showing through the facade of cool efficiency before she brought it back under control. Who was this woman, and what did she mean for the future of the pack?

"Please, handle this until we can have a proper burial," she said, gesturing to three of her companions.

They stepped up and raised their hands. Magic flowed between them, a single spell they were weaving together. Its threads twisted and intertwined, became a bright net that settled over the bodies, and then, in a moment, the bodies disappeared.

I shouldn't have been surprised; after all, one of Josh's jobs was getting rid of bodies for us. But there was a difference between one body being quietly taken away and seeing a heap of them disappear before my eyes.

I still stood tense, ready in case things suddenly turned bad. I didn't know these people or what they stood for. I didn't know if they could be trusted, and trust was something I was far warier about now.

The others joined the white witch, spreading out through the room as they cast another combined spell. This one built on what she had done before, clearing away the last of the blood, reassembling shattered furniture, restoring order to a space that had been thrown into gory chaos.

"Josh, you can relax, no one here plans to hurt you," the white witch said as she led her followers through the spell. Hers was the guiding force behind all this, her delicate fingers darting through the air, plucking at strands of magic to refine and redirect the others' work. She gave orders and they obeyed without question, turning their efforts wherever she instructed, altering their magic to match her plan.

At last, we stood in a clean, tidy room, all traces of Josh's rampage gone.

"Good," the white witch said. "I work better in a clean workspace."

She graced each of us in turn with a smile, her full lips turned up in seemingly genuine pleasure. But her followers still stood as ready for trouble as I was, and the air between us was as tight with tension as the strings on their crossbows.

Her gaze settled on Sebastian and the two of them gave each other appraising looks. His grimace had been replaced with a winning smile, our Alpha turning on the charm that was one of his biggest political assets.

"You're Sebastian, and your reputation definitely precedes you," she said. "I'm Ariel. I will be taking Marcia's place." She took a step back from Sebastian and turned her attention to Josh. "I figured it would only be a matter of time before this happened. Months ago I decided I was going to have to initiate a coup, but it worked itself out, didn't it? Civil wars are such ugly things, and it can be quite difficult to garner loyalty from those who are on the losing side. But Marcia and her antics made it quite difficult for most to be willing to pledge their loyalty to her. Her power-lust was her undoing, and the weak minds of the others in the Creed who became complicit deserved their fate."

"You coming in with your magical show, albeit impressive, might not be enough to gain their loyalty and convince them of your qualification to be the new leader of the Creed," Josh said.

"Well, if the Creed is to be made up of the most powerful witches in the country, you are looking at them. Yes, despite Marcia's many attempts to make sure we didn't exist, we managed to survive." There was anger in her voice, a bile directed not at us but at her predecessor. "Your choice not to finish magic training was made out of youthful ignorance or defiance; it was a good one. That is where they observed us, and ones they considered a threat became targets. Between the ages of ten and eighteen, I do believe I had more attempts on my life than I had candles on my birthday cakes."

She waved at her companions. Several of them nodded as if to say that they had lived through the same thing, that they knew the truth of Ariel's words and the bond they created.

"We all are bonded by more than magic—we survived the Creed. Foolish Marcia—instead of cultivating our skills and making the witches stronger, she chose to weaken us for fear of not being the great and almighty witch. Deluded woman."

The darkness and tension consuming Josh had faded away, and for the first time since I stepped into the room I allowed myself to relax a little. If he could accept what was happening, then so could I. But I would still be keeping an eye open for trouble; my brother's safety, perhaps his whole future, was at stake here.

"There are eight of you," he said cautiously, his attention turning to London. "The Creed consists of five."

If he was hoping for answers from someone he trusted, then he was only getting one. London gave him a half-smile, but instead of replying she nodded to Ariel. Her trust lay with her leader, and Josh would have to accept that.

"There isn't a rule about that," Ariel said. "There weren't always five; at one time there were more, as many as nine. The more people that are involved, the harder one person must work to control and corrupt. That's not to say it is true with all things." She turned her smile back on Sebastian. "It has worked for you. And the were-animals."

"We do things differently than most," Sebastian replied.

"So I hear," she said with a hint of laughter as she stepped closer to him. "I will say, for someone with such a terrible bark, it is my understanding the bite is just as bad, too. I personally do not want to be on the other side of that bite."

By the time she fell silent, they were so close that he could have leaned forward and kissed her.

"It's not always that bad," he said, returning her smile. That was a good sign. A deal between two leaders would be stronger if it was held together by more than just words, and the mutual attraction between these two was clear. Whether or not they ever acted on their instincts, it could help to hold us together.

"And it shouldn't be. The witches and the were-animals were not always enemies, and I hope we can return to that." Ariel stepped back from Sebastian and swept her gaze around all of us in the room, looking pleased with herself.

"Marcia and I had an alliance at one time, which she broke. Please forgive me if I'm not running to form one with the witches again. As you said before, power-lust can become a problem, and I'm not convinced you are exempt from it."

"Of course, but please let me prove my desire to make this happen." Ariel pulled a small vial from her pocket. "This is what Marcia had made to destroy your immunity to magic. I'm sure your doctor, if the rumors are as correct about him as they are about you, can find an antidote. He'll have Josh's help, and I will offer my assistance if necessary."

She handed the vial to Sebastian, and for a long moment their fingers stayed connected while their eyes locked above. Ariel flushed as she withdrew her hand and looked away.

Sebastian peered at the contents of the vial, then sniffed at it. He smiled, nodded, and handed it back.

"We already have it," he said. "And I doubt this is all that you have, or that you haven't figured out how to duplicate it. This is of no use to me."

For the first time since she came into the room, Ariel's confidence faltered. She had come in as a powerful, enigmatic force, trying to throw us off balance then win us over with the promise of peace and cooperation. She had shown her knowledge, and in doing so created an impression of advantage over us. But Sebastian had found a crack in that knowledge, had shown how reliant she was on a pre-planned spiel, and now the advantage was his.

"I suspect your offering isn't just goodwill," he said. "What is it that you want?"

That question shouldn't have been a surprise to anyone in such a position of power, and maybe it wasn't so much the question as the asking that threw her, or perhaps Ariel wasn't as used to leadership as she was leading us to believe. Witches like her might have been waiting for a long time in the shadow of Marcia, but that didn't mean that they had been preparing that whole time. For all we knew, they had only just started to organize, and our clash with Marcia had forced them to step unexpectedly into the light.

After a moment's uncertainty, Ariel stood taller and her confident smile returned.

"Go on," Sebastian said. "What do you want?"

"The Aufero is in your possession."

"You're not getting that back," Sky snapped.

"Skylar Brooks, right?" Ariel turned to her with a smile. Sebastian was the calm, focused face of the pack, and that let him control the conversation. Sky's instinctive interruption had broken that control and given Ariel back her advantage. "Once again, I must admit that the person who has often been referred to as the Midwestern Pack's doe-eyed assassin is not nearly as vicious and savage as I expected."

I almost laughed at that description of Sky. She could be

as deadly as almost anyone in the pack, but I could hardly think of anyone less suited to the calm, cold-blooded work of assassination.

Sky, however, seemed to have taken some offense, as she scowled at the comment.

"Don't be cross over the name," Ariel continued. "I'm sure it is an embellishment, just as I am sure the story of how you viciously attacked Marcia has been altered. I'm quite confident that if you did savagely attack her, she undoubtedly deserved it. And I think it is unfair and probably a misnomer to call you a killer. But if you are the one that killed Ethos, then you, too, are far more than what meets the eye, and your bite is quite impressive as well."

"Ariel, what would you like us to do for you?" Sebastian asked.

"The magic that was stolen from the witches using it. I need to make an attempt to gain their trust and loyalty. If my first act is to return that to them, I think that will be a step in the right direction."

It was an awkward thing to ask. Sebastian clearly wanted to solidify our understanding with Ariel and her people, but he'd promised Samuel the opportunity to return that magic. Of course, it was hard to hold to a deal with someone who had vanished like Samuel had. For all we knew, he wasn't even alive anymore, making the whole agreement invalid.

"Consider it done," Sebastian said. "But I will need a favor from you and your witches."

"And what is that?"

"I don't know yet."

"I don't make open-ended bargains," Ariel said with a frown.

"Not until now." Sebastian treated her to a wolfish grin and let the animal show in his eyes. "Do we have a deal?"

Ariel didn't take his offered hand.

"As I said before, I do not make open-ended bargains."

"Then, Ariel, you should have brought a better bargain to the table."

Sebastian headed for the door, and at his signal the rest of us followed. He looked back just as he was leaving, giving Ariel one more amused smile.

"I trust that when you are ready to make that deal, you know how to find me," he said.

Ariel watched us go with a smile of her own.

I should have been worrying about what this change in power dynamics meant for us. What were the objectives of the witches' new leaders? How would they get on with the other supernatural groups? Could we really make an alliance with them? But after everything we'd been through, I was just relieved to get my brother out alive.

"Interesting times," I said to Josh as we headed out.

"They sure are," he said, glancing back. "And for once, I think that might be good."

We crossed the store and were heading out the front door when footsteps followed us.

"Josh," London called out.

"What?" he asked, sounding far less relaxed than was usual between them.

"We should talk."

She fell into step with him and the rest of us dropped back, giving them space. The conversation started casually, just playing catch-up as they leaned in closer to each other. After a few minutes, she took his hand, and Josh made no attempt to resist. Not for the first time, my gaze flitted between the matching tattoos on their arms, a permanent sign of just how close these two were. They had been far more than just friends for years, even if they didn't admit it to everyone, and it was good to see that someone had the power to make Josh happy.

By now we were waiting by the car while they stood a few feet away, lost in conversation. The casual tenderness of the moment receded as the talk finally came around to what had just happened, and in particular to Ariel. Josh's expression turned to disappointment and I heard his heart rate climb with the tension.

"Do you trust her?" he asked.

"With my life," London said without hesitation. "This was a long time coming. But for years, Marcia somehow held on to some of the witches' loyalty. The more desperate she became for power, the easier it was to see that she didn't have our interests at heart. We've been planning for years to do this."

"Why didn't you tell me?"

"Because I was sworn to secrecy. Josh, your—" She paused. The awkward issue hung in the air between them, and it was a testament to London's discretion that she didn't just look straight at me and Sebastian. "Your affiliation with the pack makes things complicated."

There it was. The witches were rebuilding after years of being held down by Marcia, some of their most talented people chased into hiding by her lust for domination. London wanted Josh to be on the inside of that. She liked him, she trusted him, for all I knew she even loved him—scarring yourselves with shared tattoos seemed like one hell of a commitment to me. But it wasn't just about what she wanted. Josh's ties to the pack might come from his personal link to me, but they still raised a question mark for other witches over where his loyalty lay.

"Thank you for telling me," he said, a note of relief in his voice. He leaned down to kiss her on the forehead and the tension between them seemed to melt away. They were just a young couple holding hands and talking in the street.

"Of course," she said. She flashed the rest of us a brief, uncomfortable smile, then turned back to Josh. "We'll talk about it more tonight. Okay?"

Josh nodded.

There was clearly more than talking in Josh's future. I just hoped that he remembered to find out something useful for us.

London headed back to the store and Josh came to join us at the car.

"Very interesting times," I said with a grin.

CHAPTER 14

Jeremy was waiting impatiently for us when we got back to the retreat. He'd only had a little time to talk with his new patients and look at the records we'd grabbed, but it was enough to fix a look of grim fury and resolution on his normally placid face.

"They were given three different formulas," he said. "Some of them are getting sick. Fevers, blood pressures that I can't get down."

"Okay," Sebastian said, his calm a striking contrast to the physician's agitation. "What can we do?"

He looked at me and Josh, then toward the stairs from which the sounds of our new guests were coming. In response to the unspoken order, we headed up the stairs to check on the compound's evacuees.

The most urgent cases had been put in the infirmary, but it wasn't big enough to hold the numbers now in our care. Our medical setup was designed to deal with a few injuries when we got into a fight with other supernatural groups, not as a full-scale hospital for dozens of scared civilians. To cope with the influx, those who were well enough had been spread out among the available bedrooms, giving them some space to rest and recuperate while they waited for Jeremy to get to them.

I took the rooms on one side of a long corridor, Josh the other side. We made our way along, knocking on doors and stepping inside to check on the people we found.

In the third room I visited, a man in his thirties lay curled up on the bed. He had the feral look of the poor creatures we'd encountered in the woods, his eyes wild and his body twitching, caught in this strange half-human, half-animal state. His hair was wet from the shower still running in the en suite bathroom, but it seemed that getting clean had taken all the will he had. Instead of getting dressed, he'd curled up on the bed and pulled the sheets over him, cocooning himself in cotton.

"How are you doing?" I asked, crouching by the bed.

He stared at me and pulled the sheets tighter, as if trying to close out the world.

"I'm Ethan," I said softly. "What's your name?"

"Ray," he whispered.

"It's okay, Ray. You're safe now," I said.

He screwed his eyes shut and gave a tiny, quivering shake of his head.

"The doctor," he said, forcing the words out as if they were torture. "The doctor says you have to change us."

To change them? I looked at him in confusion. Was he seriously suggesting that Jeremy wanted to turn all his patients into weres?

"Did he say why?" I asked.

This time the tiny movements of his head were a nod.

"Only way to save us from… from… from what they did."

He turned his face into the mattress and started to cry, tears soaking the sheets as his whole body shook, overcome with the horror of what he'd been through.

I patted him on the shoulder and looked uncertainly around the room. I wasn't good at comforting anyone, never mind a grown man in tears. The idea of responding like this was utterly alien to me.

My eyes fell on the dirty, ragged clothes he'd abandoned on the way into the shower. That was something I could deal with.

"I'll get you some new clothes," I said. "And something to eat."

If Ray responded, it was lost amid the sobs.

By the time I came back with clean jeans, a t-shirt, and a sandwich, Ray was sitting up in bed, his face blotchy but his expression more composed.

"Thanks," he said as I put the clothes down beside him. "I'm sorry about earlier, it's just, this is all too much, you know? After everything we've been through, I thought we were going to be safe, but now magic is real and people are talking about turning us into werewolves and, I mean, how do I even tell my family about any of this?"

This was new territory for us, too. The hazards and pain of turning an adult into a were meant that it was a rare act. Doing it to so many people would create challenges for the pack, not least in working out what happened to those people's old lives. But I trusted in one thing above all others: Sebastian would find a way.

"From now on, we're here for you," I said. "No matter what."

I left Ray and went to find Sebastian. The Alpha was in his office, talking about the logistics of the new recruits with Joan and Cole.

"You've heard then?" he asked, seeing the look on my face.

"Jeremy's new medicine?" I asked. "Yeah, I've heard. This is going to get complicated."

"I agree, and there's one case in particular that needs careful handling."

"Kelly."

"Exactly. If it's done by anyone other than Gavin, then

Kelly's closeness to the person who changes her will leave Gavin on the outside. We all know how he feels about Kelly, and putting someone else between them would cause conflict down the line."

That thought had crossed my mind.

"Shouldn't be a problem. Gavin will be happy to bring them closer together."

Sebastian grimaced. "Based on the way he reacted when I mentioned it, I'm not so sure."

And then it hit me. We'd forgotten about Tam and Miguel.

Tam and Miguel had been neighbors of Gavin's, poor teenage kids living in the rough neighborhood Gavin called home. The previous year, Tam had tried to get out from under the fist of a local drug dealer named Simone, who had been using Tam and Miguel as corner boys. When Tam's rebellion threatened to spread through the neighborhood, Simone had decided to make an example, beating him to the brink of death. Miguel had stepped in and gotten the same treatment. Gavin tried to save the boys' lives by turning them, but it hadn't taken, and instead of being saved they had suffered the extra agony of the failed conversion tearing through their battered bodies. Gavin had gotten his revenge on Simone, and he'd never talked about it since, which was why I had been able to forget it so easily. But it seemed that the shadow of those deaths still hung over him.

"Remember Tam and Miguel," I said.

"You think he blames himself?"

"Gavin takes things to heart."

"And now we need those things to include Kelly's change."

I hesitated, considering the best way forward.

"We should get Sky to talk with him," I said. "She's our resident Gavin expert."

"I think she's trying, but it won't be easy. Can you give her some encouragement?"

A lot went unspoken between us, things that we would have discussed if we weren't in the presence of outsiders, or at least not in the presence of Cole. If we needed Sky to find her place in the pack, then this was a way to encourage her. If we could get her used to persuading other pack members of what was needed, then she might be more willing to take on a proper place of leadership. With her strong will and her powers, we needed her to do that. This wasn't just about Gavin and Kelly—it was about Sky, too.

"I'm on it," I said.

I headed out through the retreat, following the connection that told me when Sky was nearby. Her presence led me out of the building and into the woods beyond, to the bottom of one of Gavin's favorite climbing trees. But instead of seeing him up there, I just saw Sky clinging tight to the upper trunk, her eyes closed and her head resting against the bark.

"Why are you up there?" I called out.

"Gavin." The exact answer I'd expected.

Shouting up and down a tree was no way to hold a conversation, so I leapt, grabbed one of the lower branches, and clambered up the tree toward her.

"He does this a lot?" Sky asked.

"They all do. Cat." I laughed. "But he does it more often than most."

Having reached a level with Sky, I clung to the branches and smiled at her as she leaned a little nervously into the trunk.

"He doesn't want to change Kelly," she said. "He's afraid that he won't be able to do it successfully. How hard is it?"

"I figured he wouldn't," I said. "He had an incident last year and took it hard. He lives in Clayton Park."

"He enjoys the thrill of living in a questionable area."

I laughed. "Probably, but crime in his neighborhood has definitely decreased since he moved there." The laughter died inside me as I considered the story of Tam and Miguel. "He could have moved anywhere in the city for what he paid for renovations, but it's where he wanted to live. There was an incident, and two people he considered friends were injured, badly. He tried to change them both and it didn't work."

I left it there. Either Sky worked out the rest for herself, or she lived in happy ignorance. The important thing was that she had some idea of what Gavin had been through.

I sighed. The more I thought about it, the less likely it was that Gavin could get past what had happened.

"One of us can change her, it's fine," I said. "The next best choice will be Dr. Jeremy. But it would be best for this pack, for Gavin, if he does."

Sky looked at me in confusion, so I continued.

"When you change someone, a bond, a special connection, is formed. Similar to that of a recently changed vampire and his sire."

It wasn't a comparison I liked. Vampires were cruel in their acts of creation, and in the way they treated each other afterward. But Sky was still new to this world and sometimes she needed help understanding what was at stake.

"Are you sure about that?" she asked. "Because I distinctly remember Chris trying to cut Demetrius's head off with a kitchen knife. Or am I missing the special bond thing?"

"But she didn't."

"Because I stopped her!"

"She let you stop her. It's the sire bond that allowed her to show restraint."

"Oh, my fault, I didn't realize not cutting someone's head off with a kitchen knife is a show of endearment. I'm going to go drop that from the dysfunctional category."

"It's Chris," I said, all the explanation that dysfunction ever needed. "Can you imagine Gavin if Kelly is changed? I don't want to force him to do it, but they both need it. He needs to have a successful change, and I think she needs it to be him."

"You want me to talk to him, again?"

I nodded. "He responds well to you. He likes you."

"You're using both of those words wrong."

It might not have been agreement as I knew it, but Sky was going to do the right thing. Happy to see her cooperating without resistance for once, and happier still to see her finding her place in the pack, I leaned in and kissed her on the cheek.

"I have to go; are you staying up here?"

She shook her head. "I can't. I have to go talk to a weird panther who's probably skulking in the shadows somewhere, being… well… Gavin-y."

I laughed. It was a very Sky way of describing the world.

"See, you have a way with him. I just call him a pain in my ass."

By the middle of the afternoon, we were all set to apply Jeremy's unorthodox cure. Weres had been found who were willing to turn all the new arrivals and to take care of them in the aftermath, to help them settle into the pack and our life. Sky and Sebastian had between them worked the necessary magic on Gavin, who took responsibility for Kelly. A potentially overwhelming situation was well under our control.

Then Claudia phoned.

"I've picked my way through Estevez's spell," she said. "I know where to find him and how to tackle him. Are you ready?"

I looked at the gathered weres, all waiting to be told who they were converting, and at Winter, who had helped me herd them here. Someone else could handle this from now on. It was time for me to face one of our other problems.

"I'm ready," I said. "I'll pick you up shortly."

I hung up the phone and turned to Winter.

"Take this," I said, handing her the list of who was dealing with who. "Make the introductions, then leave them to it."

"That's it?" she asked, pulling a face.

"What, you thought I was going to hold their hands and offer comforting thoughts?"

I strode out of the retreat and climbed into my car. Within an hour, I was racing out of Chicago with Claudia beside me in the passenger seat.

"I should have known he was staying at that house," I said, thinking back to the grand mansion whose walls I'd stood outside twice before. "No one buys a place like that and leaves it empty."

"Oh, dear." Claudia touched my arm. "You clearly haven't paid enough attention to the truly rich. This Estevez has three places more expensive than this one in Illinois alone. I doubt he stays in any of them for more than a few months out of the year. This just happens to be the one he's living in this week."

I shook my head. I knew that my life was a good one, with enough money from legal work, investments, and pack activities to pay for a nice house and a selection of good cars. But the idea of owning multiple places like Estevez's mansion was mind-blowing, the idea of leaving them to sit empty borderline insane.

I glanced at Claudia, about to ask if she'd ever been part of that sort of high life, and realized that something was wrong. She sat stiffly in her seat, hands clasped in her lap, holding a small wooden box with brass fittings in her gloved hands. I'd seen her preoccupied before, I'd seen her angry, I'd seen her concerned, but I'd never seen her nervous like this. The idea that anything could have such an effect on Claudia left me worrying on my own behalf.

"Are you okay?" I asked.

She took a deep breath and hesitated before she spoke.

"I know that you have faced some difficult enemies, Ethan. I have faced my own challenges over many years. But this is something more than either of us is used to. Not just an angry vampire or a scheming little toad like Logan. We're about to face real power, a Tre'ase of incredible strength empowered by this magical network of his. The existing connection between him and the spirit shade inside you only adds to the risk."

"I'm ready for it," I said. Whatever it took to keep my family safe, that was a fight I was willing to face. The odds didn't matter to me. I'd find a way to beat them. "For Josh's sake."

"For Josh." Claudia smiled.

"If we keep on like this, he's going to owe you his life a dozen times over," I said.

"You're the one carrying the burden of the spirit shade that kept him alive."

"And you're the one who used it to put part of the Vitae into him. Without that, the Creed's curse on our mother would have killed him years ago."

"I have to do it," Claudia said, her expression grim. "My friendship with your mother was important to me, and it drove a wedge between her and the Creed. I put Josh in danger."

"No. The Creed were the ones who chose to inflict a terrible punishment on an innocent child."

"Whoever you want to blame, I owe it to your mother to keep him alive, no matter what it costs me."

I slowed down as we approached Estevez's country estate. I wanted a good look at the place while we drove past. Then I'd park and we could come back on foot, ready to scale the walls, break through the wards, and hopefully get in without triggering every alarm in the place.

As we drew near, the gates of the estate swung open. I

expected to see someone drive out, but there was no one there.

I glanced at Claudia.

"Should we…?"

"It would seem rude not to," she said, hands clasping tighter in her lap.

I drove through the gates, which closed with a clang behind us, past rows of flowering bushes and ornamental trees, up the gravel driveway to the turning circle in front of the house. We stepped out of the car at the bottom of a wide flight of stone stairs with a pair of oak doors at the top. As I glanced at them, the doors swung open.

"So much for the element of surprise," I said. "Do we need to rethink this?"

Claudia shook her head. "We're committed now. Let's face the music."

We walked up the stairs and through those looming double doors. A grand entrance hall opened out in front of us, with a tiled floor, sweeping stairs at the back, and sculptures on pedestals around the walls. In the center stood a single man, short and stocky, his black hair peppered with gray, a mustache bristling above his wide smile. He held his arms out wide, as if welcoming an old friend.

"You must be Ethan Charleston," he said, a predatory gleam shining through that smile. "And my dear Claudia, I've been expecting you."

CHAPTER 15

"Do you know this guy?" I asked Claudia with a frown.

She shook her head as she stared at the little man with his big grin and his bushy mustache.

"I don't recognize the face, but faces can change." She walked toward him. "Have we met before?"

"Sadly, no," he said. "But I know you by reputation. We have moved in similar circles from time to time over the years, and my accountant tells me I have invested in works from your gallery. Art can be a good hedge against more conventional markets, if you have the right experts to help."

"You're Estevez?" I asked, studying him. Though his appearance was initially innocuous, he radiated power, something dark and ancient stirring behind that smile.

"That is the name I go by these days, though I have had many others over the years, just as I have had many other faces. But then, who hasn't?"

I stayed by the doorway as Claudia advanced across the room toward Estevez. Something about this situation didn't feel right. Why would he reveal himself to us like this if he knew who we were? What did he have to gain that he couldn't have gotten by simply coming to the pack or to Claudia's gallery and introducing himself?

He held his hand out and Claudia took it.

"A pleasure to meet you," she said.

"Believe me, the pleasure is all mine."

A vicious grin split Estevez's face as he gripped Claudia's hand tight. Dark tendrils of magic shot from his fingers, wrapping themselves around her arm and writhing their way toward her shoulder. Claudia sank to her knees, her face screwed up in pain.

I ran toward them. Estevez held up a hand and a barrier filled the air between us. Hitting it was like running into tar. I found myself caught in place, barely able to move, fighting my way through the air.

"I've been looking forward to this for so long," Estevez said, leaning in toward Claudia. "Yours is such a unique and spectacular array of powers. Absorbing them will take me to giddy new heights."

Claudia gasped as the tendrils of power touched her neck. "You're killing me."

"Sometimes, sacrifices must be made. I have worked so hard to make this one happen, to draw you to a place where I have complete control, where none of your friends or allies can come to the rescue, where my strength is at its greatest and yours at its most limited.

"I thought I had you when you used my spirit shade to save Josh. By opening up to its power, you created an opening for me. I could almost taste my triumph. But then you put the shade in this one"—he gestured at me—"a were-animal with the strength to contain it, a rare thing indeed. That set my plans back by years, but years are nothing when you have centuries to work with."

As he spoke, I drew on the power inside me. I'd broken

through wards before. For all his bluster, I was sure I could break through this one.

I had to. Claudia's life was at stake.

As the power emerged from me, there wasn't the usual clash of contact with another form of magic. Instead, it seeped into the spell holding me in place, the similarity of the two letting them mix and combine. Estevez's hold over me softened but didn't shatter. I forced myself forward, one step, then another.

"Impressive," he said, looking at me. "But I have something else to deal with you."

He clicked his fingers and a figure appeared on the stairs at the back of the hall. It was only half solid, a cloud of darkness that faded at the edges like the trailing away of mist. It advanced with human movements, but its face was blank, a featureless shadow in which all personality was lost.

"I have made more than one spirit shade over the years," Estevez said. "This was to replace the one I let you have. It has been waiting a long time to meet its dark brother, and now we get to see which of you is stronger. I have to admit, I'm intrigued."

With a sudden flash of power, Estevez was flung back. He held up his hand, from which severed tendrils of magic still hung, and glared at Claudia as she backed away, her own hand glowing with power. The glove that normally covered it had burned away, ashes floating out onto the air. She looked drained, but she was at least free of his grasp.

"You thought it would be this easy?" she asked, her voice taking on a hollow boom like the sounding of an ancient drum. "I have power you can't even dream of, little Tre'ase."

"Excellent." Estevez raised his hands and magic crackled like lightning around them. "A challenge."

The spell holding me back vanished as Estevez drew the power back into himself, but before I could attack him, the spirit shade was on me. Ghostly hands grabbed hold and flung me against the wall.

I landed on my feet, head spinning and blood in my mouth. The shade charged at me, fists raised. At the last moment, I stepped aside, letting it punch the wall while I swung a fist at its head.

It was like punching a cloud. My fist went straight through, but the head remained intact.

The shade shot out a leg, catching me in the midriff. The kick was as solid as any blow I'd ever felt, but when I tried to grab its foot, my hands went straight through.

If I couldn't hurt the shade in my human form, then maybe my wolf could do better. I took a step back and let the animal emerge, clothes ripping as my body contorted. Bones stretched, muscles writhed, hair burst through my skin, and I stood on four legs, teeth bared, growling at the shade.

Without a face, there was no way to judge the spirit shade's feelings, if it even had them. The only reaction I could see was its renewed attack, lunging at me with both hands. I darted aside, nimble on four feet, then snapped at the shade. My teeth tore through its side, and it seemed more solid than before. A chunk of the cloud came away in my teeth. But it wasn't enough. The shape reformed, more of its body flowing in to fill the gap. It swung a fist and sent me flying.

My wolf had changed the odds, but I needed something more. I called upon the magic inside me, the power of another spirit shade, let it flow down my legs, through my paws, into my claws. I didn't try to shape it into any sort of spell or ward, just let it become part of my wolf form, a cold and deadly power.

I could feel my spirit shade responding to the one I faced. There was recognition there, but not a friendly kind. An animosity born of spite and jealousy, sibling rivalry turned toxic, drove these two to fight each other.

I leapt at the spirit shade, sinking my claws into its body. It was solid to me now, a real thing that I could rip and tear. It wrapped an arm around my neck and pulled me in, even as its other hand battered at my head. I clawed and bit while it punched and choked. The two of us fell to the ground, rolling over and over in a struggle to the death.

"Ethan!" Claudia cried out.

I looked up to see her caught in a magical battle with Estevez, the air between them thick with magic. I'd never seen her like this, with her true power unleashed, and there was something about it that filled me with dread.

Claudia wasn't winning any more than I was. Our opponents had been ready for this moment and they were wearing us down. Estevez's spells were tearing away Claudia's defenses and the world around me was starting to fade as the spirit shade tightened its grip on my throat.

"Do you trust me?" Claudia shouted.

I nodded my head and let out a desperate howl.

"Then let him in." She flung up a hand, dropping one of her protective spells to fling a different sort of magic in my direction. It hit the spirit shade, and at the moment of impact the spell pushed the shade into me. I dropped my defenses to let it in.

And then the world turned to black.

I woke floating in nothingness, a gray void. But even as I woke, that void was starting to change. Images flashed past, moments in my life, things I had seen and done. The world took shape around me, familiar places blinking in and out of existence, until I stood in an exaggerated image of the pack's living room. The colors were brighter, the furniture larger, the smell richer than it had ever been.

So this was my inner world, the spirit of Ethan. It made

sense. Where did I feel more at home than among my people?

Except that those people weren't here. There was just me and the opposing spirit shade.

I looked down at myself. I wasn't in wolf form anymore. Instead, I was something half wolf and half human, furred and clawed but standing upright. Instead of the abominations Dexter and Marcia had created by combining man and animal, I was something glorious—sleek, muscled, elegant—and around me shimmered an aura of power, the magic of the spirit shade inside me.

The other shade was still a black featureless figure, but it was solid now, its body given a clear outline instead of fading into the air.

"I guess it's time for the real fight," I said with a grin.

I charged across the room, clawed hands out by my sides. The shade tried to sidestep away from my attack, but I saw it coming and adjusted my course. I slammed, shoulder first, into the shade, smashing it back into the wall, then tore at it with my claws. Shreds of darkness filled the air, floating like ribbons to the ground.

The shade grabbed my arm with both hands and twisted, wrenching me around. With staggering strength, it flung me from my feet. I hurtled into a window, which shattered as I hit.

But this was my world that the shade had come into. Instead of a shower of razor-sharp glass, the window exploded into a cloud of feathers that I fell safely through, landing softly on the ground outside. I turned and tensed, ready to face my opponent.

The shade sailed through the empty window frame, its torn body trailing behind it. I leapt to meet it and we collided in midair. My fist hit the shade's face, knocking its head back, and the two of us crashed to the ground with me on top. I raised my hand, stretched my claws, and slashed at its face, tearing away until there was almost nothing left. At last, the shade stopped resisting and fell still.

I rose to my feet and stood panting over the remains of the shade. What should I do now? Had I won?

A realization hit me. This wasn't a real fight. It was my way of understanding an internal battle, a struggle for control between my shade and the invader. It wouldn't be over until I had destroyed this thing completely. As long as any part of it remained, I was still at risk.

Sure enough, the shade's body started to shift, streams of smoke slowly rising to form a new head. I couldn't give it time to recover. I needed to end this.

I flung the limp spirit shade over my shoulder and looked around. I needed some place to get rid of this, somewhere it could be gone from my life for good. Where did darkness go to die?

As I considered the question, the world around me responded, and I laughed when I saw the answer that my subconscious had found.

Demetrius's house stood before me, its door wide open.

I walked in. The interior of the house was empty—no furniture, no decorations, a hollow shell of a home just as Demetrius was a hollow shell of a person.

In the middle of the floor was a pit so dark that its very walls were nothing but blackness. I flung the shade's body into the hole and it vanished without a sound.

The house around me faded as the world turned to gray.

I woke on the floor of Estevez's mansion. The air was filled with magic and the sound of spells dispersing. I shook my head, found that I was still in wolf form, and dragged myself up onto my paws.

The shade was gone, not even a drifting remnant of its

dark fog left behind. But Estevez was still here, locked in deadly combat with Claudia.

As I pulled myself together, I watched the battle between them. Claudia's magic wasn't like anything else I had seen. Instead of blocking Estevez's spells she nullified them, creating an area around her that no magic could touch. Blasts of power vanished as they hit it. Knickknacks and furniture, flung by force across the room, stopped the moment they came close. Lashing tendrils of power fell limp at its edge.

But that bubble of nullification was receding. Moment by moment, Estevez was wearing away at Claudia's defenses, his attacks coming closer and closer to striking her. The strain of the battle showed on his face, his smile replaced with a snarl, his forehead crumpled and coated with sweat. But Claudia looked worse. Her skin was pale and she had sunk to one knee beneath the sheer unrelenting force of his attacks.

The sight filled me with horror at the thought of losing Claudia, followed a moment later by a renewed anger and determination. If their fight continued, he would overwhelm her, steal her power, and leave her as a lifeless husk. But Claudia wasn't alone anymore.

I ran across the room, teeth bared, howling from the bottom of my lungs. Estevez turned and flung a bolt of magic at me, a sizzling blast of burning power. But it vanished as it hit me, absorbed by a power that came from the same source: my spirit shade.

I slammed into Estevez, knocking him to the ground. I landed on him, two paws pressed against his chest, my teeth around his throat. Rage riding my body, I pressed my jaws closer together. Blood ran from his neck.

"Wait, Ethan!" Claudia said.

She stood beside me, clutching the brass-bound box she had brought with her.

"Remember, you can't kill him. If you do that, then we lose the spirit shade."

"She's right," Estevez croaked, a look of triumph on his face. "Destroy me and that power within you dies. That protection you've woven around your precious brother, it will evaporate and the curse will win. Keep on squeezing with those deadly teeth of yours and you'll kill him."

His gloating just made me want to hurt him more, to rip his throat out and leave him lifeless in the mansion that symbolized all his power and wealth. But then this would have been for nothing. Worse than nothing—it would have killed Josh, the person I had set out to protect.

I let go of his throat, took my paws off his chest, and took a step back, never taking my eyes off of him.

"So much better," Estevez said, sitting up. He touched a hand to his throat. The wounds healed and the blood vanished. "If you're not going to kill me, I'm afraid that you'll have to let me go. Such a pity for you both, spending the rest of your lives looking over your—"

"Oh, shut up," Claudia said, opening the lid of the box.

A wind whistled through the mansion as Estevez's power was sucked from the air around us and into the box. His smug expression turned to horror as he stared into it, eyes wide as if gazing into the abyss. His hair flapped around him and his jowls trembled as the same force dragging in the magic pulled at him.

"You wouldn't," he hissed.

"Why not?" Claudia asked. "After all, I don't want to spend the rest of my life looking over my shoulder."

The wind dragged Estevez across the floor straight to the box.

"No!" he screamed. "I promise, I'll give you anything you want. Money, power, knowledge, I have it all. Please don't—"

His words were cut short as his head hit the box. For a moment, it seemed as though he turned to liquid, his body flowing across itself as it was sucked in with the rest of his magic. Then he was gone and Claudia slammed the lid shut on him.

"Trapped," she said, patting the box. "And good riddance to a ghastly man."

"Is that it?" I asked, staring at the box. It was incredible to think that this small cube of wood had finally trapped a being of such power.

"I'll need to find a safe space to store this, but once that's done, yes, that's it. Estevez, or whatever name he prefers to go by, will be trapped in a pocket world until someone breaks the seal and lets him out. Only death is forever, but I intend to make this imprisonment last nearly as long.

"Josh is safe. Now it's time for you and I to head home."

We walked out the door of the grand house and down to the car. As we went, I felt the magic changing in the world around us. The web that Estevez had woven, the one that had given him so much power and protection, was starting to collapse. Without him at the center, the threads were unraveling.

"What will happen to all this power?" I asked.

"It will flow back into the world. Others will find ways to use it, hopefully ones that are less greedy. Hoarding so much power for so long has limited what else could be done. There's more magic available for everyone in Illinois now, and I'll be interested to see what they do with it."

I thought of Ariel, London, and their new Creed.

"I can think of some witches who would benefit from a power boost right now."

"So Ariel made her move at last?" Claudia asked as she climbed into the car.

"You knew about that?" I asked, settling into the driver's seat. "Why didn't you tell us?"

"It wasn't my secret to tell, any more than this is." She patted the box. "If word gets out that we have trapped a powerful Tre'ase, others will try to find him, so that they can bargain to release him in return for some of that power. We can't let that happen. This has to be a secret between us, understand?"

I nodded. After everything we'd done to protect Josh, keeping one more secret was hardly a strain.

CHAPTER 16

We gathered in a large room at the retreat, a gathering of all the most influential weres in North America. Every Alpha was here, along with others like me who had come to support and advise their leaders. If this worked, then it was going to be a monumental day. If not, then they needed to see what happened.

Sky and Josh stood in the middle of the room. Josh had been working on this spell for days, creating something new from pieces of existing incantations, combining modern lore with ancient Faerie magic, all with the aim of freeing us from the lunar curse.

I watched anxiously as he whispered something to Sky. I was proud of both of them—proud of Josh for creating this spell and proud of Sky for her willingness to risk herself, taking on magic of immense and uncertain power, to protect the rest of us. Seeing the way the Alphas deferred to them, if only for this one moment, reminded me of what powerful and important people they had both become.

Still, there was that anxiety, the fear for how the spell might go. We were on uncertain ground, facing great powers with experimental magic. There were no guarantees that this would work, and the hope that ran excitedly through the room could easily be shattered. But failure wasn't the worst-case scenario. The worst case was something more, that Sky and Josh might unleash something harmful, might make things worse while trying to fix them.

I believed in both Sky and Josh, believed in their skill, their courage, and their determination. But I didn't understand the spell, and that left space for a terrible doubt to flourish.

At a nod from Sky, Josh ran the blade of a knife across her hand. I winced at the sight of her being injured, even such a little thing for an important cause.

As blood welled from the wound and Josh caught it in a bowl below, Sky started to chant. I recognized the strange syllables of the Faerie language as Sky reached out to Maya. Then the words faded away and Sky stood, eyes glazed, caught in a trance.

Around the room, Alphas waited expectantly to see what would come next. As the minutes dragged on, they shuffled their feet and glanced uncertainly at each other, no one knowing how long this would last, whether they were allowed to speak or if it would break the spell. Sebastian stood in respectful silence, hands clasped in front of him, while Niimi, the Canadian Alpha, stood entranced. Cole's gaze slid around the room, watching and judging everyone's reactions. When his eyes met mine, the two of us exchanged a cold, menacing stare.

My hands started to tingle. I looked down but couldn't see any change in them. Around the room, others were doing the same, looking at their hands or patting at their faces as the sensation spread. I felt it sweep up my arms, across my head, down through my body and legs to the tips of my toes. The spell was doing something, but was it doing what we needed?

A twitch contorted Niimi's expression. Her leg spasmed and she fell to the floor, clutching her thigh.

I looked around in alarm as the tingling in my own body grew more insistent. Weres were falling to the ground, arms and legs writhing as their muscles moved against their will. Sebastian fell and I moved to catch him, but my leg twisted. I stumbled and fell as the magic overcame me.

I lay on the ground, teeth grinding, body writhing, arms and legs twitching as a series of spasms ran through me. It was like the sensation of changing into animal form, but with every point of discomfort made a hundred times worse, and without the knowledge of how it would end. My body was beyond my control, my heart racing, breath rasping. My head hit the ground and my back buckled. I wanted to cry out in pain but my throat was clamped shut.

If this magic didn't save us, then it seemed set to kill us all.

Then the tingling started to fade. The magic receded and the spasms with it. I gasped for breath and looked around.

Sky lay in the middle of the room, a bloody knife in one hand and a second cut running across the other. Josh knelt by her side, a look of concern on his face. All around, the weres were starting to sit up, clutching shaken heads and trembling limbs.

One by one, we dragged ourselves to our feet.

Was this it? Were we free of the curse?

Sebastian lifted his shirt.

"Well?" he asked.

I looked at his shoulder and shook my head. The mark was still there.

Within a few minutes, the disappointing truth stood revealed. All that pain had been for nothing. The mark was still on every one of us. True death was coming for the weres.

Sky looked shaken by her experience. Josh took hold of her hand, their fingers intertwining, and something passed between them, some moment not just of human contact but of magic. She smiled.

"Better?" he asked.

Sky nodded. Then she looked at me and frowned. Her gaze swept around the room, a look of doubt growing as she took in each of us.

"I need some air," she said and hurried out.

"Sky!" I called, running after her. But my legs were still shaking, my movements weak. By the time I reached the door of the retreat, she was gone, out of sight in the woods, leaving a trail of discarded clothing behind her.

I walked out to the edge of the woods. I could smell Sky's presence, could sense her in the distance, but I knew better than to run after her. She had retreated into her wolf for comfort, a way to escape whatever she had seen and felt during the spell. It was good that she took comfort in the wolf now, that it had become a source of reassurance instead of something she struggled against. She was truly one of us, and that acceptance would help her find her place in the pack. Better to leave her to this. The two of us could talk once she was done.

I stood at the edge of the woodland, waiting for Sky to emerge. An hour passed with her still somewhere in the distance. Another hour, and still she wasn't back. I fought back my frustration. We needed to discuss what had happened, to work out how close she and Josh had come to a cure, whether there was any chance that we could try this again. But more immediately than that, I needed to know that she was all right. We had all been through a shock, and those of us watching had been through the physical trauma of having our bodies rocked by magic, but I didn't know what Sky had seen or felt, and that worried me.

At last she came close and settled down to rest in a nearby group of trees. I approached carefully, not wanting to alarm her.

"Sky," I said softly as I approached.

She was still in her wolf form, curled up on the ground. She looked up as if considering me for a long moment, then set her head back down.

I needed the human Sky to return, to tell me what she had seen. The wolf gave her comfort, but the pack needed information.

"Sky, look at me," I said, kneeling down next to her. "You've been gone for three hours. Change."

I reached out to touch her, to re-form the connection between us and urge her back into human form. She snapped at me with her teeth and I snatched my hand back.

"Sky. Change. Now."

We didn't have time to waste. If the spell wouldn't work, if something else was needed, then the pack had to know that as soon as possible.

Sky howled and buried her head in her paws. For a moment I was angry. I expected better of her than to hide from the world when we needed her. But then I remembered that she was the one who had gone through the magic, who had faced Maya's power only to see the spell fail. Whatever she had experienced, she clearly needed help getting past it.

"Okay." I sat down next to her. I could wait, if that was what she needed.

She slid over, settled her head in my lap, and fell instantly asleep.

I sat in the woods, listening to Sky's breathing. Snatches of conversation drifted out to me from the retreat as the Alphas tried to make sense of what had happened. Part of me was impatient to get back there, to listen to their opinions and help plan our next step. But another part of me was glad to be away from it all, to have an excuse to sit and rest. With the curse looming over us, it was hard to find a moment of peace.

The problems I faced raced around my mind. The curse. Cole's politicking. The secrets between me and Sky. Not knowing what had happened to her during the spell, why she had run off into the woods. Every time I pushed one issue aside, another thrust up its head.

And yet, when I looked down at Sky and stroked her fur, those worries vanished. Just for a moment, I found peace, before all the troubles came crashing back in.

Around dusk, Sky yawned, stretched, and then shifted into her human form. I took a moment to admire the view as she lay there naked, then took off my own shirt and handed it to her. She put it on, and we started walking hand in hand to the house.

"You are going to have to tell me what happened," I said. "That's not negotiable."

"I saw the world as it once was," she said, a shiver of fear passing through her. "The original were-animals, fierce and brutal. Vampires like creatures out of nightmares. Witches wielding huge power. It was terrible to see how we began, cruel and bestial, reveling in violence.

"Then I saw the bronze man, the one I met before in the in-between, the one who looks like you. He shifted, turning from one animal to another, trying on new forms like they were clothes in a store. There was this feeling of dread all around him, of death seeping out into the world."

She fell silent for a long moment, then looked up at me.

"Ethan, what are you? Don't tell me you're just a wolf. It all just seems so wrong. You seem wrong sometimes."

I didn't know what her vision meant, whether it had anything to do with the powers in me or whether her mind had just used my face as something familiar, a way to understand what she was looking at. I hadn't felt the power of the spirit shade stirring while the spell was cast, hadn't tried in any way to resist, and I didn't think that the shade could have acted without my knowing anything at all. It wasn't part of the spell's failure, but it had been there while the magic was cast. Perhaps Sky had sensed its presence through the spell.

Whatever she had seen, she wanted the truth, and I couldn't share it. The spirit shade was still a secret too far.

"Sky, I'm not sure why that happened or why your mind has chosen to—"

She snatched her hand away from me.

"Ethan, don't."

At the edge of the woods, someone had gathered Sky's clothes and left them out for her. She snatched them up, put them on, and tossed my shirt back to me, watching me the whole time. Her every movement bristled with anger, and I was sorry that I couldn't give her what she wanted, but I had people to protect, people who included her.

As I watched her dress, I had a sudden sense of déjà vu. A fond memory came to me, of seeing Sky turn to wolf on her own for the first time, right here on this spot. The memory was so vivid, every detail painted across my mind, and I smiled just thinking about how I'd been there for a crucial moment in her life.

A realization hit me like a hammer blow: I loved Sky.

No one else was emblazoned across my brain the way she was. No one else made me feel so alive. No one else could bring me peace amid the turmoil of our lives.

"I think I've done enough to earn the pack's trust, your trust," she said. "I can't be in the dark, struggling for some glimpse of clarity, only to be blindsided when you all need me. I'm not going to do this, Ethan."

I didn't want to be the one causing her pain, yet here I was, wounding her with the secrets I used to keep her safe. I was torn in two. Telling her my secrets could hurt her and others around us, but keeping them was already hurting her, and it threatened to tear us apart.

"It's complicated," I managed, unable to drag anything else out past my conflicting desires, the need to tell her and the need to keep my secrets.

"It always is," she snapped, then strode off into the house.

I didn't follow. What would I do, tell her I loved her when I couldn't even tell her the truth?

Needing to blow off steam, I headed down into the pack's basement gym. For the next few hours I lifted weights, jumped rope, did push-ups, anything to burn off this restless energy and help my mind to settle.

Was I really this monstrous figure Sky had seen in her visions, this bronze man striding through a nightmare landscape? I didn't buy it. Yes, I had powers that other people didn't, thanks to the unique combination of dark elf ancestry, were-animal, and the spirit shade living inside of me. As the Beta of the Midwest Pack, I also had influence over the people around me, and on the politics of the supernatural across the region. But that didn't mean that our problems somehow revolved around me, or that I was some figure of destruction striding through the world. I was just one were-animal trying to do my best for the people in my care.

I'd been doing well lately. We'd rescued Kelly from Dexter and Marcia, and in the process added some talented new people to the pack. Claudia and I had fought a spirit shade and trapped a Tre'ase, ensuring Josh's safety. But where Sky was concerned, apparently anything I did wasn't good enough unless I was telling her every last detail of my life. Sometimes it seemed like she didn't even want to be with a Beta, a position that many weres would aspire to for its own sake, never mind the attraction between us.

The situation was impossible.

I was doing bench presses when Winter came in.

"Have you been down here the whole time?" she asked.

"Probably," I said. "What time is it?"

"Half past midnight."

I set the bar on its rest and sat up. I didn't have work tomorrow, but that didn't mean that I could spend the whole night in the gym.

Still, I felt restless, my body twitching for action, my mind spinning through everything that had happened over the past few days, everything that might happen now if we couldn't find a way to lift the curse.

"Here." Winter threw a wooden practice sword to me. "I need someone to spar with."

I followed her to the sparring floor. We raised the wooden blades, then took fighting stances.

To an outsider, the wooden weapons might have looked like a way of going soft on one another. They reduced the risk of real injury, made the sparring floor a safer place. But between me and Winter, they were a sign that no punches would be pulled. Without real blades, we could go at each other with every move we had, without the risk of someone ending up dead. Winter was in the mood to fight hard.

She started the fight, coming at me with a series of short, sharp strikes, her movements flowing with a deadly grace as they always had. I parried them all and then counterattacked, putting her on the defensive.

I knew Winter too well to think that this was me winning. She had just been probing my defenses, testing to see how I would respond. Now she was seeing how I attacked, what mood I was in, what strikes I preferred, judging the speed of my reactions and whether I'd learned anything new since we last fought.

Then it was time to start the contest for real.

We went at each other with furious flurries of blows, leaping and darting, stabbing and swinging. Parry turned straight into counterattack, became a complex sequence of maneuvers meant to put the other person off guard, to draw their blade away and get past their defenses. In an unarmed fight, I could get the better of Winter eight times in ten, but even on my good days she was the better swordsman. She got three hits in on me—two on the arm and one on the ribs —before I got one in against her, a glancing strike against her shin that left me vulnerable to a hit on the head.

That blow made me more determined to prove what I was worth. I feinted left then made as if to move right, but that was a second feint. The real blow followed the same path as the fake one, and by then her weapon was moving away. My blade thudded against her upper thigh.

"Good one," she said, backing off while she considered her next move. "Did you learn that from Sebastian?"

I shook my head, even as I thought back over all the people I'd sparred with recently. Where had I picked that idea up from?

"Sky did it to me," I said. "Though I don't think it was on purpose. She just forgot to switch attacks."

Winter laughed. "That's very Sky, accidentally getting through your defenses."

I went at Winter again, using a series of strikes to draw her parries away from the center, then wheeling around to stab at her shoulder. But Winter was ready, parrying every blow, easily deflecting the last one and hitting me on the upper arm. As I snapped my weapon back to a defensive posture, she brought hers around, pressed my blade so that it twisted my wrist, and knocked the weapon from my hand.

"Disarmed," she said, tutting and resting the wooden sword point against my throat. "What are you going to do now, wolf boy?"

"If you were anyone else? Kill you with my claws."

"And because it's me?"

"Same, but I'll have to work harder."

We both laughed.

I picked up my sword and got ready to fight again.

"Seriously?" Winter said. "We've been at this for over an hour, and before that you'd been working out since around the dawn of time. Don't you need to rest?"

I grimaced. Rest sounded good, but still there was that twitching in my nerves.

Winter watched me, clearly aware that something was the matter, but quite deliberately keeping that observation to herself. This sort of behavior was one of her better qualities.

"I can't sleep right now," I admitted. "Too much on my mind."

"It's a hard life being the boss," Winter said in a mocking tone. Then her expression shifted into something more quizzical. "If that really is what's keeping you awake."

"Among other things."

"Then stop focusing on those things and focus on what will relax you. Where can you find peace?"

I wanted to say that I found peace in the pack, but I was pretty sure that had never been true. I found companionship here, found purpose, found a sense of satisfaction, but I also found endless challenges and reasons to be alert.

Then I remembered sitting in the woods earlier, listening to the wind while Sky slept off her run. There was one place where I found peace, and that was with her.

"I should go," I said.

"I bet," Winter said, a mischievous grin on her face. "But don't forget to shower and change first. You stink like a man who's been working out all day."

I headed up to the bedrooms, and finally found one that wasn't occupied by our new arrivals. Most of the clean clothes I kept at the retreat had been given out to the new weres, as we struggled to deal with an influx of ragged refugees. I found a loose pair of jeans and a shirt that would just about fit, then got cleaned up, dressed, and into my car as fast as I could, before driving out to Sky's house.

I stood on the doorstep, sensing Sky's presence just beyond. The television was babbling away in the background. Apparently I wasn't the only one struggling to rest.

I knocked softly on the door, unsure whether she would want to see me. When she answered, she looked disheveled, weary from a long day, but as beautiful as ever.

"I couldn't sleep, either," I said.

Sky took my hand and led me to the bedroom. We lay down together, her head resting on my chest. I felt the softness of her skin, inhaled her sweet, familiar scent, ran a hand through her hair.

Within moments, I was asleep.

ay was the last of the new arrivals to leave the retreat. Some others would be staying with us long term, because they were struggling to adjust or had serious injuries to recover from. But many were leaving with the weres who had turned them, and who would now give them shelter and a place to stay while they adjusted to their new life.

Ray had gotten lucky. After some reluctance, Joan had agreed to turn him into a were-jaguar and take care of his transition into supernatural society. She was a good fit for him, someone who had experience looking after family, not just living the lone home life that was so common to weres. Someone who could help Ray and his family adjust to who he had become.

"Thanks for everything," he said to me, shaking my hand.

"No problem," I replied. "Joan will be doing all the hard work."

We looked over at the minivan waiting in the middle of the retreat's parking lot. Joan was leaning against the van, chatting with Ray's wife and their two kids. The family were smiling and relaxed, infinitely more at ease than they had been when we called on them three days before.

"She's amazing," Ray said, looking at Joan. "You know she found me a new job down south, so that I don't have to explain my absence or the changes in my health? Apparently it's with some company her pack part owns, so they can manage my absence if, you know, this stuff gets in the way."

He waved a hand to take in "this stuff"—the pack, our home, and the wider life implied behind it all.

"Joan's one of the best," I said. "She'll take great care of you."

"Still, I couldn't have made it through that first night without your help. If you ever need anything, just ask."

"Will do." I couldn't see a time when Ray would ever be of more help to me than I was to him. I knew this world, while he was a novice to it all, and I already had enough accountants in my life. But the thought was a kind one.

No sooner had we waved goodbye to Ray and his family than Joan and I found Sebastian walking out toward us.

"I'm glad I found you both," he said. "We need to talk about monitoring the former test subjects. Jeremy says we should be careful in case Dexter's work has long-term effects."

"Can we take this inside?" Joan asked. "I need a coffee."

Cole was standing in the doorway, looking out at us, that same smug smile as always on his lips. One more reason why I'd be glad once the curse was lifted: to get him out of here.

"Can we help you, Cole?" Sebastian asked.

"I need to talk to Ethan," he said. "But I think you two should be here as witnesses."

I tensed. There was a stiffness to his words and a gleam in his eye. I could see where this was going.

"I don't think this is the time to—" Sebastian began.

"With all due respect, Sebastian, I think this is exactly the time," Cole replied.

"Then get it over with," I snapped.

"Ethan, you went missing for hours yesterday when your pack needed you. It's not the first mistake you've made recently and it won't be the last. You're distracted, unfocused, and it's damaging the largest pack, which means it's bad for all of us. I challenge you for the role of Beta of the Midwest Pack."

"Cole," Joan began, "do you really think that you should be—"

"I accept," I said.

Bad as the timing was, I felt relieved. Cole had been dancing around this for months, building up to his big moment. Now I would have the chance to relieve the pressure his presence created, to lance a boil on the flank of the pack. All the anger I felt at his smug, manipulative behavior would finally have an outlet.

"We fight to the death," I added.

"From you, just what I'd expect," Cole said. "But I'm willing to risk it, for everybody's sake."

He turned his back on me and walked back inside.

As he went, a little worry crept through my relief. I might despise Cole, but even I had to admit that he was a damn good fighter. This was going to be a close challenge. Glad as I was to have a chance to get rid of him, I would have to be careful. If I wasn't at my best when the fight came, then I might not be the one walking away at the end.

"Ethan, you are an asset to this pack and it is stronger because of you"—Sebastian paused for several beats—"and Cole serves his purpose. But without you, the pack won't be the same. Does this have to be to the death?"

"It's a deterrent," I said. "A way to stop people from challenging just to test their luck. Besides, if I don't finish this for good, Cole will keep on issuing challenges. He's not going to be content until he's taken over."

"Then you'd better win," Joan said. "If I've got to choose

between working with the Midwest asshole or the East Coast playboy, I'll take the asshole every time."

It was good to know that my friends had my back, but that didn't stop the mix of anger and anxiety bubbling away inside me. Cole's meddling was finally coming to a peak, and I had to deal with it, just as I'd known I would do. The timing could hardly be worse. He was so caught up in his own importance, and the importance of his mission to take over leadership of the packs, that he hadn't thought about what would happen once word got around. Now, time and energy I should be committing to the curse would instead go on preparing to fight him, as well as managing other people's responses to the challenge, trying to keep order in the pack as trouble stirred.

I needed to find my place of peace, to calm my mind while I thought about the practicalities of the challenge. I could feel Sky nearby, but I also felt a tug of anxiety at the thought of seeing her. She'd made it clear that she didn't like challenges for rank, least of all fights to the death, and now I had agreed to one with Cole. I wasn't going to get any calm if I talked with her about what was happening, but it was possible that she didn't know yet. If I kept quiet, I could find the peace I needed for just a little while.

Smiling at the thought of seeing Sky, I followed my instinctive tug toward her as it led me to the door of the library.

Looking in, the smile vanished off my face. Sky was sitting there as expected, the Clostra open in front of her, but Cole was there, too, his chair pulled up close by her, leaning in as he examined the magical text. His whole posture of study was bullshit. The pages of the manuscript went blank when anyone but Sky or her cousin looked at it. Cole had just found an excuse to get close.

What was he doing here? Was he really after Sky, perhaps deluding himself that she came as part of the package for the

Beta of the Midwest Pack? Or was he getting close to her to aggravate me, to try to throw me off balance for the fight that lay ahead?

If that was what he wanted, then he'd gotten it, for all the good it would do him. Seeing him there with her made me mad as hell.

"This place is a world of wonder," Cole said, like some wide-eyed kid in a chocolate factory. He got up from his seat, took down a few books, and flicked through them before putting them back. Like I thought, all show and no studying. "I haven't heard Latin spoken often, but to my untrained ears, you speak it quite beautifully, for a novice."

"And you can learn Latin, too," I said, my voice rising more sharply than I had intended. "Why don't you take the book and go study somewhere?"

Cole looked at me like I was a bug on his windshield, just some inconvenience to be wiped away. Then he turned his attention back to Sky.

Even in my own home, he couldn't resist goading me. He wanted my position, my prestige, the woman in my life, and he wasn't even making a pretense of respecting the life of our pack. Why should I respect his challenge? I'd take him on here and now, tear him down and get this over with.

I started moving toward him, fist clenched by my side. But before I could act, Josh walked in, a coffee cup in each hand. He stepped between me and Cole, cutting off my advance, handed one cup to me and the other to Sky.

"It probably needs to be warmed up a little," he said.

I wasn't going to be so easily distracted. Ignoring him, I kept my gaze on Cole. Let him know that I was ready. Let him feel the coming of my wrath.

Sky placed a hand on my stomach, trying to usher me back out of the room.

"We should warm it up," she said, waving her cup. "I'm

about to become caffeine-less Sky. No one likes her. Right, Josh?"

"Why do you think I brought it? I can barely stand her, and since we have work that needs to be done, please get her some warm coffee."

Their antics weren't subtle, but they had worked. The immediacy of my anger was fading, though my resentment at Cole still smoldered as he watched me with a mocking frown. I would have my chance to deal with him soon enough. The challenge had been made, a fight was coming, and I would beat the smugness right out of him.

Reluctantly, I let Sky lead me out of the library and away.

A few hours later, I stood in the library again, watching Cole as he stood on the far side of the room, looking like he owned the place. In saner times, we would already have scheduled the challenge fight and I would be preparing to get him out of our lives for good. But right now, we were all cursed, and even Cole accepted that had to take priority.

We were here for another attempt to break the curse. After getting me away from Cole, Sky had returned to the library and worked with Josh on creating a new spell. They both seemed nervous about the magic they were preparing to unleash, but that wasn't going to stop them, and we had gathered to see it begin. Sebastian was standing next to me, Cole opposite, with Joan and the West Coast Alpha on the other sides of the room. Witnesses and guinea pigs, here so that it would be immediately clear if the curse was lifted—or if it somehow got worse.

In the middle of the room stood Sky and Josh, their notes for the spell set out on a table next to them, hands out toward each other as they gathered the spell's power. Sky started a singsong chant, the words rising and falling to a musical rhythm. I watched for any sign that she was in trouble again, that the magic might hurt her, but Cole's presence was a constant distraction, drawing my attention away from Sky and Josh.

Sky faltered and muttered something under her breath.

"Just try again," Josh said.

Once again, Sky started the incantation, words and magic flowing. Her eyes darted back and forth between me, Cole, and Josh. Again, she stumbled over the singsong chant and a look of frustration crossed her face.

I wanted to step in, to tell her to take a break and rest, to come back to it refreshed, anything to ease her frustration and make this easier. But we couldn't afford to take a break. If this spell didn't work, then we needed to move straight on to the next solution, and the next, and the next, until we found a way to remove the curse or we ran out of time and were all doomed.

Sky started the spell for a third time. This time, she didn't even get halfway through before she lost the rhythm and gave up.

An awkward silence fell. I felt sorry for Sky, unable to get the spell right under pressure with all of us watching, and I worried at how Cole would twist this moment to his advantage.

"I need the room," Sebastian said, looking around at the rest of us spectators.

Nobody moved. This was such an important moment, we all felt a need to be here on behalf of our packs, to see what happened and report back. And for me, there was also the need to look after Sky, to support her in her magic and help her if anything went wrong. The rest of them could leave, but surely it made sense for me to be here.

Sebastian glared around, and the amber of his wolf's eyes showed, revealing the menace of the creature that lay within. Joan and the West Coast Alpha left, then Cole. I stood my ground. Sky and Josh were both at risk here. I couldn't leave them behind.

Still Sebastian stood, glaring at me.

"I won't ask again," he said.

I had never pushed Sebastian so far that he had to deal with me by force, but for a moment I felt that I might now. This was too important not to be present.

But that importance was also why I had to let go and stop getting in the way. I pushed off from the wall I'd been leaning against and walked out of the library.

The door closed behind me and I took up a position in front of it, like a sentry standing guard. If I couldn't be there for the spell, I could at least stop anyone else from interrupting. It would also mean that I was ready to respond as soon as they were done.

Through the door, I heard Sky chanting again. Her voice rose as the spell began. I didn't understand the details of what she and Josh had pulled together, using old enchantments and magical theory, but I knew enough to get that it was difficult and powerful, and that was enough to worry me.

The chanting was joined by a sound like the wind howling. I felt magic rushing through the world around me, racing into the library as Sky drew on vast amounts of power. I forced myself to stand in place, though every instinct said to follow the magic in, to watch over Sky and make sure that she was safe.

I tried to imagine what was happening inside, as Sky mustered the magic. I trusted her skill and intelligence, but these were powerful forces, perhaps powerful enough to overwhelm her. It didn't matter how gifted she was; magic always had its risks, and she was exposing herself to them in a big way.

A force hit me like a great surge of energy taking hold of my body. I felt as though I was being squeezed by a giant fist.

The breath raced from my lungs and the blood rushed in my veins, even as the spirit shade rose up inside me. The two forces faced each other, and I found myself held between them, like a pier battered by storm waves. Then the power inside me seemed to grab hold of the magic all around, pulling a part of it in. My shoulder tingled where the lunar mark sat, then went numb.

As suddenly as it had appeared, the power vanished. I fell to my knees.

Carefully, I ran the fingers of one hand over my shoulder, feeling for any pain. Then I tugged back the edge of my shirt and, straining my neck, looked around at my shoulder.

The mark was gone.

Footsteps approached. I straightened my shirt and rose to my feet just as the other Alphas appeared around the corner.

"Is it over yet?" Joan asked.

I turned my attention back to the library. The chanting of spells and the howling of magic had ended. Instead, I heard Sebastian, Josh, and Sky talking.

"It's over," I said.

Cole pushed past me into the library and the others followed. I watched them as they went. There was no sign that they had felt what I felt, that they had even sensed the presence of the magic.

Nervous about what we were about to find, I followed them in.

Sky sat in the middle of the room, her back to me. Josh and Sebastian stood facing her. Sebastian was lowering his shirt, a look of disappointment on his face. For him at least, the magic hadn't worked.

"What about you?" he asked, turning to Joan.

She pulled up her shirt, revealing the lunar mark still on her skin. Cole and the West Coast Alpha followed suit, with the same results.

"Ethan, what about you?" Sky asked, turning on the spot to look at me.

Her shirt was soaked with blood, as if someone had cut her right across her stomach. She seemed indifferent to it, looking up at me as if nothing in the world was wrong.

"Sky, you're bleeding," I said, appalled at the sight.

She looked down, frowned, and then looked back up at me, still acting as if everything was fine.

"What about you?" she said more firmly this time. "Do you still have the mark?"

"It's gone," I said quietly.

What did this mean? Why had the magic worked on me and not on the others? Was it part of Sky's spell, some aspect of the connection between us, or had my spirit shade hijacked part of her power to protect the body it lived in? I didn't know, and I couldn't even ask without giving away more than I wanted to reveal. I could see that Sky was considering what had happened, working out what to ask me, and I felt my defenses rising.

Then Jeremy rushed in, our were-animal doctor drawn by the scent of blood.

He grabbed hold of Sky, drawing her to her feet, and led her out of the room. I watched her with concern, but at least Jeremy's presence gave me some reassurance. However she had been injured, he would take good care of her.

"What does this mean?" Joan asked. The words could have been referring to anything about our situation, but from the way she looked at me, it was clear that she was talking about the disappearance of my mark.

"I don't know," I said. I had some good guesses, but nothing so solid that I felt like a liar for hiding it.

"Well, we're going to need to work it out," Sebastian said. "If this means that you're safe, maybe we can find a way to apply that magic to the rest of us. And if not, then we need something else."

"It's strange." Josh stood in front of me, eyes narrowed, looking me up and down. "Half the problem is going to be working out why you. Is it something about you? Were you the closest one outside the room? Did we just have enough power to hit one person and the spell picked you at random?"

"You're the witch," I said. "You tell me."

"I can't." Josh flung his hands in the air in exasperation. "The spell was meant to affect everyone. If it failed, that should be the same for everyone, too. Clearly, I missed something, and now I've got to start again from scratch."

"Any thoughts, Cole?" Sebastian asked.

We looked around, but Cole was gone, and I had a good idea where. I shoved the library door open and strode down the corridor to the infirmary.

Sure enough, Cole was standing in the doorway of the infirmary, looking in as Jeremy tended to Sky. She was lying on one of the beds, her stomach bared. Most of the blood had been cleaned away, revealing a set of claw marks. Alarming as that sight was, there was also something amazing going on: the wounds were healing at remarkable speed.

"I don't say this often—I've never seen anything like that," Jeremy said. "Skylar, you, my dear, are quite the anomaly."

"That she is," Cole said with his usual smug condescension.

I strode past him to Sky and looked down at her wounds. "What the fuck?"

"Yeah, I'm right there with you," Jeremy said.

At his direction, Kelly set about taking Sky's vitals, smiling sweetly as she worked. It was the first time I'd seen Kelly in action since she was rescued and turned into a wereanimal, but I was more concerned about Sky than about her. Something had gone badly wrong with the spell if this sort of injury was the result.

"How is she?" Cole asked.

There he was again, butting in where he wasn't wanted, trying to make the pack's life revolve around him. He'd contributed nothing today, so now he was making concern over Sky a way to make his mark, and to try to get between us in the process.

I squared up to him, ready for a fight. I hadn't been able to protect Sky against the magic, but I could protect her and everybody else I cared about from more of Cole's troublemaking.

Kelly stepped between us, smiling softly.

"She's doing fine, but we really need to check her out more," she said. "When magic is involved, you can never be too sure. I'm not sure if we are going to keep her. Cole, do you mind stepping out and coming back?"

Cole looked at me, and I could see the calculation in his eyes as he looked for a way to turn this against me, maybe to get me booted out of the infirmary, too, or to use my presence to justify his staying. Perhaps he was even going to try to push me into fighting him here and now, to make people believe that I was out of control and he would make a better Beta.

This was the worst thing about facing him. I never knew what was really going on, whether now was the time to fight or to back down.

"You can do something to help me help her," Kelly continued, smiling at Cole. "Why don't you tell me everything that happened?"

She took his arm and led him out of the room. For a moment he resisted, but in the face of Kelly's gentle helpfulness there was no way he could do that and paint himself as the good guy. It was satisfying to see him stumped.

"Ethan," Jeremy said, "tell me about the removal of your mark."

"What do you want to know?" I asked, turning away from watching Cole leave.

"What happened?"

I was reluctant to answer, worried about giving something away that would lead back to the spirit shade and everything Claudia and I had done for Josh.

"When the spell ended, the mark was gone," I said.

"And before that?"

"I heard noise from the library. I felt the magic swirling around. Then the spell ended."

"You had no idea before that?"

I thought back to the sensation in my shoulder and the numbness that followed. Then I thought back further to the spirit shade drawing in magical power.

"No idea at all."

Sky looked at me with suspicion, and I felt an urge to come out with more, to justify and excuse myself. But anything I said would only complicate matters, so I kept my mouth shut.

I approached Sky, not just to comfort her after her ordeal but to find some comfort myself. But the coldness of her words cut me short.

"There is a reason that you were the only one who was fixed — are you going to tell me?"

I opened my mouth, trying to work out how to respond, but Sky held up a hand.

"I don't want an excuse, or a reality in which you want me to believe. I want the truth, Ethan. Nothing else."

Unable to look at her, I turned my gaze to the wall. I wanted to be honest, to open up to her, to lower the barriers between us. But like so many things, this wasn't just about her and me. I wasn't going to risk Josh, or my relationship with him, by letting this secret out—especially not after everything Claudia and I had just been through.

"Ethan, I can't deal with the secrets," Sky said. "It's not fair to me… and if there is still an us, I can't continue without you being honest and open."

I let out a long breath.

"I know," I said, the weight of those words bearing down on me. There was so much I wanted to say, about who I was, what I had been through, even the things that had happened in the past few days, from the fight with Estevez to the challenge from Cole. But Sky wouldn't be content with anything less than the whole truth, and that wasn't mine to give. "I can't. If that is something you can't live with, I'm sorry. You have my answer; now you need to make that choice."

I turned and walked away, feeling like the heart had been wrenched from my chest and left behind with her.

CHAPTER 18

*D*espite everything that had passed between us, the lure of Sky was more than I could resist. I knew even before I went to bed that night that I would never be able to get to sleep without her. I could have cursed Winter for the terrible truth that she'd helped me understand: that Sky was my place of peace, and now that I knew she was in the world, I could never get a proper rest without her.

Angry as I was sure Sky must be, there was clearly something mutual in that feeling. When I turned up at her door, she let me in without question, and we ended up sleeping together as we had so many times recently.

I woke to the feeling of Sky moving next to me. Resting against my body, she kissed my chest, then my neck, pushing herself in close against me as her tongue ran across my skin. I stirred in response, feeling my excitement rise with her touch, and drew my head back to expose more of my neck.

Sky kissed my neck again. Then I felt the pressure of her teeth against my skin, gently at first, playful, then harder, biting down with serious intent.

At the jab of pain I pulled away from her, swearing. Blood trickled, hot and wet, down my neck, and the salty smell of it filled the room. Sky followed me, wide-eyed, her mouth hanging open, blood dripping from her lower lip. I shoved her away and rolled in the opposite direction, ending on my hands and knees.

I stared at her, this woman who meant so much to me, suddenly transformed into something dangerous. Something vampiric. The thought made me sick.

"I'm hungry," she said plaintively.

"Clearly," I said, staring into her eyes. Sure enough, the terait was there, as bright a circle of orange as I'd ever seen on her. The sign of vampiric blood-lust.

I had to do something about this, but what? While Sky sat looking disappointed on the bed, I headed into the bathroom. Running on autopilot while I considered my next steps, I cleaned my teeth and washed my face, constantly glancing at Sky as I did so. What control, if any, did she have over the hunger? Was she going to leap on me at any moment, fangs bared?

Leaving her behind, I headed for the kitchen. I needed something to sate Sky's need for blood, but didn't know if she would even have red meat in the house. Fortunately, a quick glance in the fridge gave a positive answer—big slabs of steak just waiting to be cooked.

By the time Sky emerged, I'd cooked the steaks, extra rare to leave as much blood in as I could. As soon as she sat down, I slid a plate with two steaks in front of her and cut a piece from one of them. Sky opened her mouth eagerly to accept the piece of meat, then another and another, wolfing each one down as if she hadn't eaten in days.

Sure that she was going to keep going, I handed her the knife and fork. Soon she was tearing through the second steak, swallowing whole chunks barely chewed. I watched her the whole time, seeing the terait fade a little but not disappear. My relief at that sight was tempered by the doubt now running through me. If this had happened once, then it could happen again. I wanted Sky to take the steps needed to keep her blood hunger under control, but I was far from convinced that she would do it.

Sky finished her second steak, pushed the plate away, and looked around, a hungry look still on her face. It was going to take more than this to really appease her vampiric side. That left me wondering what she had done when the hunger came before, and deeply uncomfortable at what the answer might be.

"Have you ever tried to feed from someone?" I asked.

"Why would I? I'm not a vampire."

I leaned in toward her, smiling as I ran a finger over those full lips.

"You're not quite a wolf, either. Now are you?"

"Neither are you."

That cut me, for reasons beyond the ones she knew. Or perhaps she did know, perhaps she had worked out the truth through what she saw in the failed spells and now she was testing me, probing to see what I would reveal and what I would conceal.

My attention was drawn away from Sky by the scent of someone approaching the house, someone I really didn't want to deal with: Cole.

The doorbell rang and Sky went to answer. Cole stood there grinning and carrying two cups of coffee. Did the guy have no boundaries?

"Things can get ugly if you don't have your coffee, right?" he said.

"What are you doing here?" Sky said acidly, opening the door wider to give me and Cole a clear view of each other.

Cole looked at me, then looked away as he caught the hostility of my stare. He smiled at Sky, painting on that mask of charm he liked so much.

"Just checking on you," he said. "Your wound looked severe yesterday, but Kelly said you'd left. I wasn't sure if you were released or you went against medical advice. You didn't seem very concerned about it, but I think you should have been."

"I'm fine," Sky replied. "Thank you."

"May I come in?"

Sky hesitated. I could see that she didn't want this to turn ugly between us in her home, but I also couldn't see any way of ending it quickly without giving some ground to Cole. Let him feel like he'd gotten his dig in, then maybe he would clear off and Sky and I could finish talking about what she had done.

"Yeah, you can come in," I called out.

Sky took a step back and Cole moved into the room.

"I didn't know exactly what you like," he said, offering a cup to Sky, "but I smelled peppermint in the coffee Josh brought for you, and white chocolate, so I took a guess. Peppermint white mocha, is that your drink?"

Sky nodded. They each took a sip of their drink.

"I got regular chocolate, just in case," Cole said, holding up his cup. Then he turned to me. "Good morning, I didn't expect to see you here."

"Obviously."

It looked like he'd come to make a move on my girlfriend, and here I was sitting in the way of his plans. I could live with that.

If Cole felt any shame at being caught in the act, he didn't show it, just smiled some more. Silence fell. It was awkward, but better than the alternative of having to talk with him. I walked up to Sky, wrapped my arms around her from behind, and pulled her close, taking comfort in her touch. I could face anything, from Cole's machinations to a curse to destroy us, as long as she was there with me.

"Mine," I said.

Sky leaned into me and I felt that sense of peace, something even Cole couldn't taint.

"Of course she's yours, pretty much like all the others," he said. "But if she really were yours, she would bear your mark —she doesn't. Why don't you go ahead and add the little disclaimer 'for now' and save her the trouble and heartache?"

I glared at him. So he knew about my past. So what? Things were different now. Sky wasn't just some passing fling, she was someone I cared about deeply. Cole's attempts to prove otherwise just showed how little he understood.

He headed out, looking over his shoulder at Sky one last time before he closed the door behind him.

As I saw the look of disdain she gave him, I knew more than ever that I'd picked the right woman. Sky wasn't falling for any of Cole's so-called charm.

That knowledge, and the feeling of her pressed against me, roused a deep and passionate urge. I kissed her deeply and she responded in kind. Our tongues intertwined as we pulled each other close, and her heart raced along with mine.

I pushed her back to the counter, swept everything off it to the floor, and lifted her up. Her ass was firm in my hands, the smell of her entrancing, and the sound of her breath catching in her throat drove me wild.

I pulled away from her just long enough to tug off her underwear and my own, then pressed against her, sliding inside. She gasped in pleasure as I thrust deeper, then pulled back, settling into a slow, steady rhythm that let me relish the movement of our bodies against each other, the tightening of her legs around me, the taste of her neck as I pressed my lips against her.

Sky moved against me, the shifting of her body and the moaning of her breath matching my own. I ran my hands down her thighs and pulled them wider apart, pressing deeper and harder with each stroke. She gripped my shoulders and flung her head back, breasts swaying, hair hanging loose behind her.

I pulled her close and kissed her fiercely, wanting to join

with her like this forever. Her fingers dug into my back and her legs wrapped tight around me, pulling me in as I thrust faster and faster, our excitement growing until her whole body tightened around me and my flesh throbbed with pleasure as we reached a final peak.

I pressed my face against her neck, felt the pulsing of her blood and tasted the salt of sweat on her skin. As our breath slowed and we eased into the afterglow, I'd never been happier in my life.

There could be no one else. I loved Sky and wanted to be with her forever. I wanted her as my mate.

I kissed slowly down her shoulder, unsure how she would react to the idea. Then I set my teeth briefly against her skin, all too aware of how much like a vampire's bite this could look, while knowing how very different it was in meaning. Not possessing and devouring someone, but promising yourself to them together, joining as one.

"Mine," I whispered, pressing harder with my teeth. I knew she wanted me, knew how much we meant to each other. Surely she would accept the mark, to let all other weres know whose she was.

She tensed and a terrible doubt hit me. Was Sky not ready? We hadn't been together long, but that time had been so brilliant, I had been sure she felt the same way I did. Yet she held herself back from me now.

I waited for her to consent, and with every passing moment I became more certain that she would say no.

"Ethan," she said quietly, and her tone told me her answer.

"I know." I kissed her shoulder, then rested my head on her chest while she stroked my hair.

Everything had been so good, this couldn't just be about us.

"Is it Quell?" I asked, trying to hide the hurt that thought gave me. It made sense that she would want someone who could understand her vampiric side, someone she could face the blood hunger with.

She shook her head.

"Are you interested in Cole?"

She shook her head again.

"It's you. I don't want to do it because of you." She took a deep breath. "I've proven myself to be trustworthy. Everything there is to know about me, you know, and most of the time you know before I do. I've accepted that when it comes to you I will never have all of you, including the secrets you have. I've accepted it, but it doesn't mean I like it. And having what we have now is all I can take under those circumstances."

I leaned back against the counter and looked at her, pushing down my disappointment. If we were going to face this, we had to do it fairly, calmly, rationally.

"Have I not been forthcoming with you?" I asked. "I've made it clear that there are things that I can't tell you, nor will I. Things will not change because we are together. I'm sorry that they won't. It was a mistake for you to think that they would."

"You have to meet me halfway, Ethan, because I can't do this. It's not fair to me. Or us." She took a deep breath. "You have to choose between your secrets and me. You can't have both."

Her rejection was like a sledgehammer smashing into my chest, leaving me breathless and racked with pain. I'd never had to face a moment like this before, never been rejected by anyone I cared about so much. It was bewildering, terrifying even, to think that I might lose her not to violence but to some inability to make our lives match.

I nodded, buying time. I had to keep my secrets, for Sky's own safety and for that of the whole pack. But if we couldn't get past this, then I would lose Sky, and that thought was unbearable.

I walked up to her, took her face in my hands, and stood looking into her eyes. That beautiful face, that amazing woman within. I had no idea what to do, but one thing was clear: anything I said now would only make matters worse. I had to get out before I made a terrible mistake.

I kissed her gently, then turned away and returned to the bedroom. Struggling to hold myself together, I got dressed then headed out the door. It felt cruel to leave without speaking, but I didn't trust myself to say anything right.

CHAPTER 19

Sebastian and I gathered around the desk in the library where Josh had spread out his notes. We both knew enough to understand that we were looking at something complicated, but not to put all the pieces together. This was why the pack gained so much value from having a witch among us. Magical theory was like advanced abstract mathematics: unless you'd spent years studying it you wouldn't understand much beyond the basic numbers.

I felt Sky approaching before I heard or smelled her. Stepping back from the others, I took a deep breath. I wanted to rush to Sky the moment she came in, to feel her pressed against me and to know that everything was okay.

The thought of losing her was no more terrible than it had been a few days before, but ever since our talk in the woods, it came with the knowledge that I loved her. There was no one else in the world like her, no one who had ever made me feel the way she did. I knew that if we didn't find a way to fix things, then I would lose her. There were plenty of other men in the world who wanted Sky, and I couldn't expect her to wait forever if I couldn't give her what she wanted. Yet to give in would break the trust others had put in me.

I knew that if Sky got close, if I gave in to the connection between us, then I would break and it would all come tumbling out. But right now, we had other things to deal with. I had to hold my emotions in, had to hold my affection back until I had an answer I could give Sky, one that we could both live with. I couldn't even think about what that might be right now.

She came into the room. It hurt to see her and not touch her, but I held myself back, just greeted her briefly and then left her to work with Josh.

"You don't think there is any other way?" Sebastian asked, looking up from the paper in Josh's hand.

"We've tried everything," Josh said. "We need to get the third book from Samuel."

"I've had someone go to the last three places where his whereabouts were known. He's gone deep into hiding."

That was Samuel's way, to hide from the supernatural forces that he wanted erased from the world. The paranoia that made him so destructive also helped to keep him safe.

"Is there a location spell that we can try?" Sebastian asked.

"Not without his blood," Josh said.

"Senna, she might know," Sky said.

It would have been an odd combination—Sky's spell-wielding cousin and the man who wanted to remove all magic from the world—but our lives were full of odd combinations. If they weren't, then I would never have been with Sky.

"You think she will help?" Josh asked.

By way of answer, Sky pulled out her phone and headed for the door.

We waited tensely while she made the call. I paced back and forth while Josh shuffled through his papers, rearranged books, and generally did a terrible impression of studying.

Sebastian watched us with apparent calm, but I knew better than to be fooled by his demeanor. Our whole existence hung on this call, and while Sebastian was a master of the poker face, that didn't mean that he was devoid of feelings.

At last, Sky returned. She looked around, her whole body tense, and I realized that she couldn't look me in the eye any more than I could face talking with her.

"What does Senna say?" Sebastian asked.

"She's in contact with Samuel, though I'm not sure how much. She's going to try to convince him to call us."

"That's not a lot to work with," Josh said.

"It's a start." Sebastian steepled his fingers. "The question is, how do we turn it into the end that we're after?"

"There will be a catch," I said, forcing myself out of silence.

"There's always a catch," Sebastian said. "The question is, is it a catch we can live with?"

I looked at Sky, who sat biting her lip, a lock of hair dangling down the side of her face. Sebastian was right, and not just about Samuel.

<hr>

We went to Sebastian's office and waited for Samuel to call back. Two hours ticked by without a response. Josh and Sky kept picking away at their research, looking for new angles, different approaches to the problem. Sebastian and I paced the room, waiting for any kind of response.

In the end, it was Sebastian's phone that rang, not Sky's.

"You are interested in a trade?" Samuel asked the moment Sebastian answered the phone.

"No," Sebastian said. "I need the third Clostra."

"For?"

"Pack business."

There was a long silence. Had Samuel really been

surprised by what Sebastian said? I doubted it. More likely, he was drawing this out, making us wait while the pressure built.

"Is it true that Marcia is dead and it was your doing?" he asked.

"Yes."

Another silence. If Samuel was trying to play mind games, then he needed to learn some new tactics.

"Will Josh be taking over as the head of the Creed?"

"No. But there is someone already in place."

"The book is yours if I am given Marcia's position. It was rightfully mine before I was exiled, and I want what is mine."

It was a ridiculous request. We had no power to decide who ran the Creed, and if Samuel thought we did, then he was more detached from reality than I'd ever realized. But ridiculous or not, now Sebastian knew what he was after.

"Done. Be here tomorrow with the Clostra."

And just like that the ridiculous deal was made.

I didn't know what Sebastian really had planned, but I was confident that he would tell me when I needed to know. I was also confident that it was smarter than anything Samuel might be scheming.

Sky stared at Sebastian like he'd just pulled half a steak dinner out of his ear.

"Sky, unless you have something you need to say, you might want to close your mouth," he said. He looked around at the three of us. "Thank you for your help."

Apparently he didn't need to discuss the plan with us now. That was fine with me. I had plenty of other things I needed to work on. Josh and I headed out of Sebastian's office, but as we went, I realized that Sky had stayed behind. Of course she couldn't accept what Sebastian had said; she would be demanding answers, just like always. She was nothing if not persistent.

That thought made me smile for a moment, but then the

happy thoughts about Sky turned back into worrying about how I could handle things between us. Perhaps if I told her how I felt, it might be easier for her to accept the secrets and the strains between us. At the very least, it was one thing I wouldn't be lying about.

I turned back to wait outside Sebastian's office. A moment later, Sky emerged. I took her by the arm and led her to another room, my heart thudding in my chest. Was I really going to do this? How would she respond? There was only one way to find out.

I closed the door behind us and leaned against it for a moment of stability in the spinning world of my thoughts and emotions. Then I stepped away from the door, mustering my thoughts.

How could I start the conversation? Should I talk about what had happened that morning? About the time we had spent together over the past few weeks? About my hopes and dreams for what we might mean to each other? Perhaps this was the time to say something poetic, but I'd never been any good at poetry. Growing up around a were-animal pack, my experience of romance usually started with sparring or running through the woods, then quickly moved on to fucking wherever and whenever we could find a chance. Sharing feelings, overcoming secrets, winding our lives and hearts together, none of that was what I was used to. But it was what I wanted now. It was what I wanted with Sky.

I realized that time was getting away from me, minutes flying by while Sky stared and I struggled to find anything coherent to say. I had to break the deadlock in my head. I had to get past this.

I had to tell the truth, the only one that mattered.

"I love you," I said, the words sounding alien even as I said them.

Sky stared at me, open-mouthed.

"I love you," I said again, more softly this time, offering it up as an apology, an explanation, and a confession all in one. "It's not what I expected. Definitely not what I wanted, because it only serves to complicate things. But I needed you to know."

"What was your plan, to keep being a jackass until you, me, or both of us died?"

I felt ashamed that I'd behaved so badly she could think that. But then, I'd never offered an alternative. Until this very moment, I hadn't known that I had it in me to do any different.

To my surprise, she reached out to stroke my cheek, then kissed me on the lips. She pulled back to look at me, then leaned in to rest her lips against mine.

"Did you think the last part was romantic?" she asked mockingly.

I laughed. She was right, if I'd meant to make this a special moment, then I'd pretty much ruined it. At least it seemed to count for something that I'd tried. I could tell because she kissed me again.

"I'm just saying, if you would have left the last part off, we would have had a very kickass moment the first time you confessed your love. Now I'm going to have to take creative license with the story and rework it and take all the 'I don't want to love you, Sky, you're a complicated mess. We are a complicated mess' stuff out. Or no one is going to dote over that story."

Smiling, I kissed her on the forehead and then pulled her close.

"You know what I want, but I won't press it," I said. "I'm content just being with you, okay?"

She nodded and squeezed me tight.

The best part was, it all felt true. Admitting what I felt was like opening up a dam inside of me, and now the waters ran free. A great weight was gone, leaving me feeling energized and renewed. I might not have everything that I wanted, but I had Sky, she had me, and we would find a way through this.

For now, that was enough.

I spent a couple of hours checking in on the recently turned weres still living in the retreat. When I was done, I could feel Sky still in the building, working in the library again. I decided to go and see her, to test the waters of how we stood with each other after my earlier confession.

As I approached, I could hear her and Josh talking, discussing something about a spell.

"Do you really understand what it means for you to be a conduit?" he asked.

I didn't know how a conduit fit into their plans, but it sounded like exactly the sort of dangerous role that Sky would unthinkingly take on.

"How dangerous is it?" I asked, walking into the room.

"Not as dangerous as a challenge to the death," Josh said, glaring at me. I hadn't told him about Cole's challenge, but of course word had gotten around, and apparently now I was the bad guy for not worrying him. "Of all the times to do something so stupid—both of you. Your lives are on the line and you want to have a pissing contest. Good, I guess whoever survives the challenge gets to see if they survive the curse, too."

I sighed. This wasn't my fault, as Josh would know if he took a moment to think about it instead of acting all aggrieved.

"We've agreed to wait until after the curse is lifted."

"How admirable of you two," he said, his voice rising as he got out of his seat. "Good to know, at least you told me that. Why don't you tell me when exactly you planned on telling me about the challenge? While you were in the middle of the fucking death match?"

By now he was shouting in my face, arms waving around in fury. My own anger stirred in response, but I held it back. Getting mad at him wouldn't help. I had to calm him down, so that we could talk like adults instead of screaming at each other like we were kids again.

"I didn't tell you because you tend to act like this when I do," I said.

Josh glared at me. A wave of magic blasted out of him, wild and unfocused, like a storm sweeping through the room.

"You're an ass," he muttered as he headed for the door, a string of curses following behind.

"Josh," I called after him. "Josh, wait!"

But he kept going, and a moment later the front door of the retreat slammed.

"Sorry," I said to Sky, offering an embarrassed frown. "I should…"

Then I was out of the library and striding down the corridor, following Josh. I barged past Kelly and Gavin, who were making out in the hallway, writhing against each other so hard they might as well have been naked. Then I was in the car park, the front door swinging shut behind me, looking for where the hell my brother had gotten to.

This was typical of him, grabbing hold of a problem and making it twice the size. It was one of the reasons why we argued so often.

Josh was opening the door of his car. I strode over and slammed it shut. One of the new weres, just getting out of her own car, glanced nervously at us before hurrying away.

"You don't get to just walk away from me," I said. "I'm your older brother and the Beta of this pack."

"Yeah, well I'm not a member of your damn pack," Josh snapped. "And if you think that being the older brother somehow entitles you to respect, then you don't understand what a whiny little brat looks like."

"And you don't understand the lengths I go to in order to look after you. The things I've done over the years just to keep you safe."

"Oh really?" Josh folded his arms and glared at me. "You want to play the overprotective older brother card? Think that's a good look right now, do you?"

"What's wrong with protecting the people who matter to me?"

"What's wrong is doing it so much that you stifle them. I spent years with you and Claudia constantly peering over my shoulder, not giving me space to be myself. How would you feel if there was someone always telling you what you were doing wrong?"

"If it kept me safe, I'd be damn glad they were there!"

Now the anger was riding up through me. I couldn't help it, Josh just got under my skin. It was easier to manage my temper when I was dealing with people I didn't give a crap about. It was when I cared about the consequences, when a hurt to them felt like a hurt to me, that it became impossible to let anything go.

"Bullshit!" Josh said. "You hate being told what to do just as much as I do. You're a control junkie, constantly stepping in to meddle in other people's lives. No explaining, no helping, just telling them they can't take a risk. But when it's about you, apparently taking on pointless danger is fine. Why not arrange a needless fight to the death?"

"I didn't offer the challenge."

"No, but you accepted it, and you made it lethal."

"I've got to do it that way, otherwise—"

"You've always got an excuse. But you know what? I've got reasons why I do what I do. So has Sky. So has everyone around here. None of us treat that like it makes us exempt from the consequences or concerns of other people."

I let out a sigh. I could see where he was coming from, even if he didn't understand the difference being Beta made.

"I get it," I said. "It stressed me out seeing you run off to fight the Creed on your own."

Josh looked down, red-faced. That one had gotten to him. Then he looked back up at me, a spark in his eye.

"You don't have to do this alone," he said. "I can use magic on Cole, make sure the challenge goes your way."

A different sort of anger ran through me, icy cold.

"Absolutely not," I said.

"You'll still be doing what you have to do," Josh said, smiling as he grew in animation. "Still fighting for your spot, still putting off competitors, still dealing with the douche bag in our midst. I'll just be taking some of the risk out of it."

"No." I practically shouted the word. "If I can't win without cheating, then I shouldn't win at all."

"But what if you—"

"This isn't just about me. It's about the pack and its traditions."

"Fuck traditions!"

I slammed my fist down on his car. The roof buckled beneath it.

I didn't know if my anger was solely directed at Josh, or at myself for putting him in a position where he would consider cheating. I hated that I put him in this predicament and I despised that he didn't feel confident enough in my ability to win. But looking at him, I knew it was about more than just me winning, it was him losing me.

"Those traditions hold us together," I hissed. "They keep us safe. Without them, we couldn't even work together as weres. We'd just be the wild beasts Sky saw in her vision, fighting each other and everything else in sight."

"I don't care! Don't you get it? Saving your life trumps any rules or traditions. You're my brother, and I won't let you die."

I sighed. It was the same way I felt about him. How could I ignore that?

"It doesn't matter," I said. "Using magic won't work. The minute you try it, Sebastian or Cole will notice and stop you. I'll lose the challenge by default. You'll be ensuring my defeat."

Josh pressed his fingers to his eyes and let out a long breath.

"Fine," he said. "You win. Go die in your stupid challenge."

I laid a hand on his shoulder. Seeing his sadness like this drained all the anger out of me.

"It'll be fine," I said. "I wouldn't be Beta if I couldn't take on the likes of Cole."

"I suppose."

"Seriously, I've got this one. I need you in my corner in other ways, like breaking this curse."

"I guess you'd be screwed if you had to deal with that one yourself, huh?" Josh said, giving me a lopsided grin.

"So screwed. Now tell me, what's this conduit thing you were talking about with Sky?"

Josh looked away, unable to meet my eye.

"You're not going to like it," he admitted.

"Because it means putting Sky at risk?"

"Exactly. There's magic from the Clostra we can use, but only by channeling it through her. It'll mean drawing the full effect of the curse down on her, instead of the rest of you. Theoretically, Maya's presence should make Sky immune, so we can ground the spell without anyone suffering. But we've had a lot of things I thought could work in theory, and so far none of them have."

"Do you have a better alternative?"

He shook his head. "Nothing. This is the most powerful spell we've considered, something that wouldn't be possible without both me and Sky working on it. It's a desperate move, but we're running out of time and we've already run out of other options."

The thought of risking Sky's life in such a way was like a claw digging into my heart. I'd found the love of my life and now I had to let her risk death by wild, dark magic. But I couldn't choose her safety over that of so many members of the pack.

"We'll do it," I said. "I believe in you and I believe in Sky. Together, you've got this."

Sky wasn't in when I got to her house. Fortunately, I'd gotten her spare keys off Steven, who still had them from when he'd lived in her spare room, so I was able to let myself in. I sat in her living room, idly watching television and looking forward to some peaceful time to ourselves, until I heard her car pull up outside. I switched off the television and turned to face the door.

Sky walked in with a scowl on her face.

"How did you get in here?" she asked wearily.

I got up off the couch and walked over to her, holding out the keys.

"They're Steven's. It's really not appropriate for him to have a set."

I'd meant it as a joke, but the look on Sky's face told me that it had gone down like a lead balloon.

"More rules to make you feel comfortable. It's funny how that works."

I set the keys down on the counter.

"If you want him to have it, so be it." I leaned in close to her and caught a scent that set my teeth on edge. "You smell like Cole."

I stood back, arms crossed, waiting for an explanation.

What the hell was she doing with the asshole who wanted to kill me and take my place?

Silence stretched out as we stared at each other, neither speaking.

"Fine," I said. "Why do you smell like Cole?"

"Because I met with him earlier."

"About what?"

Again, she gave no answer, even though I'd asked directly this time. So much for wanting truth and openness between us. I'd opened my heart to her and now she wouldn't even explain what she was doing with my worst enemy.

"About what?" I asked again, trying to hold back the hostility I felt whenever I thought about Cole.

"Of the two of you, I thought he was the more reasonable," she said.

I let the silence hang, waiting for her to explain, but apparently she was feeling even more stubborn than usual tonight.

I'd burned through all my emotional energy arguing with Josh. I didn't have the will to wait this one out.

"Continue," I said.

"And he's just as confident and callous about his life."

She shoved past me and flung herself down on the sofa, pushing the ottoman away as she went. It crashed into the wall and Sky blinked as if surprised at her own strength.

"It's not just you anymore," she snapped.

So there it was. Josh wasn't the only one holding a grievance against me for something that wasn't my doing.

"Were you unaware of my position in this pack?" I asked, forcing myself to stay calm. "Did you think that I wouldn't ever get challenged?"

"I thought you would consider others," she said coldly. "Me. You're not alone. The decisions you make affect other people, too."

"Sky," I said, the word riding out of me on an exasperated

sigh. Did she really not understand, after all this time in the pack, after all the conversations we'd had? "No matter how much I want to, I can't prevent you from being affected by pack rules—"

"But it's not pack rules. There aren't any rules that say that a challenge is to the death. That's some arbitrary BS that you and Sebastian hold to just to up the ante to decrease the number of challenges. Ethan, it's not the same."

"I do wish I could make this better for you, Sky." I was so sorry to see her hurting, to witness her struggles to come to terms with our world. If there was anything I could have done to ease her understanding, to help her accept this, I would have done it. But I couldn't turn the world of were-animals upside down for her.

"You condescending prick."

"Sky." I switched to Portuguese, a reminder of the bond between us. "Desculpa por te ter magoado." *I'm sorry you are hurt.* "Tu tens o poder de o mudar." *You have the power to change it.*

She stared at me like I was a stranger, and the coldness of that gaze made me ache.

"I don't understand you, Ethan. First you tell me you love me, but not enough to do this for me."

Where had this come from? We'd had this conversation already. I thought she understood, even if this wasn't something she liked, that it wasn't something I could give up. It felt bitter to have my confession of love used against me, trying to twist me away from the principles I upheld.

"Já terminaste?" I asked. *Are you finished?*

She nodded.

I watched her. I knew she didn't mean to be cruel; Sky just wasn't that sort of person. But the cruelty was still there in her attempt to control me, to force me to live like her instead of being myself. I had a responsibility to the pack to fight against Cole's meddling, to uphold our way of life, to protect the safety and stability of all our lives. She was trying to get me to give that up, and somehow she couldn't even see it.

I had offered something precious to her when I told her I loved her, something I had never done with any other woman. I should have been furious that she was using it against me, but instead I felt flat, as though sadness had sucked all the life out of me.

I walked slowly over to her, ran a finger along her jaw, her chin, up to her lips, and then kissed her gently.

"I do love you," I said. "If you doubt it, please don't. My stance on the challenge has nothing to do with my feelings for you. I'm sorry you feel that it does. I don't respond to emotional blackmail. It is a tactic I discourage you from using again." I looked away, unable to face her anymore. "Do you want me to leave?"

She sat in stony silence for a long moment, then nodded. Not even a word in response, just that small, defiant gesture.

Heartbroken, I walked out the door.

The next morning, I stood outside the witches' headquarters with Josh, Sebastian, and Sky. Things were still tense between me and Sky, the two of us barely talking to each other. I'd told her I loved her and she'd still rejected me. I didn't know how we could come back from that, and I had no idea how to interact with her while our relationship was still so uncertain.

A car pulled up and Samuel got out.

"Where's the Clostra?" Sebastian asked.

"Not on me," Samuel replied. "Do you think I'm an idiot? I'm not giving that up until I've seen for sure that you got me what I wanted, and I'm not bringing it here just so that you can grab it off of me. If that was your plan, then you're going to be really disappointed."

"My plan was to broker a deal between you and the new Creed, and here we are."

"I'll believe it when I'm in the room with them."

"Then let's go in."

The last time we had been here, the place had been wrecked from Josh's onslaught. This time, we walked through a fully functioning shop, past a smiling attendant behind the till, and into a neatly ordered back room. The mirrors that had once lined the walls were gone, replaced in large part by shelves full of books, but runes still marked the walls, along with a vellum manuscript on which was written a Latin pledge by the Creed to honor their magic and protect those in their care. Fine sentiments, and a stark contrast with what had come before, but only time would tell if they lived up to it.

Ariel was sitting at a long table in the center of the room, along with the other witches. Another figure lurked at the back of the room, his face hidden by the shadow from a bookcase. Ariel stood as soon as we walked in and came over to greet us, calm and confident, a woman in full command of her domain after only a few days. She and Sebastian exchanged warm smiles, then she turned to greet Samuel.

"I've heard wonderful things about you."

"Then you've been hanging around with liars," he said sharply.

Ariel laughed and the whole mood of the room lifted. I felt myself rising out of the gloom that had consumed me, and even Samuel managed a smile.

"Well, Marcia hated you, so that means you can't be that bad," Ariel said. "Sebastian informed me of your wishes, and I understand that what happened to you was horrible. You are right, this position is rightfully yours. Unfortunately, you must understand that your reputation will not allow that to happen. The witches had been fractured for some time under Marcia's rule, and there needs to be a show of goodwill and faith. Putting you in any position of power will not do that."

"That was the agreement!" Samuel turned to Sebastian with a look of pure fury. "You promised."

"I did no such thing. I said bring the book."

A wild, intense look filled Samuel's eyes, and he scowled from behind his scruffy beard. I tensed, ready for a fight.

"Samuel," Ariel said in a soft, soothing tone. "I understand that was an agreement you feel he made with you; unfortunately, it is something that can't be done at the time. But your goal was to have access to the Aufero to return the magic to those it was taken from. That is something we will help you with. It will be a benevolent act that will improve your standing with others."

"That was something I was going to do anyway."

"Yes, months ago. I suspect that offer from Sebastian is no longer available. Voided by your inactivity. Not his fault but yours."

Samuel stared at her, then back at Sebastian, and the fire of anger flashed in his eyes again.

"This meeting is over."

He moved to leave, but Ariel held up her hand.

"That is my first offer to you. My second one is Eric." She gestured to a corner of the room and a man emerged, round faced with dark hair and penetrating eyes.

I knew that face, not from personal experience but from my intelligence files, and the sight of him increased the tension I was already feeling. Eric de Bono was a powerful fae, and such creatures never did anything without inserting a trick or two of their own.

Judging by Samuel's face, he knew Eric as well. His look of shock turned quickly to one of fear. Sebastian hadn't said to me that we were setting an ambush, but I had no qualms about us delivering one.

"I thought you might know him," Ariel said. "He rarely needs an introduction as one of the strongest fae on this side of the country. I think we know three or four stronger." At a signal from her, the witches closed in. "There are eight of us and a fae who can make you tell us anything we want. I don't want to do that. It's distasteful to treat someone that way."

She leaned toward Samuel and for the first time that day I saw the steely determination that she had shown in our last encounter. There was more to Ariel than met the eye.

"Let's be clear," she continued. "I find it distasteful but not reprehensible. I will do it. Will my fae friend have to work his magic and make you give us the truth and reveal the whereabouts of the Clostra, or will you do it willingly?"

Samuel stood, teeth clenched, hands twitching at his sides, his regular look of madness more visible than ever as he surveyed the room. I could see his urge to resist and was surprised to find myself feeling sympathy for him. If I'd been cornered like this, I would have wanted to refuse and fight back, no matter how desperate the odds.

"Fine," Samuel said at last. He pulled a phone from his pocket, pulled up a map app, and selected a location from his favorites, a featureless spot out in the countryside. "It's buried in a secure box here, under a flat rock with a red cross painted on the bottom."

Sebastian took the phone while Ariel offered Samuel an appreciative smile and directed him to the main table.

"Please join us while Sebastian retrieves the book," she said. "We have things to discuss. I look forward to us working together."

With the phone in his hand, Sebastian started heading for the door. Josh, Sky and I moved to follow him.

"Sebastian," Ariel called sweetly after him. "When you have all three, and you've used them for what you need, I do expect to have two of them given to the witches." She glanced pointedly at Josh. "And copies of any translations you may have."

Sebastian paused in the doorway. For the briefest moment, his smile vanished, only to reappear as Ariel walked slowly toward him.

"That wasn't discussed last night," he said.

"Yes, dinner was nice, and you are ever the charmer. You have a mirror, I don't have to elaborate." Ariel laughed as she came close to Sebastian and he flashed her his most winning smile. It seemed that he'd started early on improving diplomatic relations with the Creed. "I'm sure getting women to swoon over you is a tactic that probably has served you well in the past. I'm not one of them. It was quite an exercise in restraint for me to decline dessert."

She stepped back and winked. "I'm not comfortable with you all having them. We split the difference in our favor. We're all friends here. If you need the third at some point, something can always be negotiated, but the Midwest Pack having access to the books and someone who can read and use the spells isn't something I'm comfortable with."

Now it was Sebastian's turn to close in on Ariel, his eyes running up and down her before he spoke.

"Ariel, you know we can be trusted. I can be trusted. These will remain with us."

"Of course, Sebastian, I do believe you can be trusted; however, I guarantee that you will do whatever is necessary to protect your pack. A quality I find admirable."

She kept her tone soft, conciliatory, drawing us in to better hear her. But at the same time, her fingertips danced through the air, weaving magic out of empty space. A smoky ring of power spread out behind her, and I could sense both the strength and the deadliness of her magic. Josh was good at what he did, but Ariel was on a whole other level. No wonder she was the new head of the Creed.

"It's not a matter of trust, but checks and balances," she continued. "We all need them, which is why I increased the number of people on the Creed. I'm not above requiring checks and balances, either. Tre'ases are unrestricted; vampires are immune to daylight as well as holy water. I understand it is your pack's doing. It's never a bad idea to get a second opinion. I think you can agree with it enough to know there doesn't need to be any more discussion about it."

No one could miss the way her eyes shifted when she spoke about the pack's role in what had happened, her gaze settling briefly but pointedly on Sky. Then her attention was back on Sebastian long enough to ensure his attention as he turned away.

"Full disclosure," she said over her shoulder, "I was approached by a man who calls himself X this morning. For some reason he is seeking an alliance against your pack. His offer was tempting. If the books aren't returned to us, I don't think it will be a bad idea for me to meet with him again."

There it was, the reason why Ariel was so confident we would cooperate—because the alternative was Dexter. We could have her on our side or we could see her join our enemies, and we had too many of those already. Those volumes of the Clostra were as good as hers.

She turned back to give us a final triumphant look. "I'm sure you all can see yourselves out."

She was good at this, not just the substance of what she was asking but the style with which she delivered it. She had arranged the moment to demonstrate her mastery, to leave us obligated to cooperate, and to make sure she still had Sebastian's appreciative attention. From the look on his face, she had succeeded. Whether that was a good or a bad thing remained to be seen, but we had access to the Clostra now, providing one last way to try to break the curse, and that was the most important thing.

***

The woods behind the retreat were still, as if every animal and bird there knew that something dangerous was coming, that now was the time to get out of the way. The something in question was Sky, walking between me and Josh, heading into the woods to either save us or show the futility of our last best hope.

She had tried the new spell once already, inside the retreat. As the power had flowed from her, the walls had crumbled and the ceiling had started to cave in, threatening to crush everyone there. Despite the urgency of the need for a cure, we'd had to stop the spell before it was stopped in a terminal way. Once we'd gotten out of the weakened building, we'd seen how much more powerful the spell was, with trees around the house reduced to splinters. It had left us looking for a safe, open space to complete the spell, while we worried about what might happen when its full power was unleashed.

The eclipse was still days away, and yet I felt as though time had run out. It had taken so long to prepare this spell, we wouldn't be able to create a new one again. We had to win now or see ourselves fall victim to the curse.

Sky was trying to shrug off the concerns and advice coming from me and Josh, because she wouldn't be the woman I loved if she wasn't obstinately fighting back against any attempt to help or guide her.

"I know, under no circumstance do I stop the spell," she said. "Stay in the sacred circle, and start the spell the moment my blood hits the ground within the sacred circle..."

"Because?" Josh asked.

"Santa will put me on the naughty list."

"Sky!" Josh and I snapped in unison. This was serious stuff, all our lives on the line. The pack needed her to listen for once.

"Because my flowing blood is what will be used for the transfer. Once the last drop is spilled, then the offer is sealed."

"No matter what happens, you can't stop," Josh said, concern showing in the crumpling of his brow. "If you stop, what do you have to do?"

Sky sighed dramatically. "I must do the spell of purity, cleanse the area and myself, and start all over again."

"No matter what happens, you can't stop," I said. I had to make sure that she was safe, both for her own sake and to complete what we were doing. "Even if the world is crumbling around you, the circle is where you will be safe. Do the spell and we'll handle everything else. Okay?"

I took her hand and looked down at the wound on her palm where she'd spilled her blood trying the spell before. Though things still lay unresolved between us, for now none of that was important. What mattered to me was her safety and the success of the spell. If anyone could manage such vast and unruly power, it was Sky, but that "if" still hung over us.

We emerged from the trees into a large open field just as the sun was starting to set. Over two dozen were-animals, Cole among them, spread out around the edges, there to provide security in case any of our enemies attacked. Dexter was still out there, as were the vampires, and who knew what followers of Marcia's Creed or other old enemies of the pack might still be out there in the world, waiting for their moment to strike. Here in the open, forced to complete this spell, we would be at our most vulnerable, in the very moment when it was most important for our magic wielders to be safe.

The three of us walked to the middle of the field. Sky knelt, set a knife down beside her, and held out the Clostra. It seemed as though the weight of what we were doing had finally hit her. Her shoulders slumped and she stared at the books.

I knelt next to her, indifferent to the gazes of all the other weres around us. If Sky needed me, then I was here for her, no matter the moment, no matter how fractured our relationship had become.

I leaned in and spoke softly.

"Be careful."

She nodded, a small, uncertain movement.

I kissed her on the forehead. When she didn't pull back, I moved down and kissed her on the lips. I couldn't escape the thought that this might be our last moment together, that the power of the spell might kill her or the curse might kill me, for all that the mark was gone from my shoulder. That could just be false hope, and until everybody was safe, I had to assume that none of us were.

My heart raced at the thought of losing Sky, and I heard hers speed in response. I kissed her again, sad and desperate, then forced myself to pull away.

"Okay. Ready?" I asked.

She nodded and spoke confidently. "I have this."

That confidence was forced, a desperate bravado in the face of danger, but even if Sky wasn't convinced, part of me was. She could do this.

"Are you ready?" Josh asked.

In response, Sky gave him the thumbs-up. I stepped back to let them do their work.

Josh handed her another book, then drew a knife and ran it across his hand. With the blood, he formed a tight circle around Sky, chanting as he went. Magic rose around her, a protective barrier that seemed to shift and twist like the blowing of a storm, but that left Sky untouched. A look of peace descended over her face.

Sky arranged the books of the Clostra, then picked up the knife from beside her. She uncorked a small bottle and poured thick liquid over the blade. It was a potion to slow a were-animal's healing, to make sure that her blood kept flowing for the spell. Just the sight of it made me wince.

Slowly, carefully, Sky raised the knife, then ran its blade across the palm of her hand. She grimaced in pain and the blood flowed, spattering the ground around her as she began to chant the spell.

Dark smoke swirled up around Sky, just as it had done when we tried the spell before. It rushed out, blocking the last golden sunlight of the evening, bringing cold and darkness to the world. It wrapped itself around the trees at the edges of the field, which creaked and twisted as the magic took hold. Then a wave of power blasted out, shattering the trees. Other members of the pack ducked or raised their hands to protect their faces as splinters filled the air.

As chunks of wood rained down around me, I glanced back at Sky. The book in front of her was covered in ice, which melted away as quickly as it had appeared, leaving the Gem of Levage, one of the great artifacts of power, lying on a blank page.

Around me, the magic shifted, the wind rushing with supernatural power. The trees—those that had survived the first magical onslaught—swayed in the growing storm.

Something else was moving among the trees. Someone was approaching. I prepared myself to face whatever came next.

Sky kept chanting the spell. She ran the knife over her hand again, poured more of the potion into the wound, and let blood stream out across the books of the Clostra.

The movement among the trees grew closer. People were coming, magic flaring around their hands. Had Ariel come to see the Clostra in action? And if she had, was this support or had she turned against us? I paced back and forth, trying to see what was happening, keeping myself between Sky and whoever was coming.

Magic flew out of the woods and some of it broke against the power rising around Sky. Seeing what they had unleashed, I knew immediately that this wasn't witches' power. They would have managed something stronger. This was mages.

Sure enough, as Sky raised a book and continued her spell, I saw Dexter leading his people out from between the trees. He waved his hands and a chunk of fallen tree flew through the air, hitting me hard on the shoulder. I stumbled, kept my footing, and turned to glare at him, my teeth bared. My instinct was to charge, but he was holding back, trying to draw me in. He wanted me away from Sky.

Why?

"Keep reading," Josh said to Sky, raising his hands to counter incoming magic.

Dexter advanced again, coming out from beneath the trees with twenty mages behind him. They used their magic to fling branches and rocks in my direction and a couple of them hit me, knocking me first one way and then another. Compared with what Josh could do, the power they unleashed was pitiful, not even enough to knock me over, never mind to hurt me. But they kept coming with a confidence far in excess of their power.

What was I missing?

Led by Gavin, Steven, and Sebastian, several of the pack shifted and advanced on the mages, growling with low menace. Dexter backed away, but others stood their ground, flinging magic at the advancing weres.

Then the vampires appeared, rushing out of the woods from the opposite direction to the mages. Michaela led the charge, midnight hair streaming out behind her, crimson shining in her eyes. The weres who weren't already fighting the mages turned to engage them.

"Keep going," I said to Sky, seeing her attention drawn by the commotion around her. We needed her to focus, to continue the spell. If that failed, then everything else would be futile.

I charged at the nearest vampire. He bared his fangs and raised a fist as I approached, but I ducked as I rushed in and his punch sailed past my head. I slammed my shoulder into his chest, flinging him to the ground, and landed on top of him. He squirmed and slashed at me with long, barbed fingernails. I caught one hand, twisted, and grunted in satisfaction as his wrist snapped.

He wrapped his other hand around my throat and dragged me down to him. His head came up, snapping at me with those deadly teeth. I slammed my fist into his nose and blood spurted out with a satisfying crunch. I hit him again and again until he lay still.

Any semblance of order between the two sides was gone, the fight descending into a chaotic brawl. I grabbed a mage by the shoulders and flung him from his feet, straight into one of his companions.

A yell of pain made me look around. Two of the vampires had tried to break through the magic circle around Sky and bounced off so hard one had broken his arm. But that wasn't who the cry of pain came from.

Next to the circle, Michaela had hold of Josh. She had yanked his head back and sunk her teeth into his neck. Blood streamed out as she fed, brutally, on my brother.

With a cry of fury, I rushed at her. She saw me coming a moment before my fist collided with the side of her head, knocking her away from Josh. She staggered back and raised her fists to fight, but I was already on her, flinging her away from him, away from the circle. The poisonous bitch had chosen to attack us just as we were at our most vulnerable, but she didn't understand how dangerous a cornered beast could be.

The wind howled in icy blasts across the field, carrying great swirls of magic with it. All around, spells were flying and people were fighting as we drove the vampires and mages away from Sky. Michaela looked at me with an expression of pure venom as she saw her efforts failing, her pathetic minions driven back.

Sebastian, in wolf form and bristling with fury, ripped the head from one of the vampires. Michaela stared as the body tumbled into dust, flung around by the howling gale.

"Back!" she shrieked.

Dexter was already gone, leaving his followers to their fate. Now, as the remaining vampires backed away, the mages went with them, leaving the fallen behind.

The magic reached a new peak. Ice crystals formed across

my skin as a freezing darkness descended over the field. Sky's magic had plunged us into darkness as completely as any eclipse could have done. She screamed, a sound that pierced me to the core, and I looked around, but I couldn't see her through the gloom and the magical ward surrounding her.

Then, as suddenly as it had come, the darkness was gone. Light and warmth swept across the field.

I expected to see a victory, but instead I saw devastation. Were-animals lay motionless on the ground, some in animal form, some human. None of them stirred. In the middle of the field, Sky lay beside the tomes of the Clostra, her shirt matted with blood. Only three of us still stood—me, Josh, and Steven—the ones without the curse mark.

Sky sat up and looked at what remained. On her face, she wore the same crushing horror I felt at what I was seeing. Our friends, who had fought so hard to keep her safe, lay fallen, not even breathing, seemingly struck down by the curse.

"It didn't work," Steven said, his voice hollow.

I couldn't even move, frozen in place by the devastating sight. Sky flipped frantically through her books, pages rustling, as the last dwindling light of dusk lingered over the bodies of our friends.

"Reverse it!" Sky yelled at Josh.

"I can't reverse it, Sky."

His words fell like coffin nails into gloom. This was it. The end of the Midwest Pack. The end of almost everyone I cared about.

I heard rather than saw the swiping of a knife through flesh and turned to see fresh blood running from Sky's hand. Josh backed away from her, a strange look on his face, as she began to weave a spell. But there were no spells to bring back the dead. It was over. We had run out of time.

Time. That was it. Sky had to be casting *rever tempore*, the time reverser, one of the great forbidden spells, something so dangerous the Creed would kill anyone who used it—even the new Creed under Ariel's leadership. They were sworn to do so, to keep the world safe. The only person I knew who had ever used it was my mother, and she had never been the same after the punishment inflicted on her in response. I shouldn't let Sky do this.

But looking around, seeing Sebastian, Gavin, Winter, and so many others lying lifeless on the ground, I couldn't bring myself to stop her.

I looked away from Sky, watching the fallen and remembering who they had been, who they could be again if the spell succeeded. The sky darkened again and magic crackled around Sky.

Then I saw something. It started with Gavin, lying in panther form on the ground. His sleek black fur rippled as he took a breath. Then it was Winter, lying face down with a sword in her hand, who let out a small groan as she started to lift her head. Sebastian twitched a paw as his chest rose and fell.

"Sky, stop!" I shouted.

She kept going, magic flashing from her fingers, the power building around her.

"They're moving," I cried out. "They're alive."

The crackling in the air stopped. I rushed to the nearest were and leaned in to hear the breath rushing through her lips. I almost laughed in relief as I ran to the next, and the next, checking pulses, watching for movement, listening for heartbeats.

Gasps ran around the clearing as, one by one, the pack stirred. Winter sat up, shook her head, and sheathed her sword, then looked around as if wondering who had won.

We had. Acting as a conduit, Sky had drawn off the magic meant to kill weres all over the world. Though they had fallen for a minute, now they rose revived, the curse lifted. We were safe.

"That was not cool," Winter said.

"What?" Sky asked.

"Wherever you sent us to vacation. That place and..."

Wherever they had gone, I was glad that I hadn't followed. The looks on their faces spoke of a terrible experience, followed by the shock of returning to life.

But they were alive, and that was what counted. I smiled.

Then I saw Cole rising from the dirt. He looked at me, wearing that same smug grin he always did. This problem might be over, but another one still lay ahead.

CHAPTER 21

Of course there was a party to celebrate, the biggest party the pack had thrown in years. Were-animals and guests turned the whole retreat upside down, eating and drinking, dancing and singing, reveling in being alive.

As the party progressed, I watched Sky from across the room. Seeing her bloody and in pain at the climax of the spell had been terrible, but it seemed to have done something to wear away the tension between us. Whether it was fighting on the same side or remembering how much we had to lose, something about it had made a difference. We weren't quite back to relaxed conversation yet, but there were at least passing smiles.

That was why I noticed when she slipped out of the party and headed into the night. Following at a discreet distance, I saw her get into her car. Something gleamed on the seat beside her—a sword. It seemed like Sky had more on her mind than celebrating, and given everything that had happened, I had a good idea what she was doing instead.

Sky was going after Michaela.

By the time I figured it out, I was too late to stop her from pulling away down the driveway. I leapt into my own car and followed, pulling out my phone and dialing her number as I went. I could understand why Sky was doing this, and given Michaela's attack on the pack it could easily have seemed like an acceptable move. But things were never this easy; at the very least, we needed to talk through the consequences of attacking Demetrius's lover and the Mistress of the Northern Seethe.

The call rang out. Apparently Sky wasn't in the mood for talking. I considered speeding up to overtake her and block her way, but the more I thought about it, the less I wanted to. If this was Sky's choice, so be it. Let Demetrius try to condemn Sky for attacking Michaela after she and half his Seethe had attacked us. Let him see how far those arguments took him.

Part of me wanted to get ahead of Sky for another reason: to protect her from Michaela. The vampire was one of the toughest individuals I had ever met. It would be no easy fight, and if I took it on, then I would be keeping Sky safe. But I remembered what Josh had said about that, and I finally understood one of the things I had been doing wrong this whole time. If I wanted to get close to Sky, then sometimes I had to let her take risks, to be the best version of her she could. I had to let her have her fights against the world, or all of her fights would be against me.

Knowing where Sky was going, I lowered my speed, dropping back to make sure that she wouldn't see me. My sense of her presence would tell me if she headed off in some other direction, but I was confident that wouldn't happen.

As I approached Michaela's oversized Victorian house, I turned off my headlights and then switched off the engine, rolling to a near-silent halt just outside the heavy wrought-iron gate. Sure enough, Sky's car was waiting there, and I could see her standing in the garden of the house, sword in hand. I quietly opened the door of the car and stepped out, unseen, hidden in the deep shadow between two streetlights.

Sky went from hammering on the door of the house to peering in through the darkened windows. Then something moved in the garden behind her and a moment later Michaela emerged, dragging a tall, dusky-skinned young man behind her.

"The little pup has come to bark at me," she said in a wispy voice.

Even at this distance, I could hear Sky's heart race as she spun around, alarmed but not deterred, the sword in her hand.

"He should leave," she said, pointing at Michaela's stray.

"Don't worry, I doubt he will be bothered by the Midwest Pack's little bitch yapping and biting at my ankles. Perhaps he will enjoy the performance as well."

"He's awfully young. Has he seen someone killed before? It might traumatize him."

Now the young man's heartbeat was racing as well. I hoped he had the good sense to get out of there as soon as he saw his chance, but good sense and hanging out with Michaela didn't tend to be a match.

The two women stood staring at each other, a deadly tension between them. I forced myself to sit back on the hood of my car and watch, rather than interfere with what was going on.

"If you want an audience for this—so be it," Sky said, raising the sword.

Michaela looked at the sword, then over at the young man. She kissed him briefly then waved him away.

"We will continue this later."

The young man backed slowly away, then turned and sped up. As he emerged onto the street, he caught a glimpse of me and his eyes widened. I leaned into the light and bared my teeth, showing a flash of predatory canines, and he ran off around the corner, out of sight.

In the garden, Michaela was circling around Sky.

"What is the pack's little bitch here to yap about now?" Michaela asked, a sneering tone in her voice. "Go ahead and just yap away because you will not do anything. Might as well put your toy away, because you aren't going to use it."

Sky stood still, watching, waiting, sword gleaming.

"Skylar, put it away. We can play this little game if you'd like, but I know you will not use that sword. If Sebastian is nothing else, he is strategic, and I think it is safe to say that you are, too. If you kill me there will be a war—my created will seek revenge, and they will get it. I can go out tonight and create thirty more of us. You and your little pack, maybe two, three. We require very little to survive; you'll have a success rate of seventy-five percent at best. Even Sebastian and Ethan have failed at changing someone into a were-animal. The question remains, do you want to take the risk?"

Sky didn't answer, didn't move, just turned slowly on the spot to keep watching the circling vampire. She was calm and patient, two things Michaela could never be.

Soon, Michaela grew bored.

"Go away," she said, heading for the front door.

"No," Sky said, steady as a rock. "Michaela, Quell is gone. If you want an apology, I freely give it. You're cruel unnecessarily. You've tried to harm my pack one time too many and I will not stand for it. Either we call a truce now, or..."

"Or nothing," Michaela said with arrogant disdain. "He was mine, you took him. When I feel that you have sufficiently paid for that, I will stop. Until then, I will entertain myself with making your every waking moment a nightmare. You'll bark about it and even nip at my ankles as your kind often do. And that will be it."

A movement drew my attention down the street. A lone figure was heading for the house—Demetrius.

I had to think quickly. I didn't want to stop Sky from doing what she needed to do, but I didn't want to leave her to be outnumbered by the city's two most powerful vampires.

I took a nickel from my pocket and tossed it into the street in front of Demetrius. At the ping of metal against paving stones, he stopped and looked around. I leaned forward for a moment, just long enough for him to catch a glimpse of my face in the streetlight, then subsided back into darkness.

Demetrius stared at me, then at the wrought-iron gate. He tilted his head on one side, listening, his face full of curiosity.

Michaela chuckled as she turned away from Sky and headed up the steps to the house.

"I've lived over a hundred years and I will live even more. I don't mind taking a few years out of it to make sure you are miserable—just because it entertains me. Run along and tell Sebastian to learn to control his little bi—"

Sky lunged forward, sword swinging. Michaela turned to face her, but it was too late. It was a perfect blow, clean through the vampire's neck. For a moment, her head fell from her body, blood spraying from both. Then the pieces that had been Michaela crumbled to dust.

Demetrius stared at me in shock and anger. Then he strode through the gate into the garden.

"We underestimated you for so long," he said softly, his rage brought swiftly under control.

Sky spun around, raising her sword in a defensive stance. I stiffened, ready to leap to her aid. She had dealt with Michaela singlehandedly, I figured I was allowed to step in now.

But Demetrius knew what she didn't—that he was outnumbered two to one. He stood perfectly still, surveying the scene, making the terrible calculations that came so easily to those with power.

"You will return Chris to me as repayment for this," he said. "If not, your life for hers."

Then he vanished into the night.

It was over. I stepped out of the shadows and went to lean against Sky's car. She didn't even seem to notice me as she walked through the garden, her shirt covered in blood and ash, lost in thought.

She never ceased to amaze me. After everything else she had been through, she had just taken down one of the toughest vampires in the city and walked away to tell the tale. I had never been prouder of her, of how strong she had become, how much difference she made in our lives. She had cut through the crap to rid us of Michaela, and for all its complications, that was surely a great thing. She might cause trouble for the pack at times, but that was nothing next to the good she brought us.

She looked up and our eyes met. I stepped away from the car and brushed a drop of blood from her face with my thumb.

"Do you feel better now?" I asked.

"I don't feel bad," she said, sounding a little surprised.

"Okay." It was all we needed to say here and now. I backed away, got into my car, and followed as she headed for home.

CHAPTER 22

I set my cup down on its saucer and pushed my plate aside. Tiny Scottish cookies and a fancy cup of tea weren't exactly filling, but I hadn't come to this strange little coffee shop for the food. It was one of Claudia's favorite places, a special treat for her and a chance to talk one last time, just in case.

"How are you feeling about the challenge?" she asked.

I shrugged.

"A little nervous." I wouldn't have admitted that to anyone else, but there was little point hiding such things from a woman who'd once changed my diapers. She could see right through me. "Mostly relieved to get it out of the way. If I win, I get Cole out of the way. And if I lose… well, then he's someone else's problem."

It was a stupid, flippant comment, I knew, but it helped me not to worry about facing Cole, one of the few weres who came close to matching me in a fight.

Claudia scowled. "I hope you haven't been talking about it like that in front of Sky. It's hard enough for me to hear, but that poor girl…"

"I haven't," I said. "I promise."

I sighed.

"In fact, things have been kind of awkward between me and Sky. It's tough, being Beta and being with someone, especially someone like her."

Claudia leaned across the table and took my hand.

"I know it's hard for you," she said. "Life has forced you to be so independent, you've never learned to open up and let someone else in. But Sky could be that person. You just have to let it happen."

I nodded, not quite able to look her in the eye.

"The secrets don't help," I said. "So many things I have to keep from her and they're driving us apart. I love her, but she won't accept me as her mate while those secrets are still there, and they're not my secrets to share."

"If those secrets are a burden on you, then they're yours. Who else's would they be?"

I looked her in the eye.

"Some of them are yours as well."

"Ah." Claudia sat back and folded her gloved hands in her lap. She watched me thoughtfully, as if I was a puzzle she had to solve. "Ethan, the secrets we share have stayed secrets this long because that was in the best interests of everyone involved—you, me, and Josh in particular. But things change whether we want them to or not, and neither I nor Josh would want you to be lonely and miserable for our sakes. If keeping these secrets from Sky will destroy your best chance for happiness, then perhaps our best interests have changed."

"If word gets out…"

"Sky is a dear, sweet girl. Do you really think she would tell anyone your secrets?"

I shook my head. Of course she wouldn't. She was Sky.

"So you trust her?" Claudia asked, reaching for my hand again.

"With my life."

"Then I give you permission to trust her with mine."

I felt as though a weight was being lifted off of me. Perhaps it would be all right to share some of what I knew with Sky. Perhaps there was a way forward.

But then I thought about the world we lived in. There were magics that could be used to rip the truth from someone against their will.

"Ariel brought in a fae to drag information from Samuel. What if one of our enemies does the same to Sky?"

"Then you should prepare her for that. Encourage her to learn ways of defending herself against such magic. I suspect that Ariel can help, and I hear she is growing closer to the pack."

Claudia smiled mischievously at that last comment and took a sip of her tea. Apparently Sebastian and Ariel were the hottest gossip in town. I just wished that I could find a way to enjoy that fact instead of getting bogged down in my own difficulties.

"I hope you're right, but for any of this to matter I've got to get through the challenge." I pushed my chair back. "I should go. I have a meeting with Sebastian."

Claudia stood and kissed me on the cheek.

"Take care. I'll see you soon."

I headed out to my car and drove back to the retreat, the drive consuming my mind, making the cares and worries of the day fade away. For a short while, there was just me and the road.

Then I drew up to the retreat and saw Cole's car, like I had every time I'd come here lately. Calm vanished as I ground my teeth.

Sebastian was waiting for me in his office. As I came in and closed the door behind me, he slid a slim book back into the poetry section on his bottom shelf.

"Thank you for coming, Ethan," he said. "I know we don't really need this meeting in practice, but I wouldn't be much of an Alpha if I didn't prepare in case you lose the challenge."

"It's okay," I said. I wouldn't have been much of a Beta if I didn't make arrangements in case something happened to me. "It's all sorted."

The meeting was supposedly a formality, getting things in order on the slim chance that I might lose the fight. But Sebastian seemed strained, far from one hundred percent confident that I would win.

"Do you want to fill me in on any of our ongoing issues?" he asked.

I shook my head.

"The intelligence files are all up to date and backed up on the main servers. If Cole wins, one of the Worgen will reset the access codes so that the new ones go to him and you. Every folder has a file labeled intro, which will guide you through the rest.

"Honestly, with Michaela dead, Dexter's science experiment shut down, and the curse lifted, things are the quietest they've been in months. If there was ever a time for me to get myself killed, this is it."

I tried to laugh, but the sound came out hollow. I wasn't worried about myself. I'd made my choices and accepted the risks that came with them. But I'd had so little time with Sky, I didn't want to miss out on having more.

That wasn't a reason not to fight; it was an extra motive to win.

"There's one more thing to add to the files, and for you to deal with once the challenge is over," Sebastian said. I couldn't help admiring the way he did that, showing his confidence in me while keeping business moving. "We've had a pack of twelve weres move in from the east—a breakaway from a bigger pack. I don't know if someone hired them or if they're here to cause trouble for their own sake, but they seem to be linked to Dexter."

That name drew a growl from me. I wished we'd gotten him when he attacked us during Sky's ritual. It would have been the perfect time to take him out of the picture. But he was out there still, one more enemy scheming against us.

"Has someone explained our rule against smaller packs?" I asked. "And what happens if you ignore that rule?"

"Someone will," Sebastian said. "But you might need to follow up on it."

"Is that everything?"

Sebastian nodded. "I think so. Go spend some time with Sky. Everything else can wait."

I smiled. Why not? If I only had a little time left, then I wanted to spend it with her.

Hell, if I had all the time in the world, I wanted to share that with Sky, too.

I woke in the night to the sound of Sky's heartbeat racing in the darkness. She tossed and turned, and I knew in an instant what was bothering her: the challenge. Tomorrow, I would be fighting Cole to the death.

There was an irony to the situation. I was the one whose life was on the line. I was the one who needed to rest before the coming confrontation. But it was Sky who was fretting about the future, keeping us both awake.

I reached out a hand to pull her close.

"Sky," I whispered.

I drew her in tight, wrapping my arms around her. She wouldn't look at me, but I could see that she was struggling to hold back tears, blinking as they spilled down her face. I ran a thumb over her cheek, wiping them away.

"I'm never going to get used to this," she said.

"I don't get challenged a lot," I replied, trying to reassure her. "I've had five, and one person stepped down when I challenged him."

She seemed to relax, her heartbeat coming somewhere

closer to normal. I lay back and settled down to sleep beside her. But sleep took longer than usual to come, and just as I was starting to drift off, Sky got up and went to the living room. There was the sound of a light switch being flicked and of Sky settling down on the sofa, but to my surprise the television didn't come on.

Her agitation was making me restless, and any hope of sleep evaporated. After a few futile minutes of wishing that rest would come, I got up and went through to find Sky reading, or at least staring at the pages of a book.

Seeing her like that, remembering how much I loved her, I was struck once again by how badly I wanted her as my mate. I hadn't wanted to risk telling her the truth about me, but until I did that we would be stuck in limbo, together but not truly close. She would hold herself back because I was holding back part of me. If I wanted her to truly be mine, then I needed to tell her more about me and my magic.

First though I needed to prepare her for the challenge of hiding that truth.

"There isn't a way to counter a fae truth spell," I said, coming out of the bedroom.

I sat down next to her on the couch, lay back against the armrest, and pulled her close. She was a warm, comforting presence against my chest.

"It's not easy to fight it, but it can be done," I said. "It hurts like hell. Like a small explosion in your chest, acid on the skin. But it never lasts.

"If you clear your mind and only focus on what's happening, it makes it easier. No matter how strong they are, you can do it. I know you can do it. Don't even think about your animal half, it doesn't work. I tell you this from experience."

I paused, thinking back to the one time I'd had to do it. The pain raging through me, my inner wolf trapped and unable to help, as I struggled to hold back secrets that would keep the pack safe. Struggled and succeeded, against the odds.

"We should practice sometime," I continued. "Perhaps Ariel can help."

It was good that we had a friend at the head of the witches now. That was one less threat Sky and her magic would face, one more ally who might be able to help her. I would talk with Sebastian in the morning, make sure something was set in case I didn't make it through.

"You've been able to use the Clostra, not because of the magic you may have from your mother, but from Maya. Some spells require stronger magic; the Vitae was one of them. We didn't have the convenience of asking another witch because they all knew of the curse placed on Josh. It would have made things simpler." I hesitated, thinking back to moments from my youth, serious conversations with my mother, things I had learned far too young. "My mother thought he was a powerful witch, one strong enough to use the Vitae to keep Josh alive. It wasn't until we used his magic that we knew differently. It was different than anything I'd felt, not like Josh's magic. Not like mine.

"Then we met you, and the first time I was around you, I felt the odd magic again. I'd known about spirit shades, but at the time it was a limited knowledge. I knew witches had usually done it as a way to obtain immortality."

Sky seemed on the verge of speaking, but then she held back, letting me go on.

It was difficult. Some of the details of how we originally saved Josh were things I hadn't thought about for years, never mind spoken about. Even when Claudia and I had gone to hunt down the Tre'ase behind the spirit shade, memories had stayed locked away in a corner of my mind, safely closed down.

"Finding the host of the spirit shade was easy. Switching

hosts was harder because he was reluctant. You can imagine that the host didn't want to be divested of the power.

"He woke up, no longer a host. He was human; he couldn't even use his magic. I have no idea why he was so attached to the shade. I'm sure he's still trying to figure out what happened. But it needed to be done. I was going to do whatever was necessary to protect Josh. Then we met you and everyone predicted you would hurt the pack. I'd always figured it would be through me, or Josh. Your magic was so similar to what I had—I knew there was a connection."

"When did you find out the spirit shade was a Faerie?"

"When we first encountered the books I gave you. When Logan told me how they could be killed, Claudia and I had to find the Tre'ase who'd created him. We knew it would be too dangerous not to have him secured where no one could find him. Now the Tre'ase is secured and can never be found."

"Who are you hosting?" she asked. "Ravyn or Leonel?"

"The one that they all deemed too dangerous. Instead of killing him, they forced him to live hosted by a body he couldn't use. And that's why it is so important for it to never be known that I'm the host. Too many people want him dead, and the ones that don't will want the power he possesses."

I readied myself for one of Sky's emotional explosions—anger at me for not telling her sooner, hurt at the story she'd just heard, outrage at the hoops she'd had to jump through when I already had a similar power to hers inside of me. But instead she turned and gently cradled my face in her hands.

"Thank you," she said and kissed me.

I returned the kiss, then pulled back to look at her. I ran my thumb across her cheek as I contemplated just how beautiful and surprising she was.

I kissed her again, on the lips, along the jaw, down along the curve of her neck. She shivered as my teeth nipped at her skin, and pressed herself closer to me, running her hands through my hair.

I wanted her, just as I always wanted her. My whole body stirred in response to her touch. I ran my fingers down her and she shuddered, letting out a small gasp. My teeth pressed again against her shoulder, a gentle reminder of the mating mark, a question to be answered. We looked each other in the eye and she nodded, as eager as I was for more.

Our lips pressed together, tongues tied and wild with passion, as I ran my fingers down her body, hooked onto her underwear, and tugged it away.

She raised herself up and then slid onto me, our bodies joining. I clung to her tightly as she ground against me, moving harder and faster with each passing moment, her excitement rising in time with my own. She was mine and mine alone, this wild and wonderful woman, rising and falling in the night, her hair cascading dark waves across the two of us, her hands pressing into my back, pulling me in close. I kissed her again on the lips, on the neck, across the breasts, ran my hands down her back and gripped on tight. She kept rising and falling, panting in excitement, building toward a climax.

And then we were there, the two of us joined in a moment of sheer pleasure, our bodies radiating something more primal and more passionate than anything magic could achieve.

I sank my teeth into her shoulder, tasting her, marking her, leaving a sign to the whole world that we were one.

She was my Sky.

Sebastian had arranged for the fighting hall to be built specifically for use in challenges. It was a barren room, with unpainted plaster walls and a bare concrete floor stained from previous fights. A place as stark and brutal as the battles that took place here. Not a place for style or comfort, but for the resolution of unresolvable tensions through unrestrained violence.

The ranking weres stood around the edge of the room, waiting for the fight to begin. Winter was the last to arrive, Sky trailing behind her. Josh sat in a corner of the room, arms folded across his knees and a scowl across his face. He didn't want this, but he couldn't look away, and if I had been in his position I would have been the same.

Cole looked at Sky, that hungry expression on his face again, and then back at me. Just for a moment he licked his lips.

Always the same with Cole, trying to get into people's heads, to play mind games and get himself leverage over them. That would come to an end today. This thorn in the paw of the pack would be yanked out.

Sebastian held up an iridium cuff. I nodded and he placed it around my ankle, locking it in place. No magic in a fight like this, just were against were, fighting in the old way.

Having checked that the cuff was firmly secured, he took a step back and noticed Sky. His brow furrowed.

"Sky, you'll have to step out," he said.

"What?" she asked, her expression indignant. "I'm not going anywhere."

"Mates aren't allowed to stay during a challenge."

Sky glared at me and I looked away. I could see how bad this must seem. After all, if I'd wanted to stop Sky from seeing the challenge, then this would have been the ideal way to achieve it. But the fact was that I'd just been thoughtless, so eager to show the world that she was mine that I hadn't thought about how it would affect this moment, that she would miss out on seeing one of the most important moments in our pack's life.

I would find a way to make it up to her, but not now.

Sky stood by the door, jaw clenched, that all too familiar expression of obstinacy on her face. I stared back at her.

Was this going to turn into another spectacular Sky moment? Was she going to try to flaunt the laws of the pack?

"Sky," Sebastian snapped as she strode over to me. "Sky, get out."

She stopped inches from me. "You have fifteen minutes and then I'm coming back in."

I offered her a half-smile.

"I only need ten." I looked from her to Josh and then to Sebastian. "Josh, too."

Josh glared at me and bared his teeth, but he was smart enough in the ways of the pack to know that he couldn't win this. He walked over to Sky and together they left the room.

The heavy metal door slammed shut behind them and Winter slid the bolts shut. It was time to fight.

There was no starting gun, no announcement to take ten paces, turn, and fight. Everyone else simply backed away, leaving me and Cole facing each other across the concrete floor.

Now that I had my chance, I wanted to lay straight into him. To punch him, kick him, claw him, to wipe that smug smirk off his face. But instead I stood perfectly still, body loose and muscles ready, waiting for him to come to me. It was his challenge, he was the one who needed to fight if he wanted to be Beta. Let him make the first move and show me what he had.

Cole advanced at an angle, as if he was hoping to circle around behind me. If I'd advanced, too, perhaps he could have done that, forcing me out into the center of the room, but I just turned on the spot, watching, waiting.

At last, his patience gave in. He rushed at me, fist swinging. I ducked aside, grabbed his arm, and twisted, aiming to throw him to the ground.

As I pulled at him, Cole shifted, fur and claws sprouting from his arm. My grip loosened on a leg that was narrower than the arm of a moment before, and he rushed on past, landing on his feet.

He turned, jaws snapping, and leapt at me, claws bared. My instinct was to change to match him, but I fought it. I stayed in human form, sank at the knees, caught the leaping wolf with both hands, and used his momentum to throw him.

Cole hit the wall with a thud and a shower of plaster dust. He landed on all four feet, but before he could recover I was on him, punching and kicking, hammering at his face and chest, driving him back.

He turned human again, ducked under one of my blows, and swung around with a low kick that knocked my legs out from under me. I changed as I fell, landed in wolf form, and rolled clear as he kicked at me.

Then he became the wolf once more and it became a fight between beasts, the two of us snapping and clawing at each other, twisting and turning, our teeth and claws deadly points. Fast and strong, he drove me back across the room, keeping up the momentum and keeping me on the defensive to give him an advantage. Blood flew as we slashed and gouged at each other.

I leapt straight at him, caught a hit to the side but kept moving, knocking him back and rushing clear.

By now, we were into the rhythm of a wolf fight, all sharp edges and animal instincts. I needed to throw him off that rhythm.

I turned again, became human a moment before he reached me. He slammed his head into my chest and pain ran through me, but I kept my feet and twisted aside, grabbing him around the neck as he barged past. I wrapped my arms together and squeezed, trying to crush the breath out of him.

Caught as he was, Cole couldn't bring his claws to bear against me. He writhed and growled, flailed wildly at the air, but I had him.

Then he changed, becoming human once more, and before I had a chance to respond he slammed his foot back and down into my ankle. A sharp jolt of pain ran through me and I let go. Staggering back, I felt that pain again with every other step. My ankle was broken, staying on it agony, but I had to stand, had to keep fighting—for my life, for my pack, for my mate.

Grinning triumphantly, Cole advanced. Making the most of my limited mobility, he ducked and dived, swinging punches and kicks from every direction. Just twisting on the spot to deflect them made me want to scream at the pain in my ankle as ends of broken bone ground against each other.

I couldn't win by drawing this out. I had to do something decisive.

I shifted all my weight onto the other ankle and leapt at Cole. For a moment, there was a flash of triumph in his eyes. If I was leaping like this, I must be turning into a wolf, and a wolf on three legs was a sorry one indeed. He could beat me now.

But I didn't turn. I slammed into him in human form, my whole weight knocking him back, my forehead smashing into his nose, which crunched and streamed with blood. The two of us fell to the floor and I was on top, pinning him down. I rained punches on his body and head, beating that smug face into a mess of bruises and blood.

Victory was in my grasp. I was going to kill Cole and rid us of this poison presence.

For my life.

For my pack.

For my mate.

Thinking of Sky, I hesitated for a moment. Could I really say I was acting for her when it went against her wishes? Could I kill a man for her when she wanted no more deaths?

I wrapped one hand around Cole's throat.

"Submit," I said.

"What?" He looked up at me in bewilderment.

"Submit and you can live."

"I thought the great Ethan only fought to the death." There was the smugness again. Did he really think this was somehow a win?

Still gripping his throat tight, I punched him with the other hand—once, twice, three times, the last one bouncing his head off the concrete.

"Submit," I said. "Last chance."

The smugness was gone. All that remained was fear and desperation.

"I submit," he mumbled through a mouthful of blood.

"Louder," I said. "So that everybody can hear you."

"I submit," Cole called out.

I rolled off of him and lay back on the ground. The pain in my ankle blazed so hard I almost didn't notice the other aches all over my body.

Somebody had been pounding at the door, but it was only now that the sound sank into my brain. I laughed. I knew exactly who that somebody had to be, but this time Sky really would have to wait.

Jeremy detached himself from the wall and came over to us, first aid kit in hand.

"Who's first?" he asked.

Cole stood. He didn't look at me or Jeremy or any of the assembled weres. Ignoring even Sebastian, he limped to the door, pulled back the bolts, and walked out.

"Sky," Sebastian said.

There was no response.

"Sky," he called again. When she didn't answer, he walked out of the room. "Come in."

He dragged Sky in after him, her eyes squeezed shut, her face squirming as she built up to some dramatic protest.

"Why are your eyes closed?" I asked.

Sky opened her eyes and looked around in bewilderment.

"Did someone stop it?" she asked, looking down at me and Jeremy as he tended to my swollen and twisted ankle.

"Ethan won, and Cole is in a little hiss," Jeremy said. "He decided to leave without me looking at his injuries. Pride." He looked scornfully at the door Cole had disappeared through, then back at me. "The same pride that led him to continue when he shouldn't have." He prodded at my ankle and I stifled a wince. "This isn't going to heal right away, you know?"

I shrugged. I could afford to take my time healing now that this was out of the way.

"It was a submission fight?" Sky asked.

I nodded.

"Why didn't you tell me?"

"I decided at the last minute," I said softly. "Actually during it, when I knew I was going to win."

I did it for you, I thought, and by the smile on her face, I figured she knew that.

"All he had to do was win a damn fight," Jeremy grumbled. "I have to come in and work a miracle and make his ankle new again."

I smiled at Sky. After a close brush with death, there was something enjoyable even in listening to one of Jeremy's moans about our behavior.

Sky crouched down and nudged his cheek with her nose. "You're the best, and if anyone can make him as good as new, it's you."

Jeremy smiled despite himself, and so did I. Considering the alternatives, it wasn't bad to have a broken bone.

***

For all the pain it had left me in, I was relieved to have the challenge over. It wasn't just getting past that one threat to my life and the stability of the pack, or the feeling of triumph that came from proving my superiority over Cole. It was knowing that he had gone, running off in shame to recover with his own pack. I wouldn't have to see him around the retreat anymore, wouldn't have to deal with his smug grin and his sly politicking. I'd proven my prowess and the world felt like a better place.

Maybe Cole would have stuck around if he had the sort of care I did. As long as I sat still, Sky brought me food and drink, stopped by to kiss me on her way about the house, and generally made life easy. Perhaps it was putting the fight behind us that did it, easing the tension that had hung in the air. But I suspected it was more about mating. We were bound together now, and somehow that made everything a little easier. I knew that she would be around whenever I needed her. I felt calmer and more secure in that knowledge, less resistant to her whims and her questions.

That didn't mean I was willing to sit idle for long. I hated enforced rest and wanted to get back into action. But as Sky pointed out, most people would have been off a broken ankle for weeks if not months, their bones filled with pins. Being a were brought that down to days, and if I had to spend a bit of that time doing nothing, then so be it.

Still, I made sure to get back on the foot from time to time, just to see Sky squirm and enjoy one of her indignant lectures. She wouldn't be Sky if she wasn't trying to look after all of us.

That was why she belonged in my pack.

CHAPTER 23

I sat on Sky's couch, my feet up and my laptop on my knees. She'd insisted that I stay with her while I recovered from the fight, so that she could take care of me, and I'd felt no need to resist. We were mated now, and sometime soon we would want to move in together. This was a good way to start getting used to that.

Before heading out, Sky had set me up with a big glass of water—"Because hydration is good for healing"—and an ice pack on my ankle. By now, the water was long gone and the ice melted, but I sat in place, still busy with work.

The events of the past week, first removing the curse and then fighting Cole, had kept me out of the office. Even after I'd finished solving those two problems, I could hardly walk into a law office with a broken ankle and a battered face. Clients would have too many questions about what had happened to me, and even with a plausible cover story, my colleagues might notice how unnaturally quickly I healed. Fortunately, Stacy had a gift for covering for me, one developed through years of hard practice. She also knew which pieces of work were urgent enough that they needed my attention no matter what, and which others I could do something about without a trip to the office or risking my bruised face on a video call.

Plowing through legal briefs and evidence files was strangely soothing. Away from the pack, my life had so much lower stakes; million-dollar business deals were nothing next to the lives of everyone I loved. Solving problems without the threat of death hanging over me was a satisfying way to fill recovery time.

The sound of Sebastian's car on the driveway made me look up from the screen. Sky had gone with him and Josh to meet with the Creed, and it hadn't sounded like it would be a gentle conversation. I closed the laptop and set it aside, ready to offer Sky whatever comfort and help she needed.

She walked in, slumped with weariness, and I offered her a smile. With a sigh, she sat down next to me, and for a long moment neither of us spoke. I noticed fresh marks on her arms, the signs of the interdico. The witches had decided to restrain Sky's magic, and apparently she had accepted. I knew how hard that had to be.

Our eyes met and her expression carried the same thought that hung heavy in my heart—the cruel irony of things. Sky had stopped someone else's harmful magic, and in response hers had been taken away. I had wanted to save my brother from a terrible fate, and as a result I'd ended up cursed with a spirit shade. We both bore punishments for doing the right thing. If there was justice in the world, then it was hard to see it.

But there was still good in the world, and the greatest good I felt came from Sky. I ran my fingers along the marks on her skin, admiring the courage that let her take this punishment, and then gently kissed those spots. Like me, Sky would do whatever was needed to protect the pack.

"It's absurd," Sky said, her voice drained rather than bitter. "I didn't even cast *rever tempore* in the end, but I'm still being punished, just because I nearly did it. Ariel is set on turning the witches back into the world's protectors, and that's great, I'd far rather have that than another Marcia, but did they really have to start by protecting the world from me?"

I wrapped an arm around her and pulled her close. I didn't need to speak, didn't need to ask any questions. If Sky wanted to tell me more, then she would. If not, that was her choice.

"Perhaps I could have said no, but what then? Sebastian is building this alliance between us and the Creed, and I don't want to undermine that. After everything we've been through, it's obvious that we need people on our side, because there's always going to be another threat. We're stronger together, you know?"

I nodded. It was true of the pack's members, true of our alliance with the witches, and true of me and Sky.

"Maya tried to stop it. She doesn't like to be restrained." A bitter little laugh broke from Sky. "But I wouldn't let her stop them. We need this. No more magic for me."

"At least now maybe Maya is under control," I said softly, offering up a small bright side.

Sky smiled and curled in closer to me.

"You're right. It's not all bad."

CHAPTER 24

The next evening, I was on the couch again, like I was most of the time that week, with my feet up and a car show on the television. Sky emerged from the bedroom ready for a night out, wearing a fitted shirt, jeans, and short heels. I took a moment to admire the view as she headed for the door.

"You're going out with Steven?" I asked, raising an eyebrow. This seemed like a lot of effort for a guy whose idea of dressing up was a slightly less crumpled t-shirt.

Sky pulled a face. "And David."

Now it made more sense. David relished living up to the gay guy clichés, including his own high-effort dress sense as well as commenting on everybody else's clothes. Sky would have a far more relaxing night if she showed up in something he would like.

My way of having a relaxing night was to avoid David altogether, but there was no accounting for Sky's taste in friends.

"After everything you've done, you've earned a night out," I said, smiling. "Have fun."

"I'll try." She kissed me on the forehead then headed out the door.

I turned back to the television. A British guy in dad jeans and a scruffy haircut was enthusing about a new Mercedes. In as far as I cared about television at all, this was the sort of show for me, but I found myself distracted, thinking about Sky and wishing she was there. She would have made me watch some dumb show, but it would have been worth it to spend time with her. She'd only been gone a few minutes, but the knowledge that she would be out for hours made me realize how much I missed her.

It was ridiculous. I was a grown man, I shouldn't need to be around my girlfriend all the time. But Sky was more than that, she was my mate, the love of my life. Things were simply better when she was around.

That got me thinking about our living arrangements. Staying at her place was fine for now, but my house was larger and in better condition. It made sense that we'd move in there, but I didn't know how much Sky had considered it. Perhaps she was planning the practicalities already, or perhaps that was just me, always acting the part of the Beta, making sure life went smoothly for our pack of two.

Getting us both safely settled in one place wouldn't just be more comfortable, it would be safer. Though we'd dealt with Marcia, Michaela, and the curse, other threats lingered. Even if Demetrius himself didn't retaliate for Michaela's death, other vampires were bound to bear a grudge, and some of them might come after Sky. I wanted to be in a position to protect her, and that would be easier if we were both under one roof.

All these issues left me agitated, full of restless energy. Usually, I would have worked out to let off steam and restore some sense of calm, but I was meant to be resting. I couldn't exactly do squats and push-ups on a swollen ankle. I knew that other people had sedate lifestyles, spending most of their days resting their bodies in front of screens, but it baffled me how anyone could stay sane that way.

I looked around the room. Sky didn't have weights in the house, but she must have something heavy I could use instead. Working out my arms wouldn't be as relaxing as cardio, but at least it would get the blood pumping a bit, and if I sat down to do it then surely it counted as rest.

I was considering the weight of pans versus bags of pasta when my phone rang. Stacy was calling. That was odd for the time of night, but we had a big case prepping for court, so she could be working late. Though if that was the case, I would have expected her to call from the office number, not her cell.

"What's up?" I asked, muting the television as I answered the call.

"You need to check your emails right now," she said, her voice tight with agitation.

"Is it Tannahill again?" I asked, reaching for my laptop. "I've told him a thousand times, either he raises his offer or—"

"It's not that sort of problem. This one has more fur."

My stomach clenched. What kind of pack problem could possibly have gotten Stacy's attention before mine or Sebastian's?

I opened my inbox to reveal an email from Stacy titled "WATCH RIGHT NOW." I clicked on the link inside and waited while a video loaded.

"It hasn't been up for long," Stacy said, "but it's already getting a lot of shares. I have alerts set up, just in case, and fortunately one of them caught it."

The video started playing. It showed Steven standing in front of four unfamiliar guys. One was creeping around to the side, and Steven kept his eyes on him even as he talked to the rest.

"Do you know this guy?" Stacy whispered.

"Why do you ask?"

"You'll see."

One of the men swung a punch at Steven. He blocked the blow, punched the guy in the face, and turned around just in time to stop another attack.

The third guy made a move, coming in behind Steven, but he wasn't fast enough. Steven slammed an elbow back into the guy's throat and he fell to the ground, apparently gasping for breath but actually preparing to change into his animal form.

Steven kicked the guy over and leapt on him, wrapping himself around to get a choke hold. Then he jerked his arm, and there was a blurry moment of him twisting a were-animal with a human head.

The fight went on, Steven punching and kicking, blocking and grappling, fending off the attacks. He might be outnumbered, but he significantly outclassed his opponents, and the desperate struggle started shifting his way.

But even as I watched his efforts with pride, a sense of dread rose through me. To ordinary people, this would look like Steven beating up and even killing other humans, which was a bad thing to have out there in the world. If he had to change to survive the attack, then showing the whole world that would be even worse.

By the time I finished processing that thought, the fight was over. Two guys lay dead at Steven's feet, weres in human form, and another lay injured. The camera faded to black, and for a moment I was relieved that it was over. Then a final shot faded back in, Steven standing over the body of a small wolf.

What the hell was this? Someone had cut out the moment of transformation, deliberately sharing the sight of Steven fighting but not of his opponent changing. It made no sense.

Unless this was deliberate, part of a calculated plan to attack us, to drag us into the open by carefully planned steps.

"Who else has seen this?" I asked, my voice flat.

"Judging by the viewing figures, a couple of thousand people. And going by the comments, that includes the police."

"Shit."

"Do you want me to dig into this?" she asked, sounding concerned. "I've got a friend at—"

"No, leave it." I didn't know yet how best to handle this, and I wasn't going to get Stacy needlessly tangled up in it. "I'll call you if I need anything."

I hung up and then hit the top number on my speed dial. I needed to call Sebastian and let him know about the danger, needed to call Joan and let her know what had happened to her adoptive son. But before any of that, there was someone else I needed to warn.

There was a click as Sky answered her phone.

"We are about to be outed," I said.

<<<<>>>>

MESSAGE TO THE READER

Thank you for choosing *Moon Fated* from the many titles available to you. Our goal is to create an engaging world, compelling characters, and an interesting experience for you. We hope we've accomplished that. Reviews are very important to authors and help other readers discover our books. Please take a moment to leave a review. We'd love to know your thoughts about the book.

For notifications about new releases, *exclusive* contests and giveaways, and cover reveals, please sign up for our mailing lists at McKenzieHunter.com.